Like in Love
with You

Praise for *You're the Problem, It's You*

"Alban gives readers a fiercely romantic, splendidly sensual romance. This love story not only delivers memorable moments of wit and whimsy (a game of Spot the Scion, anyone?), but also, with great grace and incredible insight, perfectly captures the inexplicable joy that comes from finding a place where you belong and a group of people who love you just the way you are."

—*Booklist* (starred review)

"This found family story showcases the unconditional love between the varied cast of characters while playful hijinks bring a positive, uplifting tone to a subject matter that can be harrowing. A heartwarming enemies-to-lovers romance."

—*Shelf Awareness*

"Come for the *Bridgerton* vibes, stay for the fun!"

—*Book Riot*

"Alban skillfully captures James' emotions, including his absolute yearning for Bobby, in this wonderful depiction of found families and their power to heal."

—*BookPage*

"The chemistry between the two catch[es] fire in a well-drawn and compelling way. . . . Alban hits the final mark with a historically accurate possibility for everyone's HEA. . . . [A] charming queer historical romance."

—*Kirkus Reviews*

Praise for *Don't Want You Like a Best Friend*

"A 1960s Technicolor spectacle of Victorian courtship, complete with buoyant teenyboppers, a widow with all of Maureen O'Hara's mournful glamour, and an Ascot race scene straight out of *My Fair Lady*. . . . The sheer exuberance proves irresistible."

—*The New York Times Book Review*

"Emma R. Alban is a fresh, distinct new voice in the genre and her debut gives us all the top-tier wit, spice, and swoons we love in a historical romance. One to watch!"

—Evie Dunmore, *USA Today* bestselling author of *Bringing Down the Duke*

"*Don't Want You Like a Best Friend* is a funny, sweet variation on *The Parent Trap*. . . . The characters and their activities are uniformly delightful. . . . Every time I think of this book, I smile."

—Smart Bitches, Trashy Books

"Sweet, angsty, and ingeniously subversive, *Don't Want You Like a Best Friend* will have you turning the pages and rooting for Beth and Gwen to finally get the happily-ever-after they both deserve. A delightfully refreshing historical romance!"

—Amalie Howard, *USA Today* bestselling author of *The Rakehell of Roth*

"A stunning sapphic Victorian romance from an author to watch."

—*Kirkus Reviews* (starred review)

"Equal parts swoony, nail-bitingly emotional, and sizzling, *Don't Want You Like a Best Friend* sweeps readers off their feet in a wholly new and exhilarating dance. With a beautifully rendered setting, whip-smart banter, and a cast of characters that are so easy to love, Alban cements herself as an instant voice to watch in queer romance."

—Carlyn Greenwald, author of *Sizzle Reel*

Like in Love with You

with You

A Novel

EMMA R. ALBAN

AVON

An Imprint of HarperCollins*Publishers*

HarperCollins books may be purchased for educational, business, or sales promotional use. For information, please email the Special Markets Department at SPsales@harpercollins.com.

Avon, Avon & logo, and Avon Books & logo are registered trademarks of HarperCollins Publishers in the United States of America and other countries.

hc.com

FIRST EDITION

Interior text design by Diahann Sturge-Campbell

Flower illustration © Mimi Art Smile/Stock.Adobe.com

Library of Congress Cataloging-in-Publication Data has been applied for.

ISBN 978-0-06-342877-5

Printed in the United States of America

25 26 27 28 29 LBC 5 4 3 2 1

To Dani:
I'm the luckiest, to gain a sister like you

Like in Love with You

Chapter One

Rosalie

Bath, 1817

A re you listening to me?"
Rosalie looks up from her slouch on Mother's stiff pink fainting couch, the latest copy of *Debrett's* crinkled in her hands. "The Duntons would like to meet the Spokes, and their son should dance at least one set with Henrietta."

Mother narrows her eyes and Rosalie stares back just as pointedly. She may not actually care about tonight's ball, but she's still her mother's daughter. Not missing a trick is practically part of their family crest.

"Good. Miss Raught could use a few more dances, and it wouldn't hurt to turn Mr. Spokes away. Wouldn't want him getting any ideas," Mother says.

Rosalie watches Mother consider her reflection in the three-pronged mirror. She has a small dais set up in the corner of her expansive, blue-wallpapered bedroom, and she spends at least an hour at it before every ball, perfecting every single part of her outfit.

Rosalie spends her fair share of that hour primping as well, but Mother is always the last one ready to leave. Well, unless Father is attending. It's equally possible he'll be running late tonight.

They're well suited, and always at least an hour late.

But it saves Rosalie another hour at the Assembly Room, for which she's grateful. Every ball is the same people, the same introductions, the same dances. It's perfunctory.

Spending her whole night deterring men like Mr. Spokes, lest he, or anyone else, get the idea that Rosalie could be stolen away from the most eligible Mr. Dean, gets tired. Rosalie sometimes quietly wonders if she might like to be stolen.

Mother would have kittens. Mr. Dean is by far the best prize of Bath. Far better than Rosalie could do if they'd chosen to present her in London. Father's estate has a sizeable living and they're exceedingly comfortable here. But she knows her dowry wouldn't command nearly the same attention in London, nor would Father's young earldom command the same respect.

Other girls might pout, but Rosalie can't imagine going through all of this on a larger scale. Being a big fish in the small pond of Bath suits her, her parents, and her brother, Christopher, when he's at home. It used to be fun, even, running the ton, everyone catering to them, especially if Aunt Genevieve and Uncle Walter were in town.

But lately it just feels . . . hollow. Christopher's off at school and Aunt Genevieve won't arrive for another two weeks. Tonight is going to be interminable.

At least Mr. Dean doesn't fawn. He's a quiet, sturdy kind of man, of rather few words. Rosalie doesn't mind so much. She doesn't think their life together will be filled with witty conversation or sparkling attraction, but it should be a good life. She'll have a staff and the money to give her children a comfortable upbringing.

It's what her mother has had. And Mother is happy with her lot.

Rosalie should look forward to one day putting her daughter through—*helping* her daughter through—the marriage market. Presenting Rosalie, seeing her happily wed, is something Mother's dreamed about for years. Rosalie should be overjoyed with all that she has, like her mother is.

"All right, I can't do anything more," Mother declares, spinning back to get last looks from Rosalie.

"You are absolutely stunning," Rosalie says, the smile in her voice almost genuine.

Mother, of course, does look beautiful. Her cream muslin gown, overlaid with a beautiful lace covered in little rosettes, is gorgeous. Her bountiful dark brown hair is swept up against the back of her head, and the gentle curls that frame her face only accentuate her rosy cheeks and bright brown eyes.

A smaller, near-perfect copy of her mother, Rosalie knows she's equally beautiful. Has never had to doubt it. But Mother has always needed more reassurance. Rosalie wishes sometimes her mother wanted more than this. More than the most recent fashions and hair and beautiful compliments. Wishes there were more for her to want.

Rosalie wishes there were more for her to want too.

"You're sure it's—"

"Perfect. Everyone will be absolutely green with envy. Mr. Dean might even forsake me for you."

Mother snorts. "One too many. You always go one too many."

Rosalie laughs. "Come on, Father might actually be waiting for us this time." She takes Mother's hand to pull her out of her suite and down the hall to the massive staircase that wraps around and down into their grand foyer.

It's the perfect place to make an entrance, and all four of them enjoy doing so. Christopher likes to slide down the polished mahogany banister when he's at home. Rosalie used to do the same, until she turned fourteen and it was suddenly brazenly unladylike to make *that* much of an entrance.

Still, Father beaming at them as he waits for them to descend, beautiful in his own right in his navy waistcoat with a pink necktie to match the rosettes on Mother's dress, is lovely enough.

"You have outdone yourselves," he declares, meeting them at the bottom of the stairs, his grin stretching across his narrow cheeks, brown eyes crinkling.

He touches Rosalie's chin and then looks at Mother, hearts practically coming out of his eyes. He takes her hands and helps her down the final step before twirling her. Her laughter fills the foyer and Rosalie's shoulders come down just a hair.

In thirty minutes, they'll be their most prim, proper, and intimidating selves, presiding over the ton. But right now, they're just her parents as they truly are. Happy, soppy, and really far too much sometimes.

She supposes that's the real difference, isn't it? Mother may have little with which to fill her time, but she and Father do love each other.

"We're going to be late," Rosalie says after giving them the requisite two minutes of fawning over each other.

They're easier to handle when Christopher is home. Or at least she can commiserate with someone when he's here, equally exasperated along with her. It's always worst when Father's preparing to return to London for Parliament too.

"We're already late," Father says, even as he steps back from Mother, sedately offering her his arm.

"We'll miss the opportunity to make an entrance," Rosalie counters. "We can only be fashionably late so long."

"Well, you two took forever getting pretty."

"How long were you waiting?" Rosalie asks, ushering them both toward the door. Mother just eyes them with fond exasperation. They do this dance every time. Rosalie kind of loves it, and kind of hates it.

"Thirty minutes."

"Oh, George, really," Mother cuts in.

"Miss Wrigsby?" Rosalie calls out, glancing toward the servants' wing.

Their lady's maid, Miss Wrigsby, pokes her head out and looks among them, her big brown eyes narrowed, lips suppressing a cheeky smile. "M'not sure it's in my best interest to be truthful."

Mother cackles. "Less than five minutes!"

"It was at least ten," Father counters.

Rosalie winks at Miss Wrigsby before shooing her parents out the door and into their waiting carriage.

FOR ALL HIS charms, Father abandons them almost immediately for the cards room, leaving Mother and Rosalie alone to push through the stifling crowd toward the ballroom at the Upper Rooms.

Every six steps there's someone they need to greet. She can feel Mother's fingers pressing indentations into her arm even through both of their long white gloves.

Eventually, they make it through the foyer and into the two-story rectangular ballroom. With its vaulted, half-dome ceiling and tall white columns, the room is a breath of air, even packed as it is with bodies. There's space in the center for dancing, and an orchestra set up at the far end. Still, the perimeter is easily ten people deep on every side, with more packed into the alcoves created by the overhanging balcony and interspersed pillars.

Rosalie gratefully notes Henrietta Raught and Amalie Linet across the room, loitering in one of those alcoves, momentarily out of the fray. Their yellow and green dresses are easy to spot and complement each other nicely, a truly welcome sight.

"I'm going to . . ." Rosalie says over the din, jerking her chin toward her friends.

"Keep an eye out for Mr. Dean," Mother whispers, tugging Rosalie in for a moment in a wordless farewell before she sets her free.

Mother's immediately swarmed by her own circle, a group of mothers equally intent on finding their daughters proper matches. It's like watching Mother be swallowed by a sea of white muslin. Rosalie leaves her to swim on her own, lest she get sucked in as well and stuck in an endless round of thinly veiled insults dressed as compliments. Mother's much better at navigating these events than Rosalie is, even though she doesn't have bosom friends to fall back on.

Mother always has endless acquaintances, of course—and she's invited to every tea—but outside of Aunt Genevieve, it's like she's never wanted to make true friends.

But Rosalie doesn't want to feel sad about her mother's lack of friends tonight, not when she has twenty minutes of politely declining dances and pretending not to see men's advances ahead of her. Amalie and Henrietta simply watch her struggle, sipping their drinks and smirking.

They used to be a phalanx ten girls strong, all moving about the room together, making pacts and architecting charming bumbles to intersect with their chosen suitors. Rosalie adored those balls; she was always good at making sure the right girl stumbled into the right boy.

But now, it's just her, Amalie, and Henrietta—a lone trio inching toward spinsterhood and left at the perimeter of the room. Well, Amalie and Henrietta are concerned with spinsterhood. Rosalie has Mr. Dean, of course.

"Lady Rosalie—if I may, I wanted to introduce you to Mr. Thomas Pilkey."

Mrs. Thornson steps directly into Rosalie's path, her pinched face split in an overly polite smile. Beside her, the aforementioned Mr. Pilkey stands awkwardly. He's nearing thirty, at least. There's a cowlick at the back of his hair and his shirt is unevenly buttoned beneath his waistcoat.

She's sure he's lovely, but he's so far below what her mother would ever consider—never mind that Rosalie feels not an ounce of attraction to him at all—it would be cruel to even entertain the introduction.

"Mr. Pilkey, a pleasure to make your acquaintance," Rosalie says, dipping in a light curtsy to both of them. "And Mrs. Thornson, so kind of you to make the introduction. I've promised my dances for the evening, but Mr. Pilkey, I'm sure my father would be pleased to meet you, if perhaps Mr. Thornson might like to introduce you?"

Mrs. Thornson's smile turns hard, but Mr. Pilkey looks frankly relieved.

"That would be most pleasing, Lady Rosalie, I thank you," he says, his voice halting.

Mrs. Thornson nods and ushers him away, sending Rosalie a cutting look. She has a new cousin to introduce to Rosalie at every single ball. If she hasn't gotten the hint by now, she never

will. At some point Rosalie is sure Father will revoke her allot-
ted two brush-offs; it can't be pleasant for his card games to
be interrupted with inane introductions either. But for tonight,
she's grateful for his largesse.

It only takes dodging five further introductions until Rosalie . . .
not scurries, for ladies never *scurry* . . . but hurries over to Amalie and Henrietta, slipping into their alcove with true relief.

But it's hardly a warm greeting. They're both staring across
the room, and Henrietta's biting at her nails through her gloves.
Rosalie reaches out and swats her hand down. Only then does
Henrietta look over, her round face wilting, blue eyes wide.

"Oh, thank God," she says, gripping at Rosalie's hand with
her slightly damp one. "It's absolutely dreadful."

Amalie nods, her auburn curls bouncing rapidly around her
high cheekbones. "I've been telling her it's not, but it *is*, Rose."

"What, exactly, is the cause for such histrionics?" Rosalie asks.
She follows Amalie's pointed finger and looks across the
dance floor. There, surrounded by a cluster of gentlemen, stand
two dark-haired women she's certain she's never seen before.
And the gentlemen are acting like they've never seen anything
like them in their lives. It's a veritable swarm. The group includes Henrietta's latest suitor, the broad-cheeked Mr. Rile, and
his two friends, Mr. Plory and Mr. Cason. She's been planning
to keep Plory and Cason on reserve for Amalie and Henrietta.

"Mrs. and Miss Pine, new to town," Amalie mutters.

The mother is certainly striking, but it's the daughter who
catches Rosalie's attention, her breath stalling in her chest.
Dressed in a white muslin gown embellished with gold trim
and blue ribbon, Miss Pine almost glows. Her tall, lithe frame
suits the current popular silhouette in a way almost no one man-

ages, making her look like she's floating in her dress. Her light brown hair is shiny and studded with little gemstones. The capped sleeves show off her delicate arms, and the shelf on her bodice . . .

What man wouldn't be enraptured? Rosalie's having trouble tearing her eyes away. And then Miss Pine glances over, catching Rosalie's gaze. Miss Pine's deep brown eyes sparkle even at this distance, curious, and inquisitive, and far too keen. Rosalie actually has to look away.

Well. This won't do at all.

"She's so beautiful," Henrietta says mournfully. "How can I compete with that?"

"You're equally beautiful," Amalie insists.

Petite, with charming curves and a round, open face, Henrietta is perfectly handsome and lovely in her own right. But Henrietta doesn't have the captivating effect Miss Pine does simply by standing there.

"Isn't she?" Amalie prompts, nudging Rosalie.

"And smart, and funny, and winsome," Rosalie says, smiling brightly at Henrietta. "We'll take care of this, don't you worry."

She squeezes Henrietta's hand and exchanges a look with Amalie before leaving the protective cover of their alcove.

Oh, excellent, there's Mr. Ebert. He'll do nicely. Rosalie's personally responsible for his marriage. He owes her this favor, and at least five more. Not to mention his wife, Laura, is stuck up north heavy with child.

Better yet, he's talking with the haberdashery owner, Mr. Higgs, who can hardly rebuff her interruption, not when she and Mother practically keep his shop in business.

"Pardon me, Mr. Higgs, may I steal Mr. Ebert away? My

friends and I are desperate for news of his dear wife," she says, slipping in beside Mr. Ebert.

Mr. Higgs nearly jumps out of his skin. He's easily six inches taller than Rosalie, and Mr. Ebert an inch taller than that. She can be very surprising at five feet, sneaking up on people. It helps keep them off-kilter.

"Oh, of course, of course, Lady Rosalie. Please do give your parents my regards," Mr. Higgs says quickly.

"I will," Rosalie says sweetly, looping her arm through Mr. Ebert's to pull him away. She steers him back toward Amalie and Henrietta. "I need you to go grab Mr. Rile and bring him to me," she says.

"Hello to you too, Lady Rosalie. You look very well," Mr. Ebert says.

"And you look like you're having an awful lot of fun while Laura suffers bringing your heir into the world," Rosalie says, looking up to meet his light brown eyes.

He shakes his head, but can't help the grin that crosses his stupidly square jaw. She picked a handsome one for Laura. Their children should be beautiful.

"What would you like me to say to Mr. Rile to remove him from . . . whatever situation he needs to be removed from?"

"You've business in town. Make something up," Rosalie says, turning them so he can see Miss Pine's little gathering. "Now go."

"Yes, captain," Mr. Ebert mutters, releasing Rosalie's arm to march around the perimeter and retrieve Mr. Rile.

Rosalie heads back to Henrietta and Amalie. "He'll be with us presently."

"What did you have to tell Mr. Ebert?" Amalie asks.

"Only that Laura's nearly bursting with child and he's here drinking and carrying on."

Amalie snorts. "You didn't want to go with him still owing you nearly five pounds off that game of whist?"

"I much prefer my bets paid in favors," Rosalie says with a shrug. Money she has. Social capital—now that's much more important.

"If he ever coughs it up, I'd take the money," Amalie says archly.

"I'll keep it in mind. But Laura will have your hide. I gave up that debt as a wedding present."

Amalie laughs loudly. A few gentlemen turn around to look at them and Henrietta nudges them both. Amalie shrugs, still giggling, while Rosalie lets Henrietta force her back on task.

It only takes Mr. Ebert a minute to extricate Mr. Rile. Mrs. Pine looks bemused, but Miss Pine is busy talking to Mr. Finch, the account manager at the high street bank. Father mentioned Mr. Finch had cousins coming to town. The Pines must be his relations.

Mr. Finch is too old to truly tempt any of the girls, but maybe she ought to convince him into a dance with Amalie or Henrietta—make it clear that she's calling the shots here.

Mr. Ebert and Mr. Rile approach their group, and Henrietta glances at Rosalie, gratitude bright in her large blue eyes. Rosalie squeezes her hand and then gently pushes her toward Mr. Rile.

"You promised Miss Raught your first dance, did you not, Mr. Rile? How fortuitous Mr. Ebert has brought you by."

Mr. Rile's brown eyes go wide and he snaps to attention, ignoring whatever Mr. Ebert was just saying. He quickly steps forward, offering Henrietta his sturdy arm.

"Of course. You look lovely tonight, Miss Raught," he says.

Henrietta blushes and lets him lead her out onto the dance

floor for the next set. Rosalie watches them go, pleased. They look good together. Tall and burly, Mr. Rile towers over Henrietta, but he always touches her delicately, which only accents her bright, cheerful smile.

Amalie sighs quietly beside her, swishing her green dress and watching Henrietta out on the floor.

Rosalie withholds a laugh. "Mr. Ebert, we can't waste your dancing prowess. You ought to invite Miss Linet to dance, in Mrs. Ebert's honor."

Mr. Ebert quirks a brow, but gallantly offers Amalie his arm. Amalie grins at Rosalie, and Rosalie all but pushes her into him. They stride onto the floor, a graceful couple of friends, and Rosalie looks around for a drink.

She notes the drinks station has been moved to the far side of the room tonight and girds herself, preparing to take the entire four-dance set to make her way there and back. Perhaps she can even find her suitor along the way. Mr. Dean is certainly taking "fashionably late" to an extreme.

She smiles and nods as she's approached and introduced, and makes her polite excuses. She notices her mother standing amongst a cluster of her society friends across the floor, all of them glancing down the room to where Mrs. Pine and Miss Pine are still holding court. They're fresh meat, she supposes—a natural source of interest.

But in a few weeks' time they'll be old news, and some newer, possibly younger, woman will take Miss Pine's place as the curiosity of the week. Rosalie, Amalie, and Henrietta will just soldier through until then.

Though Rosalie does note Mr. Sholle and Mr. Jenkins glancing down toward Miss Pine as well. She'd earmarked them as backups for Amalie and Henrietta too, should Mr. Rile and Mr. Fortes, Amalie's current suitor, prove disappointing.

Rosalie may not be at all eager to see her relationship—such as it is—with Mr. Dean progress any further just yet, but Henrietta is getting antsy for a match. And Amalie deserves someone who will make her happy, someone who will protect and support her like she's protected and supported Henrietta all this time.

"She's a pretty young thing," Rosalie hears as she finally reaches the drinks station. She takes a waiting glass of champagne and turns, noting a group of older women loitering at the edge of the dance floor.

"The mother's a jewel as well," another woman says.

Rosalie follows their gazes across the length of the room to where Miss Pine is now chatting with Mr. Jenkins.

"I feel as if I've seen her before," one of the women says. "The daughter looks so familiar."

"Likely the spitting image of Mrs. Pine when she was young. But I can't remember her maiden name."

"We should make our way over," the oldest woman says.

The group scoffs and Rosalie hides a laugh. Getting four matrons around the dance floor could take the rest of the evening.

Rosalie battles her way back toward Amalie and Henrietta's alcove. She glances at the Pines as she gratefully slips back into her spot, most of her drink already gone. Mrs. Pine is laughing at something Mr. Finch has said. Mr. Jenkins is still speaking with Miss Pine, but she's clearly not listening. Instead, Miss Pine is watching the dancers, like she's studying the steps.

And then her eyes flick upward and find Rosalie's. They stare at each other for a moment. Miss Pine glances at the dancers, and Rosalie can see her spot Henrietta and Mr. Rile. She looks back at Rosalie, those large brown eyes narrowed, and then she turns to Mr. Jenkins, like nothing at all has happened.

This one might really be more than just a pretty face. Rosalie's going to have to keep a close eye on her. Make sure she doesn't cause her friends any problems.

And if she should keep shooting Rosalie those frustrated, heated looks, well, that will just be a side benefit, won't it?

Chapter Two
Catherine

C atherine isn't surprised to find she'd rather be home reading the final chapters of *The Mysteries of Udolpho*, but
she'd been hoping the ball would be more interesting. She's
been talking to Mr. Jenkins for a solid fifteen minutes. She likes
his gray waistcoat, and supposes that his flop of dark blond hair
is becoming. His voice isn't as grating as Mr. Helm's was, at any
rate. But he's hardly keeping her attention.

Dear Cousin Louis has been dutifully bringing eligible young
men into their circle for the last hour. Mother's hovering at her
elbow, interjecting every so often to gently interrogate the gentlemen. The gold ribbons on the lace overlay of Mother's white
muslin gown accent her light brown hair, and her warm brown
eyes suit the colors wonderfully. She looks exquisite and heads
have been turning throughout the room to look at them all night.

For all of Mother's anxiety about this evening, their first
dress ball at the Upper Rooms seems to be going decently well.
Except that, somehow, just before each gentleman is about to
ask Catherine to dance, they're abruptly pulled away.

She can even see it coming this time, Mr. Rile approaching
behind Mr. Jenkins, hand outstretched to tap him on the shoulder. Mr. Rile, of course, has some urgent business they need to
discuss, and whisks Mr. Jenkins swiftly away, the two of them
lost in a sea of tailcoats and white muslin.

Mother sighs gustily and Cousin Louis forces a smile, wiping at his shining forehead. "I'll find some others, don't you fret, Mrs. Pine," he says, squeezing Mother's arm before scurrying away.

Catherine withholds her own sigh and steps closer to Mother, offering her the final sip of her champagne. The thought of crossing the room to get more is abhorrent, but it might be better than losing yet another dance whenever Cousin Louis returns with his newest victim.

This is supposed to be Catherine's entrance to society. She's supposed to be impressing all the gentlemen, lining up outings, generally making herself as desirable as possible. Which . . . is all kinds of horrible in its own right, but at least she had a plan coming into tonight. Perhaps if Father had been feeling well enough to attend with them . . .

"I simply don't understand," Mother mutters.

Catherine stays quiet, watching Mr. Rile bring Mr. Jenkins around the floor to be handed off to the tall, auburn-haired young lady in the green dress who's been receiving half of Catherine's prospective dances for the last hour. The other half have gone to the full-figured young woman in yellow with the pretty brown hair studded with little yellow daisies.

None of her dances have gone to the mysterious petite woman loitering in the alcove behind them, but Catherine knows she's to blame. Her shiny dark brown hair, small upturned nose, and sharp cheekbones, coupled with her gorgeous light pink dress, should give her an angelic presence. But Catherine's seen her whispering in the ear of each man who's come to steal Catherine's suitors. The devil on their shoulders, so to speak.

The woman happens to look up as Catherine glances at her, and Catherine feels her breath stall in her chest. She's never seen eyes like that before—gray blue, penetrating and extremely intense, even from this distance.

Catherine wants to stalk across the floor and ask what the hell her problem is. At the same time, she'd like to just keep looking into those icy gray eyes. Which is thoroughly confusing and infuriating.

The woman looks away, leaving Catherine alone with her excited stomach. Catherine does sigh then and Mother nudges her arm.

"It's that girl," Catherine whispers.

"Who?" Mother asks.

Catherine tips her empty champagne glass toward the woman in the alcove. "She's been stealing my dances."

Mother follows her gesture and goes perfectly still beside her. Catherine glances at her and finds her face pale, back ramrod straight.

"Mother?"

Her head whips around, neck craning this way and that until she stiffens again. Catherine follows her look. That's— No, it's not the same woman. But they're very close. Wearing a cream gown with little pink flowers, the woman standing by the refreshment table across the room looks almost like an exact replica of the girl in the alcove, just twenty-five years older. Mother and daughter, and no surprise, the mother is surrounded by a throng of friends too.

"Do you know her?" Catherine wonders. Maybe Mother can introduce her to the daughter so Catherine can get to the bottom of her meddling.

"That woman ruined my entire life twenty-five years ago," Mother hisses.

Catherine's jaw drops. "Beg pardon?"

"Lady Tisend," Mother snarls quietly. "Ruined my reputation with a vicious lie. My parents could hardly go to the Pump Room. I couldn't even leave the house. If it wasn't for your father deciding to marry me and take me to Idless despite—" She breaks off, heaving in air.

Catherine reaches out, taking her hand, heart in her throat. She can barely hear the ball around them now. "How awful," she whispers. "I'm so sorry."

"My parents left Bath right after the wedding, so I hadn't heard— But of course I knew she'd be here. To have her daughter stealing your dances even now is abhorrent."

Catherine blinks. That seems an awfully damning conclusion to jump to. "Mama, I'm not sure—"

"She ruined me to protect her match then, and she's trying to do it again," Mother insists. "We have to—"

"I've a few more gents coming our way as soon as their card game has finished," Cousin Louis says, appearing on Mother's other side, blocking their view of Lady Tisend. It doesn't stop Mother from glaring, seemingly through his shoulder. "Everything all right?" he asks.

"Mother's just spotted an old . . . acquaintance," Catherine hedges. "Lady Tisend?"

"Oh, yes," Cousin Louis says, glancing over at her. "Just bumped into her daughter's suitor, Mr. Dean. The viscount's not in attendance, as usual, but his son always attempts to make an appearance."

"Lord Dean's son?" Mother asks.

"Came back from Oxford about two years ago," Cousin Louis says. "He and Lady Rosalie have been courting since last year."

So that's the petite woman with the blue-gray eyes—*Lady Rosalie.*

"Rumor has it he'll propose before the season's out, and she'd accompany him to London when he takes his father's seat. Oh, there he is, by the entryway," Cousin Louis says.

Catherine glances toward the doors, and Mother tugs on her hand, abruptly marching forward.

"Come with me," she insists.

Cousin Louis yelps, dropping the lone profiterole he'd been intent on, as Mother grabs his wrist and hauls him along as well. Catherine does her best to apologize to the myriad people they're bumping into, but once Mother's determined on something, there's rarely any stopping her.

Cousin Louis glances at Catherine, who shrugs, both of them trying to look like they're not being dragged through the room. When they reach the doorway to the ballroom, they come face-to-face with a tall, dashing young man. A strong jaw, beautiful chestnut hair, and large dark eyes—he could be the romantic hero in one of her gothic novels.

"Cousin, I know you were eager to introduce us," Mother says to a baffled Cousin Louis.

Cousin Louis glances from Mother to the gentleman and back. Mother's giving him quite a look.

"Oh, well, yes. Right. Mr. Dean, a pleasure to see you again," Cousin Louis says as he extricates his arm from Mother's grasp.

Catherine would laugh at the way he's subtly wringing out his hand if she couldn't see Lady Tisend starting to push her way through the crowd behind him.

"May I present my cousin and her daughter, Mrs. Pine and Miss Pine. They're new to Bath."

Mr. Dean looks at them, clearly caught off guard to be bombarded with an introduction without even stepping into the ballroom. Though, as the son of a viscount, Catherine figures he must suffer through introductions by the minute at these events.

Everything about him is as perfect as she imagines a suitor of Lady Rosalie's should be. So perfect that it boggles the mind to think he'd ever have an interest in Catherine, of all people.

"It is such a pleasure to make your acquaintance, Mr. Dean," Mother says, her eyes twinkling. "I've heard such lovely things. I'm told you're an excellent dancer."

Mr. Dean puffs up a little bit. Oh, that's just too easy.

"I do rather like a turn about the dance floor, yes," he says, smiling at Mother. It's a ridiculously charming smile. "Is Mr. Pine in this evening? I ought to make his acquaintance before asking your lovely daughter to dance."

That was fast. A little too fast for a man who's supposedly almost engaged to Lady Rosalie.

"He isn't in attendance tonight, unfortunately," Mother says quickly. "But he would be delighted to meet you later this week at his club, or the Pump Room, if it pleases you."

"We'll find a time," Mr. Dean agrees. "Please tell him I'm looking forward to it. And I suppose now I must be a bit gauche and offer Miss Pine my first dance, if she has any room on her card."

"She'll make room," Mother says.

Catherine winces; too pushy, too desperate, too everything— but Mr. Dean just grins and offers her his arm.

Is it that easy? She's been putting in effort all night, making sparkling conversation (if she does say so herself), and then losing her potential dances to Lady Rosalie's machinations. Does this mean she could have just stood there all night and said not a word?

Mother and Cousin Louis walk with them to the edge of the

dance floor, almost bodily blocking anyone from approaching Mr. Dean. Catherine can see Lady Tisend fighting her way toward them through the throng of onlookers, but they reach the dance floor before she can manage.

Mr. Dean walks out with Catherine and they step apart to join the uppermost quadrille just as the band is warming up for the next set. Mother grins victoriously, and a few yards away Lady Tisend stands seething, glaring daggers at Mother.

Not that it's Mother's fault, really. Mr. Dean asked Catherine to dance after all.

Catherine's grateful she remembers the steps to the minuet. There have already been multiple dances she's never seen tonight. It turns out Idless doesn't get all the newest each season.

She focuses on her footwork for the first few minutes, making sure to smile at Mr. Dean, who smiles back, but offers nothing by way of conversation as they twirl around each other. He's handsome, and he seems perfectly nice from their brief interaction, but he doesn't seem particularly special.

The reaction to their dance *is* special, though. The whole room is focused in, whispering about them while they move up and down the line of dancers. Catherine gets a glimpse of Lady Rosalie when they make it to the other end of the line. Her look of loathing rivals that of her mother's, and Catherine has to withhold a grin.

See how she likes it, having her dance stolen.

Bolstered by Lady Rosalie's reaction, Catherine looks up at Mr. Dean as they join arms to skip down an aisle formed by the two rows of dancers.

"Do you attend all of the balls, Mr. Dean?" Catherine asks.

"Most," Mr. Dean says, smiling down at her. "I enjoy a good dance and a round of cards, and here I can have both."

And then they break apart, returning to their sides of the dance aisle. She expects him to ask a question in return as they step forward and meet hands. But he doesn't.

Then she expects him to ask a question when they meet in the middle to circle each other. And then when they join in the middle to take each other's hands, spinning around once before returning to their lines. But he doesn't.

He doesn't ask her even a single question for the rest of the dance. He just keeps smiling that bafflingly beautiful smile at her.

Other couples are talking as they dance. Lady Rosalie's friend in the yellow dress with the round face and Mr. Rile are talking and laughing up a storm. They look like they're having fun. She didn't find Mr. Rile nearly as interesting as Lady Rosalie's friend seems to, nor does she find Mr. Dean as charming as everyone else.

He's very polite. She ought to be flattered he gave her his first dance.

Maybe something's wrong with her.

Then the dance ends and she's curtsying to Mr. Dean, unsure of her next move. Does she try to bring him back to her mother? Does she invite him to get drinks? She realizes with panic that she has no idea how to . . . keep a man's interest. Hasn't ever wanted to.

"Mr. Dean."

Well, it hardly matters, does it? Because Lady Tisend has found them. Mother's glaring at her from the edge of the dance floor, but Mr. Dean turns affably to bow to her.

"Lady Tisend, a pleasure as always. Have you met Miss Pine? She's a most charming new addition to our circle."

Lady Tisend's eyes narrow just slightly while she gives Catherine a broad smile. If Catherine didn't know better, it might seem genuine. But remembering her mother's words makes Catherine see the calculation behind her eyes.

"A pleasure to meet you, Miss Pine. But I'm afraid I need to steal Mr. Dean away. I had promised to introduce him to several of Lady Rosalie's and my friends."

"Of course," Catherine says, helpless to come up with a way to make him stay.

Mr. Dean gives her a bow and another handsome smile, then offers Lady Tisend his arm. Catherine stands alone on the dance floor for a moment before making her way back to her mother, trying hard not to feel the eyes of the entire room on her.

Was it a triumph to get Mr. Dean's first dance? Or is it more embarrassing to have him stolen away by her competition's mother?

"Lady Tisend was practically green with envy and Lady Rosalie looked ready to combust," Mother says, tugging Catherine in as soon as she's within reach. "You'll surely have his first dance at the next ball, and I believe we could even get a promenade out of him if we were to run into him at the Pump Room. We'll have to go each morning this week."

Catherine looks over at Mother. Something pointed and intense has come over her face. It's unsettling.

"Mama, I'm not sure I truly like him—"

"You'll be the one marrying him by season's end, mark my words."

"*What?*" Catherine exclaims.

"We are going to make that woman pay," Mother says, turning with a glint in her eye that's cold and frenzied in a way Catherine has never seen her mother look before.

". . . By stealing her daughter's suitor?"

"He hasn't offered a ring yet. You're every bit as lovely as her precious Lady Rosalie, and we're going to make you a vis-countess."

Catherine just stares at her mother. "You want me to become a viscountess"—an absurd notion in its own right—"to get back at Lady Tisend?"

She must hear how ridiculous this sounds.

"Not entirely, but it will be an enormous bonus," Mother says, grinning at Catherine.

"I don't think that's a—"

But Mother takes her hand, squeezing too tightly. She's trembling a little. "You're going to have everything you could ever want, and be the envy of the ton," Mother says softly. "Wouldn't that be grand?"

Catherine meets her eyes. She looks so animated. Ever since they arrived in Bath she's seemed . . . anxious, strange. Now Catherine supposes she knows why. But is this really the only way to help her gather her confidence?

And could she really do it, steal Lady Rosalie's suitor? Find it in herself to play the marriage mart the way her mother wants her to?

Mother loops her arm through Catherine's, starting to rattle off a list of outings and activities they'll have to arrange. It seems an answer isn't necessary; the decision's been made.

Catherine stares out at the dancers, her stomach clenching with unease. Mr. Dean seems like a man of few words and meaningful looks. She could grow to be interested in that, couldn't she?

Cousin Louis steps up on Mother's other side, looking as pleased as Mother. It's loud, and far too warm, and Catherine is suddenly rather exhausted. She decides she can let Mother and Cousin Louis guide her around the room for the rest of the evening and make decisions later. She can pretend at ease and comfort. Perhaps a few balls from now she'll truly feel it.

But after an hour of harried scheming that seems to require none of her actual involvement, Catherine needs to escape. She leaves Mother and Cousin Louis in the tearoom at a table with some of Cousin Louis' acquaintances and heads to the cloak-room with promises to hurry back.

Stepping inside is an immediate relief. The dark, green-velvet-lined room is quiet and empty. Catherine stands at the threshold, looking around at the light green settees and the large vanity mirrors over the counter along the wall that abuts the water closets. Candlelight flickers, casting everything in a warm glow. It makes her want to linger.

When she's done with her business, she goes to return to the peaceful anteroom, planning to sit for a few minutes and gather herself. But the water closet door won't budge.

Catherine jiggles the handle, pushing on the heavy wooden door, painted green like the cloakroom. It doesn't move. She puts her shoulder into it, tries to shift the door side to side, up and down, to get it to unstick. Nothing works.

She leans against the door, blowing out a slow breath. Everything's fine. This is not a dire portent of things to come. Another woman will need the lavatory before the end of the night, and she'll be rescued. The water closet isn't that small. She's fine.

She presses her ear to the door, hearing nothing on the other side. Slumping, she rests there against the door, trying to convince herself that this respite in the pungent water closet is just as good as sitting on one of the overstuffed settees out in the cloakroom.

Thankfully, just as her sanguine attitude begins to crack, she hears the cloakroom door open. Moments later, someone tugs on the door from the other side.

"Oh goodness," she hears through the door.

"If you pull, and I push, we can get it open," Catherine calls hopefully.

There's a short pause. "Are you stuck in there?"

"Terribly!"

"All right, three, two, one . . ."

Catherine pushes with all her might, and slowly, the door groans open, until it swings back into the cloakroom, and Catherine goes tumbling into her rescuer.

It's Lady Rosalie's friend dressed in yellow. Her big blue eyes are wide with surprise as she helps Catherine stand back up. There's an uncomfortable moment, before the lady in yellow starts giggling. Catherine follows suit, and they stand in front of the open door to the water closet laughing together, bright-cheeked.

"Thank you," Catherine manages after a moment.

"Of course," she says. "How dreadful to get stuck. We should tell someone about that."

"Would have been an awful way to spend the whole ball," Catherine agrees.

"Oh, gosh, yes," the woman says. "Glad I found you."

"Me too," Catherine says genuinely. She may be Lady Rosalie's friend, but she's been a colossal help, and she seems sweet. They can't *all* be mercenary masterminds, right?

"I'm Miss Henrietta Raught," the woman says.

"Miss Catherine Pine," Catherine replies, ducking in a very belated curtsy.

Miss Raught sucks in a breath and curtsies herself. "We've been watching you. I mean—it's nice to meet you, I haven't seen you at the balls before," she continues, her voice going a little meek, cheeks pinking further.

She steps backward and moves to stand in front of the mirrors, avoiding Catherine's eyes. Catherine considers her. Lady Rosalie was stealing dances for her all night. She may not have any part in Lady Rosalie's schemes and might merely be the beneficiary.

She could be a wealth of information, and it wouldn't hurt to try to befriend someone tonight. Surely Mother would approve of her trying to make a friend, even if Catherine hasn't entirely accepted her crusade for revenge yet. And if that friend can give her some insight into Lady Rosalie's intentions, all the better.

"It's nice to meet you as well," Catherine says, stepping to stand in front of the mirror beside Miss Raught's. "How long have you been in Bath?"

"About ten years," Miss Raught says, her face relaxing. "My father has a solicitor's business."

"Do you like it here?" Catherine asks, pretending to adjust her curls.

"Most of the time," Miss Raught says with a shrug. "It gets a little dull after so many years, but we keep busy."

"We?"

"Oh, my friends. Miss Linet's been here for her entire life, and Lady Rosalie. They adopted me into their group when we moved, and we've been friends ever since."

Catherine wonders what it must be like to have a friend like Lady Rosalie. To walk about the ballrooms with someone like that. To be under her care and protection . . .

"That's lovely," Catherine says. "Bath seems such a busy place. It must be nice to have such good friends."

"It is," Miss Raught says, taking a short breath before finally looking back at her. "How are you enjoying Bath so far?"

"It's been an adjustment," Catherine says carefully, watching the way Miss Raught's face is going slightly wooden, her jaw tight, lips poised for another question.

"I'm sure you'll get the hang of it quickly. You certainly have made an impression tonight," Miss Raught says, a little fast.

Catherine hides her smile. It seems she struck a nerve, gaining Mr. Dean's first dance. Though she thinks Miss Henrietta Raught was perhaps not the most subtle of friends to send on a reconnaissance mission. "I get the sense that any newcomer causes some minor fuss, but I'm sure there'll be another in a few weeks."

"Oh, but none so pretty as you. All of the suitors are interested, I can tell," Miss Raught says.

"Do you have a formal suitor?" Catherine asks.

"Not . . . officially. But Mr. Rile comes to call quite often," Miss Raught says, blushing.

"He seems taken with you from what I could see."

Miss Raught's face relaxes and her shoulders come down. "Oh, thank you."

"And your friends, are they courting too?" Catherine asks, hoping it comes off as casual.

"My friend Miss Linet and Mr. Fortes are close, I think. He seems very set on her."

"But not she on him?" Catherine wonders. She didn't get a close look at the third woman in their trio.

Miss Raught's smile drops. "Oh, well, I don't know. I'm sure she's very—she's very fond of him," she decides.

"That's good," Catherine says quickly. "It's always nice when there's mutual regard in a potential match."

Miss Raught's eyes brighten. "Was there anyone you danced with tonight with whom you think you could have a spark?"

This is what she was sent in to ask. Catherine could demur, could play it safe. But where's the fun in that?

"Well, Mr. Dean is surely quite handsome," she says, withholding a laugh when Miss Raught's face goes scarlet.

"He's courting Lady Rosalie," she says loudly, glancing at the door to the cloakroom. "Surely . . . surely he *must* have said."

"We didn't say much to each other," Catherine admits. She got her answer, no need to antagonize the poor woman. "And a single dance doesn't mean anything."

"It was the first dance, though," Miss Raught says, her words not quite a whisper, her eyes darting back to the door again. "That can *mean* things here, Miss Pine."

"Oh, well, I suppose I'll keep that in mind," Catherine says. "I appreciate you looking out for me."

Miss Raught's face drains of color and Catherine feels a pang of remorse. It's not Miss Raught's fault that she's rather bad at subterfuge.

Thankfully, the door to the cloakroom opens, interrupting whatever further questions Miss Raught might have tried to stumble through. Though the figure entering doesn't put Catherine any more at ease.

Because here is Lady Rosalie, up close, in person, and thoroughly, stunningly intimidating. Her cheeks are a bit flushed, her dark brown hair beginning to go frizzy with the humidity of the ballroom. And her eyes, oh, her eyes are simply dazzling at this distance. The whole effect is awe-inspiring. Which is quite a feat at five feet tall.

"I worried you'd gotten locked in the water closet," Lady Rosalie says to Miss Raught. Her voice is low and rich, not at all what Catherine expected.

Miss Raught looks flustered and glances at Catherine as if they've been caught somehow. Which is absurd; Lady Rosalie was clearly listening at the door.

"She actually saved me from that fate," Catherine says, her voice only a little tight.

Lady Rosalie looks over and meets her eyes. Catherine wonders if her face has gone as flushed as Miss Raught's was a minute ago. There's just something about Lady Rosalie that seems to make one a bit unbalanced, a bit stunned.

"How heroic of Miss Raught," Lady Rosalie says.

"Lady Rosalie, this is Miss Catherine Pine," Miss Raught says hurriedly. "We were just talking about this being her first ball. She says Bath has been an adjustment, but that she's enjoyed her dances."

It comes out rapid-fire, but Lady Rosalie doesn't look surprised by the delivery. Catherine wonders if Miss Raught is always this flustered around Lady Rosalie.

Catherine can hardly blame her if she is. When Lady Rosalie looks Catherine up and down, it sends a shiver of something other than cold down Catherine's spine. The sensation isn't wholly unpleasant, but it's foreign, and makes her want to blush too.

But she doesn't want to appear unsure or discombobulated. She can't show weakness here. Clearly, she stood up well enough to Miss Raught's interrogation, or she doubts Lady Rosalie would have approached her.

"We do a lot of dancing in Bath. I'm sure you'll have the opportunity to dance much more as the season progresses," Lady Rosalie says, her voice even.

"I certainly hope so," Catherine agrees. "Do you like to dance, Lady Rosalie? I didn't see you on the floor, though Miss Raught and Miss Linet danced a fair few."

Catherine feels a little thrill at the way Lady Rosalie's eyes narrow just a touch at the insinuation.

"She was dancing with Mr. Dean when I came to the cloak-room," Miss Raught says loudly.

Lady Rosalie closes her eyes for a moment. Catherine's touched a nerve just by existing somehow. Thrown what she imagines is a well-oiled social machine all out of whack, and now Lady Rosalie must repair it.

"Mr. Dean and I did dance," Lady Rosalie agrees, giving Miss Raught a very tight smile before meeting Catherine's gaze again. "And he told me you are a talented dancer yourself."

"Oh," Catherine says, surprised. "Well, that's kind of him. I wasn't entirely sure of the steps."

"No one else noticed," Lady Rosalie says.

No one except Lady Rosalie, apparently. "Oh, well, that's good. Dancing is not my forte," Catherine says humbly, wanting to put her at ease.

"And what is your forte?"

If only Lady Rosalie would extend her the same courtesy. "I enjoy music," Catherine replies honestly. "I play pianoforte rather well. And I like to read, which I suppose isn't really a skill."

Lady Rosalie considers her for a moment. Miss Raught opens her mouth but Lady Rosalie raises a hand, as if able to antici-pate whatever she would have said. "We're having a private con-cert next week. You ought to attend. Your parents as well, of course. It will be the best performance you'll see this season. My father knows the best musicians."

Catherine blinks, surprised. It's a bold move to invite Catherine to a private gathering so soon. Miss Raught looks surprised as well.

"You can enjoy the music, and then I can help you line up your dances for the next ball."

"Lady Rosalie knows everyone worth knowing. She'll find you the perfect, proper suitor in no time," Miss Raught says eagerly.

Lady Rosalie shoots Miss Raught a sharp look.

So, it's about keeping your enemies close, is it?

"I'm sure your cousin will introduce you to a good number of men, but he doesn't know the young ton like we do," Lady Rosalie says, her voice calm, but just a hair too quick, trying to undo the damage of Miss Raught's honesty. "We can help you fall in with the right crowd, if you're interested."

Catherine meets her eyes. Lady Rosalie wants to keep tabs on her, orchestrate her matches, and keep her far away from Mr. Dean, all under the guise of friendship. Killing Catherine with very precise kindness.

Two can play at that game.

She thought Mother's scheme utter madness not an hour ago. But now, she wants to meet the challenge in Lady Rosalie's eyes. She wants to find out what will happen if she lets Lady Rosalie think she's controlling her. She wants to see the inner workings of her world, and her mind, and find out how she ticks. And then she'll use it all against her while Lady Rosalie thinks she's got the upper hand.

"I would be delighted to attend your concert," Catherine says sweetly.

Lady Rosalie's lips quirk in a smile. "Wonderful. I'll have Mother send an invitation for you tomorrow morning."

"Thank you," Catherine says. "And I would appreciate your help with the marriage mart. It's so hard to know who to trust."

Catherine could get used to seeing the challenge in Lady Rosalie's eyes. It's exciting. She feels a little breathless, and hopes it doesn't show.

"You can trust Lady Rosalie," Miss Raught says.

Catherine almost jumps. She'd nearly forgotten Miss Raught was there. Lady Rosalie sighs quietly.

This is going to be interesting.

Chapter Three
Rosalie

R osalie grimaces as she swallows the last of her cup. She's never gotten used to the waters. The light smell of sulphureous rotten eggs gets her every time.

"Manage your expression, dearest," Mother whispers, pressing Rosalie's elbow into her side.

Rosalie smooths her face, gratefully depositing her cup onto the tray of a passing attendant. It's crowded in the Pump Room today, and the attendants seem to pop up every few minutes to keep things orderly.

Not that Rosalie and her mother ever frequent the bright, airy Pump Room at any time other than its busiest. Eleven each morning, they're here to sign the book, take their waters, and walk up and down the creaking wooden floorboards. Mother recounts gossip while Rosalie people-watches, or stares out the enormous floor-to-ceiling windows at the abbey churchyard below, pretending to listen to Mother's prattle.

It's dreary out today, like it is most days in March. There's a steady drizzle, and while it's nice to be warm and inside, the room is crowded. The mended cuff on her blue pelisse is a little tight, and with Mother holding her arm in a death grip, it's pinching her wrist.

"He'll be here any minute," Mother says, her voice soothing.

Let Mother think she's worried about Mr. Dean being late

for their arranged indoor promenade. It's a little mortifying that Mother's still overseeing her courtship so intently. A year of courting in, Rosalie and Mr. Dean ought to be able to manage their outings themselves with servants for chaperones.

Then again, Rosalie might forget to arrange an outing for weeks without Mother's prompting, and Miss Wrigsby has much better things to do than choke down pump water with her every morning on the off chance Mr. Dean might show.

"I've arranged for the linens, and Mr. Brook is digging out our finest stemware for this weekend," Mother continues, diving into another recounting of all the preparations they've discussed six times already for the concert at the end of the week.

Mother's rather obsessing over it. Rosalie usually couldn't care less, but she's been making plans of her own. The seating has to be perfect: Henrietta, Mr. Rile, Amalie, and Mr. Fortes in between Miss Pine and Mr. Dean. For her mother's nerves, Rosalie's going to ensure that Miss Pine has no further opportunities to speak with Mr. Dean, let alone secure any of his time or dances.

Further, and far more importantly, she has to keep Miss Pine away from Mr. Rile and Mr. Fortes. She worries about Mr. Rile. Henrietta is sweet, and delightful, and a perfect match, but Miss Pine is clever.

She talked rings around Henrietta without even trying at last week's ball; got all kinds of information out of her as if it was nothing. Rosalie knows she should have sent Amalie in instead, but Henrietta volunteered. She wanted to repay Rosalie for getting Mr. Rile to dance with her, and how could Rosalie refuse?

Now she's had to invite Miss Pine to her concert. She can't be left to her own devices, not when she's clearly so bright and observant. Rosalie needs to pick a suitor, set them up, and see

Miss Pine sorted in short order. Someone perfect, appropriate, and bound to take her far away. Rosalie's worked with much worse and made excellent matches. Miss Pine, with all her allure, and wit, and entrancing eyes, should be no trouble at all.

There's a thump near the entrance and Rosalie looks over to see Miss Pine and Mrs. Pine struggling to hold up a thin, unsteady man with gray hair. It's as if she conjured them.

Miss Pine is valiantly trying support the man Rosalie assumes is her father. He's clearly saying he's fine, but Miss Pine still leads him over to a bench at the side of the large white entrance doors. Miss Pine says something to Mrs. Pine, and Mrs. Pine turns, wiping her hands nervously on her gray pelisse before heading for the logbook.

Mr. Pine leans lightly against Miss Pine, who's pointing out the window and talking as if nothing is wrong. Her lighter gray pelisse only highlights her brown hair and eyes. She can see Miss Pine's tight grip on her father's arm from here. Rosalie feels a sudden surge of genuine concern, wanting to walk over and help distract Mr. Pine.

Surely Rosalie could do more to help than the three glasses of waters Mrs. Pine brings over to the two of them. Sulphureous vapors hardly seem like a proper cure for whatever makes a man lean on his daughter like that.

She glances at her mother, an absurd urge to ask to go sit with them on the tip of her tongue, but Mother is already looking at her, her gaze sharp. Rosalie forces a smile and turns them to walk toward the back of the room, away from the Pines.

"We don't put ourselves out for those who cannot help us in return," her father used to say when she was small. "It's not what we do."

It's a phrase that's never sat overly well with Rosalie. How can you know who could help you in return when they're in need? And isn't there value in helping those who cannot help you or themselves?

Rosalie shakes herself. She'll help Miss Pine by finding her a proper suitor. Perhaps find her someone with wealth and acumen enough to help Mr. Pine as well. And if it takes her out of the courting pool at the same time, well, no one ever said charity can't also be self-serving.

She needs someone pleasant, kind, and inoffensive, with money, and a need for marriage. Rosalie casts about the room, searching for viable candidates. They're all rather interchangeable.

Ah, there's Mr. Sholle. Son of a baron, taller than Miss Pine, with a charming smile—he'll do nicely.

Rosalie starts to guide her mother across the room to where Mr. Sholle and his friend are leaning against one of the columns talking. She just needs a good excuse to interrupt them and bring Mr. Sholle over to introduce him to Miss Pine.

"Miss Pine, how lovely to see you again." Mr. Dean's booming voice echoes around the room. Rosalie winces.

Mother's hold on Rosalie's arm goes tight again. Mr. Dean has stalled at the entrance to the room to talk to Miss Pine and Mrs. Pine, and get an introduction to her father, instead of coming further in to meet Rosalie and her mother for their prearranged outing.

"Go interrupt," Mother hisses.

She starts pushing Rosalie across the floor, as if she can just walk straight up and say, "That's my suitor, get your own!"

Rosalie pulls Mother to a halt and Mother's lips go thin. "Trust me," she says, squeezing her mother's arm before gently yanking her own away.

Rosalie composes herself and walks across the room toward

Mr. Sholle. Mr. Sholle and his companion see her coming and tip their hats. Rosalie curtsies, giving both her best smile.

"Mr. Sholle, so good to see you," she says, her voice dripping honey.

He stands up a little bit straighter, as does his friend. "Lady Rosalie, so good to see you. To what do we owe the pleasure?"

Rosalie glances at his friend, letting her smile fall just slightly.

"Ah, Sholle, I'll see you later in the week at the club, must be going now," he says, offering Rosalie a quick nod before ducking away and striding out of the room.

Mr. Sholle doesn't look surprised.

"I'd like you to meet a friend of mine," Rosalie says, taking Mr. Sholle's arm and turning to walk sedately toward the entrance. "I don't think you had the opportunity at the dress ball last week."

"I didn't," Mr. Sholle says, seeming to notice Miss Pine and her family for the first time. His back goes straight and his smile grows. "Very thoughtful of you, Lady Rosalie."

"I'm sure you and Mr. Dean have things to discuss as well," Rosalie adds, sweetening the deal as they near the group.

"Yes, I need to ask about the hunting trip in a month," Mr. Sholle says.

There's always something for the men to discuss. She can count on that.

Miss Pine looks up at them as they approach, her head tilting. Mr. Dean doesn't even notice, too engrossed in whatever he's saying to Mr. Pine. Mrs. Pine stares at them, her look bordering on a full-out glare.

But Rosalie's never cowered from an unhappy mama before. She's not about to start now.

"Mrs. Pine, Miss Pine, may I introduce my friend, Mr. Sholle," she says, smiling brightly at both women.

Mrs. Pine dips in a curtsy with a sour look on her face while Miss Pine inclines her head. "Papa," she says softly, cutting through whatever Mr. Dean was saying.

"Oh, hello," Mr. Pine says, his narrow face splitting in a charming smile that puts both Mr. Dean's and Mr. Sholle's to shame.

So that's where Miss Pine gets her sparkle.

"Mr. Pine, Mrs. Pine, Miss Pine, a pleasure to meet you," Mr. Sholle says quickly. "Lady Rosalie has been singing your praises."

So he can lie to charm, can he? That's useful.

Mrs. Pine and Miss Pine both look at her, surprised, and Rosalie smiles brightly. "I thought he should meet our new lovely society members. And Mr. Dean, you know Mr. Sholle," she adds as Mr. Dean finally looks up at them.

He blinks, as if just realizing they're all standing there. God, he can be oblivious.

"Yes," Mr. Dean says. "Been meaning to find you about the hunt, actually. You must come as well, Mr. Pine."

Mr. Pine's eyes crinkle. "That sounds marvelous, though I'm not sure my joints will allow me. But tell me of your plans."

Mr. Sholle leaves Rosalie and squishes in next to Mr. Dean, both of them intent on Mr. Pine again. Would that these boys were ever so intent on ladies as they are on talk of hunting.

Miss Pine stands, allowing Mr. Pine and the boys to scooch down the bench more comfortably. Mrs. Pine rolls her eyes and Miss Pine shrugs, making Rosalie think of her own mother. She glances back and finds her white-knuckling the windowsill halfway across the room, watching them shrewdly.

Rosalie withholds her own eye roll and turns back to the Pine women. Mrs. Pine still looks like she's swallowed something unctuous. Which, given the way the waters taste, is fair. Miss Pine looks down at Rosalie curiously.

Her gray pelisse is even more fetching up close, and while Rosalie's hair gets frizzy with all the humidity, Miss Pine's still looks sleek beneath her bonnet, her few pin curls perfectly round. How does she do that?

Rosalie needs to think of something winsome to say. She interrupted, but she hadn't exactly anticipated all three men ignoring them.

Men.

Miss Pine glances back at the men, her eyes narrowing, before she turns back to Rosalie. "It was a lovely dance you and Mr. Dean did after we returned from the cloakroom. What is it called? I forgot to ask and wanted to find a set of instructions."

Rosalie's surprised she doesn't already know it. "It's a variation on a quadrille out of London from last season," she says.

"Are there variation pamphlets? Perhaps I could borrow one from you?" Miss Pine asks, looking perfectly earnest.

Too earnest. Too beautiful. Too polite.

Miss Pine's easy regard and curiosity put Rosalie on edge. Her mother is far more open with her emotions, easier to read. Miss Pine can play it close to the chest, apparently.

Or she really does just want to learn a dance, which would be disarming in its own right. Rosalie needs to be disarming right back.

"I could teach you" comes out of her mouth before she can really think through the implications.

"You would?" Miss Pine asks, surprise clear on her face. Her mother is a moment away from gaping.

"You could come early to the concert," Rosalie suggests quickly, trying to play it off like a premeditated idea, rather than something that just fell out of her head. "We could have one of the musicians play and practice to it."

"That sounds lovely," Miss Pine says slowly. "Mama?"

They both turn to look at Mrs. Pine, who's watching them with wide eyes. "Of course, dear, as long as Lord and Lady Tisend don't mind our imposing early."

"Oh, Father would love to show you and Mr. Pine his art collection. He's very much looking forward to seeing Mr. Pine again."

Mrs. Pine's eyebrows almost seem to climb into her hairline, but she gives Rosalie a tight smile and then turns back to the men, pretending to listen to their conversation.

"We'd be delighted, then," Miss Pine says.

"Wonderful," Rosalie replies.

They stand there in strained silence while the men continue talking beside them. It's Rosalie's turn to find something banal to discuss.

"Your pelisse is lovely," she says, falling back on her mother's favorite topic: fashion.

"Thank you," Miss Pine says cheerfully. "I chose the color because it reminded me of a stormy sky. I've gotten very into gothic novels and was feeling a bit moody at the modiste, I'll admit."

That's . . . actually very interesting. "What are you reading right now?"

Miss Pine takes a step closer, leaning her neck down to whisper, "I just finished *The Mysteries of Udolpho*."

Rosalie doesn't know what's more surprising, the book or the way the scent of Miss Pine's lilac perfume momentarily stuns her. "Oh?" she manages, feeling ridiculous.

She doesn't get flustered like this. She doesn't let herself get . . . caught up in people. Men. Women. She's resigned to her life of machinating other happy endings and staying comfortably out of the way of attraction and intrigue and anything . . . complicated.

Otherwise, it's just too painful.

"It's fantastically scandalous," Miss Pine continues. "Have you read it?"

Rosalie stares at Miss Pine's pretty face, words caught in her throat. Rosalie has read it. A year ago. But none of her friends ever have. And Mother doesn't like to read. With her brother, Christopher, off at school, she hasn't had anyone to discuss it with, and of all the people in the world, Miss Pine is the first who—

"I'm so sorry, my dear."

Rosalie blinks, ripping her gaze away from Miss Pine to look up at Mr. Dean, now at her side. He leans down to take her hand and kiss the back of her glove.

"Might I take you on a walk tomorrow, to make up for my deplorable manners?"

Rosalie hesitates for a beat, pushing herself back into the present moment. She came over here to distract Mr. Dean from Miss Pine, and she has succeeded. She got distracted herself in the meantime, but no matter.

"I'd like that," Rosalie says, smiling up at him.

He smiles back, and then stands there, saying nothing. Rosalie turns her smile on Miss Pine and her mother, pretending to be disappointed they can't join. She just couldn't impose on Mr. Dean, you see. It's nothing personal.

Miss Pine looks lightly amused, but there's a glint in Mrs. Pine's eyes that doesn't bode—

"Miss Pine so loves to go walking," Mrs. Pine says, a little too loudly.

Mrs. Pine is looking at Rosalie pointedly, and when Rosalie turns back to Miss Pine, she's blushing, but there's a slight tilt to her lips.

"I do," Miss Pine agrees. "It's invigorating."

Rosalie pushes her tongue against her teeth. Oh, so it's like that? She wants to fight this in close quarters? Fine.

Rosalie looks up at Mr. Dean, but he's still just staring off out the windows. She leans toward him, trying to get his attention, and slowly his head turns back to her. She glances at Miss Pine.

He just stares at her.

She inclines her head, just slightly.

But he's blank behind the eyes, nothing there, no one home.

God, but men are useless.

She looks back up at Miss Pine, whose smirk of amusement has grown. Rosalie's tempted to roll her eyes in response. Instead, she looks past Miss Pine to Mr. Sholle, who's still locked in intense discussion with Mr. Pine. She can make this interesting.

"Mr. Sholle, would you like to accompany Miss Pine to Sydney Gardens?" she asks, interrupting. "The two of you could join Mr. Dean and myself on a walk."

Mr. Sholle's long face lights up. "I would be most pleased to accompany you, Miss Pine. As long as it's permitted, of course," he adds, looking to Mr. Pine.

"Of course. I'd join you myself if my knees were less swollen. As it is, I'm sure my lovely wife will gladly go along as chaperone," Mr. Pine says jovially.

Mrs. Pine looks distinctly dourer. She exchanges a look with Miss Pine that's brimming with meaning. And not particularly subtle.

So mother and daughter are in cahoots. Rosalie can work with that.

Mrs. Pine nods with a tight smile. "Of course," she says.

"Lady Tisend always joins us as well, so you'll have good company," Mr. Dean says easily.

Of course, *now* he's engaged in the conversation.

Rosalie will have to prep her mother to help ensure Mr. Sholle and Miss Pine stay back from her and Mr. Dean. To give them time to get to know each other. Mr. Sholle certainly looks eager.

Miss Pine is watching Rosalie, sucking on her cheek. Rosalie gives her a broad smile.

"We'll meet you at the Great Pulteney entrance tomorrow at ten, then," Rosalie says.

"Looking forward to it," Miss Pine says, turning her face toward Mr. Sholle, her eyes never leaving Rosalie's.

Challenge accepted.

MOTHER IS TEN minutes away from a fit of hysterics.

Mr. Dean promised to meet them at the Great Pulteney entrance to Sydney Gardens, but he's nowhere to be found. He's not exactly late, but for the first time in a while Mother was so anxious, they actually left with more than enough time to spare. Which leaves them loitering outside the gates to the tall, Bath stone Sydney House in a light drizzle, seagulls cawing overhead.

"We'll need to make sure the napkins match the ribbons," Mother says, her voice tight as she fiddles with Rosalie's pin curls.

Rosalie jerks her chin back and takes her mother's hands. "It's just a walk," she says softly.

"I know that," Mother says, pulling her hands back to fuss with her own outfit. "Lists keep me calm."

"But there's nothing to be nervous over," Rosalie insists. "Is this about Mrs. Pine?"

Mother avoids her gaze. She toys with her gloves, going for aloof and failing terribly. "No."

"Did you know each other well? You must have been in the same season."

Mother hesitates, meeting Rosalie's eyes. Rosalie raises one of her brows, waiting.

"We were friends, long ago, before she married Mr. Pine and left Bath. That's all," Mother says.

"Oh," Rosalie replies, a little miffed.

Mother no longer speaking to an old friend doesn't seem so odd, really. She rarely writes letters to anyone. Stands to reason Mrs. Pine might feel slighted if Mother stopped corresponding once she had moved away. Doesn't seem like a good enough reason for Mother's panic, though.

But there isn't time for further questions, because here come Miss Pine and Mrs. Pine, before either Mr. Dean or Mr. Sholle, of course. Miss Pine is wearing a beautiful blue spencer jacket over another gray gown, while Mrs. Pine is in a dark brown that highlights her beautiful hair.

They're a striking pair, and Rosalie ignores her mother's sharp intake of breath to prepare herself. She's going to help Miss Pine see that Mr. Sholle is the perfect match. And hopefully Mrs. Pine will be happy with him. The son of a baron isn't a future viscount, but it's still a title.

This walk will be a success. There's no other choice.

Though when Mrs. Pine and Miss Pine reach them, Rosalie

wonders if there's more to Mother's story than a faded friendship. Mrs. Pine is staring at Mother with much more than disappointed feelings. But there's hardly time to focus on that, not
when Miss Pine is curtsying and smiling down at Rosalie.

"Hello. Beautiful day, isn't it?" she asks slyly.

Miss Pine's hair frames her face perfectly beneath her bonnet. Rosalie has to stop herself from reaching out to move a
stray piece back behind her ear.

Oh, God. Where did that impulse come from?

"It's certainly atmospheric," Rosalie says, meeting Miss Pine's
eyes. It's time to reestablish her position. "I'm looking forward
to the poetry reading on Tuesday, nicely indoors. Will you be
attending?"

She knows Miss Pine won't be. Henrietta's mother arranged
the whole event, and the guest list is exclusive.

"Oh, we haven't been invited," Miss Pine says softly, looking
rather unperturbed.

"Yes we have, dearest," Mrs. Pine cuts in. Mother glares at
her and Rosalie looks over, surprised. "Mrs. Raught was kind
enough to invite us at last week's ball. However, we already have
dinner plans with Lord and Lady Smith, and therefore will have
to miss it."

Mother's eye is twitching. The baron and baroness are only
in town for two weeks, and Mother hasn't managed an invitation yet for tea, let alone a dinner.

"Will you be at the Teppling tea next Wednesday?" Rosalie
asks.

"I don't believe so," Miss Pine says, narrowing her eyes.

"Oh, that's a shame," Mother says, stepping closer with a
smirk that's far too transparent. "We've got the poetry reading,

the tea, dinner with the Howleys—such a busy week after Rosalie's concert this Friday."

Miss Pine and Mrs. Pine exchange a look. The whole exchange makes Rosalie's skin crawl. The four of them, fighting over a man who can't even be bothered to show up on time.

Thankfully, Mr. Dean and Mr. Sholle appear around the corner together not a moment later.

"So sorry we're late, ladies," Mr. Dean says, smiling down at all of them. It makes her height difference with him seem even more glaring, setting her teeth on edge.

She doesn't usually mind being so short, but with the past five minutes of guarded competition, even her height seems a disadvantage.

"That's perfectly fine, dearest," she says, ignoring the way Mr. Dean's head tilts at the endearment. "Shall we?"

She takes his arm and gestures toward the park, forcing Miss Pine and Mr. Sholle to fall in behind them, order restored.

Mr. Dean pats her hand in the crook of his arm as they walk down the path past Sydney House toward the interior of the park. This early in the season, the trees are only just beginning to bud, the bushes devoid of flowers. The grass is at its dullest, and the gray overcast sky doesn't help. But what the gardens lack in splendor, they make up for in silence, at least for the moment.

For all his faults, Rosalie does appreciate Mr. Dean's ability to simply be. She loves her mother, but her constant stream of conversation can grate on a person, and after the tense exchange just now with the Pines, she appreciates some peace.

Of course, it doesn't last very long.

"What is your favorite flower?" Mr. Sholle asks behind them.

"I'm rather fond of violets," Miss Pine replies. "Though I know they're not the most ostentatious of flowers."

Rosalie chances a glance back over her shoulder and watches the way Mr. Sholle is staring at Miss Pine. He certainly looks a little smitten by her beauty.

"They are a remarkable color," Mr. Sholle agrees. "What is your favorite meal?"

"I don't get to know your favorite flower?" Miss Pine asks.

Rosalie listens to their back-and-forth, silently cataloguing Miss Pine's favorite food (roast duck), favorite color (violet, again), favorite sonnet (William Shakespeare's 130), and favorite piece of music (Bach's Cello Suite No. 1 in G Major, Prelude). Mr. Sholle's answers don't interest her in the least.

Her plan is working, but it's left her with a simmering feeling in her belly, like she's won a battle but might be slowly losing a greater war. Mr. Sholle has taken more interest in Miss Pine in the last ten minutes than Mr. Dean has taken in her in over a year.

Miss Pine must be convinced that Mr. Dean is out of reach and utterly devoted to Rosalie. *That's* why Rosalie's bothered that Mr. Dean isn't talking all of a sudden, and that he hasn't ever asked her such questions. It's because it looks bad.

Not at all because Miss Pine's genuine curiosity in Mr. Sholle's answers is making Rosalie feel squirrelly inside for reasons she's can't quite name.

"Are you looking forward to your hunt next weekend?" Rosalie asks Mr. Dean, desperate for a way to shut her mind up and prove his interest all at once.

"Mr. Laghtley's lake is exceedingly well stocked and his land is full of grouse. I expect it to be an excellent weekend," Mr. Dean says, smiling off at the foliage.

She waits, but he doesn't offer anything else. "Is grouse particularly hard to hunt?"

"No, but we do spend a good portion of the day tiptoeing through the woods." He's still not looking at her, but he looks pleased to be talking about it, at any rate.

"It sounds as if you might enjoy coming home to a well-planned meal," she says, wondering if she could entice an invitation for herself, Henrietta, and Amalie. They could . . . wait at home for their men to come back from the hunt. Ugh.

"Mr. Laghtley's cook is excellent. Always puts together an impressive feast."

"Well, perhaps some sparkling conversation after the meal could—"

"We'll want to get a very early start. I've heard there might even be wild boar, which would be exciting."

Rosalie curls her free hand into a fist. Sometimes she just wants to punch his stupidly handsome face. Would it be so heinous to have her along? She wouldn't interfere.

"Oh, I've a question about the Laghtley hunt," Rosalie hears Mr. Sholle say.

And suddenly he's on Mr. Dean's other side. Mr. Dean squeezes Rosalie's hand, and then lets her go, falling into step instead beside Mr. Sholle. Which leaves Rosalie and Miss Pine watching the two men bend their heads together and amble ahead, without them.

Rosalie stands still, seething. The fact that Mr. Sholle abandoned Miss Pine equally quickly is no balm at all. Rosalie is not supposed to get left behind for talk of hunting, or anything, for that matter.

"Have you ever killed anything?"

Rosalie blinks, turning to find Miss Pine now standing next to her and looking down at her with honest curiosity.

"What kind of question is that?" Rosalie asks, laughing a little, the anger in her chest lessening just a hair.

"Would you rather discuss needlepoint patterns?"

Rosalie glances behind them, where their mothers are walking as far apart as possible, glaring at the backs of the boys' heads. At least they're united in that.

"I've done some gruesome needlepoints, actually, but no, I've not killed anything," Rosalie says, looking to Miss Pine.

She giggles, the most utterly charming sound. Goodness. Rosalie breaks eye contact and starts walking again, Miss Pine falling into step with her.

"Have you ever killed anything, then?" Rosalie asks.

"Father and I used to trap rabbits. I didn't . . . directly kill anything, I guess. But I was still responsible," Miss Pine says, rather contemplatively.

"Did you like it?" Rosalie asks, allowing her guard to come down a bit.

The men seem to adore killing animals—the thrill of the hunt clearly more important than conversation with a potential life partner.

"I liked spending time with my father," Miss Pine says softly. "And he would . . . check that the rabbits weren't suffering before I saw them. I don't relish the idea of causing pain."

Rosalie glances over at Miss Pine, whose eyes are far away. She has the absurd urge to make her giggle again—to wipe the melancholy from her face. But that's not why they're here.

"Outside of trapping game, what kind of more . . . appropriate pastimes do you enjoy?"

Miss Pine huffs a laugh. It's no giggle, but charming all the same. "The usual, I suppose. I paint, I draw, I read, I play the pianoforte, as I mentioned at the ball. And you? You must be prim and proper all the time."

Rosalie rolls her eyes at the little smirk on Miss Pine's face. She wonders what Miss Pine would say if she told her about her dirty limerick competitions with Amalie, or that she used to climb trees until she was fourteen and ruined her mother's favorite dress. Would she giggle again? Raise an eyebrow? Ask more questions?

"I also enjoy the pianoforte," Rosalie begins. She's made up some rather scandalous lyrics to an old madrigal. Maybe Miss Pine would—

"Lady Rosalie is most accomplished on the pianoforte. She'll be performing a piece at the concert on Friday," Mother says.

Rosalie and Miss Pine jump. Their mothers have snuck up on them. Mr. Dean and Mr. Sholle have gotten at least fifty feet away from them, already up the hill and over the bridge that crosses the small stream at the back of the park. She'd hardly noticed.

Rosalie withholds a glare. She's not at all excited about playing for their guests, especially after a professional performance. But Mother is insistent that it will endear her to Mr. Dean. She's been getting increasingly desperate to cement Rosalie's courtship, even before the Pines arrived in Bath. A year without a proposal, something must be afoot.

Rosalie's rather sure it's just that Mr. Dean isn't that interested in anything.

"Miss Pine used to serenade our tenants weekly; she's utterly gifted on the instrument," Mrs. Pine says quickly.

Rosalie glances at Miss Pine, who's blushing, but not entirely out of embarrassment. "More than just a hobby?" Rosalie asks.

Miss Pine meets her eyes, straightening up. "I'm good," she admits. There's a spark of confidence in her that makes Rosalie's fingers tingle.

Mother opens her mouth—

"Perhaps you should play as well," Rosalie says impulsively. All three women stare at her. "Perhaps we should all play. Mother, you play so beautifully and rarely show off your talents. Didn't you used to perform with a friend in your season?"

"Oh, Mother, you should join us too," Miss Pine says before Rosalie's mother can manage words. "You played in your season as well. Duets. Could we find your duet partner?"

Mother's surprise turns to discomfort. Rosalie glances at Mrs. Pine, who's also gone slightly white, and realizes with a flash: Mrs. Pine was the friend Mother used to play with. And now they haven't spoken in over two decades.

Oh, dear.

They stand for a moment in uncomfortable silence as their mothers refuse to look at each other. Rosalie glances at Miss Pine, who looks as discomfited as her mother, and won't meet Rosalie's eyes all of a sudden. All that challenge gone in the face of whatever happened twenty-five years ago.

"Or each of you could play separately," Rosalie says quickly. "I know you've been practicing the Haydn, Mother. It would be a shame to waste that effort."

That seems to bring her mother back. "It would hardly be a waste, as it wasn't so much effort. But as I don't believe my former duet partner would be . . . amenable, I agree. But only if Mrs. Pine will play as well."

They all look to Mrs. Pine, who hesitates.

"It would be a wonderful opportunity to reintroduce yourself to the ton," Mother continues. "As long as you've kept up with the pianoforte since our season."

The color returns to Mrs. Pine's face quickly. It seems she's as reactive as her daughter. "I would be delighted to play. Miss Pine and I both enjoy performing, don't we, dearest?"

"Yes, we do," Miss Pine says confidently, smiling at her mother before looking at Rosalie, challenge back in her eyes.

Mother hates performing as much as Rosalie does. What has she gotten them into?

But she can't show weakness, not now. "Looking forward to it."

"Yes," Mother adds, and gestures for them all to keep walking.

They turn to head up the path, Mr. Dean and Mr. Sholle nearly specks in the distance.

Rosalie glances again at Miss Pine, who's staring straight ahead. But there's a quirk to her lips, like she's won something. It's infuriating, and alluring.

Nope. No. Just infuriating.

Rosalie needs to practice. Her performance must be the best of the bunch. To impress Mr. Dean, of course.

And to wipe that smug smile off Miss Pine's face.

Chapter Four
Catherine

C atherine paces the hallway outside her bedroom on the third floor of their new townhouse, the floorboards creaking unfamiliarly beneath her feet. The sound of the pianoforte fills the house. Catherine twists her fingers together, hoping that this time Mother will get through the final few flourishes of Bach's Fugue No. 9 in E Maj—

BANG.

Mother's shout of rage rings up the staircase and Catherine winces. Mother's been practicing for hours. She wants to best Lady Tisend. Wants to rise to her cruel challenge, and utterly impress the ton, proving that she has returned triumphant after leaving Bath in such haste all those years ago. Why she's chosen such a fiddly, technical piece, Catherine doesn't know. Catherine hasn't had even a minute with the pianoforte.

She's confident in her choice of music, but it would be nice to get a chance to run through it even once before the concert tomorrow. She's not as intense as Mother, but she does want to impress the ton. And Mr. Dean, of course, the whole purported reason for the performance.

But mostly she wants Lady Rosalie to know that Catherine will meet any challenge she tosses out. She's not going to let Lady Rosalie decide her season, no matter how clever she seems nor how beloved she is in Bath. Mr. Sholle? He's perfectly respectable and nice, but not enough to distract Catherine.

Not that Mr. Dean seems much better, really. Mr. Sholle couldn't ask enough questions, but it sounded like Lady Rosalie was prying information out of Mr. Dean with a crowbar. Who walks away from someone like Lady Rosalie to talk about hunting?

Mother misses the final run, again, and screams.

It's time for a break.

Catherine pads down the stairs and heads for the sitting room, only to find her father sitting despondently on a chair just outside the doors in his housecoat. Mother starts over, yet again.

"Should I?" Catherine asks when he looks up at her.

"No, no, let her get it out of her system. When she's exhausted all her anger, she'll get it. She always does."

Catherine can't help but smile. Father loves her mother so ardently and fully, even twenty-five years after their wedding, foibles and faults and all.

"Then let's at least give her some privacy," Catherine suggests, holding out her hands.

Father hesitates, his big brown eyes unsure, brows creasing. Catherine nods encouragingly and he takes her hands. She helps him out of his chair and wraps her arm around his waist. Together they head back down the hall to his study.

Only half of Father's books have been unpacked, sitting disorganized on the deep brown shelves that line the walls. Portraits are still waiting to be hung between the shelves, and there are stacks of files and papers on his desk to go through. The light from the windows that look out on the street help make the space bright and airy. Catherine feels her shoulders come down, at peace here.

She helps Father over to his aged brown leather armchair. Rarely does she appreciate being a few inches taller than he is, but being able to help him as his condition has worsened has been a blessing.

Father groans softly and shifts in the chair while Catherine settles onto the far stiffer settee Mother insisted on buying new for the study. It's cream with red fleur-de-lis, and while it's pleasant to look at, it lacks in comfort.

"Don't judge your mother too harshly for her . . . intensity about this concert," Father says.

Catherine nearly jumps. She'd been expecting some companionable quiet. "I don't. Though I'd love to better understand what—"

"She just wants everything to be perfect for your first season."

Catherine sighs, curiosity batted down, again. "The season will be perfect. I'm here with the two of you. We're settled, and you're feeling so much better, aren't you?" she asks.

Father smiles, his eyes crinkling and cheeks dimpling. "I am, I am. The waters really do help." He laughs when Catherine grimaces, thinking of the pungent waters from the Pump Room. "You do get used to them."

"How many years does that take?"

"I think I was twenty-four?" he replies.

Catherine laughs. "But that's when you left Bath."

"Perhaps it's the absence that has made my heart grow fonder," he says, chuckling. "But they are helping, as are the baths. You don't need to worry about me."

"I know," Catherine says quickly.

As if she could stop worrying about him. He's been in such

pain, for years. And now they're here, and Mother's on this quest to get revenge on Lady Tisend, and it's taking up all of their time. She knows he'll do anything to make Mother feel better, including lying about how he's really feeling.

"And your mother will be back to her normal self," he continues. There's another loud crash of keys from the sitting room. "Once the concert is over."

For all her admonishments over the years, Mother has some very colorful expletives stored away.

"Maybe I should, or you should—" Catherine starts.

"Or maybe there's a present for you on the desk," Father cuts in, smiling sneakily.

Catherine sighs, torn between helping Mother and seeing what Father's gotten for her. Father raises an eyebrow and Catherine lets curiosity win out. She jumps up and scurries over to the desk, delighted to find a neatly wrapped package in the distinctive shape of a new book.

Catherine can't help it, quickly tearing into the wrapping. *The Old English Baron* by Clara Reeve stares up at her and Catherine grins.

"You spoil me," she says, holding the book to her chest.

"As is my right," Father says.

Catherine walks back to the sitting area and bends down to kiss his cheek. "Thank you."

"You are most welcome. Now take that upstairs and read until your mother comes out of her fugue state." He grins up at her as she groans.

"Father," she admonishes. He's always making such terrible puns.

"Go."

Catherine hugs the book once more to show her appreciation

before heading out of the study. She ignores Mother's curses and banging, forcing herself up the stairs with the promise of a good story.

She has her own library to finish unpacking in her new room, but she bypasses the boxes by her bookshelves, her freshly made four-poster bed with the new blue curtains, and her vanity.

The large picture window along the side of her room that looks out on Great Pulteney Street has a built-in window seat covered in a paisley fabric. It's the perfect cozy place to hole up and forget that she only has such a luxurious room because her father couldn't climb daily to the third floor to take the primary bedroom.

But as she starts to read about Sir Philip Harclay, she finds she can't picture him the way she ought. She should be picturing a broody, stalwart young man, returning home from knightly adventures. Instead, he's short, and fiery, and bears a striking resemblance to a certain lady dressed in breeches and a tunic.

Catherine slams the book shut, closing her eyes tight. She has to stop letting Lady Rosalie pervade her every thought. It's not healthy. It's not productive. And it's not going to help her do anything but get more bothered. Hot and bothered and—

No. Lady Rosalie is her adversary, no matter how pretty, persuasive, cunning, and witty she may be.

Catherine keeps her eyes closed and forces herself to mentally go through her own upcoming performance. She's decided to play the much less technical but far more lyrical Nocturne No. 14 in G Major by John Field. She's hoping her musicality will win points with . . . well, with whomever she decides she's trying to impress tomorrow.

Because like the hero in her new novel, the face that comes to mind when she imagines playing isn't Mr. Dean's. Instead, she keeps seeing a pair of icy gray-blue eyes beneath dark brows that are more expressive making a snide remark than most people manage when talking about love.

SHE HAD COMPLETELY forgotten that Lady Rosalie had offered to teach her a dance. But the reminder came this morning on a beautifully embossed calling card. What was she thinking, knowingly walking into the Tisend home early, with no society set around them as a buffer? And what are her mother and father supposed to do while they practice? Chat idly about the rumor that nearly ruined Mother's life?

Mother's gripping so tightly to Father's arm that Catherine's worried she'll cut off his circulation. Her own nails are digging into her arms through her gloves. But Father, cheerful as ever, knocks on the door, and there's no going back.

The door to the massive Tisend townhouse opens before she can gather any composure and they're quickly ushered into a cavernous foyer and relieved of their cloaks. Unlike their narrow townhouse, which is still half unpacked, with art everywhere while Mother dithers over placement, the Tisend foyer is immaculate. High columns ring the two-story space, with enormous ocean landscapes hanging on the walls. Catherine turns her head rapidly, trying to take them all in. The one of the ship being swallowed by waves is rather ominous.

The butler ushers them through a tall arch that opens onto an expansive ballroom. It looks almost like the dance hall at the Upper Rooms, but more lavish. Three chandeliers hang down from the ceiling, casting shimmering patterns over the assembled chairs, all wrapped in beautiful white linens. Twenty of them sit facing a raised dais with chairs for musicians and the largest pianoforte Catherine has ever seen. The whole scene is surrounded by the most beautiful flowers in blues, whites, and soft yellows.

She has to perform in this lush space. Has to impress here. Has to prove she and her mother are as worthy of regard as the Tisends. How can she possibly—how can *they* possibly—prove their worth when no level of perfect performance can make up for what they clearly lack in wealth and power?

"Got what she always wanted, didn't she?" Catherine hears Mother murmur.

She turns, noticing the pallor of her mother's face, while her father simply looks around, impressed. She tries to find words of comfort, despite the unease skittering up and down her own spine—

"You're finally here."

Catherine spins around and reflexively stands up taller as Lady Rosalie and Lady Tisend appear from behind the dais. Lady Tisend is dragging a short, dapper man with salt-and-pepper hair by the hand. Must be Lord Tisend. He has Lady Rosalie's small, upturned nose.

Behind him, a slightly taller woman follows with an older gentleman, the two of them walking more sedately. The second woman has a soft smile and looks far more relaxed than either Lady Rosalie or Lady Tisend.

"Come, come, I've got our pianist set up on the smaller pianoforte at the back," Lady Rosalie says, dipping in a curtsy to Catherine's parents before grabbing Catherine by the hand.

"It's nice to see you, Lady Tis—" Catherine manages, trying to curtsy while Lady Rosalie pulls her away.

Everyone laughs, even Mother, which is something. But she can't focus on them, not when she's trying not to trip over her own feet.

"Is there a fire?" she asks Lady Rosalie. She's decidedly not focusing on the feeling of Lady Rosalie's smaller hand in hers.

"We've only thirty minutes to learn this dance," Lady Rosalie says simply, tugging Catherine around behind the dais, where, just as she said, there's a small pianoforte and a pianist patiently waiting for them.

The man nods to her, wearing a powdered wig and dressed in a cream patterned silk waistcoat that looks like something out of a drawing of Versailles.

"That's Monsieur Claude," Lady Rosalie says, dropping Catherine's hand to gesture to the musician. "He's my father's favorite pianist."

"A pleasure to meet you," Catherine manages.

How many concerts do the Tisends throw a year?

"And you, mademoiselle," he says. "Shall we begin half tempo?"

"I'll show Miss Pine the steps and then we'll begin, Monsieur Claude," Lady Rosalie says.

Monsieur Claude sits back, happy to relax.

It's only then that Catherine gets a chance to admire Lady Rosalie's stunning outfit. Her gown is a soft pink that lays over her petite figure perfectly, with beautiful flowers embroidered along her hem and up to her knees, matching the flowers on the dais. Her shiny dark hair falls softly around her face in slightly relaxed curls, the rest gathered elegantly at the back of her head. Her short gloves, in a light pink lace, accentuate her dainty hands.

She's utterly breathtaking, which is a problem, because she's been explaining steps for a full minute and Catherine hasn't caught a word of it. No wonder people are dazzled by Lady Rosalie. Between her beauty, her intimidating countenance, and her obscene wealth, how could anyone not be?

Lady Rosalie stops talking and stares at Catherine expectantly.

Catherine shrugs guiltily. "I'm so sorry, could you . . . say all of that again?" Lady Rosalie raises an eyebrow. "It's a lot to take in!"

"It is a dazzling room, Lady Rosalie, you must admit. I nearly forgot my entire solo the first time I performed here," Monsieur Claude says merrily.

Catherine's more than willing to let Lady Rosalie think it's all the room.

"I will give you a tour another time. But we've limited remaining minutes to learn this, so will you focus?" Lady Rosalie asks, looking back at Catherine.

The quirk of her lips suggests she noticed Catherine staring at her décolletage. It's only that the lace along her bosom draws the eye, and her dress suits her exceedingly well, and it's *meant* to attract attention. She appreciates a good shelf. Bosoms are pleasing to look at.

Usually, she doesn't get caught.

"Ready?"

"Yes," Catherine says quickly, hoping her cheeks aren't bright red.

"It's four counts forward, touch hands, then four back, a cross to the right, then back to middle, then back to the left. Got it?"

Catherine nods and they step to face each other. Lady Rosalie counts off and Catherine stumbles through the easy steps. Lady Rosalie doesn't look impressed.

Catherine forces herself to focus. She's not a bad dancer. She's just usually not this distracted. The men she danced with back home were beautiful in their own right, and Mr. Dean is certainly handsome, but none of them were as captivating as Lady Rosalie. None of them had so many minute expressions.

No one has commanded her attention like this so far.

"No, do it again, you're missing the second turn," Lady Rosalie says imperiously, tugging on Catherine's hand as they stand close together, halfway through the sequence.

Catherine manages a nod and lets Lady Rosalie walk her through the turn sequence again, their hands coming together, then apart, and back.

"Better. You're not terrible at this, you just lack focus," Lady Rosalie decides, looking Catherine up and down when they finish the last step. "Think you can manage the whole thing?"

Catherine swallows against a new flutter of nerves. "No mistakes," she promises.

Lady Rosalie chuckles. "We'll see."

Lady Rosalie nods to Monsieur Claude. He begins to play and Lady Rosalie counts them off softly.

Forward, hands touch, back, turn right, center, turn left, center. Take Lady Rosalie's hand without focusing on the way it makes her arm tingle. Hop step twice, spin, take her other hand. Don't focus on the way she squeezes gently, as if in encouragement.

Then she has to circle Lady Rosalie, careful not to step on her toes in her pink ballet flats. Catherine tries hard not to notice her floral-and-citrus perfume—something different from what she wore on their walk. It's sharper, like lemon.

Lady Rosalie's countenance cracks and she smiles as they go into the last sequence, spinning around each other and hop-stepping, hands linked. Catherine finds herself breathless, laughing as they spin around. Lady Rosalie joins her and they come together one last time, a little too close, before spinning away in a final flourish.

Monsieur Claude concludes the accompaniment with two

triumphant beats and laughs along with them. Catherine smiles over at him and then looks to Lady Rosalie. Her curls are a little disarrayed, and her cheeks are pink.

Catherine's breathing hard, her own face hot, mouth still split in a smile.

"You're a quick study," Lady Rosalie says.

"You're a good teacher," Catherine admits. "Mean, but good."

Lady Rosalie cackles, her laughter ringing around the room so pleasantly. "That is exactly what I'm going for."

"You should teach children. They'd learn in days," Catherine suggests, delighted at the way Lady Rosalie snickers.

"I should not. I made a girl cry once trying to teach her arpeggios.

"It was my daughter. She still won't touch a pianoforte," Monsieur Claude says.

There's the sound of a commotion suddenly on the other side of the dais. Catherine can hear chatter beginning to echo about the room.

Lady Rosalie laughs and takes Catherine's arm. "Do give her my best, would you? Bonne performance, Monsieur Claude. Thank you for your time."

"Of course, my lady," he says, standing to give them both a bow.

Lady Rosalie tugs gently on Catherine's arm, leading her back out into the main room and toward the waiting phalanx of guests queueing at the entrance.

Lady Rosalie's parents approach the crowd, all smiles. Catherine looks for her parents and spots them standing near the entrance to a side room, chatting with the couple they saw when they first arrived. Mother doesn't look too strained, though

Catherine can tell she's still gripping Father's arm rather hard. But at least she's smiling.

"My aunt and uncle will take good care of your parents, don't fret," Lady Rosalie says.

"Of course not," Catherine says quickly, not wanting to let on that anything might be amiss. She got to practice dance moves while her mother faced her greatest betrayer.

"Now, stay close to me. I'll be sure to introduce you to all the right people. Present you to society properly."

Catherine bites back a retort. There was nothing improper about her own cousin's introductions at the Assembly Room, nor her parents' ability to introduce her to the *right people*.

But she shouldn't let on. She and Lady Rosalie have just spent a surprisingly fun few minutes together, and allowing her to think she retains the upper hand is the whole point, isn't it? Catherine will lie in wait to prove her wrong, slowly, steadily, stealthily.

Though as they join the receiving line and Catherine curtsies time and time again, she begins to wonder if it might truly be easier to just let Lady Rosalie have at it and simply give over to her power.

"And how is your cousin—Miss Getling? Has her rheumatism improved on the Continent?" Lady Rosalie asks a tall broad gentleman. Catherine thinks his name might be Mr. Darton.

"It has," he says, surprised. "I'll tell her you asked after her. It'll make her whole week."

Lady Rosalie smiles, and it's a crafted expression—nothing like the amused delight from their dance earlier—but no less dazzling. "Please do remind her about my father's friend in Lorraine. She should call and see the orchards."

"I will," the man says, bowing to them before heading off.

"Have you ever been to the Continent, Miss Pine?" Lady Rosalie asks.

There's a momentary lull in the procession of guests and Catherine allows her shoulders to come down. If she remembers one-eighth of these names, it will be a triumph.

"I haven't. Have you?"

"Twice," Lady Rosalie says, gesturing toward the chairs.

Catherine lets her lead, the two of them smiling as guests mill around them, slowly heading toward their seats.

"Was it wonderful?"

"Parts of it, yes," Lady Rosalie says with a shrug. "Sometimes it's just as boring as Bath."

There's a crack in the façade, a dimming in her eyes. It's momentary, before that practiced smile snaps back into place. But it makes Catherine wonder. Can she tease out the woman she was dancing with earlier?

"Who among your traveling party would you leave behind to make it more adventurous?" Catherine asks casually.

"My father," Lady Rosalie replies immediately. Her eyes widen a fraction and she glances at Catherine.

"Oh? I would have thought him very adventurous," Catherine admits, glancing back at the lively pair of Tisends still greeting guests at the door. The earl seems most affable.

"You haven't seen him at a museum," Lady Rosalie mutters.

Catherine stifles a surprised giggle. "My father's much the same."

That makes Lady Rosalie smile. They turn together and look out at the room.

Catherine feels a prickle of anxiety work its way up the back of her neck. She has to perform in front of all of these people. By the way Lady Rosalie stiffens beside her, Catherine figures she's thinking the same. Catherine decides to try to poke her again, get her smiling. Or, rather, put her off-kilter so she doesn't play as well, she thinks, spotting her mother and father making their way up the center aisle toward them.

Behind them, a woman and a man, both dressed rather ostentatiously with a lot of gold trim, walk with their noses in the air.

"Who are they?" Catherine asks.

Lady Rosalie doesn't need to look at her to know. "Mr. and Mrs. Fairwinter."

Catherine watches Lady Rosalie's reaction, the way her jaw tightens, as though she might like to laugh at their haughty looks.

"I bet he could make a stuffed woolly mammoth long for death with a lecture on ancient trees."

Lady Rosalie lets out a loud snort. Catherine can't help but grin as people turn to look at them. Lady Rosalie coughs into the crook of her elbow, shrugging politely at the onlookers before looking over at Catherine, eyes narrowed.

"What? He could!" Catherine insists.

Lady Rosalie's frowning at her, but her eyes are alight with mirth.

Lady Tisend appears at their side, followed by Lady Rosalie's friends Miss Henrietta Raught and the taller, sharper Miss Amalie Linet. Lady Rosalie's cheeky regard vanishes, and Catherine watches, impressed, as her shoulders roll back, and all at once she's *Lady Rosalie*, imperious and in control once more.

Mr. Dean and Mr. Sholle are at the back of the group, and Catherine wonders for a moment if she should try to find a way to—

But Lady Rosalie's already guiding Catherine far down the

row to her waiting parents. Catherine sits carefully beside her mother, watching in frustrated amusement as Lady Rosalie directs her friends the same way. Unsurprisingly, Mr. Sholle ends up on Catherine's left, with Miss Raught, Miss Linet, Mr. Fortes, and Mr. Rile seated between Catherine and Lady Rosalie. She's even put Mr. Dean on her other side, as if Catherine could somehow reach him through five other people.

Catherine would be more upset, but she realizes her mother is sitting ramrod straight beside her.

"How are you?" Catherine whispers.

Mother glances at her for a moment, eyes a little wide and harried. "I am perfectly well," she says stiffly.

"That Sir Walter Jones has such stories," Father says, leaning around Mother with a grin. "We'll have to have them over for tea."

"Sir Walter Jones?" Catherine asks.

"Lord Tisend's brother-in-law. Just arrived with Tisend's younger sister for the rest of the season. Lady Jones is a laugh and a half," he adds at a whisper. "Isn't she?"

Mother doesn't say anything, just jerks her head. The musicians are assembling on the dais in front of them, and everyone around them has sat down.

Catherine glances down the row, noting Miss Raught and Miss Linet speaking animatedly to their beaus, while Lady Rosalie and Mr. Dean sit facing the musicians, not talking.

Lady Rosalie glances over at her and Catherine sits back quickly as the musicians take the stage and begin their performance.

Mr. Dean is squandering the moment. Catherine's not sure now if stealing him away would be a triumph, or if she'd ultimately be doing Lady Rosalie a favor. Lady Rosalie is as dazzling as the soprano on stage. Mr. Dean is simply . . . mortal, in every way.

All too soon, the professional performance comes to a close. The musicians and singers sumptuously dressed in powdered wigs and Georgian gowns take their bows. Then Monsieur Claude and a porter are moving the pianoforte up to the front of the little stage.

Mother swallows audibly beside her and Catherine grabs her hand for support.

Lady Tisend rises and moves to the front of the dais. "We are so thrilled all of you could join us tonight for such a wonderful performance," she says, her voice commanding yet somehow still soft. Everyone has to lean in to hear her. "But we couldn't let tonight just be a sparkling concert! Lady Rosalie and I had planned to perform for you, but then a dear old friend returned to town."

Mother stiffens beside Catherine, her hand like a vise.

"I couldn't dare to deprive you of her talents, and that of her lovely daughter. So, what better way to reintroduce herself to Bath than for you all to hear the brilliant talents of my friend Mrs. Pine?" Lady Tisend says, smiling over at Mother.

She gestures to them and for a horrible, halting moment, it seems Mother can't make herself stand up. How dare Lady Tisend do it like this, frame it like this? As if she isn't the reason Mother is *returning* to Bath in the first place.

Father discreetly moves his hand to Mother's upper back. Catherine looks toward Lady Rosalie. Is she in on this? Does she know what happened?

But then Mother stands up. Her face settles into a blithe mask and she walks toward Lady Tisend with a broad smile. Only Catherine and Father would notice the way her shoulders are just slightly too far back.

Catherine slides over to sit next to Father, taking his hand, her own heart in her throat as Mother takes her place at the pianoforte. She adjusts the seat and sits for a moment, staring at the keys. Time stretches and Catherine's chest grows tight, eyes prickling. If her mother should falter here, she'll never forgive herself. To have returned to Bath only to be humiliated—

And then Mother begins to play. What was halting and fumbling in their sitting room becomes the most fluid, exciting, propulsive piece of music Catherine thinks she's ever heard. Mother is stunning there at the pianoforte, her mouth set in a relaxed smile, her posture tall, her fingers flying perfectly and effortlessly over the keys.

She soars through the piece, and when she hits the final note and looks up and out into the audience, the crowd erupts with applause. Catherine watches her mother's eyes sparkle, her face breaking into a humble smile. She's never seen her mother look so luminous, so excited, and so relieved in all her life.

Catherine needs to secure their place in society, heal whatever hurt lurks in her mother's heart, and wash away the ugly past, so her mother always looks this radiant. She should never fear the ton. They should fear her, just as they do Lady Tisend.

Catherine will start by winning Mr. Dean's hand.

Chapter Five

Rosalie

The audience is still clapping when Miss Pine stands and trades places with her dazzling mother. They squeeze each other's hands when they pass, their dimples rising exactly the same way. It makes Rosalie's heart clench a little to see Miss Pine so proud of her mother.

Rosalie's mother's nails, on the other hand, are biting into her arm. Neither of them expected Mrs. Pine's performance to be that technical nor that spectacular. Rosalie doesn't know how she's going to follow it, let alone how Miss Pine will manage.

Mother never outshines Rosalie in moments like these. She comes close, but keeps herself back to let Rosalie take the spotlight. Mrs. Pine made no such effort for her daughter. Rosalie almost pities Miss Pine, watching as she adjusts herself on the bench.

Then Miss Pine looks right at her for a moment before beginning to play the most beautiful rendition of Field's Nocturne she's ever heard in her life. Every note, every beat, every rest feels poignant and powerful. Her graceful, delicate fingers dance across the keys. The long line of her neck and the soft smile on her face—she is luminous.

Rosalie's every minute movement on the pianoforte is rehearsed and calculated. She feels no grace, no ease, when she's behind the instrument. It's a battle between her and the keys. She always wins, but not like this.

Miss Pine's piece is far less technical, far less impressive than Mrs. Pine's was, but she makes it sing. It's— She is—

"Breathtaking," Mr. Dean whispers.

Rosalie's awed wonder immediately sloughs away. She can't let Miss Pine's talent, and charm, wry wit, and beautiful face cloud her judgement. Make her careless when she needs to be in control, of Miss Pine, of Mr. Dean, of everything.

This girl is her competition, not something—someone—to be ogled and mesmerized by and infatuated with. The spell she's cast over the audience—over Rosalie—will end when she finishes the piece, and then Rosalie will decimate her.

When Miss Pine concludes, there's another round of thunderous applause. Miss Pine curtsies to the crowd and then steps down from the dais. Her eyes briefly catch Rosalie's, triumph on her face.

"Aren't they wonderful?" Mother asks the crowd, looking gracious and happy for the Pines. But Rosalie can see the tightness in her jaw. Mother's furious.

"My daughter, Lady Rosalie, would like to play a piece for you as well. And then my sister-in-law, the lovely Lady Jones, will serenade us. And I'll play a little something too, just for fun."

The crowd laughs good-naturedly. Rosalie takes a deep breath and forces herself to rise with poise. She walks to the dais and up to the pianoforte, smiling at the audience.

Don't look at Miss Pine. *Don't* look at Miss Pine.

Rosalie adjusts the bench forward, Miss Pine's lithe, tall body having shifted her normal setup. But she's not thinking about

Miss Pine, or her body. She's thinking about her fast, technical variation. If she can't have Miss Pine's musicality, she'll impress them with Bach.

She settles her hands over the keys, raises her head, and looks straight into Miss Pine's eyes. There's a catch in her chest, and she starts playing almost by reflex.

It's too fast.

She rips her gaze away from Miss Pine, staring straight at the wall. There's no more room in her head for girlish fancies or fancying girls right now. There is only the keys, an audience of the most important people in the ton, and the punishing pace she's set.

She manages to keep herself on track, closing her eyes to get through the fast, delicate ending. She probably makes too much of a flourish of her final notes, but she manages it, releasing the keys with a short retraction of her hands.

Slowly, she opens her eyes, turning to the clapping audience. She knows her performance was hugely impressive. But they're not clapping like they did for Miss Pine.

Rosalie stands abruptly, curtsying before returning to her seat. Miss Pine and her mother are leaning together happily. Miss Pine shoots her a bright smile, but Rosalie averts her eyes.

She sits down, her whole body shaking. She never gets nervous like this. Or rather, is never nervous *after* a performance. But her heart is pounding, and she's a little clammy. She's glad Aunt Genevieve is taking the stage. She'll play something beautiful and long, as is always her way, giving Rosalie a minute to compose herself.

"That was most impressive," Mr. Dean whispers to her.

Rosalie forces a smile and glances at him before looking back at Aunt Genevieve. Impressive, but not *breathtaking*.

The Pine women are just too good. They're a true threat, much more than Rosalie would have thought just two weeks ago.

Her heart, at least, has calmed down by the time Mother plays her tight, technical variation. She's excellent without being showy, and gives a polite curtsy to the audience as they applaud her afterward. She never disappoints, but neither does she overshadow.

Father stands and thanks the guests for attending, encouraging them to mingle and relax with passed hors d'oeuvres. Rosalie rises with Mr. Dean and girds herself for facing Miss Pine. She has to give the woman a true compliment, and, at the same time, find a way to put her in her place.

"You were so wonderful!"

Rosalie turns to find Henrietta and Amalie approaching her, dragging Mr. Rile and Mr. Fortes with them.

"Easily the hardest piece of the lot," Amalie adds, squeezing Rosalie's hand with her free one.

"Very well played, Lady Rosalie," Mr. Rile agrees.

"Though that Miss Pine, my goodness," Mr. Fortes says, his long face gone a bit dreamy.

He winces a moment later and Rosalie stifles a laugh. Amalie must have pinched him.

"She has a true gift," Rosalie says, pushing a tinge of admiration into her words. "You and she might enjoy duets, Miss Linet," she adds to Amalie.

"Oh, you certainly should. You are a true talent as well," Mr. Fortes says quickly.

Amalie winks at Rosalie.

"I wish I could play as well as the two of you," Henrietta says without malice, round-cheeked smile still perfectly in place.

"You can play circles around us on the violin," Rosalie says firmly. "I suppose we could all gather to play music."

"That sounds like an excellent idea," Aunt Genevieve says, appearing around their little group, leading Mother by the hand.

"I'm sure Rosalie could teach all of you some new pieces," Mother says. "You were perfect, darling," she adds.

"Thank you, Mother," she says, only a hint of bite there. Laying it on thick won't make anyone think she was better than Miss Pine.

"You were fast," Aunt Genevieve says.

Rosalie laughs softly at that. She adores her aunt so very much. "And you were wonderful, as always. Is there anything you can't do?"

"No," Aunt Genevieve says playfully. The gentlemen laugh, and Henrietta and Amalie giggle. "And whose did you gentlemen think was the best performance of the evening?"

Mr. Fortes, Mr. Rile, and Mr. Dean all look at her and then glance amongst themselves.

"Well," Mr. Fortes begins, narrow shoulders going up.

"Sorry to intrude, but Lady Jones, I must congratulate you on a beautiful performance." Mrs. Pine appears behind Mother and Aunt Genevieve with Miss Pine, whose cheeks are lightly pink.

"You flatter me, Mrs. Pine," Aunt Genevieve says.

Mother only barely withholds her glower as Aunt Genevieve lets Mrs. Pine and Miss Pine into their circle. Mrs. Pine looks inches taller than she did at the start of the evening. Rosalie can hear people murmuring around them, all in awe of the Pine women. The men in their circle look far too interested as Miss Pine shifts in beside her mother.

"It's not flattery at all," Mrs. Pine says to Aunt Genevieve. "I was very moved by your performance. And Lady Tisend, yours was equally impressive."

Mother manages a polite smile, though Rosalie can tell it's costing her.

"I must say, Lady Rosalie, I thought yours was by far the most challenging piece of the night," Miss Pine says.

Rosalie blinks, surprised. Miss Pine looks so earnest.

"I quite agree," Mrs. Pine says. "You must spend hours at the pianoforte every day."

"Oh, well, I—"

"She barely needs to practice," Mother cuts in. "It comes so naturally, you see."

Rosalie stares at her mother, then glances at Aunt Genevieve, whose eyebrows are raised.

"I don't mind practicing. The challenge of it is what's most exciting, for me, at least," Rosalie says, looking back to Mrs. Pine. "Miss Raught and Miss Linet get sick of it."

"We do not," Henrietta says quickly. "It's always an honor to listen to you practice."

Rosalie glances at her with a true smile. There's no guile or artifice in Henrietta at all. Which is charming, and unhelpful.

"I'd love to hear you rehearse someday," Miss Pine says.

Rosalie meets her eyes again. Is she being honest, or does she want more information out of her?

"If you'd like to hear more music, Miss Pine, you ought to join myself and Lady Rosalie at the Upper Rooms in two months' time. My father is throwing a most exciting concert, and we would be honored by your company," Mr. Dean says.

Rosalie nearly gapes. He rarely chimes in at these events. And not only is he engaging now, but he's inviting Miss Pine on one of their long-scheduled outings?

Mother's definitely glowering this time. She looks to Rosalie, opening her mouth, forcing Rosalie to intervene before she's entirely ready.

"Miss Raught and Miss Linet will be there as well. I'm sure Mr. Fortes and Mr. Rile are looking forward to escorting them," Rosalie spits out.

Her friends stare at her, surprised, but she forces a smile, ignoring them to look to both men.

"Of—of course," Mr. Fortes says quickly. "So looking forward to it. Aren't you, Rile?"

"Honored!" he says, his voice a little high, brown eyes wide.

Maybe Rosalie's glaring too.

She looks to Miss Pine, who's been watching the entire exchange, biting at her lower lip, withholding a smirk.

"I'm sure Mr. Sholle could be convinced to escort you, Miss Pine," Rosalie continues.

"I'm sure," Miss Pine says easily. "Thank you for the invitation, Mr. Dean."

Mr. Dean smiles at her, and then goes back to staring off into the distance, leaving Rosalie to stand essentially alone in the ensuing awkward pause.

Who invites another woman to a previously scheduled event, anyway?

Rosalie catches Aunt Genevieve's gaze, trusting that she can read the desperation in her eyes.

"Two months is an awfully long time to wait for further

divertissement," Aunt Genevieve says. The whole circle turns to look at her and Aunt Genevieve grins. "Tell me, do you ladies paint as well as you play pianoforte?"

"They do," Mother says quickly. "Goodness, it's been ages since we've gotten Rosalie's friends together to paint in your back garden, hasn't it?"

"It certainly has," Aunt Genevieve says.

"Lady Tisend, I recall attending a most exciting competition at your parents' home in our season," Mrs. Pine says, surprising everyone. "Are you thinking of reviving it? It was marvelous fun."

Aunt Genevieve and Mother exchange a look while Rosalie watches, surprised. Miss Pine glances over at her, and Rosalie raises a shoulder, as in the dark as she appears to be.

Mother and Aunt Genevieve's nonverbal conversation is quickly reaching comical heights. Rosalie used to think they were all rather good at subterfuge, but perhaps she's been mistaken. This is ridiculous.

Aunt Genevieve claps her hands together. "I declare we shall hold a portrait painting competition in my back garden in two weeks' time. Provided our esteemed gentlemen callers will stand as subjects?"

She looks around the group at Mr. Fortes, Mr. Rile, and Mr. Dean. They all nod slowly.

"Of course, Lady Jones. Anything for you," Mr. Fortes says. He looks a little too eager, honestly.

Amalie frowns as he stares at Aunt Genevieve. Rosalie will have to find a way to punish Mr. Fortes for that one.

"Excellent. Lady Rosalie will send out invitations. Now, I have people to watch your mother intimidate. If you'll excuse us," Aunt Genevieve says, curtsying to the group before dragging Mother off.

Miss Pine is staring at her, her eyebrow raised. Rosalie stares back. It was *her* mother who formally instigated this.

Mr. Rile leans over to tell Miss Pine how wonderfully she played, and Henrietta bites at her lip. Two weeks is too long to leave this girl to her own devices.

"Miss Pine, would you like to join Miss Raught, Miss Linet, and myself on a day of shopping next week?" Rosalie asks, cutting Mr. Rile off. Mrs. Pine frowns over at her, but Miss Pine meets her eyes, surprised. "I could use a casual outfit for this competition, and I've promised Miss Raught and Miss Linet a whirlwind of ribbons. Surely you might like to join us?"

She'll gather information while they shop, look for weaknesses. The woman must have them.

Miss Pine glances at her mother, who gives her a quick jerk of the chin. She looks entirely unsure of Rosalie's invitation— suspicious, really. But Miss Pine looks intrigued.

"I would be delighted. You'll send a note?"

"I will," Rosalie says, smiling brightly at the two of them. "I'm looking forward to it."

"Me too!" Henrietta says.

"It will be nice to get to know you better," Amalie adds, her voice much cooler. Amalie may already be in on Rosalie's plan, then.

"Thank you very much for the invitation," Miss Pine says, smiling at Rosalie's friends before meeting Rosalie's eyes again. "It's deeply appreciated."

And there's just something in her tone that makes Rosalie think Miss Pine will be using the outing for reconnaissance as much as she will. Something in her beguiling eyes.

A *challenge*.

Chapter Six

Catherine

C atherine stands in the foyer, wringing her cream gloves between her fingers. She's wearing a matching cream dress
beneath her light blue pelisse. Their lady's maid, Miss Teit, arranged her curls beautifully beneath her bonnet, which has a
blue ribbon woven into the hood. All of it will be easy enough
to take on and off throughout a day of shopping.

She looks lovely. Mother said so. Father said so. Miss Teit
said so.

Catherine wishes she felt as confident about the day as everyone else does about her outfit. But she's about to go shopping
with Lady Rosalie, Miss Raught, and Miss Linet. She'll be alone
with them for hours, rather than a few scattered minutes at a
large function. They're intimidating among a crowd. On their
own, they seem insurmountable.

Miss Teit comes out of the hallway to the kitchens, button-
ing up her spencer jacket. She smiles at Catherine, her brown
eyes bright, round cheeks dimpling in amusement at Catherine's obvious distress.

"We are going to have a marvelous time," Miss Teit says confidently, stepping up to Catherine and slowly prying the gloves
out of her hands. She hands them to Catherine one at a time to
slip on. "They're just girls."

"They're terrifying," Catherine whispers, glancing around

the foyer as she adjusts the gloves. "And they've ten years to-gether. I'm fresh meat."

"You are more than up to the challenge of a little shopping, I promise you."

Before she can spiral any further, there's a knock on the door.

Miss Henrietta Raught stands on the stoop, wearing a rose-colored pelisse, with a matching bonnet. She smiles brightly at them, her round face so open and inviting that Catherine feels her shoulders come down just a hair.

"Thank you so much for picking us up," Catherine says.

"Of course!" Miss Raught says happily. "Good to meet you as well, Miss—"

"Teit," Miss Teit says. "I'll sit up top with the driver and stay well out of your way."

"Oh, you needn't—" Miss Raught begins, but Miss Teit has already closed the door behind them and started down the steps.

"She's quick," Miss Raught says.

"My mother's on a tear about decorating the sitting room. This will be much more fun for both of us."

Miss Raught giggles and gestures for Catherine to precede her.

The waiting carriage is enormous and gilded. It must belong to the Tisends. She can just see Miss Linet and Lady Rosalie inside the open carriage door as she approaches. Miss Linet is waiting patiently, staring out the opposite window to the street. But Lady Rosalie is looking right at Catherine.

In her burgundy jacket and short-rimmed bonnet, she's striking. The look she's giving Catherine just adds to the over-all effect against her dark hair and eyes. Without doing more than sitting there with a droll expression, she's imperious and intimidating. It's enough to make Catherine hesitate there on the pavement.

Is she ready to be in such close proximity with Lady Rosalie all day? Is she really up to the task of extracting information from her without letting on that she's trying to undermine her?

"Oh my word, would you just get in already?" Lady Rosalie exclaims.

Catherine jumps and hurries to clamber into the carriage, cheeks hot.

"You look lovely today, Lady Rosalie. Thank you for inviting me," Catherine says as she sits down beside Miss Linet.

Lady Rosalie's eyes widen just a fraction. "As do you," she replies.

Miss Raught climbs in and settles beside Lady Rosalie, smiling at all of them. "I'm so excited. I love shopping," she tells Catherine.

Lady Rosalie snaps the door shut and bangs on the ceiling.

"I do too," Catherine tells Miss Raught.

There's a pause as the carriage rumbles forward, bumping on the cobblestoned street. The silence feels stifling in the small space.

"I look lovely too, you know," Miss Linet says abruptly.

Lady Rosalie snorts, and Miss Raught giggles.

"The green suits you very nicely," Catherine agrees, smiling at Miss Linet. Her green pelisse and bonnet are very fetching.

"We'll be sure to keep you well complimented throughout the day, Amalie, don't you worry," Lady Rosalie says, rolling her eyes as Miss Linet sticks out her tongue. "We're stopping at the haberdashery first, if you agree, Miss Pine."

"Oh, of course," Catherine says quickly. Who is she to dictate where they go? "I've been meaning to get a green ribbon for my favorite bonnet."

Lady Rosalie's brow wrinkles. "We'll be getting you a *new* bonnet, Miss Pine."

"That's . . . very kind. But I don't need—"

"Just say yes; it's easier," Miss Linet says in an overloud whisper.

"Rosalie loves to shop, and she has the best taste. Let her get you whatever she wants," Miss Raught adds.

Catherine watches Lady Rosalie's lips quirk upward. All right. So she's being shopped *for* today.

Discomfort pricks at her neck, but Catherine merely nods and sits back in her seat.

She and Mother have visited most of the shops on the broad, gray-stoned Milsom Street, but they certainly haven't purchased at all of them. She's brought some of her pin money with her, but a new bonnet and perhaps one pair of gloves would run through it quickly.

It seems Lady Rosalie's purse has no such limitations.

Their first stop at the haberdashery is a whirlwind. Lady Rosalie, Miss Raught, and Miss Linet position Catherine in front of a mirror and take turns roaming around the pink-walled shop, grabbing any hat they deem remotely interesting. Catherine doesn't so much try them on as the girls try them on her. Lady Rosalie stands by, approving or disapproving each choice.

Miss Raught slips a wide-brimmed straw hat onto Catherine's head that droops over her eyes. Miss Linet brings her a tiny narrow bonnet that pinches her temples. She insists it makes Catherine's head look dainty.

The overlarge brown bonnet Miss Raught brings her next

hides her face entirely and fully blocks out any peripheral vision.

"I feel like a horse with blinders," Catherine mumbles, wondering if they're intentionally trying to get her something ugly and embarrassing.

Lady Rosalie lets out a quiet chuckle. Catherine swings her head to be able to see her, which make Lady Rosalie laugh more. The way Lady Rosalie smiles at her and helps her remove the bonnet makes Catherine's skin tingle.

Her fingers graze the underside of Catherine's chin as she undoes the laces holding the hideous thing to her head and Catherine shivers.

Lady Rosalie's eyes spark momentarily. But then Miss Raught appears with a little lace cap and Lady Rosalie turns away, placing the brown monstrosity to the side.

Miss Linet returns as well with an even bigger bonnet, but they all stop moving as Catherine situates the lace bonnet on her head.

"Now, that has promise," Lady Rosalie declares.

It does sit well against her brown hair, and Catherine likes how delicate it looks.

"I haven't a dress to go with this," Catherine admits.

"Nonsense," Lady Rosalie says dismissively. "You'll take that."

"But—" Catherine starts.

Miss Raught touches her shoulder. "Give in, I swear it's easier."

Catherine meets her eyes in the mirror while Lady Rosalie glances at Miss Linet. Miss Raught smiles at Catherine and Catherine tentatively smiles back.

"Okay," she says, carefully lifting the bonnet from her head. "Aren't you going to try something?"

"There is a pink bonnet I've been eyeing for a few weeks," Miss Raught says, pointing across the store.

Catherine turns and spots the most hideous dark pink bonnet rimmed in pointy little rosettes, which would make her head look like a pink soup spoon.

"Uck, no, you'll look like a flattened tulip," Lady Rosalie says brusquely.

Catherine can't help but huff a little laugh. Lady Rosalie's eyes find hers and she smirks. It makes Catherine's chest clench in a strangely pleasant way.

"I think something in blue or green would suit you better," Catherine tells Miss Raught.

Miss Raught sighs loudly. "I suppose."

"I found you three, come on," Miss Linet says, rolling her green eyes at Catherine and Lady Rosalie before pulling Miss Raught across the room.

"Let's buy this, and then we'll find you matching gloves and have a dress fashioned to go with," Lady Rosalie says, taking Catherine's arm.

Catherine fights another shiver. "You really don't need to—" Lady Rosalie silences her with a look. "I mean, thank you, Lady Rosalie. That's very kind of you."

"That's better," Lady Rosalie says, making Catherine laugh.

When they exit the shop, Miss Teit catches Catherine's eye as she passes over the box with her new bonnet. Catherine shrugs subtly. It seems to be going well, at any rate. Though it's hard to tell, really.

At the cobbler, Lady Rosalie sits them all down and then walks the display with the proprietor, Mr. Deetson, directing him to pull shoe after shoe for them to try.

"Is she always like this?" Catherine asks, glancing between Miss Raught and Miss Linet on either side of her.

"Yes," Miss Linet says.

"No," Miss Raught says at the same time.

They glance at each other. "She does this every time," Miss Linet insists.

"Yes, but she doesn't have so much fun when it's just us," Miss Raught says simply.

Miss Linet frowns and Catherine squirms in her seat. "The three of you seem wonderful friends. I'm sure Lady Rosalie enjoys your outings immensely every time."

Miss Linet smiles at her, though it doesn't quite reach her eyes.

"She's making jokes with you, though," Miss Raught says.

"Henrietta," Miss Linet says firmly.

"You're funny, is all I mean," Miss Raught tells Catherine. "And you have very dainty feet."

Miss Linet and Miss Raught look down at Catherine's feet and Catherine tries to stop the flare of heat in her cheeks. It does feel a little good to think Lady Rosalie finds her funny. And not only funny, but funnier than her oldest friends.

Lady Rosalie returns with the obsequious cobbler, his arms laden with shoes, and begins directing him to lay them out in front of each of them. She's picked out the prettiest shoes for Catherine, by far.

"These are beautiful, but they pinch," Miss Linet says, considering her foot, now scrunched in a low-heeled and very narrow brown boot.

"Beauty is pain," Lady Rosalie says immediately.

Miss Linet moves her foot side to side, her long face set in a frown.

Catherine glances at Lady Rosalie and then decides to take a chance. She needs to win over Miss Linet and Miss Raught as well. She needs to get them talking, get them to trust her, so they might share something useful—faux pas Lady Rosalie has made, preferences Mr. Dean has made clear—something she can use to her advantage.

"Those will be awfully hard to walk in, though," Catherine says carefully. "Mr. Fortes likes the outdoors, doesn't he? You want to be able to keep up with him."

Miss Linet looks over at her, surprised. "I suppose."

"Beauty is pain, but practicality, in this instance, might ultimately be more alluring, don't you think?"

Miss Linet stares at her for a moment, and then nods slowly. "You know, I do. I'm sorry, Rose, I think these aren't for me."

They both look up at Lady Rosalie, who's watching their exchange curiously.

"If that's all right," Miss Linet adds softly.

"I'm not going to buy you a pair of shoes you hate, don't be daft," Lady Rosalie says. "Mr. Deetson, please put those back."

Mr. Deetson hurries to oblige, removing the pinchy brown boots and scurrying away. Miss Linet glances at Catherine with a little smile and Catherine returns it.

Catherine looks up, but Lady Rosalie has already returned to wandering the shop, completely unperturbed. A small win, then.

When they arrive at the modiste's shop, Miss Linet is giddy over the new black boots Lady Rosalie purchased for her, Miss Raught is ecstatic over her new dancing slippers, and Catherine is the proud new owner of a pair of white lace slippers, which will match the white lace gloves and white lace bonnet Lady Rosalie has gotten for her as well.

Lady Rosalie hustles them into Madame Florent's shop, directing Henrietta to look for gloves while Miss Linet is to try on the dress her mother recently had commissioned. And Lady Rosalie herself goes to check on the status of her next ball gown.

Catherine still feels a bit other. Which is how she *should* be feeling, given she didn't come on this trip to make friends. But having now been in their orbit for an entire day, Catherine might not mind actually being friends with these women, Lady Rosalie's matchmaking machinations aside.

"So, what do you think of Mr. Sholle?" Miss Raught asks.

Catherine turns and finds Miss Raught watching her as she thumbs through the display of gloves by the window. It puts her on a slightly more even keel. They've been asking questions about her life near Idless and her family all day. Finally, they're going to go in for the kill.

"He seems kind," Catherine hedges.

"He is," Miss Raught agrees immediately. "Once, I fell on a walk, and he carried me all the way back to my house to spare my ankle."

"How chivalrous."

"It was," Miss Raught says a bit dreamily. "And he came to call to make sure I was all right the next day too."

Catherine watches as she goes back to looking at the gloves. "It didn't turn into . . . more?" she asks carefully.

It certainly sounds like the start of a romantic novel. Something right out of *Sense and Sensibility.*

"Oh, we didn't have much in common. And he has these two enormous hunting dogs. I'm terribly allergic," Miss Raught says with a shrug.

"Oh," Catherine says. She's not one for large dogs either.

"Don't let Henrietta's fear of dogs dissuade you. They're beautiful animals," Lady Rosalie says, coming to join them at the front of the shop. "And he has such eyes for you, Miss Pine, you really ought to capitalize on it."

Catherine watches Miss Raught busy herself with the gloves. "I wouldn't want to—"

"Mr. Sholle's father vehemently opposes Henrietta's father representing a particular member of his opposition in the Lords. It had little to do with Henrietta's aversion to two average-sized hounds."

"They're huge," Miss Raught exclaims. "They're as big as you!"

"They're—" Lady Rosalie starts.

"A mere few inches shorter when sitting," Miss Raught insists. "It would have been a poor match regardless of my father."

"He wasn't that interested anyway," Lady Rosalie says dismissively. "He never looked at you the way he's been looking at Miss Pine."

Miss Raught's eyes dim, her round face falling. It's a backhanded compliment fully at the expense of Miss Raught, and it prickles at Catherine's skin.

"You deserve someone who looks at you like he's been looking at Miss Pine," Lady Rosalie continues.

Lady Rosalie and Miss Raught stare at each other for a moment, before Miss Raught puffs up with a little pride. She turns back to Catherine, her cheerful smile right back in place.

"You should definitely let him court you. He's quite a catch. He'll be a baron someday. And his lands are extensive. Your father would love to go hunting with him. The dogs are very impressive at that. And he's funny. He told me a joke this one time that—"

"Henrietta, go give Amalie your opinion on her dress," Lady Rosalie says.

Miss Raught goes a bit pink and mumbles, "All right," before scurrying from the room.

Catherine watches her go, unsure of whether to feel bad that Lady Rosalie cut her off, or be grateful Lady Rosalie had the gumption. Protesting a bit too much about Mr. Sholle, she thinks.

"Your father and the baron would get along well," Lady Rosalie says.

"Yes, that is the most important part of a marriage, the groom getting along with the father-in-law," Catherine says.

Lady Rosalie lets out a startled laugh. "It's a benefit, certainly."

"Hardly my most pressing concern," Catherine admits. Lady Rosalie raises an eyebrow and Catherine decides to push. "If he's such a catch, why didn't you catch him?"

Lady Rosalie sucks on her cheek. She reaches out and takes Catherine's hand. It's like a bolt of lightning courses up her arm and Catherine withholds a gasp. But Lady Rosalie's too busy dragging her into the fitting room to notice. Her delicate fingers are gentle around Catherine's.

She settles them both on the padded pink benches across from the dais where Miss Linet will model her gown. Her fingers leave Catherine's slowly, and Catherine looks down to meet her eyes.

"Mr. Sholle is a wonderful match. He's charming, monied, in line for a title, and good enough to look at."

"That doesn't answer my question," Catherine presses.

"My father—"

"Could likely get on with anyone, and given Mr. Sholle was at your concert, I'm assuming they're aligned politically," Catherine says. Lady Rosalie purses her lips. "You're pushing him on me; I at least deserve to know why he wasn't good enough for *you*."

Lady Rosalie takes a breath and glances at the fitting room curtain. "We didn't agree on books, music, or art. And Mama thought I could do better."

Catherine considers the slightly haughty look on Lady Rosalie's face. Considers how hard she wants to prod her, how many cards to show.

"What makes you think he and I will agree on anything, then?" Catherine asks.

Lady Rosalie opens her mouth, but Miss Linet and Miss Raught bustle out of the fitting room.

Catherine and Lady Rosalie turn, eyes ripping slowly from each other, to watch Miss Linet step onto the dais in a mustard-yellow dress overlaid with brown floral lace.

It's hideous. Catherine didn't think Madame Florent could make anything hideous.

"Mama insisted on the colors," Miss Linet says balefully, turning to face them.

Madame Florent slips out of the fitting room and looks Miss Linet over in the light coming in from the back windows. Her round face is drawn, considering the dress, hands on her ample hips. "The craftsmanship is some of my best, but I don't know, dears, what do we think?"

Miss Raught has a hand pressed to her mouth to keep from laughing. Catherine glances at Lady Rosalie, who looks back at her, equally horrified.

Miss Linet's green eyes are round and wet. Even her auburn curls look like they're sagging.

"No," they say together.

Miss Linet nods and looks to Madame Florent. "I'm so sorry, madame, but I just—I just—"

"Maybe with some green?" Catherine suggests quickly. Everything about the dress is gorgeous, save for the colors. It must be salvageable.

"And dusty orange flowers?" Lady Rosalie agrees quickly.

"And green gloves to match," Miss Raught puts in.

Madame Florent's concern melts into a smile. "I think that would help immensely," she agrees. "Miss Linet?"

"Please, oh, lord, please," she says, her voice choked.

Madame Florent takes her hand, disappearing back into the changing room with her. Miss Raught follows them, mouthing *Oh my God* before slipping behind the curtain.

Which leaves Catherine and Lady Rosalie sitting alone again, aghast. The moment their eyes meet, they burst into quiet laughter. Catherine tries to calm herself down. She doesn't want to embarrass Miss Linet, but good lord, that dress was terrible.

After a minute, they slowly stop giggling.

Catherine meets Lady Rosalie's eyes, deciding to push, just a little more. "It seems we have much in common in terms of taste."

Lady Rosalie's eyes narrow. "I suppose so. Does that mean, then, that you plan to pursue my tastes?"

Catherine blinks. Does she plan to—

"In gentlemen suitors," Lady Rosalie continues quickly, her cheeks lightly pink.

Her words ignite something in Catherine's chest—their tête-à-tête catching fire against her skin, tingling and bright. "What would you do if I did?" Catherine asks, her voice rougher than she means it to be.

Lady Rosalie's eyes seem to glint in the dim fitting room. She bites at her lip and glances at the curtain. Then she leans in to whisper, her breath warm on Catherine's ear. It sends a shiver straight down to Catherine's toes.

"That would mean war," she says huskily.

Catherine swallows hard. "Aren't—aren't we already at war?" she whispers back.

It's heady, and intimate, and *exciting*.

"Our mothers clearly are. But we've yet to formally declare, wouldn't you say?"

Catherine can feel herself flushing, the tone of Lady Rosalie's voice dancing across her body, every nerve ending alight in a way she's never experienced from a conversation. Or . . . possibly ever, actually.

But she can't let herself be clouded by whatever this feeling is. By Lady Rosalie's beauty there in the shadows. She has to stay strong. She has to match Lady Rosalie quip for quip.

"Oh, well, if it needs a formal declaration, then we're at war," Catherine manages, her voice trembling just a hair.

Lady Rosalie's lips curl in the most delicious smile. "War feels good."

Catherine finds herself nodding. It does. This feels good. Whatever the hell this charged, combustible, sparkling tension actually is.

"What do you think of this for the flowers?"

Miss Raught's voice splits the silence and Catherine and Lady Rosalie wrench backward from each other.

It's awkward. Oh, it's awkward.

Lady Rosalie hesitates for a moment, her body going taut, before she stands and strides over to Miss Raught, like nothing at all has happened. Like the air around them isn't still crackling.

Does she do this a lot? Declare flirtatious war with new friends? So often, it's easy for her to put that mask in place in an instant?

Because Catherine's pulse is still thrumming. She tries to school her features as Miss Linet exits the fitting room, thanking Madame Florent over and over.

A declaration of war over Mr. Dean isn't . . . exciting. Not like this. It's a challenge. It's a gauntlet. It's not . . . thinking about how Lady Rosalie might look in that back changing room without her clothes on.

She's had thoughts like this before, of course. In passing. Momentarily.

When she and Millie, one of the farmer's daughters, kissed behind the barn when she was fourteen, it felt like this—shimmering and simmering and consuming. But it passed. It had to. It was abundantly clear that the kiss meant more to her than it did to Millie. Millie thought it a lark. And Catherine thought—well, she didn't think. Hasn't thought. Hasn't focused on it in years.

The pounding in her chest, the heat at her throat, the tingling in her fingers every time she and Lady Rosalie touch—it's absolutely, thoroughly inconvenient, and confusing, and startling. Of all people, why is *Lady Rosalie* the first person she's felt this for as an adult?

She's meant to be stealing her suitor. They're in competition. They're at *war*.

Lady Rosalie looks over her shoulder from the front of the shop, the light catching her face in a way that makes her almost glow.

Holy shit, is she in trouble.

Chapter Seven
Rosalie

E ven with most of her flowering trees and vines not yet in bloom, Aunt Genevieve's garden teems with verdant leaves and bushes. Divided into three long sections, the garden extends off the back of Uncle Walter's townhouse along the Royal Crescent, stretching all the way to the other side of Church Street.

In the first section just beyond the back patio they've set six round tables covered in white linens and arranged for a formal tea. Aunt Genevieve and Mother usually sit out here to gossip, sipping lemonade spiked with whatever Uncle Walter has pulled from the cellar. Sometimes Father even joins them. Those are Rosalie's favorite afternoons, listening to Father and Aunt Genevieve bicker and tease each other while Mother sits there smiling.

But Mother's not smiling today. Instead, she's leading a parade of maids around the tables, pointing out little mistakes while Aunt Genevieve watches from the patio, smirking.

For her own sanity, Rosalie walks back into the second section of the garden. Aunt Genevieve has had a large platform erected beneath the enormous oak along the eastern wall of the garden where Rosalie used to curl up to read as a girl.

Around the platform, easels with canvases and paint sets have been arranged in a horseshoe, each with a dainty chair covered in white linen behind. Today, they'll be capturing the likeness of the young society gentlemen, who will be posed on the platform.

Rosalie tries to sketch out the scene in her mind. She should use every ounce of advantage she has, because once everyone arrives—once Miss Pine arrives—she knows she'll be distracted.

She hasn't been able to get Miss Pine out of her head all week. The way her eyes darkened, the huskiness of her voice, the challenge in her smile have left Rosalie befuddled since their shopping trip. And the way Miss Pine looked in the mock-up Madame Florent made of the dress Rosalie insisted on buying her?

Rosalie might actually die when it's finished.

"Now, I want you to seat the girls, Gen."

Mother and Aunt Genevieve approach Rosalie, Aunt Genevieve watching her mother with fond exasperation.

"Rosalie should be here," Mother says, moving around Rosalie to place a hand on the fifth chair from the right, not quite at the apex of the horseshoe, but close. "And Mr. Dean will be right there," she adds, pointing at the tree.

"Right where?" Aunt Genevieve asks, pointing about six feet to the left.

"No!" Mother says, her voice edging toward that shrill tone that could summon dogs.

"So, so sorry, yes, I see now," Aunt Genevieve says, glancing at Rosalie with a wink.

Rosalie grins back. Everything's always better when Aunt Genevieve and Uncle Walter are in town for the season. It makes Rosalie long for her brother, Christopher. They aren't complete with him off at Cambridge, and she knows he'll be disappointed to miss some of Uncle Walter's visit in particular.

They've always been close. Uncle Walter just understands him in a way it feels like Father never has.

But her brother's complicated relationship with their father isn't the point today. Today, Rosalie needs to impress Mr. Dean. Truly impress him.

Their promenade two days ago was an utter failure, according to Mother. They walked for over an hour along the Avon, didn't say a thing to each other, and agreed to do it again next week.

She wonders what it would be like to promenade with Miss Pine, just the two of them. She wants to see more of that playful spark Miss Pine showed when they shopped—more of her cutting insights and smart observations. She wonders what it might be like to slip her hand into Miss Pine's. To maybe find their way under a bridge, out of sight, out of mind. To push Miss Pine up against a—

"Miss Pine should sit—"

"Third from the left," Aunt Genevieve repeats. "I know. I'll get it done. Would you just calm down?"

"I am calm," Mother insists.

Aunt Genevieve gives Rosalie a pointed look. Rosalie feels her shoulders go up, as if her aunt could possibly know about her treacherous, confusing thoughts. But Aunt Genevieve just pats her shoulder and heads toward the front of the garden, where the first guests are now arriving.

"Just focus on your own canvas, and you'll be the best," Mother says. "Mr. Dean will pick you as the winner, and they'll all fall in line with him."

The gentlemen get to judge the winner of the contest, as payment for posing for them. Or so Aunt Genevieve says is always the rule.

Rosalie isn't sure they have much right to be judging the paintings. Mr. Dean *should* choose hers. But Mr. Dean is . . . Mr. Dean. It's always hard to tell.

"You'll be the best. You're always the best," Mother says.

Rosalie nods reflexively. Henrietta and her mother, Amalie and her mother, and Miss Pine and Mrs. Pine have just entered the back garden, all six of them chatting. Henrietta has her arm through Miss Pine's elbow and Miss Pine is laughing at something she's said, her face bright and pink.

Rosalie's stomach clenches. It should be jealousy coursing through her, that Miss Pine has charmed her friends. But it isn't. She isn't feeling any of the things she should, and what she is feeling—hot along her neck, flushed up to her ears, tingly—is inappropriate in the extreme.

Something is clearly wrong with her.

Miss Pine is a *threat* to everything Rosalie's built.

So, she has to go over there. To oversee the afternoon. To guide Miss Pine to the right suitor. To ensure she's making the proper connections.

Not to see if she's wearing the same perfume she was when they sat close on the bench at the back of Madame Florent's shop. Floral and fresh and—

"Welcome," Rosalie says, approaching the trio. She hopes she looks confident and aloof, and that no one can hear the infatuated pounding of her treacherous pulse.

"It looks splendid," Amalie says, gesturing to the garden. "Though I wouldn't expect anything less."

"Lady Jones throws the best fetes," Henrietta tells Miss Pine.

"I believe it," Miss Pine says, staring around, her big brown eyes wide and delighted.

Rosalie should not be feeling any pride from that look whatsoever. Even if it is her aunt's garden. It's not like she had any-thing to do with it.

"Come see where we'll be painting," she says, taking the hand of Henrietta, who tugs along Miss Pine, who grabs Amalie, so they're a traipsing train across the lawn. It loosens something in Rosalie's chest.

"The boys will be there, and we'll all have—I think it was two hours?" Rosalie says as they come up on the platform and easels.

"Two hours exactly," Aunt Genevieve says, appearing behind them and grinning when Miss Pine and Henrietta let out little gasps of surprise. She likes to stalk her prey at these events, stealthily popping into conversations. It's how she gets the best gossip. "Then the boys will choose the winner, and while they fawn over her, the rest of us will drink and drown our sorrows in tea cakes."

"We'll get biscuits and sweets too," Henrietta tells Miss Pine. "When Rosalie wins."

Rosalie bites her lip while Amalie swats Henrietta. "I don't always win everything," Rosalie says, going for humble. She does, but Henrietta doesn't need to brag about it.

"Of course I'm rooting for my niece, but I do love a good dark horse," Aunt Genevieve tells them. "Miss Linet gave me a wonderful sketch the other year, and you yourself have painted multiple watercolors I've hung in my parlor," she tells Henri-etta. Both of her friends blush. Rosalie grins at her aunt. "And who knows, Miss Pine is a new variable in our midst."

"I could beat you all," Miss Pine agrees.

Rosalie meets her eyes, enjoying the challenge. "You think so?"

"My mother certainly does," Miss Pine says with a shrug. "Though mostly I want to see your paintings," she adds, looking to Amalie and Henrietta.

"I'm sure yours will be wonderful," Henrietta says, while Amalie looks back and forth between Miss Pine and Rosalie.

Henrietta's warmed to Miss Pine in the way Henrietta warms to everyone—trusting and giving her full self at a whiff of kindness. But Amalie's remained steadfast in their mission; Rosalie's winning the season, she'll see to it. But she can like the girl.

Miss Pine is charming, and kind, and listening to her and Henrietta begin discussing shading and which ratios to mix to get the exact green of the giant oak leaves is practically warm and fuzzy.

It's making Rosalie soft, which is a problem as the gentlemen enter the garden. What if Miss Pine is actually as good as she says? What if she's not just being playful? What if, like with the pianoforte, she's gifted and Rosalie merely has hard-won practice on her side?

Thankfully, she doesn't also have to put on a show for Mr. Dean and his friends, because Aunt Genevieve snags them first. She positions Mr. Dean against the oak tree, staring off into the distance, not unlike how he spends most balls.

The broad Mr. Rile she places in a contemplative pose in a chair center stage, with the tall and narrow Mr. Fortes on Mr. Rile's right on the floor, leaning back against the side of his chair. Rosalie rather hopes he'll fall asleep with his head on Mr. Rile's thigh.

Mr. Plory she plunks down on the front of the stage, legs over the side, hands on his thighs. "Look down, you're sad," she tells him.

He giggles and does as he's told, clearly enamored of her. All of the boys are watching Aunt Genevieve, jumping to do her bidding. Who can blame them? The twinkle in her eye as she directs them around is infectious.

Rosalie glances back at the mothers, who have clustered on the patio in chairs to watch the proceedings. They're all holding drinks already and laughing. Even Mrs. Pine looks amused.

Rosalie looks back at the stage just in time to watch Mr. Sholle gamely lie down on the floor on his stomach in front of Mr. Rile, a notebook and old quill in hand.

"Knees bent, legs kicking, as if you're writing to a sweetheart," Aunt Genevieve instructs.

Mr. Sholle looks up at her, then out at the group of women, his eyes wide. Aunt Genevieve hums, waiting, and Mr. Sholle gives a comical shrug before bending his legs and swinging them back and forth while pretending to write in the notebook, looking just like a schoolboy working on an assignment on holiday.

The girls giggle, including Miss Pine. Rosalie feels her cheeks heating up. In pride, obviously. Her plan is working.

Aunt Genevieve steps off the platform and walks backward to peruse the scene. The boys look ridiculous.

"Just as I imagined," she says, making the entire garden laugh. "Now, ladies."

She turns and begins directing each girl into a specific seat. Rosalie waits with Henrietta, Amalie, and Miss Pine, watching Aunt Genevieve place some of her acquaintances at the furthest seats on either side of the horseshoe.

Aunt Genevieve will give Rosalie the prime chair, like Mother wanted, but she clearly also wants a true competition, seating Henrietta and Amalie between Rosalie and Miss Pine, the four of them at the apex of the horseshoe of easels.

Rosalie slips on the apron from the back of her chair and sits down, taking in the tableau. Mr. Sholle's actually writing something in the notebook, while Mr. Rile pulls contemplative faces. Mr. Fortes has let his sandy-blond head rest back onto

Mr. Rile's thigh, and at intervals they look at each other and grin. It's adorable.

"No moving, gentlemen," Aunt Genevieve says imperiously.

The boys quickly drop their smiles, looking seriously out at the girls, or down at the ground. Mr. Dean's still staring off into the distance, not in the least interested in the women at the easels.

"You'll have two hours," Aunt Genevieve says, turning back to the girls. "On your mark, get set, paint!"

There's a flurry of movement all around. Rosalie forgoes her paints to start. She picks up a charcoal and does a quick sketch of the tree, the platform, and the general location of each boy.

She knows she needs to focus in on Mr. Dean, so her painting is most impressive to him. A perfect likeness should score her a win. Which is a shame, really, because Mr. Sholle is clearly the star of the show. He's still writing in the notebook, gently swinging his feet in the name of authenticity.

He does glance up and over at Miss Pine from time to time, which is very promising. Rosalie forces herself not to follow his gaze. She needs to get to work.

She quickly mixes her colors and begins painting in earnest, forcing dedication into each and every stroke of her brush.

Usually, she and Aunt Genevieve put on old dresses and get intentionally messy, laughing and telling stories and sharing. They're some of her favorite afternoons, when Mother lets her come over with no agenda and nowhere to be, and she and Aunt Genevieve can just talk, or sit in true companionable silence.

But today isn't usual. Today isn't about fun, or comfort. Today is about having the best painting. By bounds.

She takes a moment to glance around the group, noting Henrietta frowning at her canvas and Amalie going in with smudged fingers. They both look adorably determined and Rosalie hopes their finished products impress Mr. Rile and Mr. Fortes. And their mothers too.

But then her eyes flick over to Miss Pine and Rosalie's breath whooshes out of her chest.

The way Miss Pine is staring at her canvas with such intention, the way her hands are moving, the way she's got a smudge of green on her cheek and her tongue just between her lips . . .

Aunt Genevieve coughs behind her and Rosalie starts, her brush jerking across the canvas, wiping a streak of green right across what should be Mr. Dean's chest. She bites back a curse.

"Eyes on your own canvas, Lady Rosalie," Aunt Genevieve whispers, extending a clean cloth for Rosalie to carefully wipe away the fresh green paint. Her smirk is far too knowing for Rosalie's liking.

Rosalie hopes she didn't look as . . . stunned as she felt. She should look competitive, like she was checking on Miss Pine's progress, not . . . not whatever it was she was doing instead.

"Don't sneak up on people," Rosalie whispers haltingly, her cheeks flushing.

"Thirty minutes" is all Aunt Genevieve says in return, smiling playfully before returning to her prowling.

Rosalie looks back at the empty space where she should be painting Mr. Dean. Miss Pine wasn't even trying to distract her that time. The woman is just too magnetic.

Of every person here, all the men on display, all her lovely friends, Miss Pine is by far the most beautiful, and captivating, and clearly deserves most to be memorialized. Rosalie can imagine all kinds of scenes to paint her in. She might defy portraiture altogether, too complex and full of too many different simmering layers to capture perfectly.

But she's not who Rosalie is here to paint. She needs to paint Mr. Dean. She needs to focus on Mr. Dean. She needs to win.

She blows out a slow breath and looks up to study him. He's beautiful too. Differently from Miss Pine, of course. But his jaw is sharp, his brow line fluid, and his eyes have their own depth, in their way. His hair is luscious, his stature strong and lithe and commanding. He's everything a girl should want.

And she can capture that. Even if he looks bored. She can highlight that part of his charm. He's consumed by interior thoughts, unruffled by the frippery of man.

Good God.

Maybe she can't make him into poetry, but she can give his likeness half the spark she sees in Miss Pine. She can force herself to see the same in him. She can make him into something worthy of memorializing. She can make him worthy of her, she thinks.

Chapter Eight
Catherine

Catherine can feel Lady Rosalie's eyes on her like a hot iron, but she forces herself to concentrate. She won't give Lady Rosalie the satisfaction of distracting her.

Won't give herself the satisfaction of meeting her gaze and getting lost in her challenging eyes either. She's here to win Lady Jones' painting competition. Not to let herself be beguiled by her insanely hot niece.

Her portrait is going well, she thinks. She's captured each gentleman's likeness, and they all appear dynamic and distinct, while remaining part of a larger whole. She even thinks she's managed to make Mr. Dean look contemplative rather than bored or mad, though he does look a bit of both, just staring off like that, oblivious to everyone around him.

She hopes the other women have managed nothing more elaborate than she has. Two hours is not really long enough to do anything excellently, but she supposes that's part of the challenge.

She can allow herself one sneaky glance over at Lady Rosalie before she starts to finesse all of her details. What could it hurt?

Only when she looks over, Lady Rosalie is staring straight back at her. Catherine's breath catches and they sit there, like time has frozen them in place. Catherine knows she should scowl and look back at her painting, but she's as curious about Lady Rosalie as Lady Rosalie seems to be about her.

And she's much more interesting to look at than anything, or anyone, up on the platform. She could stare at Lady Rosalie for hours, if only no one would notice . . .

Someone coughs behind her and Catherine jolts in her seat. Lady Rosalie looks back at her canvas, smirking. Catherine blows out a calming breath before turning to look up at Lady Jones.

The woman smiles and nods toward her painting, as if she hasn't just caught Catherine staring at her niece.

"Very good indeed, Miss Pine," she says.

Catherine feels herself flush. "Thank you."

"Certainly a contender, if you can keep your focus."

That flush makes its way up to her hairline. "Yes, Lady Jones," she mumbles, looking back at her canvas, feeling chastised and caught. But then again, what's wrong with scoping out her competition?

No one, not even Lady Jones, can know half of the time she's staring at Lady Rosalie she's just in awe of her beauty, and not at all thinking about their competition over Mr. Dean.

"Five minutes," Lady Jones says, winking at her.

It's hard for Catherine to reconcile the playful, funny Lady Jones with Mother's history with Lady Tisend. By Miss Linet's account, Lady Tisend and Lady Jones get on like a house on fire, but all Catherine's seen of Lady Tisend is her austerity. And her history with Catherine's mother, the rumor she spread . . .

Beside her, Miss Raught groans and wipes feverishly at her painting, bringing Catherine back out of her thoughts. She needs to win this to assuage whatever happened twenty-five years ago. To put Lady Tisend, and Lady Rosalie, and even lovely Lady Jones below them.

All too soon Lady Jones calls out, "Brushes down!" and Catherine sits back.

It's good. But is it good enough?

"All right, aprons off and step back, ladies. Gents, you may resume normal human movement."

Catherine undoes her apron, watching with amusement as the men all stand up stiffly, stretching aching joints. Mr. Dean blinks a few times and then helps Mr. Sholle up, the two of them smiling and exchanging some small talk.

Catherine turns to wander behind the horseshoe of easels like the other girls, perusing the competition before the boys come to judge. She keeps her mouth in a neutral line as she looks over Miss Raught's and Miss Linet's paintings. They're lovely, but nothing compared to her own. She might even venture that hers is the best of the lot.

Until she comes to Lady Rosalie's painting. While Catherine tried to perfect each gentleman's pose, making them into parts of a greater whole, Lady Rosalie fully highlighted Mr. Dean. The other boys around him are less distinct, making him the center of attention. The detail, the shading, the way she's captured his far-off gaze, making him wistful—it's incredible.

Catherine wasn't thinking about the competition as solely a way to impress Mr. Dean. Lady Rosalie's clearly cleverer than she is.

Could she sneak over, add some gilding to Mr. Dean's tie, or give his hair an extra little flip in the front? Catherine glances back toward her own portrait.

And there Lady Rosalie stands, stock-still, a nail between her teeth, staring at Catherine's canvas. She's frowning, looking how Catherine imagines she did only a moment earlier. Perhaps she thinks Catherine is more competition than she is?

"Your portrait is amazing."

Catherine drags her eyes away from Lady Rosalie, turning to

face Miss Raught and Miss Linet. "Yours are both beautiful," Catherine says honestly.

"Not nearly as good as yours," Miss Raught insists.

"You've a real talent," Miss Linet adds, offering her what looks like true smile, before blowing at a lock of auburn hair that's escaped her bonnet.

Catherine smiles uncomfortably. All this attention is still foreign, and her natural reaction is to shrink away. "Your shading is marvelous," she tells Miss Raught. "And the way you captured the light is really striking," she tells Miss Linet.

Both girls smile, surprised.

"Amalie and Henrietta are very talented," Lady Rosalie says, appearing behind them, head high, all that concern and contemplation now gone from her face. "I'm glad they can hear it from someone else as well."

Miss Raught and Miss Linet preen under Lady Rosalie's attention. So it's not just her. Lady Rosalie ensorcels everyone around her.

But the way her stomach flips when Lady Rosalie meets her eyes—she rather thinks Miss Linet and Miss Raught aren't feeling quite what she is.

"Your work is stupendous."

Catherine's whole body goes warm. "Thank you. Yours is too."

Lady Rosalie's lips quirk upward. "Thank you."

Catherine opens her mouth to say more, but Mr. Dean, Mr. Sholle, and the rest of the gentlemen are heading toward them. Miss Raught and Miss Linet stand up straighter, smiling for their suitors coming behind Mr. Dean.

"I thought the way you captured Mr. Sholle's likeness rather striking. You made his playfulness really come to life. It's very charming," Lady Rosalie says loudly, almost straight toward the approaching Mr. Sholle, whose admittedly handsome face splits in a delighted grin.

Lady Rosalie turns and smirks at Catherine before grabbing Mr. Dean's arm, swinging him away from their group to go look at Lady Rosalie's portrait. That sneaky, devious—

"I caught your eye?" Mr. Sholle asks Catherine, looking so absurdly pleased.

"You were the star of the show, I can't lie," Catherine replies without thinking. His grin doubles in size and she feels her chest clench. She's not sure she wants to please him. "However, I do think Miss Linet captured you best, though Miss Raught really got your twinkling eyes. You clearly caught their attention more than anyone else."

Miss Raught and Miss Linet turn to look at her, their eyes wide, while Mr. Rile's and Mr. Fortes' smiles simultaneously dim.

Oh, oh no. She didn't mean—she was just trying to get out from under Lady Rosalie's—

"You did a splendid job," Lady Jones proclaims, taking Catherine's arm. "Excuse us for a moment," she adds to Mr. Sholle, pulling Catherine away from the mess she's just made.

Catherine glances over her shoulder while Lady Jones drags her toward her canvas, watching as Miss Linet and Miss Raught hurry to assuage their suitors' hurt feelings. Mr. Sholle just stands there, staring moonily after Catherine.

"It's absolutely perfect," Mother says as Catherine and Lady Jones stop in front of Catherine's painting. "He looks wonderful."

"All of them do," Lady Jones says, squeezing Catherine's arm.

Catherine gives them both a weak smile.

"I think this puts to shame the competition both of us were a part of, Lady Jones," Mother says.

"Who won that one?" Lady Jones asks.

"That horrid girl. Miss . . . Lysa?" Mother asks.

"I don't remember—oh, do you mean Miss Lystra?"

"Yes!" Mother says.

"She *was* horrid, wasn't she?" Lady Jones says.

"Truly terrible. Do you remember when she insisted on that awful game of charades? Lady Tisend nearly took an eye out . . ."

Catherine really should be listening. It's the first time Mother has spoken about the past with anything other than anger or terror. And to Lady Tisend's sister-in-law of all people.

But Catherine can't pull her eyes away from Mr. Dean and Lady Rosalie as they wander closer and closer to Catherine's easel. Unlike previous outings, Mr. Dean is prattling on today, presumably commenting on each woman's painting skills, while Lady Rosalie nods and smiles at all the right places. It looks like a well-rehearsed activity—him talking, her listening.

Which seems absurd, because she always has such things to say.

Like her well-timed comment about Mr. Sholle. Did she mean to get Catherine to insult her friends' suitors? Would she actually root to hurt her friends to get one up on Catherine?

Then again, look what her mother did to Catherine's all those years ago. It might run in her blood.

"Miss Pine," Mr. Dean says, slowly dropping Lady Rosalie's arm to step in front of Catherine's painting. "Look at the detail you achieved in only two hours. It's exquisite, isn't it, Lady Rosalie? She's captured each and every likeness."

"And so she has," Lady Rosalie says through gritted teeth.

Catherine watches her stare darkly at Mr. Dean, until he turns her way. Her face clears instantly, replaced by a complacent smile that doesn't reach her eyes.

"You have a talent, Miss Pine," she says.

"Thank you," Catherine says. "We had—"

"After the judging, I want to hear all about your methods. Who did you paint first? Did you decide on the lighting before or after filling in the figures? And what technique did you use to tap in the leaves?" Mr. Dean continues, finally turning to look at her.

"Of—of course," Catherine says, going for bright.

He smiles, his cheeks dimpling dashingly, before walking to the final two easels.

Catherine glances at Lady Rosalie. She's staring after Mr. Dean, crestfallen. He never asks *her* questions.

Mother steps forward to grab Catherine's arm. "Did you hear that? You impressed him," she whispers.

Catherine's still watching Lady Rosalie. Her dismay slowly hardens, and she turns to stare back at Catherine, muted fury in her eyes, her mouth pressed into a thin line. Behind her, Lady Tisend stands back from the easels, glaring as well.

Catherine stares back. Lady Tisend wanted a competition, she brought one.

Lady Rosalie wanted a war. She *brought* one.

Lady Rosalie turns and walks back to her mother, practically stomping. It lights something a little wild and brazen in Catherine's chest. Lady Rosalie fired the first shot with Mr. Sholle, who'll be even more eager now. She's just attacking back. This is what war is. And she came to win.

And when Lady Jones steps up on the platform a minute later, that's exactly what she does.

"By unanimous vote, the gentlemen have crowned Miss Pine the winner of the day. Congratulations, Miss Pine." Lady Jones, at least, is beaming at her while all the other girls clap politely.

Catherine allows herself one true, proud smile.

Mother hugs her hard. "I knew you could do it," she whispers.

"Thank you," Catherine says, pulling back to meet her sparkling eyes.

She looks so happy. So Catherine has to harden her shell. Has to meet Lady Rosalie's challenges with true gusto. They're going to win. She can make it happen.

She schools her face quickly. A lady mustn't *gloat*, after all.

"Thank you," she says to Lady Jones, hoping she sounds humble and grateful.

"Now, losers, go eat your sorrows in cake, and Miss Pine, we shall toast to you when the next round of champagne arrives," Lady Jones says happily.

There are laughs all around and Mother squeezes Catherine's arm before stepping away.

"Miss Pine, you simply must tell me about your painting," Mr. Dean says, gesturing for her to step back up to her easel with him.

Catherine sneaks one last glance at Lady Rosalie, who's still glaring back at her. She's not sure where the playful urge comes from, but she winks. Lady Rosalie's cheeks turn red and Catherine mentally pats herself on the back.

"How did you manage such fine detail in so short a time?" Mr. Dean asks.

"Well, I didn't give nearly so much attention to the tree or the platform," Catherine says honestly. "With another hour I could have done more."

"But the lack of specificity in the background is what makes the picture so striking. You know, it's almost an inversion of the Romantics, wouldn't you say? I simply must have it for my collection."

"Oh, um, of course," she says.

It should feel like a victory. Should feel better than making Lady Rosalie glare. It should ignite excitement and anticipation in her belly that Mr. Dean wants to take her work home.

But why on earth would he choose her portrait over Lady Rosalie's, which highlights him so expertly?

"You know, when I was abroad, I took tea with so many of the great painters. I've never had the talent, like yours, to paint, but I have quite the discerning eye."

He lightly touches her elbow, turning them to head toward the tables set up in the first section of the expansive back gardens. Somehow, this compliment about her work feels suspiciously like the entrée into one of her brother Richard's endless diatribes about his world tour.

"When I was in Italy, I visited the Doria Pamphilj in Rome, and I saw the most exquisite portraits . . ."

Catherine bites back a sigh. Richard visited the Doria Pamphilj collection as well. She imagines there must be a guide or tutor in Rome who gives the same speeches year after year after year.

Mr. Dean continues his monologue and guides Catherine over to one of the tables, where Miss Raught, Mr. Rile, Miss Linet, Mr. Fortes, Lady Rosalie, and Mr. Sholle are already seated.

Her pride and triumph over winning are quickly outweighed by a deep sense of looming awkwardness. Catherine glances behind her, hoping there might be someone to divert them. But everyone is already seated for the tea service, save for Lady Jones, who appears to be setting up her own easel to capture the tea itself.

Catherine's not sure how she feels about Lady Jones immortalizing this afternoon. She's gotten the impression Lady Jones fully understands each and every social dynamic at play at this garden party. Catherine's not sure she wants to see any of them in paint.

Mr. Dean pulls out the chair one away from Lady Rosalie and graciously helps Catherine into it, plopping himself down between them like he's never heard or seen a bad look in his entire life.

He's moved on to monologuing about France now.

Catherine glances across the table at Miss Raught and Miss Linet, who are staunchly not looking at her and continuing to speak to their respective suitors. Mr. Sholle, seated almost directly across from her, keeps trying to catch her eye, and Catherine, without other recourse, forces herself to tune back in to Mr. Dean, lest Mr. Sholle get the wrong idea.

"I found myself lingering in the Galerie Médicis at the Louvre for hours. The way Rubens paints ethereal fabric was entrancing."

Richard says *ethereal* too.

"I was always more partial to the Egyptian exhibit myself," Lady Rosalie says when Mr. Dean takes a breath.

"You've been to the Louvre?" Catherine finds herself asking.

"The way he captures light, as well, seems to come down from the heavens, casting his subjects in a Godly presence," Mr. Dean continues, as if Lady Rosalie hasn't spoken.

Catherine finds herself leaning forward in her seat to see Lady Rosalie's face, their eyes meeting while Mr. Dean continues to talk. And for a brief moment, they're not fighting over Mr. Dean at all, but simply united in the same bemused suffering.

God, this *guy*.

But it passes just as quickly. Lady Rosalie sits back in her seat, leaving Catherine rather alone beside the *still talking* Mr. Dean.

She looks across the table and finds Miss Linet momentarily looking over at her, anger still clear in her eyes. Catherine can fix this. Surely Mr. Dean will give her an opening.

As if on cue, Mr. Dean switches from exaltations about the Louvre to beginning a speech about the merits of Paris. It's perfect.

"Miss Linet was telling me how much she loves poetry the other day, and wished to go to a salon in Paris to hear some. Mr. Fortes, don't you write sonnets? Have you ever shared them with Miss Linet?" Catherine asks, a little overloud, because Mr. Dean will not shut up.

The whole table turns to look at her, and Mr. Fortes' narrow cheeks stretch in a smile. "I haven't had the opportunity, Miss Pine. But knowing Miss Linet might appreciate them, perhaps I should send them along with a letter tomorrow?"

"That would be lovely," Miss Linet says. She glances at Catherine, a smile on her face, and Catherine lets her shoulders come down just slightly.

"I found the Champs-Élysées too congested for real enjoyment," Mr. Dean continues to no one.

Miss Linet rolls her eyes toward Mr. Dean, as if perhaps she's heard him say this before.

"Mr. Rile, didn't you do a wonderful sketch of the Champs-Élysées with the foundation for the Arc when you were there last summer?" Lady Rosalie cuts in. "Perhaps in exchange for her painting, Miss Raught might like to have it?"

Miss Raught looks across at Lady Rosalie, blue eyes wide, a smile spreading slowly across her face as Mr. Rile bumbles to accept the offer. Catherine blows out a breath. All right, they fixed it together. She supposes she can live with that.

She looks around Mr. Dean and finds Lady Rosalie staring back at her curiously. And Mr. Dean is STILL BLOODY TALKING.

Lady Rosalie's lips quirk upward and everything seems to melt away. The way the sunlight hits her bonnet and outlines her face in a soft white glow—the way her eyes spark with amusement at their tandem frustration with Mr. Dean—the way her chest, her glorious chest, is rising and falling just a bit faster than it was moments ago—how can any of their friends or acquaintances be doing anything but staring at Lady Rosalie right now?

"Miss Pine?"

Catherine blinks, wrenching her gaze away from Lady Rosalie. Mr. Dean is apparently waiting for a response. He stopped talking, *and* asked a question?

"I'm so sorry, Mr. Dean. Could you repeat that?" she asks, hoping her voice doesn't sound choked.

She refuses to acknowledge Lady Rosalie smirking behind Mr. Dean.

Perhaps she wasn't in that wonderful moment with Catherine after all. Perhaps she meant to distract her, and Catherine's been snared in her web yet again, getting herself fanciful and dazzled all on her own.

"If you could go anywhere on the Continent, where would you go?"

Catherine meets Mr. Dean's eyes. They're a perfectly lovely brown, and ignite exactly zero feeling in her.

"Florence," she says by rote. She's not sure if that's where she'd most like to go, but Mother always wanted to see it.

"What a city. You'll have to start in the Piazza della Signoria . . ."

Catherine sighs softly and looks across the lawn to find Lady Jones watching her from behind her easel. She smiles at Catherine, though from this distance it almost looks like a smirk. But that's silly, what would she have to be smirking about?

SHE LISTENS WITH one ear as Mr. Dean moves on to what will hopefully be his final city of Luxembourg. The rest of her watches with glee as Mr. Rile approaches Miss Raught's mother, carrying her painting and gushing about Miss Raught's talents.

Lady Rosalie rises with a quick excuse and heads their way. Mr. Dean barely notices. Catherine's frankly not sure Mr. Dean is still talking to either of them. Mr. Sholle is the only one who's been making noises of interest for the past hour.

Lady Rosalie and Lady Jones meet up to see Miss Raught off with her mother and Mr. Rile. Miss Raught is beaming and bright, her round face lit up with joy, practically floating along in her bright yellow dress.

Just when it looks like she might well leave without any formal farewell, Miss Raught pauses by the back gate and shoots Catherine a huge smile. Catherine returns it, a little swell of pride washing across her chest, which only grows when Lady Rosalie glances her way, pensive, and then turns away.

This may be her only chance to escape.

"I ought to find Miss Linet to say goodbye," Catherine says, jumping in when Mr. Dean takes a rare breath.

He and Mr. Sholle don't even nod, and Catherine leaves them behind without an ounce of regret. Mother frowns at her from where she's loitering on the patio with a few of the remaining mothers, but Catherine ignores her. She might well stab Mr. Dean if she doesn't get a break.

Miss Linet and Mr. Fortes are ambling back toward the patio, Mr. Fortes holding Miss Linet's painting. Miss Linet slows to speak with Catherine, smiling.

"I'll hang this in pride of place," Mr. Fortes says kindly, leaning in to kiss Miss Linet's hand before striding off, the painting held carefully, but not particularly dearly, by his side.

"That went well?" Catherine asks.

Miss Linet is staring after him thoughtfully. "It did," she agrees. "And for you as well, it seems," she adds, looking back to meet Catherine's gaze.

"I suppose," Catherine says.

Miss Linet chuckles. "He did *try* to tailor the soliloquy to your tastes, at least. Not everyone gets so lucky."

"Did he?" Catherine asks before she can stop herself.

Miss Linet lets out a pealing laugh and Catherine can't help but giggle along with her.

"What's so funny?" Lady Rosalie asks, stepping up behind Catherine.

"Nothing," Miss Linet says, smiling at Catherine before taking Lady Rosalie's arm. "Come see me out. My escort left without me."

"He took your painting," Lady Rosalie says consolingly, nodding to Catherine before leading Miss Linet out of the garden.

Which leaves Catherine standing alone on the lawn behind the tea tables. Lady Jones' canvas is still drying on her easel. Catherine walks over to see what she's made of their teatime tableau and can't help but smile.

She's painted the patio and tables in muted whites, so every outfit stands out against the setting. Those people she knows well, or found interesting, have detailed faces and poses, while some of the guests are mere silhouettes.

Catherine searches the painting, curious as to what Lady Jones has seen in her, and her breath catches in her chest. Because there, looking around Mr. Dean, sit she and Lady Rosalie, staring at each other.

Their eyes, the pensive set of their brows, the rigidity to their posture—something is passing between them there on the canvas. It could be their shared annoyance at Mr. Dean. Or it could be something . . . else.

She captured it perfectly.

Because it felt like that. Like she was staring at Lady Rosalie with no one else in the garden, *something* there between them.

It's startling to see it laid to canvas. Alarming, she should say.

"She's talented, isn't she?"

Catherine jumps. "Stop doing that," she says loudly, turning to find Lady Rosalie smirking at her.

Lady Rosalie steps up beside her to look at Lady Jones' painting. Catherine watches her look, waiting. Will she see what Catherine does? Will she comment? Will she pretend it's not there, and nothing's strange or revealing about their poses?

She can tell by Lady Rosalie's soft inhale when she finally sees it.

"Doesn't miss a thing, does she?" Lady Rosalie says softly.

Catherine blinks, not sure how to respond. If she even could without making some embarrassing sound, or saying—God, what would she—should she—even say?

But Lady Rosalie's a step ahead. She reaches out and picks the painting up.

"I'll keep this. I've got a collection of my aunt's best paintings. A wall of gossip, if you will, up in my hallway. You can get a whole season's worth of stories just by walking down it."

Catherine still doesn't know how to respond. Are they gossip?

She decides avoiding the topic altogether is likely safest. "You should hang yours as well."

"Mother can put it with the rest. We've a graveyard of my paintings in the basement," Lady Rosalie says, dismissive.

"You should hang that one. Somewhere Mr. Dean will see it," Catherine insists. Lady Rosalie meets her eyes, surprised. "If I cannot overcome the allure of a portrait, I'm a poor competitor," she decides. "And you're talented."

"Oh, that I know," Lady Rosalie says, fluffing her hair.

Catherine laughs, startled, and Lady Rosalie cracks a real smile. She wants to say something else, make Lady Rosalie laugh too. Something to end this afternoon well. To give them both something more than this strange feeling of limbo between them, and Mr. Dean's droning voice.

Which has stopped.

Catherine glances toward the tea tables and finds her mother walking toward her, Mr. Dean on her arm. Mr. Sholle is nowhere to be seen.

"Catherine, dearest, we should see Mr. Dean out," Mother says. "Lady Rosalie, you have a true gift. Your mother should have you painting more often."

Catherine watches Lady Rosalie smile genuinely back at her mother. "Thank you," she says sweetly. "I know it meant a lot to my aunt for you to be here, and Miss Pine was delightful competition."

"Perhaps you'll beat me next time," Catherine says.

"Perhaps," Lady Rosalie says, meeting her eyes before curtsying to Mr. Dean and Mother and then taking her leave.

Catherine watches her go until Mother takes her arm, guiding her back over to her painting while discussing details for a walk Lady Jones is apparently going to chaperone for all the young people next week. Mr. Dean is looking forward to attending and seeing Catherine.

Watching him pick up her painting like it's precious should ignite something in her. Feeling his lips along the back of her still-ungloved hand should make her blush. She never remembered to put them back on.

But there's nothing there in her chest. No tingles, no anticipation.

Nothing like the feeling of Lady Rosalie's eyes on her when they leave a few minutes later. She can feel her gaze all the way up the back walkway and onto the street, long past when she's no longer in sight.

Chapter Nine
Rosalie

I t's not just that the poem was bad, Rose. It actually gave me a headache!"

Rosalie dabs her face with her lace handkerchief, which does very little to wipe away the sweat and humidity sticking to her skin.

"Mother is dead set on another three outings with Mr. Fortes before she'll allow me to change my mind, but I'm not sure I'll get through it," Amalie says, nary an auburn hair or breath out of place as they tromp down the path through the budding woods.

Rosalie's trying to listen, she is. Though this is the third such walk since the painting competition where Amalie has bemoaned her mother's continuing interest in Mr. Fortes. Amalie decided at the tea that he wasn't for her. But convincing her mother otherwise will take longer, and require more subterfuge and careful planning than Amalie generally likes to give any social function, let alone her own courting.

"We'll distract you," Rosalie promises.

Rosalie needs a real distraction herself.

Every time she tries to think about Mr. Dean, her mind fills instead with Miss Pine's inquisitive gaze, her pretty blush, the way her willowy body looks in her beautiful dresses—how she might look beneath those dresses, in just her shift, or less . . .

Rosalie balls the handkerchief up in her fist. She can't let her whole life fall apart because a pretty girl came to town. A *very* pretty girl, who is smart, and disarming, and witty, and sly and quick and—

"Are you listening at all?"

Rosalie looks over at Amalie, startled.

"Of course," she says immediately. "Mr. Fortes writes atrocious poetry, and you'd like me to provide cover for you to distance yourself from him on our walk with Aunt Genevieve."

Amalie stops walking and stares at Rosalie. "I asked if you'd like me to order you a copy of *The Shipwreck.*"

"Oh," Rosalie says, smiling guiltily at her friend. "Thank you. And I will also provide said cover on our walk."

"All right," Amalie says, eyeing Rosalie a bit too knowingly.

But she can't possibly know anything about what Rosalie was thinking. Her stomach clenches guiltily as they hike back up to her house. She should be giving Amalie her full attention. She should be thinking longingly of alone time with Mr. Dean. She should be attracted to men is what she should be.

But ugh, men.

"Stay for tea?" she asks Amalie as they head for the solarium to shed their damp outer layers.

"Will there be cake?" Amalie asks seriously.

"There's always cake when you come over," Rosalie replies, equally serious.

Amalie cracks a smile and the two of them tromp inside.

When they come through the library doors, Rosalie longing to lie down, Amalie pulls her to a stop with a gasp. Rosalie looks up and Christopher turns from one of the shelves along the back wall.

"Surprise!" he says, his voice deeper than it was even three months ago when he left for the winter term.

"Oh, how lovely," Amalie says happily.

But Rosalie just stares. What is her brother doing home?

"You couldn't have written?" she asks, letting go of Amalie. Christopher rushes across the room to sweep her up in a spinning hug.

"Where's the fun in that?" he asks as he puts her down.

"Mother's going to kill you for arriving while she's out," Rosalie says, pushing him back to hold him by the shoulders. "You've grown again."

While no great height, he's gained another half inch since Yule, making him frustratingly a full head taller than Rosalie. She *hates* that her baby brother got taller than she did by the time he was twelve.

He has a bit of stubble on his cheeks, his brown hair has gone a bit curly, and he's lost more of his baby fat, his heart-shaped face narrower, features sharper. He looks a proper young man now. Almost dashing, just over nineteen—he'll be the catch of the late season.

How did that happen?

"I do keep telling myself to stop, but it rarely works. Miss Linet, you look lovely," he adds.

Rosalie looks over her shoulder in time to catch Amalie's bright blush.

Well, that's interesting, isn't it?

"Doesn't she?" Rosalie agrees. She steps back from Christopher and ushers both of them into the sitting area at the center of the library.

With tall bookshelves lining the walls, the space can sometimes feel a bit narrow, but in the center of the room, Mother smartly arranged two settees and two deep, comfortable armchairs, all in a pale blue that catches the light from the thin but enormously tall windows on the far wall.

The whole effect is cozy, and private, and inviting. A perfect place to sit her brother and best friend down and make sure they end the day with at least two outings planned. Rosalie doesn't know why she hasn't thought of them together before now.

"What's brought you back so early?" Amalie asks, beating Rosalie to it.

"Father called me back," Christopher says. Rosalie stares; that's certainly news to her.

"Is something the matter?" Amalie asks, looking between them.

"No, no, just another attempt to sway me to accompany him to London for part of the season so I may *learn the ropes*."

"Oh, so you'll be leaving soon, then," Amalie says, sounding absolutely dejected, which makes Christopher perk up a little in his seat.

How long have they been secretly interested in each other? And why has neither of them ever said?

"He's asked that I attend. I haven't yet said yes," Christopher says quickly. "I'm not sure I want to miss the end of the season here, when my sister might get *engaged*."

Rosalie narrows her eyes. "What has Mother been telling you?"

"You don't think he'll propose?" Amalie asks at the same time.

Mother certainly thinks Mr. Dean will. But with Miss Pine, and her mother, and Rosalie's generally waning enthusiasm for all things subterfuge . . .

"Mother's dead set on it, apparently," Christopher says. "Says she and my sister have all kinds of plans to thwart a new threat?"

"Ah, Miss Pine," Amalie says. "She really is very pretty."

Christopher's eyes cut to Rosalie and Rosalie intentionally doesn't meet them. If anyone in the world could look at her and know, it would be Christopher.

"Well, I never want to miss my sister putting someone in their place. She gets ever so bossy, don't you think?"

Rosalie gasps while Amalie giggles. "I do not!"

"Oh, but you do," Amalie says, grinning at Christopher. "But it's always for the best. You're the smartest of us by far, and you see everything. We need your bossiness. You're *always* right, after all."

"You protest too much," Rosalie tells her, shaking her head as the doors to the library open and Miss Wrigsby comes in with one of the porters, carrying a ridiculous number of pastries along with their tea set.

Rosalie would be more insulted by Christopher and Amalie's teasing, but she's just so glad to have him home and, hopefully, staying for the rest of the season. Everything else aside, they'll get all his favorite meals every night, and more treats with tea. Mother's always focused on keeping Rosalie trim and healthy, but Christopher gets the goodies.

She loves him for it, and hates him for it.

"Thank you, Miss Wrigsby, Mr. Stone," Christopher says around a mouthful of biscuit.

Miss Wrigsby shakes her head and smiles at him. She meets Rosalie's eyes as she leaves, grinning, and Rosalie can't help but smile too.

"Do you have any plans while you're in town?" Amalie asks.

"Not many," Christopher says, pouring all of them tea. Such a little gentleman he's become.

Amalie's smile is wide when he hands her a cup. He's not so little anymore. He looks like a man now. A man who could make her friend happy.

"You'll come with us on Thursday, then," Rosalie says, ignoring the way both of them snicker. Fine, she's bossy. It's for their own good. "Aunt Genevieve has organized a group walk."

"I'd be delighted," Christopher says at once. "I hope you'll be there too, Miss Linet?"

"I will," she says.

It's perfect. Christopher can be another set of eyes. Help her determine if she can truly pair off Miss Pine and Mr. Sholle. And he'll be honest. He can tell her if Miss Pine is really as special as Rosalie thinks—as distracting as she thinks.

THEY'RE A ROWDY group as they clamber through the woods, heading for the Palladian Bridge in Prior Park. Aunt Genevieve has insisted they step off the road and rough it through the underbrush as much as possible. Rosalie's hemline will be ruined, and her boots will need polishing for ages, but it's been invigorating.

She's walking with Mr. Dean and Aunt Genevieve, a bit behind Christopher and Miss Pine, who made the head of the pack almost immediately. Henrietta, Mr. Rile, Mr. Sholle, and Amalie are behind them, which doesn't do much for her plans for Christopher and Amalie, but does seem to be providing Christopher with ample time to get to know Miss Pine.

He's peppering her with questions Rosalie can't quite hear. She wishes she could get the answers right away, rather than needing to figure out how to get them out of Christopher later without letting on that she's developed this massive, inconvenient crush.

Though she supposes there's always the off chance Christopher will fall for Miss Pine. Which she hadn't considered, bafflingly, until just now.

Why wouldn't he? She looks so fetching in her green walking dress and brown spencer jacket. She's taller than Christopher, but bears it so gracefully. Her hair is curling more than usual with the humidity beneath her short brown bonnet, and it only makes her whole face that much more welcoming.

What if Christopher falls for her? Surely Mrs. Pine wouldn't allow her daughter to marry Rosalie's mother's son. Not with . . . whatever animosity lurks between them. He may not have a subsidiary title now, but he *will* be an earl. That would be better even than a viscount.

What has she done? What about Amalie?

Mr. Dean coughs softly, nodding to something Aunt Genevieve's saying. Rather playfully, Aunt Genevieve has been on a solid ten-minute diatribe about how much she hates the Louvre. Mr. Dean clearly has no idea she's taking the piss, which is fabulous.

Because while Christopher and Miss Pine have been all chat, as usual Mr. Dean has said nothing but "Hello" to Rosalie since they met up with the group at the Southgate Bridge to cross the river.

Aunt Genevieve finally finishes her rant about museum acoustics and winks at Rosalie, who stifles a laugh. Aunt Genevieve then speeds up to join Miss Pine and Christopher, leaving Rosalie and Mr. Dean to walk together, only the crunching of lightly frosty grass and leaves beneath them, and the chatter from their group ahead and behind.

Rosalie thinks about engaging Mr. Dean in conversation, but decides she needs some quiet to get herself under control. To convince herself that Christopher won't fall for Miss Pine. She's catastrophizing. She must be.

"Are you looking forward to attending the theatre tomorrow?" Mr. Dean asks.

"I am," she says, looking up at him.

"I am as well," he says, and then turns his head back to their path, saying nothing else.

A wonderful opportunity to discuss the play. To ask questions about what she's seen recently. To bring up even something he saw on his engrossing world tour. And *nothing*.

He is beautiful, and stable, and such a smart, pragmatic choice for a future husband. But she has to admit to herself, he isn't fun. And everyone around them sounds like they're having fun.

Christopher glances over his shoulder again and it's like he can instantly tell she's upset, even though Rosalie's fairly sure she hasn't moved a single facial muscle. Christopher still slows down all the same, which brings Miss Pine and Aunt Genevieve with him.

"Miss Pine tells me you have stories about Barcelona," Christopher says to Mr. Dean.

"Oh, it is such a beautiful city. Have you been?" Mr. Dean asks, releasing Rosalie's arm immediately to fall into step with Christopher. Any chance to bring out his favorite hits. He hasn't had fresh ears since he started courting Rosalie.

Christopher leads Mr. Dean ahead of them, which leaves Rosalie and Miss Pine walking alongside each other, Aunt Genevieve on Miss Pine's other side.

"I should fall back, make sure those boys are being gentlemen," Aunt Genevieve says, her face serious but eyes alight, as if she knows this is putting Rosalie in an uncomfortable position.

Which she probably does. Though there's no good reason Rosalie *should* be uncomfortable with Miss Pine.

But as Aunt Genevieve slows down to join Amalie, Henrietta, Mr. Rile, and Mr. Sholle, Rosalie feels her shoulders going up. She doesn't know how to talk to Miss Pine, not after the garden party. Not after Aunt Genevieve's painting. Not after the dreams she's been having. Inappropriate, scandalous, delicious dreams.

She wants to distract herself—ask Miss Pine a safe question.

"You and my brother certainly found things to discuss" is what pops out of her mouth. Not a question, and frankly accusatory in tone.

Miss Pine only laughs. "He's a delightful young man. I see a lot of you in him, actually."

"Do you?"

"I imagine he says everything you wish you could in polite company."

"Goodness, what was he telling you?" Rosalie asks, breaking her own rule and looking over at Miss Pine, who grins back at her.

"Oh, just thoughts on a few acquaintances I've noticed you don't particularly like."

That could be any number of people. "Which ones?" Rosalie asks, shooting a glare at the back of her oblivious brother's head.

"Mr. and Mrs. Plory," Miss Pine whispers.

Oh, Rosalie does hate them. Their son, Thomas Plory, is a lovely young man. But his parents are the most vituperative, snide, judgmental people she's ever met.

"He was telling me about the time Mrs. Plory tried to say

you were too short to rear healthy children and you managed to make a server fall into her with a tray of champagne glasses?"

Rosalie's mouth drops open. She has half a mind to box her brother about the ears, until she realizes Miss Pine is giggling. It's such a ridiculously pretty sound.

She looks back at Miss Pine, who has her lace-gloved hand over her mouth. "It's *true?*"

Rosalie just blinks. She—oh—Christ.

Miss Pine's giggles turn to full-out laughter. Mr. Dean and Christopher look back at them and Rosalie can't help but start to laugh herself. Ahead of them, Mr. Dean rolls his eyes and keeps walking, while Christopher smiles at her and then hurries to catch up.

Miss Pine reaches out to clutch at her arm so they don't fall down. "How wonderfully wicked of you," she says.

Rosalie shrugs, her cheeks aching from smiling and laughing, her arm warm beneath Miss Pine's palm. "What, like you've never done something similar?"

Miss Pine's eyes go wide. "I could never."

"After your performance at the garden party, I highly doubt that. It was very *Emma* of you."

"It was not. If anyone is like Emma Woodhouse, it's you," Miss Pine insists, letting go of Rosalie's arm to brush at her curls while they amble behind Christopher and Mr. Dean, who are now almost at the pond through the thinning trees.

Rosalie feels the absence of Miss Pine's fingers keenly. "I surmise you found Emma's conduct questionable, then?"

Miss Pine gives her a look. "You didn't?"

"I thought her motivations admirable. Her execution was . . . unfortunate," Rosalie decides.

"Or perhaps her staunch belief in her own self-assurance and ability were merely hubris, hiding her inner desire for the same companionship, and proving her as fallible in love and relationships as anyone else," Miss Pine counters.

Rosalie blinks. "That is an astute reading of the themes."

Miss Pine snorts and rolls her eyes. "It is the basic reading."

"Ask a man, he'll give you a different one entirely," Rosalie replies.

"Oh? Did your brother think differently?"

"A few of my brother's friends determined it an excellent example of women needing to listen to their betters and allowing cooler male heads to prevail."

"Bollocks," Miss Pine says.

Rosalie laughs, surprised, and Miss Pine grins. "What did your brother think?"

"Richard?" Miss Pine asks. "I doubt he's read it. It would be too . . . frivolous for him. Though he'd probably side with Mr. Knightley."

"Typical," Rosalie says with a sigh.

Miss Pine nods. "But he's a good brother. Not quite as fun as yours seems."

"Do you miss him?" Rosalie finds herself asking. "I take it he doesn't live nearby."

"He's north of London now, with his own home and wife and I suppose children soon," Miss Pine says, her voice softer, more contemplative. "It must be nice to have Mr. Tisend home for the season."

Rosalie glances ahead at Christopher. "It is."

Miss Pine smiles and they walk toward the end of the tree line that will open onto the pond. Shadows dance across her face. Rosalie has to look away.

"Now, tell me, did you really used to put on a pair of his

breeches and run through the woods every day until you were fifteen?"

Rosalie splutters, catching herself on a narrow yew tree before she falls over in surprise. "What?" she nearly shrieks.

"So it's true," Miss Pine says, grinning at her.

"I will kill that boy," Rosalie says, her voice rough. How *dare* he? She glares at Christopher where he and Mr. Dean are now standing at the edge of the pond.

"Oh, I used to do the same with Richard. You're hardly special," Miss Pine says.

Rosalie looks up at Miss Pine, who's smiling a bit mischievously. "And what excessively unladylike activities did your brother wheedle you into?"

"Sorry, Mr. Tisend already told me that you were nearly always the instigator."

Rosalie shakes her head. "What did you get your brother into, then?"

"There may or may not have been days where we nearly got lost in the claypit mines when we went to work with Father and subsequent nights we didn't get dinner," Miss Pine says with a shrug.

"And were you dressed as a good little girl the whole time?" Rosalie pushes.

"Oh, no, I looked like a common mine boy. It was delightful."

Rosalie can't help but smile, imagining a smaller Miss Pine dressed in dirty pants and a shirt, mucking about in the mine with her brother, causing all kinds of trouble. She wants to ask Miss Pine about her childhood. Wants to talk more about *Emma*. Wants her opinion on *Pride and Prejudice*. Wants to know what she thinks of the assertion that the author is a woman.

But the rest of their group are quickly catching up, stomping through the underbrush to emerge on the shore of the pond in a rowdy, lightly sweaty crowd. Henrietta and Mr. Rile look rather cozy, while Mr. Sholle is leaning around Amalie to get a glimpse at Miss Pine.

Aunt Genevieve finally steps out of the woods behind all of them, giving Rosalie a look. She really ought to be commanding her suitor's attention. It's why they're here.

Rosalie's just going to ignore how every single part of her body screams in protest as she steps away from Miss Pine. She beckons everyone forward until they're all standing in a semi-circle by the edge of the pond. Mr. Dean is *still* talking about his world tour.

"I thought perhaps the gentlemen could teach us to skip rocks. We're the only ones here and we won't be bothering anyone," Rosalie suggests.

"A marvelous idea," Aunt Genevieve says, a little overloud, causing everyone to giggle.

"Mr. Rile, you'll show Miss Raught. Mr. Sholle, Miss Pine. Mr. Dean with me, of course," Rosalie says, ignoring the pleasure she gets in the narrowing of Miss Pine's eyes. "And Christopher, perhaps you could show Miss Linet, as Mr. Fortes was busy this morning."

Christopher grins at her and leaves Mr. Dean to sidle up to Amalie. Mr. Rile and Henrietta head right for the edge of the water, bending down to find the perfect smooth rocks. Mr. Sholle bounds over to Miss Pine, who gives him what seems like a genuine smile and takes his arm to walk down a ways to find their own rocks.

Rosalie watches them go before tearing her eyes away to look across the lovely small pond. To the right sits the Palladian Bridge, a beautiful Bath stone–covered walkway with arched, open walls that casts part of the pond in shadow even at the height of midday. The grounds across the pond are manicured and verdant, sloping gently up to tall, just-budding trees. It's a lovely tableau.

"Good show!" Mr. Rile's loud encouragement to Henrietta breaks the silence and Rosalie can't help but laugh.

"Shall we?" Mr. Dean asks.

"Please," Rosalie says, taking his arm and letting him lead her down the row to the other side of Christopher and Amalie, who are bickering over the best stone to choose.

Amalie's hem is muddy and Christopher's standing in the water, but they look so happy. Rosalie watches in amusement as they elbow each other for the best spot to throw. Meanwhile, down the line, Mr. Rile and Mr. Sholle are using this opportunity to wrap their arms around Henrietta and Miss Pine.

Henrietta's blushing grin is visible even at a distance. She and Mr. Rile make a good pair, his broad chest at her back, both of them bright-cheeked. Miss Pine looks distinctly less comfortable with Mr. Sholle, though Rosalie thinks she'd step away if she felt truly ill at ease.

Still, it niggles at Rosalie's brain—maybe it's a step too far to encourage Mr. Sholle. Maybe she doesn't like the idea that Miss Pine might not hate having him wrapped around her.

A massive plop pulls Rosalie from her spiraling thoughts and she looks down the line to find Henrietta pouting.

"It's all in the wrist, I promise," she hears Mr. Rile say, taking her hand tenderly to help her wind her arm in and then throw another stone, which skips twice before falling gracefully into the water.

Henrietta positively beams while Mr. Rile whoops in congratulations.

Mr. Dean flicks his wrist, sending his rock gliding across the water. It skips three times before plopping into the lake.

"Well done," Rosalie says.

Mr. Dean just hums and gestures for her to toss her rock. She manages a respectable two skips.

"More flick," he says, before looking down to hunt for another stone, offering her nothing else.

"EIGHT!"

Rosalie looks over to find Aunt Genevieve jumping up and down as Miss Pine, Christopher, and Amalie congratulate her.

"What's your secret?" Amalie asks.

"Height," Aunt Genevieve says, winking at Rosalie, who huffs good-naturedly.

"Well, we can achieve that, can't we?" Christopher asks, turning and encouraging Amalie to climb up onto his back.

Amalie hesitates, but Aunt Genevieve is giggling, and Henrietta's watching her from Mr. Rile's arms, grinning, so she goes for it. Together, Amalie and Christopher rear back and throw their stones, Amalie clinging to his back with one arm, her legs around his hips, with him scrabbling to keep her in place with one arm.

And of course both stones skip four times.

Christopher and Amalie cheer and Rosalie shakes her head. They are absurd. Perfectly absurd. And so right for each other.

As her brother and Amalie struggle to bend down to get new rocks without falling, Rosalie notices Miss Pine watching them as well. The look on her face is wistful, even with Mr. Sholle standing beside her, a hand on her back, explaining the perfect wrist flick without realizing she's no longer paying attention.

Rosalie looks away before Miss Pine can notice her. She

laughs when Aunt Genevieve steps in to steady Christopher before he and Amalie tumble predictably into the pond.

They're falling for each other, just starting, she can tell. Christopher's baby crush is growing into full adoration, while Amalie's seeing something in him she's never noticed before. And Rosalie gets to watch it all firsthand. Take credit.

She glances back at Mr. Dean, who's now just standing there, staring off across the pond.

What must it be like to actually fall for someone who falls for you back? To be so irrational and emotional and . . . infatuated? To risk falling into the pond to make a pretty girl laugh?

She can't help but look past Christopher and Amalie to Miss Pine again, and finds her staring back. She raises a slightly glum shoulder and Rosalie wonders what's on her own face. Miss Pine rolls her eyes in some kind of commiseration, and then turns dutifully back to Mr. Sholle, giving him her attention.

Rosalie sighs and bends down, picking up a smooth, gray stone. She blows out a breath and tosses it across the pond, trying to fling away all the confusion swirling in her brain with it. It doesn't skip even once, landing instead with an enormous splash.

Everyone turns to look and Rosalie feels her cheeks go pink. Christopher and Amalie seem dangerously amused at the frustration on Rosalie's face, but Miss Pine is giggling.

Rosalie's stomach swoops. She has such a damn infectious laugh.

Maybe falling for someone feels like this. Unsettling in a way that's rather addictive.

What would it be like to just . . . let herself fall? Enjoy the tingle of something real, even if it's going to crash and burn later. Who would it hurt?

It's not like Miss Pine would really be an option anyway, even for a short while.

But then her eyes catch Rosalie's, so much there in her gaze. Miss Pine can't be an option. She doesn't feel how Rosalie feels. She's just . . . competitive, and sly, and witty.

But the look she's giving Rosalie is the same one from Aunt Genevieve's painting. The look that keeps her up at night. What is she supposed to do with that?

Chapter Ten
Catherine

Catherine leans back in her chair, shifting in her stiff burgundy gown. Mother keeps nudging her to sit up straight, as if Mr. Dean might look over at any second and be overcome by her posture.

She hardly thinks he'll be looking at her. The theatre is absolutely stunning. The gold-plated railings around the rounded boxes, the domed ceiling, cream walls, and deep red curtains that frame the stage and separate the boxes from the aisles are all beautiful. The three chandeliers over the stage cast everything in a warm yellow glow, and watching the audience file into the standing room in front of the stage has been quite amusing.

But Mother can focus on nothing other than the Tisends and Mr. Dean in the opposite box on the second level across from them. It's slowly driving Catherine mad.

Her escort, Mr. Sholle, doesn't seem to mind her posture, and has been complimenting her repeatedly. He looks dapper in his dark wool waistcoat and cream pantaloons, with dark knee-high boots. His chestnut hair has a lovely little flop to it, and his eyes and cheeks are bright as he talks at her. He keeps nudging into her shoulder like he's hoping to take her hand if she puts her arm on the armrest. But she doesn't want to encourage him.

Catherine's at least looking forward to *Romeo and Juliet*.

She's hoping it will be a spirited performance. Because while Mr. Sholle has been talking, and Mother has been whispering, Catherine's been trying not to stare across at Lady Rosalie.

She's wearing a beautiful yellow gown, her hair wrapped and braided elegantly onto the back of her head, with loose curls falling by her sharp cheekbones. Her diamond necklace and hair ornaments twinkle in the light from the chandeliers.

She's absolutely entrancing, and Mr. Dean is paying her zero attention, which just boggles the mind. He and Mr. Tisend have been talking for the past half hour, while Lady Rosalie looks perfectly bored.

Having only allowed herself a few seconds of ogling, Catherine goes to look away, but Lady Rosalie's eyes suddenly find hers. They stare at each other for a long moment, the rest of the room falling away. Then Lady Rosalie tips her head toward Mr. Dean, who is nearly fully turned away from her to talk to her brother, and rolls her eyes.

Catherine has to stop herself from laughing. Lady Rosalie's lips quirk upward, and then she looks pointedly away at the stage. Catherine gives herself one moment longer, enjoying their little exchange, before forcing herself to turn back to Mr. Sholle.

To Lady Rosalie's credit, he seems *very* taken with Catherine, which is flattering, but little more. Mr. Sholle is perfectly lovely, and a month ago she might have even been excited by his attention. But his isn't the attention that's making her blush.

Worse, Mother is planning her marriage to another man in front of him—it's hardly fair, and a little sad that he hasn't noticed. It's very confusing, and it's making her tired.

Mr. Sholle, thankfully, is a fan of the Bard and pays careful attention when the play finally starts, so she can relax into her seat and unclench her hands. Her anxiety slowly fades away to almost nothing. She should accept invitations to the theatre more often.

But midway through the fourth scene of the second act, she glances across the theatre, quite without thinking. Or at least, that's what she's telling herself.

Mr. Tisend is watching the stage with rapt attention. Lady Tisend's equally engrossed. But Mr. Dean—Mr. Dean is *falling asleep.*

She can't help a quick giggle escaping, overly loud in the hush that's fallen over the room. Mother nudges her and Catherine bites at her lips, giving a guilty shrug. Mr. Sholle hasn't noticed.

But Lady Rosalie has. She peers curiously across the theatre at Catherine, then glances at the stage, but there's nothing comical going on. Catherine can't help but jut her chin in Mr. Dean's direction. She watches Lady Rosalie look sideways and let out an enormous sigh.

Catherine keeps her lips clamped together. Lady Rosalie looks back at her, exasperated. They keep staring at each other, even though important things are happening on stage.

It feels like the look they exchanged at the pond. Her chest starts to go warm, a flush creeping up her neck as Lady Rosalie's regard turns from playful to . . . something decidedly different. It makes Catherine want to squirm in her chair.

She wishes she fully understood the overwhelming space Lady Rosalie takes up in her brain. The way a single look ignites something that tingles from the top of her head down to her toes. She doesn't feel that for anyone else. Not for the men. Not for the women. What is it about Lady Rosalie that does this to her?

There's a crash on stage and they both jerk, looking back to watch the third act. Catherine forces herself to keep her eyes on the stage. Forces herself not to wonder if Lady Rosalie is looking at her. She's flustered enough already.

It's a great relief when the curtain falls, signaling the start of the interval. She needs a moment to herself.

Mother turns to her, mouth open, and Catherine hurries out, "I need to visit the cloakroom."

"Of course, dear," Mother says immediately. "Mr. Sholle and I will escort you."

Mr. Sholle rises gallantly and the three of them make their slow way around the back of the theatre and over to the women's cloakroom. Catherine slips inside, leaving Mr. Sholle and her mother talking in the hall, and breathes a sigh of sweet relief.

The cloakroom is sparsely populated, and Catherine heads for the water closets. It's quiet, if not the best of locations, and when she's done, she lingers in the outer cloakroom, staring at her still-flushed reflection in the mirrors over the vanity.

Neither Mother nor Mr. Sholle have noticed, but she's remarkably discomposed. All because Lady Rosalie *looked* at her?

And like she's conjured her out of the air, Lady Rosalie sweeps into the cloakroom, brushing her curls from her face, her expression pinched.

They stare at each other. The noise from the hallway and the few other ladies in the cloakroom registers like a dull roar, but Catherine's not sure she hears it at all. After a long, charged, strange moment, Lady Rosalie walks smoothly over to stand beside Catherine, so they can watch each other in the vanity mirror.

"A good performance," Lady Rosalie says, and her voice is rough.

"Very," Catherine agrees, her own voice a bit high. She

searches for something else to say—something witty, or observant, or—

"I cannot believe Mr. Dean fell asleep," Lady Rosalie says in
a loud whisper.

"I know!" Catherine says, turning to her. "How can you fall
asleep during Shakespeare?" *How can you fall asleep next to
someone so beautiful?*

"He was nodding off before the play even started," Lady Rosalie grumbles. "Christopher was keeping him awake, but once
the play began, there was no getting him back."

"Your brother, or Mr. Dean?"

Lady Rosalie laughs and Catherine can't help but smile.
"Both," she says. "Christopher would have become an actor if it
wouldn't have ruined the family, so he *loves* the theatre. It's one
of the few things he and my father agree on. That and opera."

Catherine bobs her head, not quite sure how to respond.

"Anyway," Lady Rosalie says, shaking her head. "How is
Mr. Sholle?"

"Awake," Catherine replies with a shrug. Lady Rosalie laughs
again. "Enjoying the performance, if his conversation with my
mother is anything to go on."

"He's not talking to you?" Lady Rosalie asks, sharper, meeting her eyes in an instant.

Catherine swallows, her throat suddenly tight. "Not just
now. I'm in here with you, you see."

Lady Rosalie snorts, and it's almost as lovely a sound as her
laugh, which is absolutely absurd.

Why is this silly moment in the cloakroom her favorite of the
entire evening so far? They've barely spoken, they're standing
near the water closet, of all places, and she doesn't want to leave.

The chatty women at the other end of the vanity bustle out, leaving them alone in the quiet together.

"He should be talking to you," Lady Rosalie says firmly.

"Mr. Dean should be awake," Catherine returns.

Lady Rosalie sighs. "Some evening."

And somehow, it is. Here. In the cloakroom. It's . . . lovely. This brief moment between them—no competition, no artifice, no mothers looming. Just Catherine talking with a beautiful woman who looks amazing in the candlelight with her face all flushed with excitement, and whose eyes are so—

Lady Rosalie reaches out to brush one of Catherine's wilting pin curls from her face. Catherine sucks in a breath at the contact. Even with her thin gloves, it's like a spark skitters over Catherine's skin. Soft, and tingling, and unexpected.

Their eyes lock. In the quiet stillness of this room, something shifts. Somehow they're leaning toward each other, and the butterflies in Catherine's stomach are rioting and—

The door opens for another group of women to enter.

They step back unsteadily, Lady Rosalie's arm dropping. Catherine twists her fingers together, and they hover there while the group titters around them. Catherine glances at Lady Rosalie just as Lady Rosalie's looking away from her, both of them flushed. Catherine doesn't know what to do with her hands, with her breath, with her face.

What was just about to happen? Were they really going to—

"Darling, are you well?"

Catherine flinches as Mother comes through the cloakroom door. Her voice is like a bucket of ice water and Catherine feels instantly guilty, as if she's done something wrong.

But she hasn't. Has she?

"Lady Rosalie. Hello."

"Mrs. Pine," Lady Rosalie says, her voice even rougher than before, her curtsy unsteady.

"Sorry, Mother, we were . . . talking about the performance. Enjoy the rest of the play, Lady Rosalie," Catherine says quickly, giving her own halting curtsy before hurrying across the room to follow her mother out of the cloakroom.

The door swings shut on Lady Rosalie behind her. It feels like there's something crawling over Catherine's skin, an unease that's almost too much to bear.

Or is it disappointment?

It felt like— But that's absurd. Lady Rosalie wasn't about to kiss her. Lady Rosalie can't want to kiss her.

Catherine must be confused.

Chapter Eleven
Rosalie

D oes she prefer flowers, or shall I get her pastries? I know
   it's not the most common, but my friends at Cambridge
had much better luck with pastries than flowers. Granted, it
was winter, so that might have had something to do with it.
Would she like a good tipple, instead?"

"Breathe!" Rosalie chides, squeezing Christopher's arm.

Christopher looks over at her, chagrined, his cheeks pink.
Though that could be sun. It's unseasonably warm and lovely
outside, hence their walk through Sydney Gardens this afternoon.

Rosalie wanted to stay in bed all day, lamenting that Mrs. Pine
walked in before Rosalie could take Miss Pine's mouth and
know how sweet she might taste. Grateful that she walked in
before Rosalie went and made a terrible fool of herself.

"Are you listening to me?"

"Yes," Rosalie lies. Christopher nudges her with his hip.
"Take Amalie on a promenade to start, bring her daisies if you
can get them—they're pedestrian, but her favorite. And she
likes macarons and marzipan."

"Good, good," Christopher says. "You're sure?"

Rosalie forces herself to focus on her brother. "I am positive.
Amalie will certainly be wooed if you follow my directions."

"She wouldn't prefer Mr. Fortes? He's older, and more distinguished—"

"And she doesn't want him," Rosalie says firmly, tugging Christopher to the side of the walking path so they can stand beneath a weeping willow tree, out of the sun. She meets his eyes. "You are a catch, dearest little brother, all right?"

Christopher's face splits in a slow smile. "Really?"

"Don't make me say it again."

He laughs, his cheeks dimpling, and squeezes her arm into his side. "Thank you. That is high praise indeed."

"Don't get used to it," she says gruffly, holding on to his cuff with her free hand as he guides them back out onto the path.

Rosalie tries to focus on places to suggest for their promenade—to bury herself in Christopher and Amalie's impending courtship—and ignore all other concerning thoughts, feelings, and urges about a certain tall, willowy, beautiful—

"We should plan some outings so you too can spend time with your . . . person of interest," Christopher suggests.

Rosalie glances up at him, wrinkling her nose. "Just call him Mr. Dean. He doesn't suggest such . . . florid language."

"Were I speaking of Mr. Dean, I would have called him your absentminded, reticent, interior, tall dark brood of a man."

"Christopher."

"*That* is florid language. I was merely trying to be circumspect, but if I must be blunt," he begins, dragging her off the path yet again so they can loiter by the embankment down to the stream. "What are we planning to do to get you more time with the lovely, charming, statuesque Miss Pine?"

Rosalie freezes beside him. "I . . . don't know what you mean."

"Don't you?" he asks, turning to look down into the stream, clearly giving her a moment.

Rosalie hesitates. It's not that he'll care. Or rather, not that he'll be scandalized. He wasn't the day he walked in on her and Jane kissing in the solarium four years ago. He simply said, "Oops," and shut the door, standing guard until they settled themselves. Then he peppered her with endless questions for two weeks until Jane abruptly announced her engagement.

He let her cry on his shoulder for a fortnight, until she'd tucked her sorrow and confusion and anger into a little box in her head. Until she decided never to give her heart to someone who would leave her for someone else, someone better, someone more . . . acceptable.

She's been doing a damn good job of keeping her heart and her desire safely tucked away for the past four years. Mr. Dean is safe. Mr. Dean is acceptable. Mr. Dean won't leave her for a man, at any rate. And he'd certainly never suspect that her scrutiny of Miss Pine is anything other than comparative.

But Christopher doesn't miss a trick. Still. Telling him is giving voice to the ridiculousness in her head.

Then again, keeping it bottled in her head isn't doing anything to persuade her treacherous heart and desire. She almost kissed the girl in a cloakroom, for God's sake.

Maybe it would be safer with Christopher to keep watch—to save her from trying something with Miss Pine and seeing her married off anyway. Or worse, discovering Miss Pine is more like most people than she seems. Rosalie probably imagined the want in her eyes in the dim light of the cloakroom.

"Am I so obvious?" she asks, her voice barely more than a whisper.

Christopher squeezes her arm. "Only to me. Everyone else

is far too wrapped up in their own affairs. Well, everyone except Aunt Genevieve." Rosalie looks up at him in surprise. "Her painting does rather give it away."

"When were you in my room?"

He laughs. "I wanted to go through your new books and Mother was going on and on about the walk."

"She's gotten rather zealous about it," Rosalie agrees, putting worries about Aunt Genevieve away in the box in her head for later.

"Mother has told you to pay Miss Pine little attention and make sure she spends her time with Mr. Sholle, and you've talked with her every moment he wasn't within earshot. You never disobey Mother."

Rosalie blinks. "I disobey her all the time."

"Not when it counts," Christopher insists. Rosalie shrugs, unsure of how to take his razor-sharp observations. "So you must really like her."

She wants to protest, wants to argue, but there's something so absurdly comforting about Christopher just *knowing*.

"It's dreadful," she says, leaning into him dramatically.

Christopher laughs and bends his head to rest on hers as she slumps against his shoulder. "It seems rather fun to me," he says.

"Fun?"

"The two of you flirting right under Mr. Dean and Mr. Sholle's noses with neither of them any the wiser?"

"It is a little bit fun," she admits in a whisper. Christopher laughs, the sound ringing around them. "Mother's going to kill me, though."

"She wouldn't be too upset, would she?"

"If Miss Pine not only doesn't marry Mr. Sholle, leaving Mr. Dean available for me, but I also forsake him to . . . what, run away and live in some city boardinghouse with another woman?"

"Oh, please, I'd put you up in a hovel, don't be dramatic," Christopher says, and Rosalie can't help but laugh. "Mr. Sholle is a poor prize for the funny, bright, engaging Miss Pine, even putting you aside."

"We're putting me aside?" she asks, affronted.

"I'm just saying, you couldn't have given the poor girl even a *chance* at happiness? Mr. Sholle is so—"

"Perfectly adequate?" Rosalie supplies.

"Yes! Should she be consigned to a life of matrimony, Miss Pine deserves someone far more interesting. As do you."

"Are you perhaps a little sweet on Miss Pine too?" Rosalie finds herself asking.

She wouldn't blame him. How could anyone not be?

"Are you admitting you're sweet on her?" Christopher returns gleefully.

"I— We are talking about you and your hypothetical crush now, not me."

Christopher narrows his eyes and Rosalie endeavors to stare back menacingly. Which is so much more difficult now that he's gone and gotten even taller than he was just last year, while she stays annoyingly petite.

"I would never pursue a lady who interests you," he says seriously. "Unless you needed me to for appropriate cover, of course."

Rosalie blinks, punched in the gut by his sincerity and kindness. She can do nothing more than lean up to kiss his cheek.

"I just want you to be happy," he says with a little shrug, cheeks pinking.

She loves him so dearly.

"And I would love to foil Mother's plans. It sounds like the best way to spend the spring. Miss Pine and Mr. Sholle? It's almost as absurd as you spending forever with Mr. Dean."

"Don't start," Rosalie says, her affection dimming. "You're meant to be going to London with Father next week."

Christopher's been against Mr. Dean since the beginning. For not . . . insubstantial reasons. But she can only deal with one heavy courting issue today.

"What's one more year at home?" Christopher says dismissively. "Surely we can *at least* architect more group outings so that you and Miss Pine may spend more time together; determine if she's really worth risking all of Mother's machinations."

And Rosalie's heart. But that feels too vulnerable, even for this supportive conversation.

"When do you imagine I'd get the chance to ask Miss Pine if she shares my unnatural inclination with Mr. Sholle and Mr. Dean always about?" Rosalie asks.

"It is not unnatural," Christopher says, sharp and fast. Rosalie blinks. She didn't mean— "You are not unnatural. I don't ever want to hear you say that again."

"I—"

"That the world doesn't accept two women in love is a travesty. You are a wonder, you deserve far more than horrid Mr. Dean, and I won't hear a bad word about you, all right?" he insists, his face hard all of a sudden.

Rosalie stares at her not-so-little brother. "Cambridge has made you much more assertive."

His lips twitch. "Promise me."

"I promise," Rosalie says, reaching out to take his hand for a brief squeeze before letting go. "I really didn't mean anything by it. It's simply how it's discussed."

"Then we'll find better words," he says firmly. "Together. Oh!"

"What?" she asks, reluctant to continue. It makes her insides twist, to try to think about the way the world might react to her wanting to take Miss Pine publicly in her arms.

"What if I pretended to court Miss Pine? Then you could be *our* chaperone, and I could just . . . conveniently sod off."

That's brilliant, but . . . "What about Amalie?" Rosalie finds herself asking.

Christopher hesitates for just a moment too long and Rosalie sighs. She can't let him jeopardize whatever this burgeoning thing is with Amalie. Christopher will be an excellent husband, and Amalie deserves an *excellent* husband.

But, then again, if Christopher looks like he's interested in Miss Pine . . . maybe that would light more of a fire underneath Amalie, increase her interest in Christopher. A little emotion, a little jealousy, could be just the trick.

"Perhaps if we ensure for every outing you take Miss Pine on, you have two with Amalie?" she suggests.

"Perfect. That's perfect," Christopher says, his face splitting in a beaming smile. "Where do you want to go with her first? Another hike, where I could get lost in the woods? Ooh, or, I could get food poisoning in the market and leave you to fend for yourselves? No, that could backfire. Let me think—"

"I have missed you," Rosalie says, smiling as he blinks, looking back at her, so caught up in scheming.

"I've missed you too," he says, reaching out to take her arm again and begin walking out of the park and down the sunwarmed, broad street toward home. "I can't wait to graduate and return full time."

"You won't miss school?" Rosalie wonders. "Wouldn't prefer London?"

Christopher shakes his head. "I'm eager to learn to manage the estate," he says firmly. "I want to do right by our tenants, and our staff, and by you, I hope you know that."

Rosalie looks up to find him watching her. "I do."

"If you decide marrying Mr. Boring doesn't suit you, you can stay with me forever, just so you know."

Rosalie wraps both hands around his arm and leans into his shoulder. "Don't call him that. And *thank you*. That—that means the world," she says, her voice tight.

Maybe that future he talked about isn't totally out of reach. The one where they find better words for how she might love someone.

"SECOND-CLASS HONORS?" FATHER asks, his eyebrows creased as he stares at Christopher later that night at the dinner table. "For this, you forwent accompanying me to London in the fall?"

Mother looks down at her dinner, picking at her pheasant while Christopher keeps sitting tall, unflinching in the face of their father's disapproval.

"I'll keep trying," Christopher says, his voice strong, but just the slightest bit raspy.

Second-class honors is jolly good. Rosalie's sure she wouldn't do even half so well in the classes Christopher takes. He'll make an excellent earl. Does it really—

"This is not what we do."

Christopher nods and looks down at his plate.

"Perhaps when we get to London, I ought to find you a tutor."

Christopher glances at Rosalie and she shakes her head. It'll only make him angrier if Christopher—

"Actually, Father, I should like to stay in Bath for the remainder of the season."

Father looks up, eyes narrowing.

"I feel I can do more for the family here," Christopher says firmly.

"Oh?" Father says, leaning back in his seat. "And how is that?"

"I would like to court Miss Pine."

Mother gasps, her fork falling to the table.

"We just thought that Mr. Sholle's affections for Miss Pine clearly aren't making an impression on Mr. Dean," Rosalie jumps in quickly. "Perhaps a little more competition might deter him, and Christopher offered to help." She hopes it comes off casually.

Father considers her, then looks to Christopher, and then over to Mother, who's red-faced and still spluttering.

"That . . . is not the worst idea I've ever heard," Father says slowly.

Christopher perks up in his seat and Rosalie stares at Father, surprised. That was easier than she expected.

"Why?" Mother adds, her voice strangled.

"Rosalie is right—we don't want Mr. Dean getting any ideas that Miss Pine might be available," Father says simply.

"We've already been pushing Mr. Sholle as her match. Certainly we don't need Christopher involved," Mother argues.

"You must admit, Mother, a man in line to be earl poses much more of a threat to Mr. Dean than a mere baron's son," Rosalie says quickly, the rationale slimy on her tongue.

She's rather hoping Miss Pine doesn't care a whit about titles, or gender.

"She has a point," Father says, glancing at Rosalie approvingly.

In any other situation, she'd be proud to have him on her side, but none of this feels *good*.

Mother gapes around at all of them. "You can't be serious."

"I don't plan to marry the woman," Christopher assures her.

"But I think protecting Rosalie's future prospects is a worthy way to spend the rest of the season, and then once we've all seen her settled, we can move on to other matters," he says, looking to Father.

"I suppose there are worse ways for you to spend the spring," Father says reluctantly.

"Do we actually think Mrs. Pine would ever allow it, or believe it?" Mother asks Father.

"Surely the blood can't really still be poisoned between the two of you. She's a wealthy woman with a successful husband and a married son. Her daughter is lovely," Father says.

Rosalie wonders whether Father has been paying any attention at all to their goings-on over the last month.

"Bad blood?" Christopher asks, giving Rosalie quite a look.

They had more pressing matters to discuss earlier.

Mother sighs and looks across at Christopher, her face softening. Sure, tell *him* what happened. Forget that Rosalie's been asking her for over a month. Mother will always give in to baby Christopher.

"When I was a young woman—"

"You're still a *young* woman," Father cuts in.

Mother rolls her eyes, but it does soften her just a touch. "When I was in my first official season here, Mrs. Pine and I were friends."

"The best of friends, actually," Father says.

"Are you going to let me tell this story?" Mother asks.

Father puts up his hands, leaning back in his chair.

"We were dear friends, and then we started being courted by the same man—a Navy captain. And of course, we promised that we'd stay friends, whoever won him," Mother explains.

Rosalie's stomach clenches. She'd hate to think that all

this drama, all the hatred—an entirely lost dear friendship—happened over a man.

"Soon enough, I met your father, and well, you know there was never anyone else for me," Mother continues, smiling over at Father, who blows a kiss back in return.

He may often be rather harsh with Christopher, but Rosalie's never seen him be anything but loving toward their mother. Rosalie wonders if Mr. Dean would ever be half so affectionate with her. She rather doubts it.

"If you married Father, surely your rivalry with Mrs. Pine couldn't be the source of so much animosity. She didn't end up marrying some Navy captain either," Christopher interjects.

"No. No, she didn't," Mother says slowly.

She has the same look on her face right now as she does whenever she tells Rosalie something for her own good. "Because you stopped her," Rosalie says. "You knew better, so you stopped her somehow."

Mother meets her eyes. "Your father knew things about the Navy captain. Horrible things. I kept hoping Eleanor would simply fall for Mr. Pine, the far better option, but the captain was . . . persuasive. He left me little choice but to intervene."

"She's angry you saved her from a dangerous man?" Christopher wonders.

Rosalie watches the way her mother's face shifts. She glances back at Father, who's no longer playful, and is instead looking down at his plate, frowning.

"You didn't tell her, did you?" Rosalie asks. "You just chose for her."

"I made sure that Mr. Pine was her only option," Mother replies firmly.

"How?"

"Your father encouraged him to propose, and given her situation, it was a swift marriage and they left Bath."

"What was her situation?" Christopher asks, before Rosalie can suggest something far more accusatory.

"I suggested the captain had taken certain advantages, which scared him off," Mother says.

There is a long, awful pause.

"You ruined her?" Rosalie asks, aghast.

"Mr. Pine swooped in not two days later. It was hardly ruin. And he's a wonderful man. Isn't he, dear?" she asks Father, refusing to meet Rosalie's eyes.

"He is indeed. I think if you ask Mrs. Pine and Miss Pine you'll find them happy with their lot in life."

"Why didn't you just tell her?" Rosalie implores. "What if Mr. Pine hadn't proposed? You could have ruined her life, her family's life."

"I saved her," Mother says, her voice tight.

"Seems she doesn't see it that way," Christopher says archly.

"Yes, well, her finding out it was me was an unfortunate consequence," Mother says stiffly.

"You couldn't have written? You couldn't have explained? She was your *friend*," Rosalie says, her chest tight and painful.

Mother is conniving and manipulative, but Rosalie never thought she'd go so far as to ruin a woman, for her *own good* or not.

"It was for the best."

Rosalie looks over at her father, who's now sitting straight in his chair. "Father, it—"

"Is in the past, and there will be no more said about it. Perhaps Christopher courting the daughter will thaw any remaining ill will."

"After all these years, doesn't she deserve to—"

"No," her parents bark together.

Rosalie and Christopher jump. They never raise their voices.

"You'll not speak to anyone about this," Father says firmly.

"But—"

"Do not ever discuss this with anyone," Father repeats, looking Rosalie dead in the eye.

Rosalie can do nothing more than nod. She doesn't want to say she's frightened of the look he gives her, but it's a close thing. She's rarely ever seen him so serious.

There's something missing from the story. There has to be. Something that would make her mother ruin her best friend instead of explaining why she couldn't marry a man. What did the Navy captain do that was so horrible it couldn't be spoken about?

Or worse, what did her parents do? And what now about Miss Pine?

Rosalie's been party to another scheme of Mother's—another planned arrangement—deciding for another Pine woman whom she should marry. Because she and her mother know *best*, don't they? Is Rosalie really going to participate in repeating this cycle? Manipulate Miss Pine until she does what Rosalie wants?

She needs to get a letter to Miss Pine. Invite her on an outing with Christopher, so they can talk. So they can figure out how to right the wrong that was done to Mrs. Pine.

But once Father has excused them from dinner, Mother grabs Rosalie before she can get even halfway up the stairs.

"You cannot tell her." Her grip on Rosalie's wrist is firm, anchoring her there on the stairs. "Mrs. Pine can never know. No one can ever know."

"What could possibly be so secret twenty-five years later?" Rosalie implores, tugging at her mother's grip. But Mother won't let go.

"It would damage our family. Invite questions into our reputation we do not need. Possibly even ruin your chances with Mr. Dean," Mother says, her voice quiet but sharp.

The hair on the back of Rosalie's neck stands up. "Mother, did he—did that man hurt you?" Rosalie whispers.

"No," Mother says, her eyes widening. Her grip on Rosalie's wrist slackens. "No. No. It's not that."

"But it's still damaging to the family," Rosalie confirms.

"Yes. Promise me you won't tell Miss Pine."

Even with the threat of familial ruin, this is still so wrong.

"If we don't tell Mrs. Pine, she'll keep pushing Miss Pine on Mr. Dean, trying to get back at you," Rosalie tries.

"She won't win. Mr. Dean will be yours, we'll get Miss Pine married off, *not* to your brother, and we'll be done with this."

Her mother's face is set, her shoulders high, eyes a little wild. She's held this secret for longer than Rosalie's whole life—lived with having ruined (having to ruin?) her best friend.

"Don't you want to tell her?" Rosalie can't help but ask. "Don't you want to apologize? Make it right?"

Mother sighs, sliding her hand down to take Rosalie's. "Is there anything you wouldn't do for Miss Raught or Miss Linet?" Rosalie hesitates, just for a second. "If it would save them from pain—from harm—wouldn't you do everything in your power, whatever the cost, to protect them?"

"Not if it would cause them more pain in the meantime," Rosalie replies instantly.

But there's a squeak of doubt there at the back of her head.

Even if it made them hate her—even if they never spoke to her again—if it was for the right reason, wouldn't she? She'd protect them no matter what the cost to her. Even if it left her alone.

Mother's never had any other friends.

"Of course you would," Mother says, digging the knife further into Rosalie's already twisting stomach. "You make choices for their well-being all the time. Guiding them to the right men, making sure they make the right connections. It's what we do."

Rosalie's breath catches. "It's not the same," she says, and even to her own ears her words are thin.

"Sometimes being right and being nice are mutually exclusive," Mother says, squeezing Rosalie's hand again. "And sometimes causing harm for the right reasons is the kindest thing you can do."

Rosalie doesn't want to believe that.

"Now, the kindest thing to do for Miss Pine is to ensure Mr. Sholle makes her a proposal by season's end. This . . . plot you have with Christopher may encourage Mr. Sholle to man up and stake a claim, so I'll allow it," Mother says.

Rosalie tries to let hope drown out the horror of Mother's ethos on the world. An ethos Rosalie has followed unquestioningly since her infancy.

"A few outings," Mother clarifies. "Don't let the girl fall in love with him."

Rosalie snorts, quite out of her control.

"Your brother is charming," Mother says, chiding. "Stranger things have happened."

If only Mother knew the strange things Rosalie and Christopher are planning.

"I'll get invitations sent for an outing," Rosalie agrees, trying to push the words out around her discomfort.

Mother's gaze turns hard again. "Promise me."

In the face of her stern, unyielding expression, Rosalie can do nothing more than nod, even as anxiety crushes her chest. "I won't tell her."

"Good. Now, get some sleep. All that worrying will give you wrinkles."

She lets go of Rosalie's hand and heads back downstairs, leaving Rosalie there alone, staring after her, wondering what in her past—what kinds of dark family secrets—could have caused her mother to have become this Machiavellian.

She climbs the stairs slowly, walking mechanically back to her room to fall onto her bed. She stares up at the ceiling, a hand to her tight chest. Is she truly capable of the same ruthlessness as her mother? As her father?

She's always been imperious and bossy and commanding. She knows what's best for her friends, and she sees that it happens. It's always been for their own good, for the right reasons . . . hasn't it?

Rosalie rolls onto her side and looks across the room to where Aunt Genevieve's painting hangs over her small settee, she and Miss Pine staring at each other captured there in oil paint.

She's been acting under the assumption that what she wants for Miss Pine—with Miss Pine—is what Miss Pine ought to want as well. Rosalie closes her eyes, dropping her head to rest against her arm. She pulls her legs fully onto the bed, curling into herself.

She can't do to Miss Pine what Mother did to Mrs. Pine. She can't choose the future that's best for her. Even if it's choosing a future that allows them to kiss in dark corners and steal away on hikes to lie down in the tall grass and—

Rosalie opens her eyes and stares at their pose in the painting. Miss Pine has to want to choose it herself. They have to make a choice, whatever choice, together. Rosalie can only hope that what Miss Pine truly wants might align with what she wants. That Miss Pine might want her in return.

Chapter Twelve

Catherine

The invitation to a tea in Miss Raught's back garden is a lovely surprise.

Catherine wishes she weren't so anxious. She's still riled up just thinking about that moment in the water closet last week. Was Lady Rosalie really leaning in? She felt something. Something tingly, and confusing, and exciting. She doesn't know quite what to call it, other than *want*.

But she hardly knows if Lady Rosalie felt the same way. They haven't seen each other since. And it's not likely there will be a moment to pull her away at this tea.

What would she even ask?

"Were you about to kiss me in the cloakroom?"

"Do you like to kiss girls?"

"Would you like to kiss me?"

"You'll need to lose him."

"What?" Catherine asks, blinking across the carriage at Mother as they trundle toward the Raught house.

"Mr. Sholle. I want you to distance yourself from him. I think Mr. Dean may think Mr. Sholle's intentions are serious and might be backing off in deference. You need to make it clear that you're not interested."

That seems a bit cold. Mr. Sholle is perfectly nice. But perhaps avoiding him would give her more time to suss out what's going on between her and Lady Rosalie.

"And don't spend all your time with Lady Rosalie. Clearly the side-by-side comparison isn't helping us either."

Catherine sucks on her cheek. "Thank you."

Mother scoffs. "Don't be daft. You are the most stunning girl around. It's simply that we cannot compete with her wealth. I'd rather he see you amongst a group so you can shine properly."

She's not sure it's much less of a slight, that she must look shabby next to Lady Rosalie. But Catherine keeps her face blank and nods.

Perhaps she can convince Mother to let her go on a walk with just Miss Raught, Miss Linet, *and* Lady Rosalie? And then maybe Lady Rosalie might come up with some clever reason to send Miss Raught and Miss Linet off together to give them time to talk. Or . . . whatever.

The idea of *whatever* makes Catherine hot around the ears. Mother's too distracted to notice as they arrive, looking around the Raughts' lovely back garden, which has been set up for tea and lawn games.

It's not as picturesque, nor as grand, as Lady Jones' garden, but clearly Miss Raught, her mother, and their staff have worked very hard to put together a charming and inviting spread for Miss Raught's friends, their mothers, and their sons.

A prickle of guilt eats at Catherine. Some dedication to friendship she's showing, planning how to manipulate Miss Raught into giving her alone time with Lady Rosalie.

"I'll go speak to the mothers, see what suggestions they can make for good outings. You should go mingle," Mother says conspiratorially.

Catherine smiles tightly, even as she wants to scream, *Can we just give up on this already?*

Catherine doesn't want a man who falls asleep at the theatre, and only seems interested in talking to other men. Catherine doesn't know if she even wants a man at all—no, no, there is so much more time lying awake at night to grapple with that thought.

But it's hard to ignore when even now, Mr. Dean is just standing in a cluster of other young men, ignoring the ladies, who have clearly worked so hard to look beautiful.

It's hard to want to want a man—any man—who cares so little.

Catherine let Miss Teit do her up in her best tea gown with her prettiest green bonnet rimmed with pink ribbon. She secretly wondered the whole time whether her outfit might make Lady Rosalie's eyes go that littlest bit dark again, her cheeks so prettily pink.

She spent not a single second thinking about Mr. Sholle or Mr. Dean.

But Lady Rosalie probably won't notice. The thing in the cloakroom probably didn't mean anything to her and—

Lady Rosalie is staring straight at her, ignoring something poor Miss Raught is saying while they stand over by the hedges in the back garden. Her eyes are *incredibly* hungry and—

"Back straight," Mother whispers before pulling away from Catherine.

Was she saying something just now?

Catherine walks as sedately as she can make herself across the small back lawn to where Lady Rosalie, Miss Raught, and Miss Linet are clustered across from the men.

Lady Rosalie hangs back while Miss Raught steps up to her, and Catherine endeavors to give Miss Raught her full attention. Her yellow dress is very charming, and her round face so excited.

"Thank you so much for the invitation," Catherine says.

Miss Raught beams at her, taking her hands and squeezing before dragging her back to Miss Linet and Lady Rosalie. "Of course! We wanted you here, and we need to spend much more time together. It's really a shame your mother's kept you so busy. You would have made a wonderful addition to our walking party the other—"

"We ought not overwhelm Miss Pine, nor remind her of events to which she wasn't able to attend," Lady Rosalie cuts in.

Miss Raught blushes and drops Catherine's hands, nodding quickly in Lady Rosalie's direction. Catherine has half a mind to swat at Lady Rosalie for taking the smile off Miss Raught's face. But at the same time . . . the look Lady Rosalie is giving her—the way her eyes sweep slowly up and down Catherine's figure—

"Perhaps a round of battledore, to prevent any more verbal mistakes?" Miss Linet suggests, pointing over toward the set of rackets and the small bucket of birdies by the fence.

Catherine blinks, rather having forgotten Miss Linet was here at all. She looks quite lovely in a soft green dress and short white bonnet. The fact that she's looking between Catherine and Lady Rosalie rather pointedly, and Lady Rosalie keeps shooting glares at her, probably doesn't mean anything.

Why should it?

"Oh, that sounds perfect. I adore battledore," Miss Raught agrees.

They both look to Lady Rosalie.

Lady Rosalie smiles. "That's a lovely idea." She glances at Catherine and then at her friends. "All of us playing together should finally draw the boys over."

Catherine can practically feel all four of them deflate with the thought.

She just *hates* this. Hates that she and Lady Rosalie are forced to fight over the oblivious Mr. Dean. Hates that Miss Linet and Miss Raught must watch their every word. They're worth so much more than the attention of that pack of silly boys.

"My brother and I used to play with friends, facing off in pairs. Whoever misses the birdie loses a point, and it switches pair to pair," Catherine suggests. "Adds a bit of competition, if you're willing," she says, looking among them.

"Miss Linet and I against you and Miss Raught?" Lady Rosalie asks.

"If you dare," Catherine replies, smirking as Lady Rosalie's eyes darken with challenge.

"Oh, we dare," Miss Linet says.

"As do we," Catherine agrees, glancing at Miss Raught. "Right?"

"Yes!" Miss Raught says quickly. "We're, um, we'll, ah—"

"We're going to slaughter you," Catherine says, grinning as Miss Raught cackles.

Lady Rosalie's eyes narrow so, so deliciously. "Are you now?"

"Yes," Catherine says, letting the *s* sit tauntingly on her tongue.

Lady Rosalie steps closer, staring up at her. "You're on."

She reaches back, grabs Miss Linet's wrist, and stalks over to the cleared area at the back of the lawn where buckets of croquet mallets, battledore rackets, and various other lawn games have been spread out.

Miss Raught giggles and takes Catherine's arm. "This is going to be such fun."

"I'll go first," Miss Linet says, grabbing a birdie from the basket off to the side. "Come on, Henrietta, show me your stuff."

Catherine and Lady Rosalie watch Miss Linet and Miss Raught bat the birdie back and forth with their rackets. It starts daintily and low, neither moving overmuch, but quickly, Miss Raught begins to show a surprising competitive streak.

Catherine watches gleefully as she shoots the birdie this way and that, forcing Miss Linet to lunge side to side, back to front, to keep the volley going. Catherine glances at Lady Rosalie, who doesn't look the least bit surprised, nor particularly worried. Which must mean she thinks she's better than Catherine.

Catherine bounces on the balls of her feet to warm up and hears Lady Rosalie snort. But when she looks over, Lady Rosalie's rolling her wrists and cracking her neck.

Their eyes catch and Catherine can't help but smirk. Screw the boys, *this* is war.

After a minute, Miss Raught scores the first point, sending the birdie down and low in a hit that Miss Linet just misses.

"One, nothing!" Miss Raught exclaims, her words ringing around the garden.

"Take her down, Rosalie," Miss Linet insists, passing the birdie to Lady Rosalie.

Catherine bends her knees, racket at the ready. Lady Rosalie stares at her for a long pause, and then lightning quick, the birdie is up and they're volleying.

Immediately, Lady Rosalie has Catherine dodging to one side. Catherine does her best to aim her return high, so tiny Lady Rosalie has to jump to hit the birdie. Which she does with impeccable reflexes. But Catherine didn't spend her entire childhood locked into tournaments with Richard and her father for nothing.

"Come on, Rosalie!" Miss Linet exclaims.

"You've got this, Miss Pine," Miss Raught counters.

Catherine lunges as far as her dress will allow to bat back Lady Rosalie's latest shot. She hopes she hasn't torn it.

"I could do this all day," Lady Rosalie says, faking a yawn.

Catherine flicks her wrist to hit the birdie toward her knees, forcing Lady Rosalie to bend at an absurd angle to bop it back into the air. "So could I," Catherine says.

But she's breathing pretty heavily. At least Lady Rosalie is as well. Her beautiful chest is heaving, her throat all pink, cheeks red, eyes wild, hair going frizzy beneath her pretty bonnet.

She can't let herself get lost in Lady Rosalie's beauty. Not now. She needs to win. For Miss Raught. To wipe the smug look off Lady Rosalie's face. To continue to see the challenge in her entrancing gray-blue eyes.

"Come on!" Miss Linet shouts.

"Get her, Miss Pine! You can take her, I know you can," Miss Raught returns.

"Miss Pine's got nothing on Rosalie; we're going to win," Miss Linet argues.

Catherine and Lady Rosalie exchange a heated series of volleys, gasping and panting and making more noise than they should, but it's *fun*. The four of them shouting and making a ruckus is delightful. And Lady Rosalie is just so . . . glorious.

After five more minutes, Catherine is sweating and suddenly aware that they've attracted a crowd. She can hear the gentlemen chiming in with Miss Raught's and Miss Linet's increasingly competitive calls.

They should stop. Should act ladylike. Shouldn't exert themselves or be so loud and boisterous. But damn if she's going to let the boys prevent her from beating Lady Rosalie.

Lady Rosalie, whose eyes are alight, brows down, jaw set, parrying back and forth with Catherine as if the glory of England might hang in the balance.

"Come on!" Miss Raught yells.

And Catherine finally manages to get the birdie past Lady Rosalie, sending it sailing so far over her head, it hits the hedge and bounces to the ground.

"Ha-hah!" Catherine exclaims, jumping up and down.

Miss Raught nearly tackles her in a hug, shrieking in glee. It's only two points total, but it must have taken fifteen minutes.

Catherine holds on to Miss Raught's arm, beaming and sweaty and victorious.

"Ugh!" Lady Rosalie shouts, throwing her racket toward the hedge.

There's a brief silence where Miss Raught, Miss Linet, Catherine, and all of the surrounding men stare at Lady Rosalie. Lady Rosalie looks across at Catherine, scowling.

It starts slowly, the joy and amusement and sheer wonder of seeing Lady Rosalie so discomposed making her laugh. And then Lady Rosalie's lips twitch, and Catherine loses it altogether, until they're both laughing, Miss Raught and Miss Linet joining in.

Lady Rosalie wipes at her eyes and walks over, extending her hand to Catherine. Miss Raught lets her go so Catherine can take her palm in a sportsmanlike shake, even though they're both still teary with laughter.

Catherine knows the whole party is watching them—can practically feel her mother's glare from the patio where all the mothers have gathered—but it all falls away the moment their hands meet.

The touch of Lady Rosalie's palm feels like lightning shooting up Catherine's arm, tingling. She never wants to let go.

"You are, in fact, a worthy opponent," Lady Rosalie says.

Catherine can't help but snort while laughter titters around them. "Glad to have lived up to such low expectations."

"Oh, I had high hopes. You . . . have exceeded them," Lady Rosalie says. Her palm squeezes Catherine's, softly, almost like a caress.

Catherine swallows, her throat tight. She knows—*she knows*—Lady Rosalie doesn't mean anything by it. Knows that she's not speaking some kind of code. But it doesn't stop Catherine's treacherous stomach from clenching.

Do they have the same expectations?

Lady Rosalie's brother, Mr. Tisend, pushes through the crowd of onlookers, and they hastily drop their hands. His entrance seems to disperse the rest of the gentlemen, which pulls Miss Raught and Miss Linet into other conversations, leaving Catherine, Lady Rosalie, and Mr. Tisend alone on the battledore court.

Catherine clenches her fist, trying not to think too hard about how Lady Rosalie's touch might feel all over her body.

"Finally, a worthy competitor to join my battledore team," Mr. Tisend says gleefully. "Excellent show, Miss Pine."

"Thank you," Catherine says, proud that her voice doesn't crack.

Lady Rosalie's still staring at her, as if their hands touching might have affected her just as much as it did Catherine. Which is *thrilling*, and complicated.

"We'll need to stage a game expediently. I've been dying to beat her for years."

Catherine looks over to meet his excited smile. "I'd be delighted. It'll give Lady Rosalie a chance to reclaim her title."

"Gladly," Lady Rosalie says, bringing Catherine's gaze back to her narrowed eyes. Good lord, that look sends almost as many tingles over Catherine's body as her touch did. What's happening to her?

"But first, some refreshment," Lady Rosalie says. "And then we might entice Mr. Dean to fill out the court?"

Catherine reluctantly looks over at Mr. Dean. He doesn't so much as glance their way, too busy talking with Mr. Fortes and Mr. Sholle. Mr. Sholle notices her looking and Catherine turns back to Lady Rosalie, whose eagerness has dimmed.

She doesn't like that Mr. Dean has that much power to influence the mood of someone like Lady Rosalie. "We'll rematch at the next event. If Mr. Tisend can wait that long to give you a thorough trouncing."

"I've been plotting my victory against my dearest sister for years. It can wait another few weeks. However, the crab puffs won't. We should get over there before Mr. Rile eats them all."

And suddenly he has both Catherine and Lady Rosalie by their elbows, dragging them across the lawn to grab plates of hors d'oeuvres.

Miss Raught and Mr. Rile are chatting by the canapés. Catherine glances back at Miss Linet and finds her wandering toward the tea tables with another gentleman Catherine doesn't know. Mr. Fortes is still talking with Mr. Dean and Mr. Sholle. Perhaps she's given up on him, then. For the best, really; he seems as inattentive as Mr. Dean.

It's good to see both Miss Linet and Miss Raught smiling, getting well-deserved attention. Though Catherine wishes they were still playing battledore, all the gentlemen be damned.

"Between your athletic prowess, your artistry, and your musical aptitude, you two may be the most impressive ladies in all of Bath," Mr. Tisend says, hurrying to pull out both of their chairs as they settle at one of the white-linen-covered tea tables.

"You're laying it on too thick," Lady Rosalie says, swatting him away until he plops into the chair between them.

Catherine wishes she and Lady Rosalie were side by side, and is grateful at the same time that they aren't.

"I just didn't think we'd meet another lady as talented at athletics as you are," he says to Lady Rosalie.

"I simply had a good opponent," Catherine says, watching Lady Rosalie blush.

"Oh, please. I bet you're that competitive with everyone," Lady Rosalie says, passing her a strawberry macaron.

They're her favorite. How did she know?

Catherine takes it, shaking her head. "It's always been a problem with my brother. Embarrassed our parents with our shouting at more than one company picnic."

"Oh, I'd like to meet your brother," Mr. Tisend says. "Perhaps that's the true match to be had."

"He'd like you," Catherine says, glancing at Mr. Tisend. "And you as well, Lady Rosalie."

Lady Rosalie's smile is suddenly soft and Catherine feels heat climbing up her neck. She does think her brother would like her. He might not understand how much Catherine likes her, but still. She wants them to meet.

She passes her cucumber sandwich over to Lady Rosalie to

push the strange, warm feeling out of her chest. But that just makes Lady Rosalie smile more. Catherine's noticed she favors them, is all.

"Oh, please do join us."

Catherine looks up to find Mr. Dean standing beside Lady Rosalie. And only Mr. Tisend noticed. Whoops.

Mr. Dean sits down on Lady Rosalie's other side. The air at the table changes immediately. Lady Rosalie sits up a bit straighter and Catherine forces herself to sit back, so she and Lady Rosalie aren't leaning around Mr. Tisend anymore.

It's quiet for a minute, neither of them coming up with anything to say, even though they should both be trying to engage him in conversation.

"We were just saying we'll need to have a rematch between Lady Rosalie and Miss Pine," Mr. Tisend says. "Perhaps we could play next weekend. Lady Rosalie and I have been planning a trip to Blaise Castle. I'd be delighted to accompany you, Miss Pine, if Mr. Dean will accompany my sister?"

Catherine blinks down at him. His eyes are twinkling. She glances at Lady Rosalie, who doesn't look the least bit surprised by the invitation.

"I'd be most pleased," Mr. Dean says. "I can arrange for my aunt to join us as chaperone, if you'd like."

"Our aunt would like to come," Lady Rosalie says, her voice perfectly calm.

"How wonderful. I'd love to discuss art with her," Mr. Dean says.

Catherine notices Mr. Tisend wince and has to bite her lip against a laugh.

"Miss Pine?" Mr. Tisend asks.

Catherine glances over her shoulder at the patio, where Mother is watching them, frowning.

"I actually got a chance to ask your father this morning at the baths, but haven't had a moment to ask your mother," Mr. Tisend adds.

"And my father said yes?" Catherine asks, pulling her gaze away from her mother's clear disapproval.

"He did," Mr. Tisend says brightly.

Catherine should interrogate why he asked her father about an outing before her. Why Lady Rosalie never mentioned anything. Why her *father* didn't mention anything before she and Mother left for the tea.

"It would be an overnight. Our aunt knows the current owner of Blaise Castle, who has invited us for dinner on Saturday. We'd travel early Saturday, see the castle, have dinner, and return in the afternoon on Sunday, if that suits?"

It's exactly the kind of outing Mother doesn't want—Lady Rosalie and Catherine "competing" directly for Mr. Dean's attention, with only Mr. Tisend and Lady Jones there for comparison. But it would be *rude* to refuse the invitation. A missed opportunity to spend that much time alone with Mr. Dean. How could she possibly say no?

And on top of it, an invitation from Mr. Tisend, who has already spoken with her father? Were he anyone else, Mother would be dumping Mr. Dean for the son of an earl.

Not that either of them would truly be winning. Catherine thinks marrying Mr. Tisend would be like flaying herself alive forever, forced to marry the wrong Tisend sibling.

Not that she wants to *marry* Lady Rosalie.

All the heated looks in the world don't mean that Lady

Rosalie wants what Catherine wants. But at least with this trip she could know for sure.

"Would you like to accompany us?"

Catherine swallows, embarrassed for getting so caught up in her head, and with such thoughts. "I'd be delighted," she says, smiling as wide as she can.

"Excellent!" Mr. Tisend says, grinning at her, and then turning to grin at his sister.

"I wonder if the current owner might give us a tour of the woods. I've been meaning to organize another hunting party and it would provide a good change of scene," Mr. Dean says, pulling Mr. Tisend into conversation around Lady Rosalie.

Lady Rosalie leans back and Catherine mirrors her without a second thought, so they can see each other around Mr. Tisend's back. Lady Rosalie smiles and takes a bite of her sandwich.

The following weekend now seems ages away. Catherine needs to know what Lady Rosalie is thinking. Whether her smirks and smoldering looks mean what Catherine wants them to, what Catherine hopes they do.

She notices Mr. Tisend nudging Lady Rosalie. Lady Rosalie swallows and Catherine's momentarily distracted by the bob of her throat. Why is that so . . . alluring?

"I need to pick up my new traveling cloak for the trip, and imagine you might need some accessories as well," Lady Rosalie says before Catherine can gather herself. "Would you like to go to the shops on Tuesday?"

"I would," Catherine hears herself say.

Lady Rosalie nods and Mr. Tisend nudges her again. Catherine watches her nudge back, her lips tilting up. Something rises in Catherine's chest that feels suspiciously like unfounded hope. Catherine doesn't know what they're about, but they've orchestrated the picture-perfect outing. Just the four of them, and the mischievous Lady Jones.

Catherine and Lady Rosalie might find all kinds of reasons to be alone. Especially if Mr. Tisend can keep Mr. Dean talking like they are now—like she and Lady Rosalie aren't even there.

This is going to be something, isn't it?

Chapter Thirteen

Rosalie

Miss Pine stands on Madame Florent's pedestal, being fitted into a burgundy spencer jacket Madame Florent "just had lying around," and it's possibly the most fetching thing Lady Rosalie's ever seen. The way it hugs Miss Pine's shoulders, the way it accentuates her bust, the way it highlights her dark eyes—

Rosalie's mouth feels thick, her fingers fumbling. There are so many things she might like to say, but none she can push beyond her lips. At least, not with Madame Florent right there.

And even if she *could* say what she's thinking, she's not sure Miss Pine would like to hear it. She hopes she would. She thinks she would. But she can't be sure. The not-knowing is frankly killing her.

"What do you think?" Miss Pine asks, fingers twisting together.

Madame Florent steps back. "As if it was made just for you," she says, smiling brightly.

"Lady Rosalie?" Miss Pine asks, her face so hopeful.

It unties Rosalie's tongue. "It's incredibly fetching," she says, a little breathless.

"Agreed," Madame Florent says. "Now, give it back to me, I'll make these few stitches and send you on your way."

"Thank you," Miss Pine says, her cheeks a little pink. She helps

Madame Florent slip her out of the jacket, leaving her in just her cream day dress, which is distractingly flattering enough on its own. "I appreciate you modifying the display for me. I needed more fashionable outerwear; everything I have from our estate up north is a little too . . . pastoral for Bath's sensibilities."

Madame Florent grins. "You just come back to me, and we'll keep making you as fashionable as Lady Rosalie here. Maybe more," she says before swanning into the back of the shop.

"Do you miss the country?" Rosalie finds herself asking.

Miss Pine looks over at her, surprised, and comes to sit with her on the small settee across from the pedestal by the mirrors. She's close enough that Rosalie can smell her lilac perfume and see the little baby hairs peeking out from the bottom of her bonnet rim.

"Sometimes," Miss Pine says. "Everything was simpler in the country."

"Like what?" Rosalie wonders.

"Everything here is both more formal and somehow laxer. It gets hard to keep track," Miss Pine says, looking down at her hands and pulling her dainty white gloves back on.

It must be strange, coming from somewhere so different. Miss Pine's vulnerability tugs at Rosalie's heart. She's been making it worse, she's sure.

Miss Pine looks up and turns her neck toward the curtains to the back room. But Madame Florent doesn't emerge.

"Like this trip with your brother and Mr. Dean," Miss Pine continues, slowly turning back to Rosalie. Rosalie's chest tightens. "What kind of trip is it? Is it a courting outing, or just friends visiting a castle?"

She's braver than Rosalie's been all day, which should make it easier to push the words out of her tight throat, but Rosalie still struggles. "Ah, Christopher just thought it would be a good opportunity for all of us to talk."

"All of us," Miss Pine repeats.

They're seated even closer together than they were in the cloakroom. She wants to say it plainly—wants to admit that Christopher decided to engineer an opportunity for Rosalie and Miss Pine to be alone together. But with Madame Florent hovering just out of sight, she doesn't know how to say it.

She's not sure how she should phrase it, anyway. *I'd really like to push you up against a wall and kiss you silly? Would you like that too?*

"All of us," she says instead, her stomach twisting. "We can get to know each other better. And Christopher wants to get to know you more, and make sure Mr. Dean is really good enough for . . . me," Rosalie says haltingly. Miss Pine's eyebrow goes up. Is it obvious Rosalie's only telling half-truths? "You're less pressure than Amalie or Henrietta with Mr. Dean and Christopher, really."

Miss Pine snorts, the sound loud in the small back room. "Miss Linet and Miss Raught aren't competing for his affections, so wouldn't they be *better* choices?"

"Are we, really, still competing?" Rosalie asks, unable to keep the words from spilling out.

Miss Pine's eyes widen. "Do you want a détente?"

More than anything in life.

Rosalie opens her mouth—

And Madame Florent walks back into the room.

They spring apart, standing up awkwardly and smoothing down their dresses.

Madame Florent doesn't seem to notice, bringing them into the front of the shop to package up Miss Pine's jacket and Rosalie's cloak. Rosalie hovers next to her, desperate to continue their conversation and unwilling to let the afternoon end.

Miss Pine was brave enough to ask. She can be brave enough to give them the time they need, can't she?

Madame Florent bids them good day, and Rosalie haltingly follows Miss Pine out onto the street. They stand for a moment beneath the awning in the light afternoon drizzle.

"Would you like to come back to mine for tea?" Rosalie spits out, fast and too loud. Miss Pine looks over at her, surprised. "My mother and father went to a function, and Christopher is at the club. We could . . . talk more?"

"Yes," Miss Pine says, her answer just as fast and overloud.

"Good, good," Rosalie replies, gesturing for them to head back toward her house.

After a moment of walking, Miss Pine slips her arm through Rosalie's. Their elbows lock tightly together. Rosalie can't tell if she's the one shaking, or if it's Miss Pine.

Maybe they *are* on the same page, after all.

They don't look at each other, but Rosalie can feel every minute movement of Miss Pine's body. It's thrilling and terrifying, and by the time they get back to her house, Rosalie's nearly sweating with nerves.

Her housekeeper, Mrs. Lowry, meets them as they come into the foyer.

"Mrs. Lowry, this is my friend, Miss Pine. We'll take tea in the sitting room, please," she says, her voice high.

But Mrs. Lowry doesn't seem to notice, smiling politely at them both and hurrying off to the kitchens. Which leaves Rosalie to bring Miss Pine up and back to the sitting room.

She could have said, "I have something to show you in my room." She could have said, "I need to show you the library" or "Would you like to see the study?" She could have proposed a million ideas other than forcing them into the sitting room, waiting to be interrupted.

Miss Pine looks around in fascination, while Rosalie paces into the sitting area. Miss Pine can peruse the bookshelves, stare at the paintings, consider the fabric Mother's always saying she wants to change on the settees. But Rosalie just looks at Miss Pine, quietly panicking.

It wasn't so complicated with Jane all those years ago. But then again, with Jane, Rosalie didn't really realize what was happening until they were kissing. Didn't understand herself so well. Didn't know what or who she really wanted, so kissing Jane—admitting she wanted to kiss Jane—wasn't so fraught.

Now, there's this beautiful, lithe, clever, funny woman sitting down across from her, smiling like she hasn't a care in the world, and Rosalie *knows*. She knows how dangerous a relationship like this could be, to her reputation, to her heart. She knows what it would feel like to be rejected.

Well, she knows how it felt when Jane got engaged and moved away. When Jane dismissed what they'd shared as a folly, a lark, when it had meant the world to Rosalie. She doesn't know how much it would hurt for Miss Pine to rebuff her now. To tell her it's all been in Rosalie's head this whole time, again. It might destroy her.

"Does your father read as much as you do, or is he more of a collector?" Miss Pine asks.

Rosalie blinks over at her. "He does. Not so much novels, but he reads all the time. And brings me books every time he goes to London. Hopefully he brings a bunch back this time."

Miss Pine has such a beautiful smile. "My father does the same."

"That's nice," Rosalie says.

They stare at each other for a moment. To Rosalie, it feels like the air is crackling between them. Anticipation and hesitation and desire flitting around the room. But then Miss Pine gets up and Rosalie slumps into the couch. She watches Miss Pine wander the bookshelves, looking at the titles.

"Have you read *The Italian*?" she asks.

"No, I haven't," Rosalie says, close to groaning. She didn't ask her back here to look at books, or take tea, or—

Thankfully, Mrs. Lowry barges in with the tea service, and Rosalie gets a brief reprieve from her nerves, helping her set everything out on the low table between the settees.

"Do you ladies need anything else? I've got to get to market for a few things. We weren't expecting visitors," she adds, smiling over at Miss Pine before shooting a look at Rosalie.

Rosalie just shrugs guiltily. "I think we're fine, Mrs. Lowry, thank you."

"Ring for Mr. Lowry if you do," Mrs. Lowry says. "You might need to ring a few times. He's organizing wine in the cellar. Your father's got a new categorization scheme."

Father and Mr. Lowry's never-ending quest for the most properly organized wine cellar is a topic of much debate among the staff. Usually, it's a nuisance. But today it means Rosalie and Miss Pine are likely not to be disturbed, at all.

Rosalie listens as Mrs. Lowry's footsteps fade away. She stares at the tea and biscuits, her heart racing. They're alone. She can ask whatever she wants. Do whatever she wants.

Anxiety tugs at her throat, so she pours them both tea, the pot and cups rattling in her hands. It sounds so loud against the silence. When she's done, she looks up and finds Miss Pine watching her, still standing half a room away by the bookcases, that tension hovering between them again. She's wanted this opportunity for weeks. Since before the moment they had in the theatre, if she's honest.

Eloquence and formality are failing her. She can't talk her way into or out of this one. And she can't stay sitting here in this silence for a minute longer, she just can't.

Rosalie stands up and sees Miss Pine's breath hitch. There's a blush climbing up her long, elegant neck. Her eyes are wide and dark and Rosalie finds herself walking across the room until she's right there, right in front of Miss Pine.

Miss Pine steps back, bumping into the bookcase, and Rosalie hesitates. What if she imagined every look and touch and question and suggestion, and she's about to make the most horrible mistake of her—

Miss Pine's delicate fingers trace along her jaw. Rosalie blinks up at her. Miss Pine hesitates, her thumbs stroking at Rosalie's cheekbones, and Rosalie nods into her hands, her heart soaring. She pushes up on her toes, leaning into Miss Pine as she bends that beautiful neck and their lips finally, wonderfully, crash together.

Soft, and needy, and delicate, it's better than Rosalie could ever have imagined. She places her hands on Miss Pine's waist, feeling her narrow hips beneath the lace of her dress. Miss Pine sighs into her mouth, one of her hands gliding back so she can cradle Rosalie's skull, her other hand stroking at her jaw.

It makes Rosalie shiver and she curls her hands around Miss Pine, pressing them closer together. Miss Pine sucks on Rosalie's bottom lip and Rosalie groans. She wants more, she wants to stay just like this forever, she wants everything.

Suddenly Miss Pine spins them and Rosalie squeaks against

her mouth. Miss Pine giggles, still kissing her, and slides her hands all the way down Rosalie's body, fingers leaving trails of heat and tingles as she goes. Her hands bunch up Rosalie's skirt and Rosalie releases her mouth, her head tipping back in shock and delight.

Miss Pine lifts Rosalie with surprising ease, pushing her back into the bookshelves. Rosalie gasps and wraps her legs around Miss Pine's waist reflexively. Suddenly they're the same height, Miss Pine's long, lovely hands holding the backs of Rosalie's thighs.

She's never thought about being picked up by a woman. Never even crossed her mind. It's fantastically arousing.

"Is this what you were thinking about at the modiste?" Miss Pine whispers before sipping another kiss from Rosalie's lips.

Rosalie toys with the hair at the nape of Miss Pine's neck, breaking from Miss Pine's mouth to trail kisses along her jaw, pressing their chests even tighter together in a delicious friction that's not enough and also so much all at once.

"I've been thinking about this for weeks," Rosalie admits.

"Me too," Miss Pine says, her voice husky and rough.

She drives her hips into Rosalie's and Rosalie can't help but let out a long, low groan. She squirms, trying to gain friction to grind back against Miss Pine. Their combined wriggling rattles the bookshelf. Delicate metal and glass objects tinkle around them.

"Should we move this somewhere less precarious?" Miss Pine whispers.

Rosalie nods, preparing to slide down to touch the floor. But Miss Pine just steps back, bringing Rosalie with her. Rosalie clamps her legs tighter around Miss Pine's hips and wraps her arms around her shoulders, laving kisses down her neck to show her appreciation.

Rosalie had never thought about being carried by a woman either. Who knew so much strong muscle lurked beneath Miss Pine's fetching gowns?

They plop roughly onto the settee, Rosalie cradled in Miss Pine's lap, legs straddling her waist, skirt pushed up nearly to her bum, chemise messy between her legs and Miss Pine's lovely dress.

It's heady and humbling and wonderful. Rosalie can't help but rock against Miss Pine's lap, both of them moaning into each other's mouths. Their kisses are growing sloppy, all lips and teeth and tongue and wonderful, overwhelming sensation. Rosalie tries to wriggle her hand down the front of Miss Pine's bodice.

She grunts in frustration to find her stays so perfectly fitted that she can't quite get her fingers down to naked flesh. But Miss Pine bucking up into her lap, her mouth going slack against Rosalie's, is reward enough.

Someday, she wants to feel Miss Pine's perfect breasts bare in her hands.

Miss Pine's delicate fingers trace along the back of her thigh, where she *can* caress naked flesh, and Rosalie's mind temporarily goes blank. Every nerve ending is alight. She's full of want, and she feels lightheaded in the most swoony way, and she wants—

But they're still in the sitting room. Anyone could walk in and find Miss Pine with her fingers—

Every single ounce of self-restraint goes into stilling Miss Pine's hands as those wonderful fingers slip up up up toward—

"We can't," Rosalie rasps.

Miss Pine blinks up at her. Rosalie's momentarily distracted by how nice it is to be looking down at her for once.

"Right, of course," Miss Pine says quickly, pulling her hands back. She holds them up as if Rosalie's a robber and Rosalie can't help but laugh, falling into her.

Miss Pine giggles and wraps her arms more complacently around Rosalie's back, so they're simply resting there against each other, Rosalie slumped on top of Miss Pine, cradled in her lap.

And this is rather nice too. They can risk this pose for a few minutes, can't they?

"Was it as good as you imagined?" Miss Pine asks softly.

Rosalie snorts. "So much better. And that's not even everything we could do," Rosalie hears herself say.

Miss Pine's breath hitches and Rosalie feels heat spread up her chest, her neck, her cheeks. She didn't mean to be quite so tawdry.

"I'd like that," Miss Pine whispers, sending shivers down Rosalie's spine.

She arches back to meet her eyes. "Yeah?"

"If you can come up with more ways to get us alone. I'd feel rather . . . queer about doing this somewhere in public."

Rosalie laughs and reaches up to smooth the mess she's made of her hair. "I'll talk to Christopher."

Miss Pine's eyes widen. "Your brother knows?"

Rosalie nods. "Christopher was the one who came up with the idea to go to Blaise Castle. He wanted us to have time to talk. He told me that I should pursue you, Miss Pine."

She watches in amusement as Miss Pine works through every implication. Her eyes zip this way and that, hand squeezing Rosalie's. She could stare at her for hours.

"Catherine."

"What?"

"My hands were— You ought to call me Catherine now, I should think," she says, looking up at Rosalie with such sass that Rosalie can't help but dip down to give her a quick, fierce kiss.

"All right," she says, pulling back when they're both breathless. "Then you drop the *Lady*."

"Gladly, just Rosalie."

Something warm and tingly spreads through Rosalie's chest. Oh, she's so thoroughly done for.

"Your brother thinks you should pursue me?" Catherine asks.

Rosalie shrugs. "Apparently we're not as subtle as we think we are, and he's never been very happy with Mr. Dean."

"But he thinks you should court *me*?" Catherine insists.

"He thinks we should get to know each other, and he's happy to help facilitate. *He* can 'court' you, I can chaperone, and he'll make himself scarce."

Catherine's eyes light up, but she wrinkles her nose. "Not for this, I hope."

"No!" Rosalie squeals, letting go of her hand to reach down and tickle her.

Catherine shrieks in surprise and they both go still, eyes flying to the doors. But no one comes in.

"Christopher will facilitate talking, and genteel outings for us, is what I meant," Rosalie says, her voice softer.

Catherine's other hand comes to rest on Rosalie's hip, toying with the fabric of her still rucked-up skirt. "I'd like that."

"Good," Rosalie says, smiling when Catherine laughs.

They sit for a minute, fingers roaming innocently, simply

basking in the stillness of being so close to each other. She wants to kiss Catherine again, of course, but she wants to sit like this too. To be alone, and calm, and simply together.

"And if we should want more time . . . like this?" Catherine asks, her hand trailing down to rest on Rosalie's thigh. Still innocent, but tempting, taunting.

"We'll go shopping again. Or walking. Or . . . anything that could need an afternoon respite afterward," Rosalie decides.

Catherine smiles slowly. "I'll convince my mother that I'm going to convince you into an unflattering dress, or that I've gotten close enough to you to gather real, meaningful intelligence . . ."

"So your mother *is* trying to sabotage me," Rosalie confirms.

Catherine bobs her head back and forth. "Your mother, really. But you've been the . . . main target, yes. For which I apologize." She hesitates before adding, "Though it has been just the slightest bit fun?"

Rosalie snorts, which makes Catherine grin. "I should probably be more insulted, but it *has* been rather fun."

"I've been trying to get her to let it go, but she's rather . . . determined. I still don't fully understand it."

The idea of her family's secrets burrows against Rosalie's stomach, threatening to pop through the bubble of the delightful afternoon they've been having. She doesn't even have enough information to explain if she wanted to—and she *promised*. So she'll figure out a way to explain later. When she's not in Catherine's lap. When she can think clearly, instead of wasting this precious moment—

She leans down to kiss Catherine again, letting her worries melt away, for now. Catherine is so soft against her mouth, beneath her hands. So supple and lovely. What's another five, or ten, minutes of kissing, really?

"I wish we could do away with the entire charade of it," Catherine says when Rosalie finally pulls back . . . clearly far too many minutes later, given the beautiful way Catherine's lips are lightly swollen.

"Which charade?" Rosalie asks hazily.

"Pursuing Mr. Dean, as if he's some great prize," Catherine says, a pout gracing those plump, pink lips.

She's certainly more coherent than Rosalie feels at this moment.

"But my mother is absolutely hellbent on me . . . winning him. I wish I could get her to focus on anyone else. Not—not that I *want* someone else," she adds quickly.

The hazy, warm, trickly feeling in Rosalie's chest grows larger. "I know," Rosalie says softly.

She doesn't know what this is, not really. But she doesn't want anyone else either. Not now that she knows what it feels like to touch Catherine, to taste her, to be with her like this, quiet and private and lovely.

What else there could be for them together is a question for a more cogent, alert, contemplative Rosalie.

But something Catherine's said pokes at Rosalie's kiss-happy mind. "Why don't we just make the best of it, then. Steer into their obsessive competition?"

"Submit ourselves to *more* of Mr. Dean?" Catherine asks, looking genuinely horrified.

"Pretend to submit ourselves to more of his . . . charming company. The outings with Christopher could be double outings. We can . . . I don't know, pretend to fight over him, and then Christopher can walk him away when we get too heated and we can just . . . talk, or not, or . . ." Rosalie trails off, frowning.

The logistics need some finessing, but it would at least be

more time together, to decide what exactly more of each other would look like.

"My mother's just barely allowing this overnight trip to Blaise Castle, and only because my father said yes before she could stop him. She—" Catherine breaks off, looking up at Rosalie, biting at her lip.

It's an unreasonably fetching look. "What?"

"She thinks that being alone with just you and Mr. Dean puts me at a disadvantage, because you have the wealth to always look better than everyone else," Catherine says sheepishly.

Rosalie blinks. "She thinks that when we're together *I* am the one coming out on top?"

"Well," Catherine says, her hands sliding around to cup Rosalie's arse.

Rosalie laughs and Catherine's face blooms into a bright grin. "Tease," Rosalie says. "And she's wrong. Next to you, I'm nothing."

Catherine's grin falters and she stares up at Rosalie, almost frozen. "That might be the most ridiculous thing you've ever said."

"We can't get into a 'No, you're prettier' contest. It's too juvenile. And I'd win."

"Yes, you would," Catherine says.

"Oh, we'll be here all day," Rosalie says, stroking the hairs at the nape of Catherine's neck.

"Right, and we need to figure out how to do this again. Mother's determined that you and I not spend much time in direct comparison—however irrationally," Catherine says as Rosalie frowns at her. "Mother and Father actually quarreled over the trip to Blaise Castle, and they never fight."

"Really? My parents squabble all the time."

Catherine shrugs. "I'm not sure I'll be able to convince Mother into letting me go on any other trips or outings that include you *and* Mr. Dean. We may get away with just your brother."

Rosalie sighs, and then sits up, a flutter of excitement coursing through her. That's exactly it.

"Then we make sure you keep bumping into Christopher while you're out with Mr. Dean."

"What will that accomplish, exactly?" Catherine asks.

"Well, I'd be with him," Rosalie says simply. "*And*, we've told our mother that Christopher should court you to 'distract' you and your mother from Mr. Dean and make him feel like he doesn't have a chance, so it's a win-win with my mother."

"You and your brother are rather wily, aren't you?"

"Exceedingly. You'll fit right in," Rosalie says happily. "And, because Christopher got permission from your father for the trip, I think he should start writing you lots of letters, so you can let us know where you'll be with Mr. Dean. Then he'll distract him, and you and I shall have a lovely time together."

Catherine smiles, nodding excitedly. "Perfect."

She leans up and captures Rosalie's lips again and Rosalie grins against her mouth. Now that they've ironed that out, there's no reason they can't spend the whole afternoon kissing. Rosalie lets her hands slide back down to Catherine's lovely, wonderful breasts. Maybe there actually is enough time for them to—

There's a creak outside the door and they wrench apart. Rosalie nearly falls off the settee as she scrabbles off Catherine's lap, landing on the seat beside her and managing to get her skirts back down just as someone knocks on the doors.

"Come in!" Rosalie calls, looking wide-eyed at Catherine, who looks very freshly kissed.

She can't look much better.

The doors open and Christopher strolls on through, hair still a little damp from the misting drizzle outside, cheeks pink. He takes one look at them and his face splits in a delighted grin.

"I knew it!" he says, spinning to close the doors while Rosalie groans. He nearly flies across the room to bounce down onto the opposite settee. "Tell me everything," he demands gleefully.

Rosalie glances at Catherine and finds her sitting very straight, looking between them uncertainly.

Something clenches in Rosalie's chest. Something painful but at the same time utterly, wonderfully free. She reaches out and takes Catherine's hand, smiling at her as Catherine turns wide eyes to look at her. "I promise, Christopher is entirely Team Catherine and Rosalie."

Which makes Catherine gasp out a laugh and Christopher chortle across from them. After a moment, Catherine nods, squeezing Rosalie's hand. Together they look back at Christopher's eager face.

He leans forward, rubbing his hands together. "All right, so, what's the plan?"

Chapter Fourteen
Catherine

The light is just fading when they arrive at Blaise Castle House. The rain has let up and the last of the sunlight breaks through the clouds, casting the verdant, well-trimmed trees and manicured green rolling lawns that lead down to the edge of the forest in a beautiful orange hue.

Catherine stands beside Lady Jones' mud-splattered carriage in front of the large, sandstone stucco two-story main house. She tries to take deep breaths, a little nauseous from the winding end to their ride. Or it's the butterflies rioting in her stomach.

Sitting beside Rosalie for the past few hours, swaying into each other, hands touching briefly, eyes meeting fleetingly before they looked away—it's left Catherine riled up, and eager, and terrified, and excited.

They're finally here. It's almost nighttime. And she and Rosalie are going to be truly alone again, soon.

"Ah, Lady Jones!"

Catherine turns. Lady Jones has just stepped down from the carriage and is smiling brightly at the approaching owner of Blaise Castle House, Mr. Tarton. Lady Jones looks remarkably put together despite her discomfort from the journey.

"Mr. Tarton," she replies, taking his hands as he reaches her. "So wonderful to see you. We thank you for your hospitality."

"I would not pass up a chance to hear your stories for all the world. And I am always excited to share my grounds with new friends. I fear it's a little late to head to the castle, but we'll sup and talk and get up early tomorrow for a full tour?"

His long, narrow face is split in a charming smile, blue eyes sparkling. His white hair catches the sunlight almost like a halo.

"Wonderful," Lady Jones says, taking his arm. "Young people, follow us."

Rosalie loops her arm through Catherine's, interrupting her brief fantasy about Rosalie grabbing a saber and running through the woods, Catherine's hand in hers, to escape to the castle, chased by thieves, or pirates, or something equally ridiculous. The very touch of her arm makes Catherine shiver.

"Pretty, isn't it?" Rosalie asks calmly.

"Very. You, ah, came here as children?" Catherine asks, trying to push the fantasy from her mind.

"Mr. Tarton has always been fond of Aunt Genevieve," Rosalie says, walking them so frustratingly sedately through the front portico of Blaise House, beneath the immense white columns. "She's brought us here most summers for at least a week. Sometimes we stay in one of the cottages, sometimes in the house. Mr. Tarton's a lovely man."

"That sounds wonderful," Catherine says, trying to imagine visiting such a property each summer, before or after being home at an estate the size of the Tisend lands.

The Pine estate is sizeable in its own way, but hardly this grand. Most of their land is rented out. She's missed the rowdy dinners they used to throw for their tenants.

"Christopher and I once played a game of hide-and-seek that lasted over a day," Rosalie says, her voice ringing around the grand entryway to the house.

Catherine takes in the high, two-story ceiling; the marble

floors; the white walls covered in enormous landscape paintings. If the rest of the house is this grand, it wouldn't be hard to
hide somewhere sneaky.

"If I recall, Mother nearly had a fit when they couldn't find
me," Christopher says, appearing at Catherine's side.

"We had to search for seven hours. It was dreadful," Rosalie
replies.

"Where were you hiding?" Catherine asks, noting Mr. Dean
following Mr. Tarton and Lady Jones toward the dining room
without a backward glance at their trio, as usual.

"There's a little attic door hidden by an armoire at the back
of one of the dressing rooms in the largest guest suite," Christopher says, smirking while Rosalie sighs.

"He shimmied behind the armoire and managed to tug it
backward so it was nearly flush with the wall. Lucky he didn't
get stuck in there and starve to death, honestly."

"Oh, that was horrible," Lady Jones says.

They've caught up with Lady Jones and Mr. Tarton in the
massive, red-wallpapered dining room. Historic crests and more
landscape paintings line the walls between the tall windows
looking out on the sprawling lawn. The table is nearly three
times the size of Catherine's at home, bedecked with expensive
silver candlestick holders and enormous floral centerpieces. It's
set for just the five of them, but so opulent.

"Please take your seats," Mr. Tarton says, beckoning them to
join him at the far end.

Catherine ends up between Rosalie and Lady Jones, with
Christopher and Mr. Dean across the table, Mr. Tarton at the
head.

"You were both banned from playing anything in the house
after that, weren't you?" Lady Jones asks.

"When young Mr. Tisend sent us on a wild goose chase? Indeed," Mr. Tarton agrees.

"My only defense was that I was seven. I think the mandatory history lessons for the rest of the visit were punishment enough," Christopher says.

"He could recite the entire chain of ownership in his sleep," Rosalie says.

"Certainly made your father happy," Lady Jones adds as the servants appear with the first course, a warming and decadent white soup perfect for a rainy day.

It's served in gorgeous bowls with what looks like a gold-leaf finish. Catherine barely wants to touch them, but her hungry stomach forces her to daintily sip at the soup. It's delicious, with more layers of flavor than any white soup she's ever had before. She can't even identify them all.

"My wonderful chef, Mr. Partly, just returned from a month on the Continent. He got this recipe in a tiny village in Tuscany. Isn't it marvelous?" Mr. Tarton asks.

"It's delicious," Catherine tells him, enjoying his pleased nod, before he turns to Mr. Dean to discuss the various game on the property.

"Were you ever one for hide-and-seek?" Lady Jones asks, ignoring that they've clearly lost their host's attention.

"With my brother, Richard," Catherine says. "But there weren't nearly as many good hiding places as there are here."

"Fewer opportunities to break things, I'd wager," Christopher says with a grin. "I broke a Grecian urn once that a friend of Father's had bought at auction. I don't think he spoke to me for a month."

Catherine watches Rosalie and Lady Jones laugh. She didn't realize there were items of such value at the Tisend house.

Then again, how could she? It's not like she's been brought up with an eye for antiquities.

"Isn't there a similar vase here?" Rosalie asks. "I know there's a collection of Greek artifacts."

"Really?" Catherine asks.

"Oh, Mr. Tarton has one of the best collections of art and antiquities. He's considering turning part of the estate into a museum."

"Or selling the relics off to larger museums, certainly," Mr. Tarton puts in.

"I'm sure there are Greek museums which would be eager to have the artifacts back," Catherine says. "You could make an expedition of it yourself."

The whole table turns her way. Mr. Dean looks almost pitying, Mr. Tarton amused. Catherine stares back, unsure of what misstep she might have made.

"The British Museum would be the first approach," Mr. Dean says, his tone soft. "Mr. Tarton would receive the best return on his sale with them. The Greeks would be far down the list, and who knows if they would even display the items properly."

Catherine shrinks in her seat, uncomfortable with his patronizing look. Uncomfortable with his superiority. How would he know which museums would do the best justice to an ancient artifact?

But as the silence stretches longer, Catherine's self-assurance begins to wane. These people visit houses like this constantly. Mr. Dean has traveled the Continent, as has Christopher. And while her brother did too, she certainly hasn't. What does she know, really?

"I think Miss Pine's point is well taken. The Greek museums

would certainly want an opportunity to reclaim their artifacts," Rosalie says, her shoulder brushing Catherine's comfortingly as she leans close to grab the salt. "Perhaps not the most lucrative of sales, but an opportunity for travel, and who doesn't enjoy travel?"

"Yes," Lady Jones jumps in. "Did Mr. Partly make it to Greece?"

"He did," Mr. Tarton says. "Then made his way back across the Continent. He did a meal for us that was all of the flat-breads he encountered; it was to die for."

Lady Jones begins peppering Mr. Tarton with questions, and Mr. Dean and Christopher fall into a conversation about various collections they saw on their world tours.

Which leaves Catherine, red-faced, staring at her dinner. Rosalie and Christopher know everything about the history of this house. Christopher and Mr. Dean have traveled, seen things, *done* things. And Lady Jones clearly knows just about everything, and everyone.

Catherine's just a simple girl from the country, playing at a station she'll clearly never reach. How could her mother ever think she'd be sophisticated enough for Mr. Dean?

How could she privately think she'd be sophisticated enough for Rosalie?

Her chest grows tight and squirmy, and Catherine puts down her spoon. They're not even through the soup course. All the tension, all the questions, all the uncertainty that she's been boxing up in her mind is spilling out and she's stuck at this table with nowhere to go.

"You were going to tell me what you thought about *The Romance of the Forest.*"

Catherine blinks, slowly bringing her eyes over to Rosalie, who's looking back at her, a hint of a crease between her eyebrows. Catherine forces a smile, not wanting to worry her. At least one of them should enjoy the meal.

Just then, Mr. Tarton's staff comes out to take away their soup bowls and remaining dishes. Catherine sits back, watching the elaborate resetting of the table. They've never stood on so much formality in her house, and certainly not with so many servants. She wonders if Rosalie's dinners are like this.

"The woods here remind me of all the chapters in the abbey. It feels like you could wander off forever," Rosalie says.

Catherine forces herself to focus on the one person at the table who wants to talk to her. The one person she wants to talk to. Rosalie, who looks so pretty, even after a day of travel.

"It really does," Catherine agrees. "Though I think you and I would be much more capable if left out in the woods. You'd think Adeline might have made more attempts at escape."

"I don't know. I'd have wanted to explore the abbey more. Maybe hidden away until everyone was forced out, rather than become a pawn in everyone else's game," Rosalie says, giving a grateful nod to the kitchen server who places a plate of spiced lamb down in front of her.

Catherine smiles at her own server and looks down at the lamb. More potatoes, this time whipped into a creamy puree, over which two spiced lamb chops have been artfully laid—it smells absolutely divine. Mr. Tarton takes his first bite and Catherine quickly follows suit, trying not to groan.

It's utterly delicious, like nothing she's ever tasted before.

She absolutely doesn't fit in with the rest of the table. Can't possibly keep up with the discussion happening among Tarton,

Lady Jones, Christopher, and Mr. Dean—something about exchequer bills—but at least the food is good.

Rosalie keeps asking more questions about *The Romance of the Forest*, pulling Catherine into a safe, special little world, filled with spices and fabulous food and Rosalie's enthusiasm. If it could be just like this, just the two of them, all the time, she wouldn't be so worried.

Then again, when dinner finally ends, all of them stuffed to the gills, that sense of ease disappears. It *is* about to be just her and Rosalie again. And she doesn't know what she's meant to do, or say, or not do, or not say.

She doesn't know what she wants, other than that she *wants*, a flare of need scorching up her chest and down her belly as Rosalie looks over her shoulder at her. Catherine's following behind while the housekeeper shows her, Rosalie, and Lady Jones to their rooms, on the opposite side of the manor from Christopher and Mr. Dean.

She can't look at Rosalie as they walk into their room. If she does, she might combust, or burst into tears, or scream. There's a large, four-poster bed with deep red curtains at the center of the room, with a small sitting space off to the side, all of the furniture in the same dark maroon. An armoire is set along the wall with a large window overlooking the lawn. There's just a hint of moonlight filtering in, and the flickering light from the fireplace opposite the bed casts everything in a warm, shimmery glow.

"Try to get some sleep," Lady Jones says, standing in the doorway, the housekeeper behind her. "Don't be talking books all night."

"We won't," Rosalie promises.

Lady Jones smiles and gives a little wave, then closes the door. They can hear her footsteps just down the hall, and the creaking of the door next to theirs.

They're really alone. In this beautiful room. Just her, and Rosalie. Who looks so incredibly beautiful, backlit by the fireplace, standing in front of the big bed.

What comes next? What comes after? How can she know who she's supposed to be, or if she's good enough, if she doesn't know what this could be, what this means, how Rosalie feels?

What if she's bad at this? What if, what if, what if, what if . . .

Chapter Fifteen
Rosalie

Rosalie turns from the closed door, her heartbeat fast, palms a little sweaty. Excitement floods through her and she looks to Catherine, only to find her pale, hands twisting together.

"Catherine?" she prompts. Catherine drags her eyes from the door and they're wide and bright with unshed tears. "What's the matter?"

Rosalie reaches out to still her hands. Catherine gives a sharp intake of breath as their fingers touch, but doesn't pull away. She's breathing fast too—too fast.

"Here, come sit," Rosalie says, taking a step to draw her toward the bed. But Catherine doesn't move, eyes growing even wider.

She doesn't know what's wrong, but the bed clearly isn't the solution. Rosalie doesn't think this—whatever this is—is something she can simply kiss away.

So she turns them and guides Catherine to the little sitting area, settling them on the surprisingly soft burgundy settee. Rosalie keeps one hand on Catherine's still tightly clenched fists, and uses her other to brush the hair out of her eyes, letting her fingers slip to rest on the back of her neck. She hopes it's steadying.

"What's the matter, darling?" she whispers.

"I don't know," Catherine whispers back, squeezing her eyes

shut, her hands tense beneath Rosalie's. "It's just . . . rather a lot."

"The house?" Rosalie asks tentatively, unsure if she wants to know the true answer.

She's heard this speech before. It's too much—what she wants is too much—*she* is too much.

"The house. The history. The dinner setting. I'm . . ." Catherine opens her eyes and meets Rosalie's gaze. "I don't belong here."

"Of course you do," Rosalie says reflexively.

The excitement in her chest is rapidly turning to panic. She knows it can all disappear in an instant. She lived it once with Jane. Found herself alone in her want and her confidence and her affection. She wasn't enough for Jane—couldn't be enough for her, in every way.

She wanted this time to be so different.

Catherine shakes her head, the baby hairs on the back of her neck brushing Rosalie's fingertips. "I don't have the money, or the breeding—I'm far outside my station."

"What?" Rosalie asks with a startled laugh.

Catherine stiffens beneath her hand. "It's not funny."

Rosalie blows out a breath, cupping the back of Catherine's neck more firmly. Relief courses through her that this isn't about *her*, but that doesn't mean it's not important. How could Catherine ever think— "I thought you were about to say something else. And that's ridiculous."

"It's not," Catherine says, her hands unclenching beneath Rosalie's palm. "I don't know how the courses come out, or how the laws work, and I've never traveled. You and your brother, and Mr. Dean—you've all had so much experience. I can't keep up. I don't know why my mother thought I could ever compete with you, or travel in your world," she whispers.

Rosalie shakes her head, taking one of Catherine's twitching hands in hers and squeezing. "You are far smarter than Mr. Dean. Far more compassionate than Mr. Tarton. And if you could have gotten my brother's education, you'd be dancing circles around him in Latin. You lack nothing but opportunity."

Catherine stares at her, her face softening just a hair, and Rosalie feels some of her confidence come swelling back. "You are extraordinary, and I'd rather talk with you than any of them any day."

Catherine's lip twitches upward in a half smile. "Thank you."

"And that's the point, right? Why we're here? To spend time together?" Rosalie encourages, trying to reclaim the looks they shared at dinner, the press of Catherine's shoulder in the carriage.

But it has the opposite effect. Catherine bites at her lip and flits her gaze away, looking toward the fireplace.

"Is . . . there something else?" Rosalie asks, fear creeping back into her chest.

"I just— No matter how much you like me, I'm not—I'm not like Mr. Dean. In . . . more ways than one."

"Ways I like very much," Rosalie says quickly.

Catherine huffs a little laugh. "But what comes next?" Catherine asks, meeting Rosalie's eyes again. "What can I be to you? Just a country girl. Just a girl, at that. How does this work?"

Rosalie hesitates. They're questions she's been asking herself. Questions she decided didn't need to be answered this weekend. A choice she made for them both, it seems.

She has to stop doing that.

"I don't know," Rosalie says softly.

"If you were a man—"

"We wouldn't be alone together right now," Rosalie says with a snort.

Catherine giggles, the sound a welcome relief.

"But if you *were*, it would all be very simple, wouldn't it?" Catherine continues. "Get engaged, get married, have children."

"All laid out and plain," Rosalie agrees. "Is that something you want?"

"Something simple?"

"A man," Rosalie says, more serious. If they're having this conversation, then she wants to have it.

She's never gotten to before. Jane didn't give her the choice to even try.

That's a wrong she wants to right with Catherine. So they both have a choice.

"It's what Mother says I should want," Catherine says slowly.

"But is it? Do you want a man, a husband?" Rosalie presses.

Catherine's other hand closes over Rosalie's, holding tight. "I've never wanted anyone like I've wanted you."

Rosalie's breath whooshes from her lips, heat flushing up her neck. "That's lovely," she says. To be the only person Catherine has ever felt this way for—it's incredibly heady.

"Have you?" Catherine asks.

"Felt like this for someone?"

"For a man."

Rosalie hesitates. She's never said it out loud, to anyone, not even Christopher. But Catherine's let Rosalie see her weak and wanting, and Rosalie doesn't want her any less for it. In fact, she might . . . feel more for her.

Catherine's trusting her to be as honest as she's asking Catherine to be in return. Choosing, together, to trust each other.

"I've never wanted the future my mother wanted for me. Never felt the things she says I should feel. I keep—I kept waiting to meet a man who made me feel the way my mother does for my father, or my aunt does for my uncle—all . . ." She trails off, struggling to describe it.

"Butterflies and giggles and giddy anticipation?" Catherine suggests.

Rosalie meets Catherine's eyes, wanting to trust her, wanting to share. "I've never met a man who makes me feel what I do when you touch me."

It comes out soft and secretive. Almost like shame. Almost, but not quite, because the way Catherine's face breaks into a smile, the way her eyes light up—it makes Rosalie feel all those butterflies, makes her want to giggle, makes her want to pounce and push Catherine into the settee and kiss her silly.

And they're alone, so she *can*.

It's quieter than the butterflies want, leaning in, drawing Catherine to her by the nape of her neck, pressing her lips against her achingly soft ones.

Rosalie sucks on Catherine's bottom lip, relishing her breathy groan. She scoots just the slightest bit closer and Catherine's left hand leaves Rosalie's to rise up and cup her cheek. Rosalie lets her tongue slick across Catherine's bottom lip. Catherine gasps.

Rosalie's whole body is warm and tingling. She lets go of Catherine's hand to press on her shoulder, tipping them sideways so she can stretch out along her glorious body as they kiss, languid with sloppy open mouths.

Catherine cradles her jaw in her hands, sending trickles of warmth down Rosalie's neck that make her shiver and smile and squirm. Catherine moves with her, the two of them squished there on the settee, everything pressed so deliciously together. But it's still not enough.

Rosalie breaks from Catherine's mouth, rearing back to stare down at her there on the settee—at the plump red of her lips, her bright pink cheeks, her eyes blown wide.

It would take a lot of work to get her down to her chemise right now, which seems needless when Rosalie can simply shuffle off her and slip to the floor. Catherine sits up, staring down at Rosalie as she begins running her fingers up Catherine's calves, rucking up her dress as she revels in the silky feel of her skin, in the soft hair on her legs, in the way Catherine's panting already.

Catherine blinks down at her as Rosalie rests her palms on Catherine's thighs. "All right?"

"I haven't done this before," Catherine whispers.

"Do you want me to stop?" Rosalie asks, smiling up at her. "We can."

"No, no, God, no," Catherine breathes out.

Rosalie can't help but laugh. "Okay."

"But you— I'll take your lead," Catherine says, cheeks going even pinker. "If you'll show me."

Rosalie can feel the smile that stretches across her face. "I'll teach you absolutely everything I know, and the rest we'll learn together, yeah?"

"Yeah," Catherine says, her hesitation melting away.

"Just tell me if you want me to stop," Rosalie says, waiting for Catherine's eager nod before she glides her hands around Catherine's thighs until she can grip at their backs, fingers pressing into luscious flesh. She drags Catherine to the edge of the couch.

Catherine squeaks, laughing, and Rosalie grins up at her before she slides one hand to push Catherine's skirts out of the way. Which leaves her bare and beautiful and so incredibly tantalizing from the waist down. Catherine stares at Rosalie, her entire face flushed.

"You're so beautiful," Rosalie tells her, leaning forward to rest her chin on Catherine's strong, lean thigh.

She watches Catherine's face as she glides her hand up to the crease between hip and thigh. Catherine swallows hard, her chest rising and falling rapidly, and Rosalie takes that as a good sign, letting her fingers move up up up until Catherine's head falls back on an overwhelmed sigh.

Rosalie grins and touches her gently, exploring, watching every little twitch and movement of her face, waiting until the thigh beneath her cheek untenses, until Catherine is lax with pleasure. Rosalie dips her head forward, swiping her tongue against Catherine's center.

Catherine moans, low and deep, and Rosalie smiles against her. She watches her face, memorizes her reactions. She holds Catherine's hip with her free hand, her other sinking down to tease against Catherine's entrance. Catherine's head jerks up as Rosalie gently sucks, her eyes meeting Rosalie's.

She wishes she had bothered with the dress now, so she could see Catherine fully bare. But still, the way her eyes, wide and searching and blissful, watch Rosalie—the way her hand comes down to cover Rosalie's on her hip, her other hand rising to squeeze at her breast—the way she moans quietly, breathily, beautifully—she is utterly glorious.

Rosalie could stay like this forever, her fingers sinking into Catherine, lips and tongue moving delicately, Catherine grinding softly into her face. To watch as the pleasure rises, feel the

way Catherine's muscles tighten, delight in the way she's bab-
bling nonsense, her other hand falling to hold Rosalie's head, to
urge her forward—

Catherine tenses, clenching around Rosalie's fingers, a soft,
keening whine escaping her lips as her hips press up against Rosalie's mouth. Rosalie keeps going, drawing as much pleasure as
she can, relishing in Catherine's moans and squeaks and sighs,
until the hand previously clenched into her hair gently shoves
her face to the side.

She withdraws her fingers, laughing as she reaches up to
wipe them on Catherine's chemise. Watching Catherine slowly
blink her eyes open, she feels powerful, and vulnerable, and so
close and connected to her all at once.

"My God," Catherine whispers, her voice a little hoarse.

"Yeah?" Rosalie asks.

"Yeah," Catherine says, reaching down to cup Rosalie's shoulder. "Get up here."

Rosalie smiles and rises on her lightly aching knees, leaning
forward so Catherine can pull her into a deep, searching kiss.
Rosalie relishes the feeling, squirming there between Catherine's legs, suddenly aware of her own aching want, and the fact
that there's a bed not feet away.

"Shall we move somewhere more comfortable?" Rosalie suggests as Catherine breaks from her mouth, dragging kisses up
Rosalie's jaw.

"Only once you're naked," she whispers, her hands gliding up
Rosalie's back to undo the laces of her dress. "Arms up."

Rosalie laughs and raises her arms, allowing Catherine to
pull her dress and petticoat up and over her head. It's a little
awkward with Rosalie still kneeling on the floor, but the hum

of triumph Catherine lets out when they finally make it over Rosalie's hair is so damn endearing.

"Fair's fair," she says, pulling Catherine forward so she can undo the laces of her dress and gather the bunched fabric.

Catherine raises her hips and together they make quick work of her dress and petticoat, leaving them both in stays and chemises, tangled together on the settee. Catherine giggles, leaning in for another kiss. It's a breathless few minutes of tugging at laces, exchanging rough, open-mouthed kisses, before Rosalie manages to get Catherine's stays off. She doesn't even notice Catherine's beaten her to it until Catherine's deft fingers are tripping up her stomach and coming to settle firm and lovely on her breasts.

"Stand up," Catherine says, a finger swiping over Rosalie's nipple.

She groans. She doesn't want to move anymore, just wants to stay here with Catherine's hands on her all night.

"Now," Catherine says firmly.

Rosalie's not sure why she finds her clear, commanding tone so attractive, but it does something to her—warmth pooling in her belly, between her thighs, tingling down to her toes.

She stands, looking down at Catherine, until Catherine follows suit. Rosalie watches her rise, tipping her head back to meet her gaze as Catherine brushes her whole body against Rosalie's on the way up.

Her fingers gather Rosalie's shift as she goes, and Rosalie finds herself raising her arms until Catherine tugs off her chemise. And then she's completely naked there in the firelight. She feels herself flush, but she's unashamed, watching Catherine take her in, her lip between her teeth, a smile tugging at her mouth.

"*You* are beautiful," she says, her hands skating down Rosalie's back, bare fingers on bare skin. Rosalie shivers, and then groans as Catherine's hands come to cup her arse. "Jump," she whispers.

Rosalie does as she's told, gasping against Catherine's mouth as she hops, wrapping her legs around Catherine's hips. Catherine holds on to her thighs and walks them confidently across the room until her knees hit the bed.

Rosalie kisses her messily, her core grinding into Catherine's lower belly, body alight with her touch and taste and scent and humming voice.

And then she's falling softly to the mattress, staring up at the dark canopy.

"Scooch."

Rosalie rises on her elbows just in time to watch Catherine peel off her own chemise. She's a goddess. Ethereal and lithe and staring at Rosalie rather incredulously.

"Move."

Rosalie turns on the bed, scooting up until her head hits the down pillows. The comforter is soft against her back, the pillow a cloud beneath her head, and Catherine is crawling toward her.

Rosalie could die happy right now.

Instead, Catherine stretches out over her, coming in for a consuming kiss as their naked bodies press together in delicious, tortuous friction. Rosalie goes to wrap herself around Catherine, but she doesn't stay still, sinking down Rosalie's body with a trail of kisses to her throat, and then her clavicles, and then her lips close over Rosalie's nipple.

She doesn't know if she's ever made that sound before, rough and throaty and wild. But the feeling of Catherine around her,

her hooded eyes looking up from Rosalie's breast, her beautiful body stretched out against her—it's almost too much.

But there isn't time to revel, not when Catherine's fingers are skating up her thigh, not when she's sinking down lower to return the favor.

"Tell me what to do," Catherine whispers, pressing a firm kiss to Rosalie's hip bone as her fingers stroke playfully at Rosalie's center.

Rosalie swallows hard, her mouth parched, overwhelmed with glorious sensation.

"Tell me," Catherine insists.

She rather likes being bossed around, it turns out.

"Kiss me," Rosalie rasps out. "At the top. Slow and firm."

Catherine does, pressing long, slow kisses as her fingers tease at Rosalie's entrance.

"Li—lick me," Rosalie whispers, hips lifting off the bed as Catherine complies.

She's never asked for what she wants before. Never had the chance. It's wonderful, and terrifying, and utterly, sinfully, fantastically hot.

"Your—your fingers," she manages. "Curl—curl up and—ah!"

She slaps a hand over her mouth, looking down at Catherine, whose lips are quirked upward even as she continues to lap at Rosalie, needing absolutely no further instruction.

Rosalie tries, she does, to keep giving suggestions, but the sensation is too great. The perfect curl of her fingers, the languid pressure of Catherine's tongue, the hand she presses onto Rosalie's hips to keep them down as she strains up against Catherine's mouth—

That it's Catherine making her feel this way. Catherine teasing and testing and learning and thriving as every single part of

Rosalie's body tightens, as everything narrows to the sensation of Catherine's face and fingers between her legs, the feel of the down comforter clenched in her hand, and the beat beat beating of her hammering heart until—

White-hot pleasure explodes from Rosalie's center, her belly clenching, legs shaking. She's seeing stars, and galaxies, and waterfalls, and explosions, and she keeps her hand plastered to her mouth, just barely holding in a shout of ecstasy.

Slowly, after what might be hours, she comes back to her body, floating into herself on a cloud of pleasure, and wonder, and Catherine wrapped around her.

She turns her face and meets Catherine's very smug grin.

"You are far too good at that for a first time," Rosalie says, her voice low and scratchy.

Catherine smirks, leaning in to kiss her. Rosalie can taste herself, can still taste Catherine between their mouths, and she groans, reaching out to pull Catherine on top of her.

"There must be dirty books somewhere in your house."

"I may have studied up, yes," Catherine says, shrugging a little.

"You need absolutely no instruction," Rosalie insists. "That was incredible."

"I'm glad," Catherine says, smiling at her, relaxed and comfortable and clearly more than a little proud of herself.

Which forces Rosalie to lift her still tingling arm and glide her hand down Catherine's taut, smooth stomach.

"You don't need to—"

But Catherine's already squirming, already so ready and wet when Rosalie glides her fingers between her legs. She moves slowly, watching Catherine's face go slack, then tense.

"It's wonderful with lips and tongue and teeth *and* fingers, but when I think of you at night, this is all I do," Rosalie whispers, proud when Catherine gasps, her eyes opening to stare into Rosalie's. "Have you ever touched yourself thinking about me?"

Catherine's lips part on a pant as Rosalie changes the angle, remembering exactly which way made Catherine's hips buck— just like that—on the settee.

"Have you?"

"Yes," Catherine breathes out.

"Tell me," Rosalie says, slowing her fingers. It's her turn to direct.

Catherine whines. "Keep going."

Rosalie strokes her very slowly, nothing like the pace she knows Catherine needs. "Tell me."

Catherine growls and bucks her hips into Rosalie's hand. "I lie on my stomach, with my hand between my thighs. Sometimes I—I read *Fanny Hill* first."

"The first scene, or the second?"

Catherine forgets to keep scowling and Rosalie rewards her with a few quick strokes that make her groan.

"Both," Catherine admits.

"You get yourself ready for imaginary me?" Rosalie presses, moving her fingers in circles.

Catherine's whole body undulates against her.

"If I'm not distracted before bed, just thinking of you gets me ready," Catherine whispers. "I think about that afternoon and—"

". . . how I could have gotten on the floor right there, and crawled up your skirts, and pressed my mouth right here?" Rosalie suggests, rubbing firmly.

Catherine gasps, her body jerking. Her thigh slips in between Rosalie's legs and Rosalie groans. Which makes Catherine smirk, which forces Rosalie to change the angle of her fingers so Catherine's jaw goes slack.

She can't stop herself from rubbing against Catherine's thigh, and after a moment, Catherine's mouth crashes onto hers, and it's a fast, hot minute until they're falling apart together, Catherine's hips pressing Rosalie's hand into her hip bone, Rosalie grinding furiously against Catherine's thigh until they're messy and spent and laughing against each other again.

They lie there breathing for a long, contented moment before Catherine slips to Rosalie's side and sprawls on her back, blissful and so incredibly beautiful. Rosalie turns, wrapping her arm over Catherine's stomach. She props her chin up on Catherine's chest and looks up to meet her flushed, blinking gaze.

"You look incredibly pretty splayed all over my sheets," Rosalie decides.

Catherine flushes more, if it's even possible. "Well, you look like a goddess when you come," she says, tugging on Rosalie until she shifts, stretching out on top of Catherine, legs tangled.

"I hope this lived up to your imagination from all those nights alone in your bed," Rosalie says. The moment the words leave her lips, she realizes just how desperately she wants them to be true. Wants to be sure Catherine enjoyed this—that it was good for her—that she'll want to do it again.

Catherine snorts and threads their fingers together on her chest. "My imagination could never have imagined." She frowns. "Or something cleverer than that."

Rosalie feels herself grinning, her chest so light and full and *happy*.

"And just think, with more practice, and some trips to the more salacious bookstores, we can dream up more imaginative things together," she says, already wondering if she can get Aunt

Genevieve to share where she gets the tawdry novels she never lets Rosalie see, but Rosalie knows live somewhere in her dressing room.

Catherine's smile dims a little. "That sounds wonderful," she says softly.

Rosalie's breath is finally slowing down, but the look on Catherine's face threatens to make it start up again. "What's the matter?"

"It's nothing. This is magical," Catherine says quickly, running her fingertips up and down Rosalie's back.

It would lull her into sleep if she weren't more in tune with Catherine's expressions. But she's spent the last two months watching the woman, and the last hour cataloguing every minute twitch of her brow, smile, giggle—she can't let this go, not now.

"What is it?" Rosalie asks, firmer.

Catherine sighs. "I don't want to ruin the mood."

"A little too late for that," Rosalie says honestly. "We're already naked, what's the use in hiding from me?" she adds, trailing her fingertips down the side of Catherine's face. "Can't be that scary when our tits are pressed together."

Catherine laughs, surprised, and Rosalie can't help but grin back. She wants to know—needs to know—what's troubling her . . . lover? But it doesn't need to be grim.

"I want to just lie here and catch my breath, and then go another round, or two, and kiss you until dawn," Catherine says, shrugging a little. "But I also want to know what happens after dawn."

"What's between this and the simple engagement, marriage, husband of it all," Rosalie surmises.

Catherine nods, lip between her teeth, and Rosalie sighs. She doesn't know. Were one of them a man, they'd be having this moment after already committing to a lifetime together. There would be no questions, no varied outcomes. Marriage. Children. Forever. They'd get to know each other afterward, and hope they still liked each other.

"Maybe that's it," Rosalie mumbles.

"What's it?" Catherine asks, a hint of panic in her voice.

Rosalie scooches up to plant a firm kiss to her lips, then pulls back to meet her eyes. "We get to know each other."

"What?"

Rosalie sits up, waiting for Catherine to shift up as well, resting against the pillows with Rosalie in her lap.

"If you were a man, we'd get married before we really knew. Stuck together forever. But us, what we have—maybe it's lucky? Maybe it's beautiful that we get to be together just to be together. Not chess pieces to be traded for a business deal, not a prize to be won as the season's catch. I like you, you like me, and that's enough for now."

Catherine considers her and Rosalie smiles back, a lightness in her chest she's never felt before.

"Just . . . kiss in secret, and find ways to be alone together—"

"And very, very naked," Rosalie adds.

Catherine giggles. "Just kiss, and be naked, and spend time together . . . until what?"

Rosalie shrugs. "Until we know what comes next. Until we're ready to . . . ask for help with what comes next. Until we have enough money or power or . . . whatever . . . to decide what comes next for ourselves."

"You're okay with not knowing?"

All her life, Rosalie's been told she'll marry rich, have a bunch of babies, and then make sure *they* marry rich. She's never wanted that future, not ever, not once. This—with Catherine—

whatever it is—isn't nearly the same answer. There's no finality. No goal to strive for. No race to run.

She feels so free. So incredibly, incandescently free, to be exactly who she is with someone who likes her just as she is. To be naked and unashamed and happy.

"It's not not-knowing. It's choosing to find out together," she says, a surge of joy coursing through her.

"Choosing to find out together," Catherine whispers, a smile blooming slowly across her beautiful cheeks. "I like that."

"I like you," Rosalie says, her voice light, a giggle bursting forth.

Catherine giggles back, reaching out to draw Rosalie in. "I like you too. So very much," she whispers, before crashing their lips together.

And then they do just as Catherine says. They kiss, and they touch, and they choose together to forgo sleep to see the sun rise out the window, wrapped in each other's arms. Bare, and free, and together.

Chapter Sixteen
Catherine

She wishes they were still in bed. Wishes she were still waking, naked, peaceful, and lightly sweaty, with Rosalie wrapped around her back, arm tight over her stomach. Wishes she could still roll over and kiss her soft lips, hold her close, and glide her hand down—

"Now the chapel was fully demolished by 1707, but we still have records of the art dedicated to Saint Blaise, from which this folly now gets its name," Mr. Tarton says, marching them around the folly castle that rises out of the deep green in an enormous clearing.

Nearly four stories of gray ashlar stone, the castle has three towers surrounding a central turret, all with parapets and designs in limestone set at intervals. There are a number of inlaid crosses on each tower, and big arched windows.

Catherine should be fascinated by the history, but she can't stop sneaking glances at Rosalie, imagining her as a roguish knight, dressed in full riding gear. The kind of tiny knight no one would mess with. The kind of knight who could sweep Catherine off her feet, save her from brigands, take her back to one of the cottages through the surrounding forest, and ravish her.

Rosalie seems to know Catherine's thoughts are far, far from architect Robert Mylne and Gothic Revival architecture. She keeps stopping to stare up at the towers, a hand on her hip, her other at the back of her neck, or stretching out to point toward something, beckoning Lady Jones' attention.

It's thoroughly distracting, and the slightest bit cruel, which just makes Catherine long to pick her up and slam her (gently) against the rough stone and take her mouth.

"He can go on, can't he?" Lady Jones asks, leaving Rosalie to her fetching perusal of the large cross on the nearest tower. "I think I've heard this speech about fifteen times."

Catherine forces herself to look up at Lady Jones. "You visit often, then?"

"Mr. Tarton and my husband are old friends. We stay here anytime we're traveling toward the coast, or back toward the city. It's a charming little monument, but Tarton's made it his life's mission to introduce everyone he can to it, and it is tiring. Still, for that dinner?"

Catherine laughs. Lady Jones takes her arm, linking their elbows to keep following after the men. "It was delicious," she admits.

"And the rooms are spectacular. Were you and Rosalie comfortable?"

Catherine swallows, keeping her smile steady. "Very."

"Good," Lady Jones says brightly, apparently unable to feel the anxiety that rolls off Catherine in waves. "I'm glad the two of you are getting to know each other better. You seem kindred spirits, and Rosalie can always use more of those."

Her kind smile is wide, cheerful, but somehow also knowing, in a way that makes Catherine's insides twist.

There's no way she can know. Rosalie says she sleeps like the dead, and they were very careful to be quiet just in case. Lady Jones can't know Catherine spent most of the previous night with her tongue between Rosalie's legs.

Last night it seemed a wonderful solution, to simply move forward, spend more time together, and leisurely figure out their mutual future, whatever that is, however serious, however difficult, as they go.

But in the harsh light of day, all the worry starts to flood back into her system.

They're here, with Lady Jones, and Christopher, and Mr. Dean, whom they're both supposed to be chasing. . . . One of them is supposed to end up marrying him at season's end.

How do they avoid that?

"Mr. Dean and Mr. Tarton are thinking about walking the hunting trails, but I thought perhaps the three of you might enjoy an amble through the hamlet instead," Christopher says, jogging up to them and beckoning Rosalie to join them.

Mr. Tarton and Mr. Dean keep walking toward the forest without even a backward glance. Rosalie catches Catherine's gaze, rolling her eyes. Mr. Dean has made absolutely no effort to engage either of them in conversation this morning. Catherine's been too anxious to give it much mind, but really, how ridiculous.

"Ah, the hamlet. Yes. Let's amble," Lady Jones says, leaving Catherine to take Christopher's waiting arm. "And let's make up lots of scandalous stories about the staff who inhabit the house."

"Should the housekeeper be in a secret tryst with the carriage driver, or the cook?" Christopher asks.

"Oh, the cook would be far more interesting," Lady Jones agrees, walking them off in the opposite direction.

But Catherine's not listening, too distracted by Rosalie striding up to her, all confidence and sly smile.

"We could get lost in the woods for a while. Your dress could snag on something and it could be ages getting untangled," she suggests.

In her cream walking dress and her green-ribbon-rimmed bonnet, her curls frizzy and cheeks lightly flushed, Rosalie looks like a decadent dessert. When it's just the two of them, Catherine's worries fall clean away. And they're blissfully alone right now. Would be a shame to waste the opportunity.

So she lets Rosalie drag her off the path into the dappled green shade. Lets her press her against a tree. Takes her chance to spin them and press Rosalie against the trunk, using their height difference to hike Rosalie up on her thigh, giving her purchase. Lets herself watch Rosalie grind herself to a quick release, head thrown back in glorious pleasure.

It's almost enough to keep her calm when they're back in the damned carriage, pressed up against each other with Christopher and Mr. Dean across from them again, and Lady Jones on Rosalie's other side. Rosalie's pinky brushes hers on the seat while they both nod at . . . something Mr. Dean is saying. Maybe about horse racing?

Rosalie's skin is so soft and warm against hers, even at that tiny point of contact. Catherine's never felt like this before, for anyone. This rush of feelings, the joy of laying with her, the excitement of her touch and her taste and her smile—it's intoxicating.

It would be so easy to fall head over arse in love with Rosalie. All it might take is a few more kisses and another few hours spent talking about books and silly men and their favorite places.

There's no diagram for the life she and Rosalie could share together. They'd literally have to dream it up and make it come true. Catherine's not sure if they're really clever enough to find a way to outsmart society and find true happiness together. But she so desperately wants to try.

When they finally reach Bath, Lady Jones has the carriage drop Catherine off first, and Rosalie hops out to see her to her door, as if she might get lost walking the eight steps, and the driver might get similarly lost bringing her small travel case behind them.

Rosalie seizes the opportunity to take Catherine's arm, standing a hair too close on her doorstep. The street is empty and gray with rain.

"We'll see each other soon," she promises.

"We will," Catherine agrees, trying to soak up the way her eyes sparkle in the lamplight. The way her cheeks are still lightly pink. The way she looks, travel-worn and still sated from last night.

It might not be love just yet, but she thinks she wants a future with Rosalie.

Rosalie briefly takes both her hands, squeezing tight. "Soon," she insists.

Catherine opens her mouth, feeling a light tug, like Rosalie might be trying to pull her in—

"Catherine, is that you?"

The door opens and Rosalie pulls away, their hands falling empty between them. Catherine's mother smiles at her through the now-open doorway and then turns to Rosalie, her eyes dimming.

"Thank you for returning her safely. And please thank your aunt, Lady Rosalie."

"I will," Rosalie says cheerfully. "I look forward to seeing you both soon."

With that, Catherine watches her walk back to the carriage and climb in. Watches her settle next to Lady Jones while

Mr. Dean snaps the carriage door shut. Watches her rumble away down the street. Too far to touch, or hold, or talk to.

"Come in, come in, your father and I want to hear all about your trip," Mother says enthusiastically, dragging Catherine inside.

She's well and truly back at home, all that openness and freedom in the countryside replaced by Bath stone and bustle and high, narrow townhouses. But they're going to change that, somehow, together. They have to.

Chapter Seventeen
Rosalie

Rosalie growls to herself, pacing beneath the large green oak tree at the back of their yard, hoping Mother's still engaged with her correspondence so Rosalie can get a handle on her "sullen" attitude.

It's getting harder and harder to listen to Mother's plans about Mr. Dean without screaming that she doesn't want him, never has, and wants the daughter of her former best friend instead. Ardently. Passionately. Physically.

She lies awake at night, driven wild by memories of Catherine's touch, and taste—the way she held her, the way she kissed her—the way she—

But each alluring, titillating, scalding memory is accompanied by an instant douse of cold water thinking about how to make it happen again.

Before Catherine, she could always see all the possible outcomes of any given situation, could architect the world to fall to her whims. But that was for socially acceptable outcomes. "Match this girl with this boy, happily (if sometimes only financially) ever after."

It makes her mad, and flushed, and uncomfortable in her skin to not be able to figure out what should come next, what she wants, and how to get it. They need more than a month to decide what they want the rest of their lives to look like.

"You appear positively vexed." Rosalie spins around to find Christopher leaning against the big oak tree, grinning at her.

She purposefully hasn't gone to find him over the last two days, because she didn't know how to talk about it. Still doesn't.

"Are you going to kiss and tell, then?" he asks, grinning wider as she splutters. "It's clear as day that you did."

Rosalie covers her face with her hands, cheeks flaming. "Shut up."

She peeks through her fingers to find him holding up his hands, still smirking. "Then do you want to discuss how we're going to ensure you get to see her again, and perhaps delay Mr. Dean by another year, if not forever? And I vote for forever."

Rosalie lets her hands drop. "I—we don't have a plan in place, and we didn't decide to . . . be together forever or anything like that. It could still be premature."

She's rather sure there's nothing premature about how she feels for Catherine. But she wants more time before voicing any of her confusing, titillated, overwhelmed feelings.

"Well, even if you haven't decided—and I rather think you're a liar—I certainly have," Christopher says, pushing off from the tree to walk over to her. "You cannot marry that absolute bore. I don't know that there's a match for you that isn't the lovely Miss Pine, but it absolutely can't be him."

Rosalie stares at her brother, relieved, and anxious, and grateful, and hesitant. "Father and Mother—"

"I don't care," Christopher says immediately. "You deserve to have a happy life that's more than . . . this," he says, gesturing to the house.

She wants to feel like wanting more isn't wrong. Wants to silence the little voice inside telling her she's ungrateful and strange to want more than what most women dream about. To want a life that's not *perfect* in the eyes of everyone around her.

Rosalie meets Christopher's earnest gaze. "It isn't like asking to go to school or get a tutor."

"No," Christopher agrees, squeezing her hands tightly. "It's so much braver than that. You're asking for them to let you be who you are, exactly as you are."

"If Catherine and I don't decide to— If whatever this is isn't forever, then I—"

"If you *want* to ask them, I'm here. I'll ask them with you if you want. And if you don't—even if you never do—I'll be here. You never have to ask me, at least, all right?"

She lunges forward, pulling him into a hard hug. Christopher laughs into her hair and then pulls back, reaching out to wipe her traitorous eyes.

"First step is making sure you don't end up in a horrible marriage. And we'll get to the second step, making sure you can spend forever, or at least a little while, with the wonderful Miss Pine."

Rosalie laughs, snuffling. "Okay."

"Okay," he replies, grinning. "Any thoughts so far? You've been pacing a trench out here, you must have *something*."

"Going boating," she admits.

"Boating?"

"I'm thinking of arranging a punting trip and being so ridiculously needy and demanding that he won't want another outing."

Christopher chuckles. "You're very well suited."

To Rosalie's confusion, he pulls a packet of letters from his pocket. He removes one and waves it with a little smirk. Rosalie snatches it from him, confused, only for a waft of Catherine's lilac perfume to hit her like a wall. Looking down at the letter, it's a small square folded carefully, with Rosalie's name in Catherine's loopy script.

"Mrs. Pine would never allow Miss Pine to write to you willy-nilly, but her father did allow her to send a thank-you for the outing, and I've written back to ask permission to continue exchanging letters."

Rosalie glances up to find Christopher bouncing on his toes, so proud of himself. "You could have simply led with that," she says, shaking her head as he giggles.

She carefully unfolds the letter, looking down at Catherine's beautiful script, her heart beating embarrassingly fast.

Dearest, darling Rosalie,

A flush immediately climbs up her cheeks.

It's strange to say I miss you when we've seen each other just two days ago, but I do. I long for your smile, and your touch, and your embrace. I hope we are able to arrange for at least an outing most urgently.

To that end, I have devised a plan. Our mothers will never forsake their quest to see one of us married to Mr. Dean. But Mr. Dean has made no such promise.

Would you care to join me in a contest of terrible manners? Perhaps if we are horrible enough, he will simply walk away from both of us, leaving us but one choice: to drown our sorrows together and force our mothers to give up the feud by way of our enduring "friendship."

My mother is planning to hold a tea for the whole ton at the Upper Rooms in a month's time. I think we can enact a suitable campaign before then, don't you?

*Please send your reply back with your brother's, as he and
I will begin a correspondence. Does he like chess? I thought
perhaps we might play a game in our letters.*

*I eagerly await your response, and look forward to hope-
fully matching you in a game of atrocious manners. And after
that . . . we'll decide what comes next, together.*

Ardently yours, and thinking of your face in the firelight,
                                                    Catherine

Her heart is racing now. She wants to laugh. She wants to
run all the way to Catherine's house and tell her she's brilliant,
and they've had similar thoughts, and she is absolutely going to
win the game of terrible manners, to make sure that she gets to
use only her very best on Catherine until . . . until Catherine
tells her to stop, really.

"I do think you might put your considerable brain power together to concurrently repel Mr. Dean *and* decide on a future
you might like together," Christopher says.

Rosalie looks up, surprised.

"What, you thought I wouldn't be peeking at your letters?"

"You better not," Rosalie says quickly, her voice higher than
she means it to be. "They're . . . private."

He laughs. "Just this one. But I demand to be in on the
scheming. In fact, I think I'll invite Miss Pine along for this
boating outing, so you can begin to repel Mr. Dean together."

Rosalie sucks on her cheek, carefully folding Catherine's letter and tucking it into her stays. He's a sneak, but at least he
didn't mention the lip print beneath Catherine's beautiful signature.

She's not at all thinking about that print, and those lips, and—

"Do I have your full attention?"

She loves him, she hates him. But more, she and Catherine need him. "We should invite Amalie and Henrietta as well," she says.

She hasn't forgotten her promise to Christopher. He deserves his happy ending too. Amalie would hate to be left out anyway. And anytime she can get Henrietta an outing with Mr. Rile is a good opportunity.

"Perhaps we can get the two of you in one boat, and me and Amalie in the other. She and I can heckle," Christopher says brightly.

"When did you become so devious?" Rosalie teases.

"I learned from the masters," Christopher says, gesturing to Rosalie and then to the house.

"You'll use your powers for good," Rosalie insists. "Take charge of the Lords, make them pursue the betterment of society."

"You sound a bit like Father," Christopher says. It's only then that she notices the other letter in his hands. He follows her gaze and taps the letter against his palm. "Another disgruntled entreaty to join him in London this season."

"You could go," Rosalie says softly.

"Nope. He can be mad all he likes, can say I'm squandering my time, but we both know differently."

"Christopher," Rosalie entreats.

"When we're ready, you and I will build a better future for the whole of England, side by side. Father can wait until I've seen you settled."

"I hardly think I'll be of much help to anyone," Rosalie says softly. She doesn't like the idea of Christopher digging his heels in with Father, courting more disappointment.

"If you can build a life you want, you'll be helping your-self, and any young women you know see there's another path," Christopher says immediately. "It's important," he adds when she lifts her eyes to his. They feel suspiciously wet.

"And Father's daft if he thinks I can follow him all on my own. I will demand you help me once I'm in the Lords. You'll need to help Amalie throw all my parties. And hopefully Miss Pine will be there to play pianoforte too."

Rosalie wants to scold him for putting the cart so far before the horse, but the image is too tantalizing to refuse. "If you say so."

"I really do," he says, slinging his arm around her shoulder to bring her inside. "Now, talk to me loudly about how much Mr. Dean enjoys punting."

WHEN SHE'S ROCKING gently in a punting boat on the still-frigid River Avon three days later, Rosalie finds herself slightly less confident. The wind is brisk, and Mr. Rile keeps splashing her with the oar.

Catherine, Christopher, Mr. Sholle, and Amalie are ahead of them in the next boat, while Rosalie floats along with Mr. Dean, Henrietta, and Mr. Rile paddling. Henrietta and Mr. Rile have been talking quietly the whole time, leaving Rosalie alone with Mr. Dean, who, as usual, is simply staring off into the distance, thoroughly at ease and entirely uninterested in her.

Catherine's boat, by contrast, is a riot of laughter and chatter. Mr. Sholle looks rather pouty, but Catherine, Christopher, and Amalie are having a wonderful time.

Meanwhile, her mother and Catherine's mother are walking along the blooming riverbank, ten feet apart, chaperoning them from the shore. Mother keeps moving her hands, as if trying to send Rosalie a coded message, *Talk to Mr. Dean, make the most of being in his boat.* But she's so far away, it's hard to be entirely sure.

Were Rosalie in Catherine's boat, she'd laugh at the absurdity of it all. But she's not. Instead, she's on the good ship flirty with Henrietta and Mr. Rile.

Catherine looks back at her, eyebrow raised, and Rosalie sighs. It's clearly her turn to make a bad impression, she just needs to figure out how.

"It's rather chilly," Rosalie says loudly. She turns to Mr. Dean. "Don't you think?"

"It's nice and brisk," he says.

"You can have one of my blankets, Rosalie," Henrietta says, passing one over to her with the sweetest smile.

It's hard to be mad when she looks so happy. But she's really cramping Rosalie's style. Still, she wraps the blanket over her shoulders, protecting her arms from the misting spray of Mr. Rile's rather erratic paddling.

"I wish there were more sun," she tries again, forcing her voice into an unnatural whine.

Mr. Dean glances at her. "Better to protect your lovely skin."

Uck, gross. But his attention doesn't hold, and he turns back to the river.

She thought it would be easy to make herself annoying, but it's perfectly nice out, save for the splashing water. And she's normally not one for loud complaints. Why did she think she could do this?

Rosalie looks to Catherine's boat and finds Catherine and Christopher looking back at her, frowning while Amalie tells a story. They're nearing the dock where they had planned to stop for a light luncheon in the nearby park. She's running out of time to dissuade Mr. Dean.

She wishes she could talk to Catherine about this. Wishes they were in the same boat. Wishes they were simply punting along together, with no one else, able to talk and laugh and spend time with each other.

She wishes she could clear this with her. Or Christopher. Or hell, even Amalie. Because the idea that comes to Rosalie is completely ridiculous. Utterly atrocious. But it's all she's got.

With a silent apology, she turns to Henrietta. "I bet I can stay standing for longer than you can," she says, awkwardly interrupting a story Henrietta was telling Mr. Rile about her family's horses.

"I'm sorry?" Henrietta says, turning to Rosalie, fully confused.

"I bet I have better balance than you do. We'll both stand and see who can stay standing the longest. What do you say?"

Henrietta stares at her with wide eyes.

"That's a ridiculous notion," Mr. Dean says swiftly.

"It could be rather dangerous," Mr. Rile adds.

Henrietta can never deny Rosalie what she wants. And usually, it's always in Henrietta's best interest. But today, Rosalie needs to play on her goodwill.

Please, she thinks, hoping it comes through in her gaze.

Henrietta reluctantly nods. "All right, I guess," she says, removing her blankets and taking Rosalie's outstretched hand.

Together they clamber up and stand there, holding hands, rocking far more than Rosalie anticipated.

"All right, on the count of three, let go," she says, trying to sound more confident than she feels.

This is so frivolous, and dangerous, and ridiculous.

"You need to sit down," Mr. Dean says, his voice sharp and focused for the first time all day.

But it's working.

Rosalie counts down. Henrietta's grip on her hands tightens, but she dutifully lets go on *three*, and they start to balance. Mr. Rile has stopped rowing and they're left to the whims of the river, drifting peacefully and rocking with the light current.

"Stop it this instant," Mr. Dean insists.

"Miss Raught, really, I don't think—" Mr. Rile starts.

Henrietta teeters and quickly sits down, breathing heavily and gripping at her seat. Rosalie withholds her wince and throws her arms up in the air, wobbling dangerously.

"I win!" she says, forcing gaiety into her voice.

"How marvelous. Now. Sit. Down," Mr. Dean snarls.

If she looks at him, she'll fall over. But the tone of his voice is encouraging. Maybe a minute or so more and she'll have entirely ruined all the admiration he has for her.

"I want to see how long I can go," she says.

"That is—"

"What are you doing?" Amalie calls out.

Their boat comes into her limited view about twenty feet to their left. Christopher's trying not to laugh, and Catherine looks shocked but amused, her eyes wide, lips twitching.

"Fine. Fine, be ridiculous and thoughtless," Mr. Dean grumbles.

Rosalie risks a glance his way and finds him staring broodily down at the water, no longer watching her. Shutting her out.

She needs to escalate. How can she escalate from here?

Her mother is shouting something from the dock, but she can't hear that. She *won't* hear that.

"I bet I can stand on one leg," she says loudly.

"No!" Henrietta says.

"Rosalie, that's a terrible idea," Amalie shouts.

"You need to sit down right this—" Mr. Dean starts.

But she's already lifted her left leg . . .

And promptly goes toppling sideways into the freezing river.

Rosalie comes up spluttering, gasping with shock and laughter. It's painfully cold. And wet. How wonderfully ridiculous. She's fallen into the river. Of course she knew it was a possibility, but she didn't think it would actually happen.

Damn, it's cold!

She blinks up at her boat to find Mr. Dean glaring down at her. Henrietta and Mr. Rile are scrambling beside him to throw something to her while she treads water. Her skirts are heavy, and her bonnet is making it hard to see all that much. Her chest clenches painfully in the cold.

A thought comes to her unbidden: A man who was in love with her would be concerned. A man who was in love with her would put aside his frustration and do something to help. A man who was in love with her would be jumping into the—

SPLASH.

Rosalie revolves in the water, leaning her head back so she can see under the rim of her bonnet. And there's Catherine, bonnetless, swimming toward her, glowering.

"What on earth are you doing?" Rosalie calls. Of all the absurd, silly—

"Getting you into the boat, you absolute fool," Catherine hisses as she reaches her.

She ducks under Rosalie's shoulder so she's half supporting her, dragging her quickly back toward Henrietta and Mr. Rile's reaching hands. She's helping Rosalie swim, even though she doesn't need it.

Just as they reach her boat and each grab on, lightly, careful not to tip Mr. Dean, Henrietta, and Mr. Rile over, Christopher's boat pens them in on the other side.

"Miss Linet, come over to our boat so you don't get wet," Mr. Dean says, beckoning Amalie to step over their heads and into his boat, even as Henrietta gapes over at him. "Mr. Tisend, help Miss Pine and your sister into yours, so the other ladies don't get wet and sick."

Rosalie glances at Catherine, who looks back, still glaring, but with a twitch to her lips. That is perhaps the least chivalrous, rudest thing he could possibly have done.

"Get in here," Christopher says.

Rosalie and Catherine twirl around. Rosalie helps push Catherine up and into the boat with Mr. Sholle and Christopher's help. And then clambers up herself, fully clumsy and not at all ladylike.

They sit there, sopping wet and freezing cold, staring at each other, eyes wide. Catherine starts laughing when Mr. Sholle places a blanket around her shoulders, and Rosalie can't help but follow. Christopher drapes another blanket over her shoulders and undoes her bonnet. He pulls the blanket over her head, laughing, and Rosalie adjusts it, looking back at him with a grin.

"Back to the docks, as fast as you can," Mr. Dean grunts to Mr. Sholle and Mr. Rile, gesturing for them to paddle quickly.

"What on earth were you thinking?" Christopher asks Rosalie as they speed toward the dock, where she can see both their mothers waiting, furious.

"It seemed like fun. I haven't been having enough fun lately," she says with a shrug that just makes him laugh harder.

"That's absurd," Catherine says.

Rosalie looks back at her, her wet hair plastered to her cheek, the blanket wrapped up and over her head, her fingers lightly blue.

"Why did you jump in?" Rosalie asks.

"I wasn't sure you could swim."

Rosalie's chest warms even as she shivers. Mr. Dean yelled at her, but Catherine—Catherine's trembling, and could catch a cold, and her mother's going to kill her, but she jumped into the river anyway.

Rosalie reaches out and squeezes her hand. "Thank you," she says.

Catherine's glare melts into a little smile. "Couldn't let you have all the fun," she says softly, squeezing back before dropping her fingers as the boats bump the docks.

Christopher and Mr. Sholle hop out to secure them.

Rosalie watches her mother and Mrs. Pine exchange a glowering look of commiseration, united in a shared anger and disappointment as they stand there side by side, hands on their hips. But *united*.

A beautiful girl jumped into a river to save her, and maybe their mothers hate each other a little bit less. Despite it all, today has been a good day.

Chapter Eighteen

Catherine

Catherine tugs the blanket tighter around her body, still shivering.

"I just don't understand why you jumped in," Mother bemoans.

"She thought she had to save the girl," Father says, rolling his eyes in Catherine's direction from where he's comfortably settled in his favorite armchair.

They've got her in the other armchair pushed as close to the fire as possible without singeing anything. Mother's lying prostrate on the settee. If she weren't still interrogating Catherine, it might be a nice evening.

"She could swim," Mother protests.

"Yes, but I didn't know that," Catherine says, snugging the slightly scratchy wool blanket tighter over her head. "And it's not like Mr. Dean was any help."

"I still think it was a good sign he didn't jump in for her."

"You don't think it's rather a black mark on his character that he wouldn't jump into a river for a woman he's been courting for a year?" Catherine asks.

"I think Lady Rosalie was being high-handed and ridiculous, and he lost his temper. Men lose their sense when they lose their temper."

Catherine sucks on her cheek and looks over at Father. "If

Mother was at her most obstreperous, would you refuse to save her because she was being difficult?"

Father sighs and then looks to Mother. "Shall I lie, dearest?"

"Oh, stop," Mother says, shaking her head.

Father grins at Mother, and then winks at Catherine.

"As ridiculous as it was, your heroics rather endeared you to Mr. Dean. I think we might see his affections shift permanently onto your worthy shoulders," Mother says.

Catherine bristles. Her heroics were for Rosalie and Rosalie alone. For her smile, and her bright eyes, and her happy, slightly hysterical giggles. But she can't think too long about that or she'll start blushing, and it wouldn't do to look anything but lightly pathetic right now.

There's a soft knock on the door and Miss Teit enters with a small tray.

"Letters for you," she says, padding into the room to hand one to Father and the other to Catherine.

"Who are they from?" Mother asks.

Catherine takes hers, noting Christopher's familiar script. "Mr. Tisend."

"Mr. Dean," Father says at the same time.

Catherine looks up, surprised. Why would Mr. Dean be writing to Father?

"Why is the Tisend boy writing to her? Did you give permission for this?" Mother asks.

"I did," Father says as he opens the seal on Mr. Dean's letter.

Catherine hastily cracks Christopher's, determined to read it and, if need be, dispose of the evidence. Her letters are meant to be personal, especially if Father's given his permission for Christopher to write, but she wouldn't put it past Mother to try to intervene.

"He's clearly keen on the Linet girl. Playing it awfully fast to be writing to Catherine as well," Mother says shortly.

"I hardly think a few letters from Mr. Tisend will dissuade Catherine from your quest," Father says, glancing up at Catherine.

"Right," Catherine agrees, smiling innocently over at Mother.

"And it must bother Lady Tisend something fierce to know her son is writing to your daughter," Father adds.

Mother's lips twitch and Catherine withholds a sigh.

But her smugness at least gives Catherine enough cover to slip Rosalie's tightly folded message inside her pile of blankets and into her stays to read later. She wishes she could run upstairs and read it right now, but she'll settle for quickly scanning Christopher's missive.

"Mr. Tisend writes:

I hope you will accept my apologies on behalf of my sister for your untimely swim in the Avon this afternoon. It was not her intention to drag you into her frivolity, and we are both very sorry for your distress.

Please allow me to escort you on a promenade tomorrow in penance, and for the chance to see your delightful person.

With hopes and further apologies,
Mr. Tisend.

"That's kind of him, isn't it?" she asks Mother.

"Very kind, but you'll have to postpone," Father says.

Catherine looks over, surprised. She'd been counting on his encouragement.

"Mr. Dean has invited you to Sydney Gardens to hear a string quartet play tomorrow."

"Oh, well," Catherine starts.

"Write back and say yes," Mother tells Father. "And you needn't take the Tisend boy up on his offer. His sister did you a disservice. You aren't obligated to accept his apology on her behalf."

"What if I want to?" Catherine asks, frustrated and tired. Father's already penning a response to Mr. Dean.

"We ought not reward that girl's behavior," Mother says, frowning over at Catherine.

"Would you have just let Lady Tisend drown if she'd fallen into the river when you were my age, before everything happened?"

Mother's eyes widen. "I— It— You are not close friends with Lady Rosalie," she says tersely.

Mother has no idea how close they've become, but that truly shouldn't matter.

"You would have swum the Channel for Lady Tisend once upon a time," Father says softly, looking up from his letter.

Mother jerks her head to meet his eyes, frowning. Her father's talent for remaining calm and collected when tempers are high is one of his greatest strengths. Someone smiling serenely when you want to scream can been utterly maddening.

"Fine. You may allow the brother to apologize, but it needn't be a public outing," Mother says, her voice rough.

"But if I'm seen publicly with Mr. Tisend, especially after this . . ." Catherine trails off, swallowing hard. It's just a white lie. She can do this. "Especially after Lady Rosalie's antics, might it push Mr. Dean toward me if he's made jealous?"

She's playing along, see? She's buying into the scheme, into the revenge. Her stomach twists as Mother's shoulders come down. As she's placated by Catherine's lies. They used to always be on the same side. A team. Girls together. It does something funny to her insides to lie to her like this.

"One promenade. But tomorrow, you go to the concert with Mr. Dean."

"Yes, Mother," she says, smiling wide enough for it to hurt her cheeks. "I'll write to Mr. Tisend tonight."

Mother nods and then turns to stare into the fire, body still tense.

Catherine just needs to dispatch of Mr. Dean, then the largest of the lies can end. And then maybe her stomach won't feel so twisted, and she can do more than squeeze Rosalie's hand on the frigid river. Somehow.

WERE SHE JUST here to listen to the beautiful music, the dreary afternoon wouldn't seem so bad. They're standing to the right of the back patio of the Sydney Hotel on the soft grass. A grand orchestra has been set up in front of the hotel's solarium, and she's been deeply enjoying their performance of Mozart's twenty-ninth symphony.

But her legs are starting to ache, as is her back. She'd slouch, but Mother's directly behind her, and anytime she's so much as shifted, Mother's poked her with her fan.

It's made it exceedingly difficult to search the assembled crowd for Christopher's top hat. There's no chance of spotting tiny Rosalie among what must be half of Bath's ton. Each time she's tried to glance around, Mother's given her a look, encouraging her to make polite conversation with Mr. Dean.

He looks perfectly dapper today, in a clean gray suit with a shined top hat. But she doesn't want to engage in more conversation.

"You were most heroic."

"I was so impressed by your poise."

"It was kind of you to help Lady Rosalie, though we ought to discuss your skills of self-preservation."

Mother looks over the moon. Mr. Dean does seem further infatuated with her. How shocking that the only time she wasn't trying to gain his affection (or pretending to try for her mother's sake) is the only time he's given his praise, now, when she doesn't want anything to do with it.

Outside of discussing yesterday's events, he's spoken very little. That they both enjoy music might have charmed her earlier in the season, but now it's simply not enough.

She needs more from someone with whom she's supposed to share a life than a vague mutual interest in music and a beautiful physique. Looking at Mr. Dean doesn't do half as much for her as simply holding Rosalie's letter against her chest last night.

Her darling letter, hidden deep in Catherine's desk, still threatens to heat her cheeks.

Rosalie's beautiful looping script, her thanks for Catherine's heroics and her admission of how much it meant to her that Catherine jumped in to save her, when no one else did, made Catherine grin. Her sly words about how lovely Catherine looked sopping wet, and how much she wanted to rip Catherine's clothes off and huddle with her by the fire—

Suddenly everyone is clapping and Catherine realizes the concert has ended while she's been lost in daydreams of Rosalie.

Mr. Dean has her arm and Mother's on her other side before she can blink, already walking her toward the exit to leave the park and head home. So much for intelligent discussion of the concert. The viola was flat the entire time. Doesn't anyone care?

More importantly, she hasn't seen Christopher. She can't leave until he and Rosalie find her.

Mother's pace increases. They must be close and Mother's intentionally trying to keep them apart.

She finally spots them about eight couples back. Rosalie raises her hand. She looks so beautiful, in a light pink gown with a white spencer jacket, her dark hair curling around her face beneath her pink bonnet. She's all smiles, waving far too enthusiastically.

Catherine has to snap her gaze forward as Mother practically yanks her ahead, dragging Mr. Dean with them. He looks entirely unperturbed, which is frankly maddening.

She needs to stall. "Do you know where the stones for the hotel were quarried?" she asks Mr. Dean, slowing her pace to force him to look down at her.

"I don't," he says with a shrug.

"Do you think . . . it was difficult to construct in the rain?"

"Not sure," Mr. Dean replies.

Usually, architecture is an excellent bet with Mr. Dean. She's heard him discuss it before with Christopher, and at the balls.

"Did you notice that the violist was a bit flat?" she asks, really dragging her heels. Enough for Mother to sigh at her.

"I didn't," Mr. Dean says affably.

Now she knows how Rosalie must have felt on the boat. You can't get a rise out of this man for anything.

Nothing else for it. Catherine blows out a breath and trips over absolutely nothing, careening forward so that Mr. Dean and Mother have to catch her.

"I'm so sorry," she says. People bump into them as they get her back to standing, now fully stopped in the middle of the path.

"Young ladies do seem to be particularly clumsy," Mr. Dean mutters, holding her arm steady. "Are you all right? Do you need to sit?"

"No, no, I'm fine," Catherine says quickly.

"Miss Pine, are you quite all right?" Rosalie calls, dragging Christopher up to them.

"I'm really just fine," Catherine repeats, turning to smile at her. Thank Christ. "Just overwhelmed by the beauty of the music and the architecture. The hotel really is striking, isn't it?"

"I was thinking the very same thing," Christopher says, tipping his cap to her and her mother. "Mrs. Pine, I hope you're very well."

"I am," Mother says tightly. "Though rather tired."

"I hope you weren't up all night with chills, Miss Pine," Rosalie says quickly. "I am so dreadfully sorry that my actions put you in danger. And I'm so sorry, Mrs. Pine, about the damage done to her dress. Mother and I would be happy to replace it."

Mother looks like she's swallowed something sour, but forces a smile. "That is kind, but deeply unnecessary, thank you."

Rosalie looks back at Catherine. "And you're sure you're all right?"

"Just fine," Catherine assures her, trying not to laugh. She can't tell how much of Rosalie's words are true or just to keep them stalled there. "In warmer weather it might actually have been fun."

Mr. Dean scoffs and Catherine suddenly remembers he's still standing next to her. Still holding her arm at that.

"It was a ridiculous and dangerous stunt no matter the weather."

"I'm really fine—"

Mr. Dean squeezes her arm. "You might strain to consider

the effect your lapses in judgment can have on others more often, Lady Rosalie. To think of anyone other than yourself and your frivolous whims. Miss Pine did you an act of service, showing only her generosity and magnanimous personality."

So there is some kind of fire, some kind of personality, hiding beneath all of those manners and blithe disregard. And it's *ugly*.

She can't let Mr. Dean talk to Rosalie that way. Even if they weren't—whatever they are—she'd want to defend her. No one talks to her friends like that. And certainly no one gets to talk to her lover like that.

"While I . . . appreciate your fervor, Mr. Dean, I don't hold any ill will toward Lady Rosalie and think she showed great consideration in making sure I got out of the river first."

Rosalie's wide eyes slowly find Catherine's and her lips quirk upward, while Christopher just grins over at her.

"You are too polite," Mr. Dean says with a sigh. "But if you can kindly forgive such foolishness, who am I to argue? Lady Rosalie, I apologize for my harsh words."

His mood swings could give a person a sore neck.

"Thank you, Mr. Dean," Rosalie says, her voice a bit high.

"That said, I must take my leave. If I may escort you and your mother home?" Mr. Dean asks.

"Oh, well," Catherine starts.

"You may," Mother says over her. "Mr. Tisend, Lady Rosalie, we have a dinner to attend. Good day."

Catherine looks worriedly at Rosalie, who stares back, equally at sea while Mr. Dean and Mother turn Catherine around. This wasn't the plan. She wasn't supposed to—what, impress him by having decency? She didn't *do* anything!

She glances over her shoulder as Mr. Dean escorts them away, doubt creeping up her spine. Rosalie and Christopher watch them go, Christopher's arm coming up around Rosalie's shoulders.

Who knew basic human decency was Mr. Dean's seemingly only soft spot? Especially as she's no longer sure he's all that decent himself. Who says such things in a public park? And then changes their opinion in just a moment? Does he have no conviction?

Worse, what if his only conviction is asking her to marry him?

Chapter Nineteen

Rosalie

In any other world, if a man spoke to her the way Mr. Dean did last week, she'd never see him again. And yet here they are in her parents' foyer, smiling stiffly.

She'd entirely forgotten about the concert her mother agreed to nearly two months ago. Lord Dean has paid for an afternoon of music at the Upper Rooms with a small string ensemble and a few opera singers. Father says it should be very good.

Which would be nice, after the bitter ending to the concert last week, if Mr. Dean wasn't the one who ruined the afternoon, and if he didn't look so thoroughly unhappy to be escorting her today.

She should be celebrating the demise of his affections, but she can't. Mother's been worrying all week. Amalie's mother and two other society matrons swore that Mr. Dean has made nearly daily house calls to the Pine residence since the concert. He's gotten to be there every day, and Rosalie and Catherine haven't so much as seen each other in the last week.

All she's gotten are two rushed letters in Catherine's tidy script. And no matter how lovely, and frankly dirty, they're no substitute for real time spent together.

If nothing else, the time apart and the constant yearning feeling that's almost like a physical ache is proving to Rosalie that what she feels for Catherine is real, and lasting, and fervid. She thinks she's feeling the way you ought to feel about your betrothed.

Which is wonderful, and terrifying, and altogether very confusing.

To be one hundred percent sure, she'd need to have time to spend with the woman, instead of being ferried about by Mother, shopping and primping and listening to her constant worry about the betrothal Rosalie absolutely doesn't want.

Mother was so excited about the concert today. About Rosalie's big, important opportunity to win back Mr. Dean's favor after her deplorable behavior on the punting outing. Father even came back from London to attend.

Mother thinks Mr. Dean writing to confirm he would escort her to their previously agreed-upon outing is a good sign, but one look at his pinched face and blank eyes proves otherwise. But a gentleman doesn't go back on his word, so even if it's clear to everyone in the room that there won't be another outing after this, here they are.

"I hear the ensemble your father has assembled is the best of the season," Mother says, her voice unnaturally high.

"Father does have excellent taste," Mr. Dean replies. Rosalie thinks he's not even meeting her mother's eyes. "He unfortunately won't be able to attend, however. He's taken ill."

"Oh, I do hope it's not serious," Mother says.

"No, no, the doctors are optimistic, but, given that he cannot attend, we should—"

"Quite right," Father says, gesturing to Mr. Dean to lead the way out of the house.

The carriage ride is a stilted nightmare. And standing at the doors to the dance hall in the Upper Rooms, her arm looped through Mr. Dean's as they bow and curtsy to an endless line of acquaintances, is somehow even worse than she imagined.

"What a lovely couple you make," Lady Hanting says, smiling as she steps up to them.

Mr. Dean doesn't even acknowledge the statement, merely bowing his head.

"Thank you, Lady Hanting," Rosalie says softly, hoping her voice comes out calm and polite. "We hope you enjoy the concert."

"Oh, I always enjoy an event thrown by the viscount. So sorry to hear he won't be in attendance. But I'm sure he'll be very proud of his son, and his potential new daughter-in-law."

"Thank you, Lady Hanting," Mr. Dean says curtly.

Lady Hanting blinks, glancing between them, before she gives Mr. Dean her own false smile. "Yes, thank you, Mr. Dean. Lady Rosalie," she adds, her eyes a bit narrowed, as if in pity.

Rosalie watches Lady Hanting walk away, feeling a weight come off her shoulders. For so long, she'd been preparing herself for a calm, vaguely disinterested life with Mr. Dean. To find that the only emotions beneath his apathetic façade are ugly and rude, abrupt and mean-spirited—she has more to thank Catherine for than she realized.

"Mr. Dean, may I borrow my daughter for a moment?" Mother asks, appearing at Rosalie's elbow.

How many people has she greeted while thinking about Catherine? Lovely, beautiful, just-arriving Catherine. She can see her at the end of the receiving line, wearing a lovely green dress with lace gloves, her hair braided delicately over the top of her head, tendrils falling against her sharp cheekbones.

"Are you intentionally trying to lose his favor?" Mother hisses, yanking Rosalie away from the doors.

Rosalie tears her eyes away from Catherine. Mr. Dean's still greeting people as if she hasn't moved. Like she was nothing but a column beside him this whole time. Rosalie turns to Mother, pushing confidence to the front of her mind. *Yes.*

"Not at all. I was simply greeting guests."

"He hasn't so much as spoken to you this entire time, and the guests inside are saying he's angry with you."

"I don't know how they'd know," Rosalie says honestly. Sure, they're not talking, but how different is that from their old normal, really?

"Well, fix it," Mother insists. "Before that Pine girl reaches him."

"I don't think there's any fixing it," Rosalie hears herself say, watching the way Mr. Dean notices Catherine at the end of the line. That perpetual look of annoyance melts off his handsome stupid face. He's standing straighter, his face brighter—

"Go," Mother says, practically shoving Rosalie toward the doors.

Rosalie goes, slipping back in beside Mr. Dean. But he doesn't even glance at her, or acknowledge Mr. and Mrs. Leon, thanking him and his father for hosting the event.

Rosalie's relief curdles into dread the closer Catherine and her parents get to the entryway. Rosalie's free of Mr. Dean, regardless of what happens next. But Catherine's not free yet.

Whether she and Catherine figure out a way to live together forever, or for a time, or whatever they want—*forever*, Rosalie thinks, unbidden—Catherine surely cannot marry this man.

This man who so openly regards another woman while standing next to the one he's courted for a year, grinning as Catherine and her parents step up to them, the last in line, everyone else already inside and seated for the concert. Given how smug Mrs. Pine looks, Rosalie wonders if that wasn't her plan all along.

"Miss Pine, Mr. and Mrs. Pine, how wonderful of you to join us. Come, I have seats all saved for us," Mr. Dean says.

"So lovely to see you," Rosalie says quickly, smiling at Catherine.

"And you as well," Catherine agrees, her smile forced but eyes bright. "Mr. Dean, thank you for the invitation," she adds, turning her head a moment after her words, like she's having trouble looking away from Rosalie.

"We ought to go in," Mrs. Pine says. "Wouldn't want to delay the performance."

"Of course," Mr. Dean says, stepping away from Rosalie to offer his arm to Catherine.

Catherine glances at Rosalie askance. He really is just going to abandon Rosalie in public like that. Walk into the hall with a different woman on his arm. A full, emphatic dismissal.

Rosalie wouldn't mind. But Mother's jaw has dropped.

"Let's all go in together," Catherine says quickly, stepping to the side to take Rosalie's arm.

Mother's jaw snaps up, Mrs. Pine glowers, Mr. Dean looks surprised and not much else. And Mr. Pine . . . well, Mr. Pine is chuckling into his handkerchief.

Catherine's arm is warm against hers, skin to skin, both of them in small kid gloves. Catherine starts walking, forcing Mr. Dean to hurry ahead to lead them inside.

"Catherine," Rosalie hears Mrs. Pine hiss as they follow him.

Catherine holds fast to Rosalie's arm. "Can you believe him?" she whispers.

"You made a late entrance," Rosalie hears her mother say.

"And you a very early one," Mrs. Pine counters.

"Well, we arrived with Mr. Dean," Mother replies. "He escorted my Rosalie."

"Only because my Catherine is too polite to let him make his preferences plain," Mrs. Pine says quickly.

"Dearest, let's focus on the concert," Mr. Pine pipes up as they walk toward the waiting sets of chairs facing an erected podium where a small string orchestra waits.

He really was planning to leave Rosalie to walk all the way through the audience after he'd escorted Catherine inside.

"What a jerk," Catherine whispers as they sit down, Catherine next to Mr. Dean on the aisle, Rosalie on her other side.

Rosalie withholds a laugh, reluctantly letting go of Catherine's arm so they can get settled. But Catherine stays close, their shoulders pressed together while Mother sits on Rosalie's other side.

Rosalie doesn't know where her father is, and Catherine's parents have settled across the aisle from them. What a tableau they must make to the ton. At least there's an hour of music and Catherine's wonderful warm presence between her and that pathetic public scrutiny.

Mother's leg jiggles beside her. Rosalie looks over at her and finds her jaw tight, eyes shining. She's twisting her hands together in her lap hard enough for her gloves to go taut. She keeps turning her head, glancing back into the rest of the audience.

Rosalie does the same and realizes mothers all over the room are glancing at them, speaking behind their fans, more focused on Rosalie and her mother than the beautiful concerto.

Rosalie knew getting Mr. Dean to forsake her would be a challenge, and she rose to the occasion. But now there's a price being paid that she didn't consider.

What there is of Mother's social life might hang in the balance of her own happiness. She's so proud of their position in Bath. And in one short boating trip Rosalie totally upended the careful balance her mother has spent her life achieving.

"My mother looks deranged," Catherine whispers against Rosalie's ear.

Rosalie nearly jumps in her seat. Mother glances at her and Rosalie fakes a shiver with a tight smile. Mother doesn't react, her eyes a little glazed over.

Rosalie turns in the other direction, looking over toward Mrs. Pine and Mr. Pine. Mrs. Pine does look a bit triumphant, almost maniacal.

"Going swimmingly, isn't it?" Rosalie whispers back.

Catherine's lips twitch up and Rosalie goes back to watching the concert, trying to enjoy the brief respite of Catherine against her.

She hopes she'll come up with something clever to protect her mother's reputation, to save Catherine from a terrible marriage—to give herself the chance to spend a potential forever with her lover. But when the concert ends, Rosalie's no closer to a mastermind plan. All she has is a desperate urge to somehow fix everything.

"Lady Rosalie, might you fetch yourself and Miss Pine a refreshment?" Mr. Dean asks as they step away from the chairs so the attendants can clear the hall for mingling.

A month ago, Rosalie would have balked, but now she goes gratefully, exchanging a look with Catherine, who rolls her eyes, her head turned away from Mr. Dean even as he takes her arm. Short of Catherine throwing food on Mr. Dean, Rosalie's not sure what they can do to deter him. Even Mother wanders away from Mr. Dean, hopefully in search of Rosalie's father, since everyone seems to be giving her a wide berth.

Rosalie grabs a plate and a few finger sandwiches and pastries, enough to share with Catherine and Mr. Dean. He may be publicly dissing her, but she's not about to leave him alone with Catherine.

It's only when she's walking back to the two of them, now standing in a group of Mr. Dean's friends, does Rosalie notice that not one person has stopped to talk with her. It's the first time she's crossed a room without interruption . . . ever. She doesn't know if she's relieved or concerned.

She steps gratefully into the circle on Catherine's other side. Everyone in the circle gives her a confused look.

"The cucumber is on the left," Rosalie tells Catherine.

Mr. Dean reaches across Catherine and grabs that exact sandwich without even looking at her, which raises more than one eyebrow around them.

"Thank you, Lady Rosalie," Catherine says, a little overloud. "Very generous of you to think of both of us."

"Of course," Rosalie says with a bright, forced smile. "Good to see you all, gentlemen," she adds to the circle.

A hoarse, loud cough startles everyone. Rosalie looks over to find Mr. Dean's eyes wide, his hand scrabbling at his throat. The greedy, rude jerk is choking on a cucumber sandwich, how gauche.

Then his eyes start bulging.

"Mr. Dean," Catherine says, grabbing what's left of his sandwich and shoving it back onto Rosalie's plate while everyone else just stands there. "Mr. Dean, can you breathe?"

Mr. Dean shakes his head, his cheeks going red as he coughs to no avail.

"Call a doctor," Rosalie hears herself say.

WHACK. Catherine's hand comes down on Mr. Dean's back, forcing him to bend at the waist. He coughs, but nothing comes out. Catherine whacks him again, her open-palmed slap ringing around them as everyone in the room turns to watch.

Rosalie looks to the grown men across from them, just staring at Mr. Dean and Catherine, eyes wide, disgust and confusion smattering their useless faces.

"One of you go call a doctor," Rosalie insists.

She's asking for help, and no one's doing *anything.* There's just the horrible sound of Catherine thumping Mr. Dean, and the gurgling of his rasping breath—

Catherine brings her fist down on his back with a mighty *thwump* and Mr. Dean finally coughs out his bite. It falls with a splat as he gasps in air, Catherine's hand still on his back, his face almost purple.

"Oh, Mr. Dean, are you all right?"

Mrs. Pine's voice rings around the silent hall. She appears on his other side, her hand falling to rest next to Catherine's, her other hand grasping his arm.

"Catherine, thank goodness for your quick thinking," Mrs. Pine continues.

Rosalie watches Catherine stand stiff in shock, her eyes large and bright. Rosalie loosens her own grip on her plate. Mr. Dean slowly stands up, leaning into Mrs. Pine and Catherine.

"Yes," he says, his voice rough, breath still ragged. "Miss Pine, I owe you my life. How can I ever thank you enough?"

Catherine looks at Mr. Dean askance, cheeks going pale. "I—I simply did what anyone would—"

"Let's find you a seat and some water, Mr. Dean," Mrs. Pine

interrupts, looking far too smug. "Come, Catherine, dear, help me get him settled."

Rosalie watches, helpless, as Mrs. Pine brings them across the room to a bench on the far side, fawning over Mr. Dean the whole way. Catherine glances back at Rosalie, looking just as stricken as she feels.

What now?

Chapter Twenty

Catherine

A delivery for you, Miss Pine."

Catherine looks up from where she's been pushing porridge around in her bowl to find their valet, Mr. Archer, standing in the doorway to the dining room holding the largest floral arrangement she's ever seen. He totters into the room, depositing the enormous vase beside her place setting.

"And the *Chronicle*, sir," Mr. Archer adds, a little breathless, handing the paper to Father.

Catherine stares up at the giant arrangement. The flowers are a riot of color, peonies and roses and hydrangeas all vying for beautiful attention. She stands slowly, noticing a card sticking out from the top of the bouquet. A bizarre hope rises in her chest, but Rosalie wouldn't have sent these. They're gorgeous, but far too showy for her taste. And it would raise a number of questions she's not yet ready to answer.

Upon seeing the tidy script on the card she knows immediately they're not from Rosalie. Worse, when she breaks the seal, she finds a note from Mr. Dean.

My dearest Miss Pine,

Please accept these flowers as simply the beginning of my thanks for your quick-witted heroics. Were it not for you,

I would be lying among these flowers today. I owe you my life.

Generations of Dean heirs and their wives thank you. My mother would thank you, as would hers; both of them were strong, quick-witted women, like yourself. They would be most gratified to know that the Dean line will not end with me, thanks to you.

The card goes on, but Catherine stops reading, all that hope turning leaden in her stomach. He's just being self-aggrandizing, speaking about his family. His favorite topic. It can't—it can't be more than that, surely.

"Who are they from?" Mother asks, far too close.

Catherine jumps and Mother plucks the card from her hands. She looks to Father for help, but he's peering at the paper, totally oblivious.

"Mother, it's not—" Catherine starts.

"Darling, you've got him," Mother says, beaming at her, the letter clutched to her chest. "He wants you to be the next Dean woman. To bear his heirs!"

"He does what?" Father asks, looking up from the paper, Catherine caught between them and her rapidly growing nausea.

"Mr. Dean has written to thank Catherine for saving his life and here, look here," Mother says, rounding Catherine to thrust the letter under Father's nose. "He'll propose by the end of the month, I'm sure of it."

Catherine's tempted to smash the vase to the floor and run out of the room. Damn it all to hell. All she did was save him from choking. Any reasonable person would have. If Mr. Dean had been less focused on being absolutely atrocious to Rosalie, maybe he wouldn't have choked at all.

Father looks up and meets her eyes. "He wasn't the only one impressed," he says, passing her the paper while Mother leans over his shoulder, pointing to the note.

Catherine takes the *Chronicle* with trembling hands. What on earth does that mean?

She scans the front page, moving down to the notations of the weekly events. And there, staring up at her in print:

At the Dean concert held yesterday at the Upper Rooms, great commotion was seen when the young Mr. Dean, standing in as host for his father, appeared to choke on a small finger sandwich. He was promptly saved from asphyxiation by the quick action of the object of his rumored affection, one Miss Pine. New to Bath, not much has been ascertained about the young Miss Pine, but surely now the ton knows the measure of her mettle as one poised, quick-thinking, and heroic young woman.

"Oh, my dear, you'll be the talk of the town! We must arrange a meeting presently, somewhere very public."

Catherine jumps again, Mother now staring over her shoulder. She passes her the paper and shifts down the table, hiding her face in her enormous collection of flowers.

She didn't want to impress anyone. She didn't want to attract attention. She didn't mean to make Mr. Dean fall for her, or worship her. He was just choking. She would have done the same for anyone. Mother, Lady Tisend, Rosalie—

Catherine shudders at the very thought of whacking Rosalie like that. The image of her in the river still hasn't left Catherine. She was perfectly fine then, and Catherine's still had nightmares of her drowning. Now she supposes she'll be adding bleak visions of Rosalie choking to her repertoire.

"That was very quick thinking on your part," Father says, pulling Catherine from her spiraling thoughts.

"It wasn't worthy of all of this," Catherine says, feeling a little relieved when Father gives her an understanding smile. "It shouldn't be so heroic to help someone."

"People are naturally cruel," Mother says. "Which makes you stand out even more for your kindness."

Mother's still staring down at Mr. Dean's note, pacing behind Father's chair.

"Do you really believe that?" Catherine asks. "That people are naturally spiteful?"

Mother looks up at her, her face going soft too. They're both looking at her like they did when she was a child with a wild fancy.

"People rarely choose to help others when given the chance in a place like this," Mother says gently.

Catherine forces herself to nod and sit back down. She stares into her porridge, thinking about how Christopher jumped at the chance to help Catherine and Rosalie. How Amalie and Henrietta take every opportunity they can to talk Rosalie up, to invite Catherine into their friendship. How Lady Jones so kindly invited her to join them at Blaise Castle.

People aren't inherently selfish. At least, not all people.

"Well, we should all go get ready for the baths, should we not?" Father suggests.

Catherine nods, leaving Mr. Dean's letter on the table, as if she can leave him behind for the day as well.

The soaking dress Mother and Miss Teit help her into is hardly the most fetching. Made of the same brown linen as Father's soaking suit, it hangs simply on her frame, weighted down by the small iron pieces sewn into the hem to keep her modest. Mother and Miss Teit slip a tailored brown jacket over her shoulders as well, which lightly accentuates her waist.

She looks just like any other woman on her way to bathe, until Mother reveals the most ridiculous bonnet, done in white and blue with an enormous gray feather. Catherine will look like a drowned peacock.

Rosalie would adore seeing her in this monstrosity. She'd laugh and laugh.

Not that Catherine would even be able to find her once they're at the baths. The vaulted stone bath chamber is full of gently rising mist, members of the ton floating in and out of sight in their own silly hats and wigs. It's impossible to see anything distinctly.

Catherine walks down the entry steps carefully, grimacing as the warm water rises up her costume, sticking it to her legs and pressing in. She breathes slowly in the steam, unnerved by the murmur of unidentified voices.

She follows Father as he wades across the expansive bath, heading to his favorite perch where they'll sit and nibble on the little bowl of nuts Catherine's clutching hard above the water. She knows the copper bowl will float, but she never trusts it. She tries to relax, just a little, and take comfort in the anonymity of the steam.

That is until Mr. and Mrs. Pilney pop out of nowhere. "We must congratulate you, Mr. Pine, on your most remarkable daughter," Mr. Pilney says, his round face red and sweating.

Mrs. Pilney nods rapidly, her own rather extravagant blue bonnet bobbing precariously close to the water. "Such quick thinking."

Catherine grimaces a smile.

"We are most proud of her," Father agrees, while Mother beams beside her, her curls already going limp beneath her less-ostentatious bonnet.

Catherine tries to focus on how comfortable Father seems, standing in the warm water. On how much better he's been doing since they came to Bath.

"What a compliment to your house," another gentleman says, stepping up on Father's other side. "I hope Mr. Dean has written to thank her."

Catherine's shoulders are steadily climbing toward her ears, discomfort swirling in her stomach.

"He has," Mother says quickly. "And sent an enormous bouquet of flowers."

"Oh, how lovely," Mrs. Pilney crows.

Catherine looks around as more and more of the bathers seem to take note of them, rushing over to compliment her parents. With the hot, sulphureous steam, the sweat dripping down her neck, the warm water pressing on her clothes—she's starting to hyperventilate.

"Mr. Pine, might I have a word?"

Catherine turns, surprised and almost relieved to see Mr. Sholle pop up beside Father.

"Of course," Father says, wading to the side, which only closes the crowd in further around Catherine and Mother.

Catherine turns her head, just able to hear as Mr. Sholle leans closer to Father. "I realize Miss Pine's attentions have fallen elsewhere and simply wanted to make known that I formally rescind my intentions to court her. I would not want to compete with a friend in Mr. Dean, nor foist unwanted attentions on your dear daughter, but neither did I want you to wonder why I have made myself so scarce."

Father says something inaudible. Catherine's stomach roils. Mr. Sholle is formally withdrawing his courtship, like the rumors about Mr. Dean's imminent proposal mean she is somehow already his property.

Anger slithers up her spine. She wants to snap that she is the only person who should be deciding whether or not she gets courted. What right does Mr. Sholle have to decide this on her behalf?

Not that she wants him to court her either. But still. They're all acting like she's a prize, complimenting her parents. As if it's their accomplishment that she . . . did the simply decent thing and prevented a man from choking.

"Mr. Tisend will rescind next, you mark my words," Mother whispers, turning her head toward Catherine, even as she smiles to someone on her other side.

Catherine stands there, hands curling into fists below the water, the bowl of nuts bobbing on the surface in front of her. Mr. Sholle shakes her smiling father's hand and looks back at her once before wading away. Didn't even bother to say goodbye to her, after pursuing her for two months.

Is she worth so little to everyone but Rosalie?

She tries to take a deep breath, tries to remind herself that Rosalie *is* fighting for her—for a chance to be with her and figure out what would come next. And Christopher is helping. There are still people on her side. People who see her as more than a prize to be given from parents to husband.

"Oh, is that the lovely young Miss Pine?"

Catherine turns to find Mrs. Raught coming out of the steam, dragging Henrietta behind her. Thank Christ, a friendly face. Maybe she can escape this and sit with Henrietta until she no longer wants to use her fists to push everyone away.

"Hello," Catherine says, her voice high and rough. "Mrs. Raught, Miss Raught," she adds, dipping in a little curtsy that sets the copper bowl rocking again.

"Would you mind if I stole Miss Pine for a moment?" Henrietta asks Mother.

"Of course, of course," Mother says, obviously distracted by the three other mothers vying for her attention.

Henrietta takes her hand and Catherine gratefully follows Henrietta through the water, excited to find herself in a far corner where Amalie is already waiting. They're both in the same brown soaking dresses, but Amalie's bonnet is rimmed with green ribbon, Henrietta's with her signature yellow.

"So, is it true?" Henrietta asks, ushering Catherine to sit on the vee created by the ledge.

Henrietta and Amalie sit on either side of her, close and tight. She's so grateful to see them, even as she's disappointed Rosalie isn't hiding back here too. She doesn't feel squished or trapped at all now.

"Is what true?"

"It's all over town that Mr. Dean will be proposing within a few weeks."

Catherine gapes at Henrietta. "What?"

"Our mothers both heard that he'd sent an enormous bouquet with a letter of intentions for your father," Amalie says.

Catherine looks askance between them. "How do you know that already?"

"So it's true?" Henrietta asks, her voice squeaky.

"He sent a bouquet, but not a letter of intention," Catherine corrects.

"But he did send a card with the flowers," Amalie presses.

Catherine sighs, tipping her head back to look up at the ceiling. She's getting a headache, whether from the close, damp air or the stress of the morning. "He sent a card thanking me for saving his life, that's all. He didn't ask my father anything, and my father and Lord Dean haven't had any conversations of which I'm aware."

"That's good," Amalie says.

Catherine raises her head to meet her eyes. "Is it?"

"Rosalie would be devastated," Henrietta puts in.

Catherine blinks. Do they—oh. Right. Yes. She and Rosalie are fighting over Mr. Dean. Amalie and Henrietta—Rosalie's closest friends—don't know anything about anything . . . else.

"I'm sure she's not, seeing as nothing has actually happened," Catherine says, trying to sound casual.

"Well, her mother certainly will be," Henrietta says.

"You're probably right about that. But I'm sure Lady Rosalie won't be upset."

"I'm sure she won't either," Amalie says. "As least she won't if you haven't said yes to him."

"I haven't," Catherine insists. "There's nothing to say yes to. There won't be," slips out unbidden.

"You're sure?" Amalie asks, her green eyes sharp, gaze somehow too knowing.

Does Amalie know? Christopher wouldn't tell her, not unless Rosalie gave him permission. Would he?

Catherine and Rosalie have been spending all their page space being gushy. She hasn't thought to ask about Rosalie's friends.

Her own friends.

"I'm sure," Catherine tells Amalie.

"Well, you might want to tell Mr. Dean that," Amalie says simply.

"And Rosalie," Henrietta adds from her other side.

"Lady Rosalie already knows," Catherine says.

"Discussed it on the trip to Blaise Castle I've heard nothing about, did you?" Amalie asks.

Catherine meets her eyes and wonders if perhaps she and Rosalie haven't been as subtle as they thought. But she can't be the one to tell them. They *are* her friends, but Rosalie should tell them. If she hasn't already told them. God, she and Rosalie need to meet.

"Enough about Mr. Dean choking on a sandwich. Tell me about Mr. Rile," Catherine says, turning away from Amalie's knowing gaze to look at Henrietta. Who is blushing already.

"Well, Mr. Dean may not have made his intentions clear, but Mr. Rile has. He spoke with my father yesterday, and I think he might propose on the weekend," Henrietta says, her pretty, round face breaking into an enormous grin.

"And you let me go on about Mr. Dean?" Catherine scolds, reaching out to take her hands in genuine excitement. "How wonderful. I'm so happy for you!"

"Thank you," Henrietta says brightly. "My parents are elated."

"And you?" Catherine asks immediately.

"Yes, are *you* happy?" Amalie asks, shifting closer on Catherine's other side.

"I am," Henrietta says, almost dreamily. "So happy."

"Good," Catherine says.

"If he hurts you, I will lance him with Mr. Tisend's saber," Amalie says.

"Have some real access to that saber, do you?" Catherine can't help but ask.

Amalie chuckles. "I have more access than you know."

"Amalie!" Henrietta shrieks, sending them all into giggles.

Catherine lets herself get lost in their gentle teasing. She pretends for one blissful hour that people aren't watching her. That Mr. Dean isn't intent on proposing like Mr. Rile is. Pretends for just an hour that her precarious plans with Rosalie aren't going wildly, spectacularly off track.

Chapter Twenty-One
Rosalie

Everywhere they've been this morning, she's heard the whispers. Titters about how Mr. Dean has forsaken her. Snickers of how he's mere weeks, if not just days, away from proposing to Catherine. Snide remarks about her mother hidden by fans and bonnet rims.

Only Aunt Genevieve, walking tall and going on loudly about her latest travels has kept Mother from breaking into pieces. Rosalie's clung to her stories all day, desperate to ignore the cacophony of anxiety in her head.

Because she and Catherine haven't seen each other in days, and haven't managed to exchange even a single letter. Amalie and Henrietta saw Catherine at the baths, but Amalie says she overheard Mrs. Pine's schedule and it's jam-packed until next weekend, when the Pines are throwing their tea party at the Upper Rooms.

Mr. Dean might be polishing up his late grandmother's ring as they speak. And Rosalie's stomach might eat through her body.

Mother's planning to walk into that tea with her head held high. She still believes Rosalie can win Mr. Dean back with a large enough show of wealth. She can't. But neither can Rosalie take Mother's fragile hope.

So here they are, adding needless embellishment to their dresses, huddled together in the sitting area outside the dressing room in Madame Florent's shop.

"I would bet creams and blues. With Miss Pine's complexion, it would be the most complementary," Aunt Genevieve continues.

"What would?" Rosalie asks, having lost the thread of her eighth question about décor for the tea, of which Rosalie and Mother know nothing at all.

"A cream-and-blue color scheme would go nicely with her skin, and her eyes," Aunt Genevieve says. "For the tea, or a wedding, I suppose."

"There won't be a wedding," Mother bites out.

Rosalie barely withholds her own snapped retort. There just can't be a wedding. They need more *time*.

"Mrs. Pine seems awfully determined," Aunt Genevieve says, her voice slightly lilting, like she's intentionally needling them.

"Well, of course she is. She wants to ruin my life," Mother snaps.

Rosalie sighs. She's so sick of this stupid feud. Whatever happened—

"Explain," Aunt Genevieve says.

Rosalie turns to look at her, surprised. "You don't know?"

"Know what?" Aunt Genevieve asks, face turning serious. "I figured the two of you had just gotten competitive," she adds, looking to Mother.

"We can't discuss this here," Mother says quickly.

Aunt Genevieve raises a sculpted eyebrow. "Madame Florent had to go by carriage to get your lace. We've easily thirty uninterrupted minutes. Explain."

Mother shrugs. "It's just competition. Mrs. Pine made up her mind that she had to have Mr. Dean for her daughter, and we've let her win. She must be beside herself with triumph."

Rosalie looks between them. If anyone can get the secret out of Mother, it'll be Aunt Genevieve. It has to be. This might be her only opportunity.

"It's not merely competition," Rosalie says.

"Rosalie," Mother warns.

Rosalie turns to Aunt Genevieve. "She won't tell me *why*, but Mother prevented Mrs. Pine from marrying a man. A naval captain? Back when they were young. And it ended in scandal, and because of *that*, Mrs. Pine arrived determined to sabotage my marriage prospects."

Rosalie waits, expecting Aunt Genevieve to lay into Mother. Expecting her to make some sarcastic remark. To make light of Mother's feud. To call her out. Something.

Instead, Aunt Genevieve's eyes go wide. Rosalie forgets, sometimes, that Aunt Genevieve is five years younger than her mother. But in this moment, she can see every one of those years on her face, and something clicks sickeningly into place.

"Why didn't you tell me?" Aunt Genevieve asks Mother.

Rosalie's stomach turns over. She never would have— She would have been more tactful— Oh, God, it was—

"Did he hurt you?" Rosalie whispers.

Aunt Genevieve blinks and meets her eyes. The smile on her face is a cracking thing, but she takes a breath and reaches out to take Rosalie's hand. "No, darling. I—I let him charm me, and seduce me, but he was— My honor was ruined, but I wasn't hurt."

"I . . ." Rosalie starts, her words curdling in her throat as she hangs on to Aunt Genevieve's hand.

"Your father got me out of Bath, and no one ever knew. And then a few years later I met your uncle. Everything—everything turned out for the best."

Rosalie tries to divine the truth of her words just from her soft smile. Being cast out of your life because a man made promises and didn't keep them—she doesn't think that ever goes away.

"You understand now why I couldn't tell Mrs. Pine."

Rosalie turns her head to meet Mother's shining eyes.

"You never told her?" Aunt Genevieve asks.

Mother leans around Rosalie, her hand falling to rest on Aunt Genevieve's on top of Rosalie's, so they're a close press of sniffles and shaking breath.

"I promised your brother I wouldn't. I trusted her, but he—he asked me not to tell, and I couldn't break his confidence. I wanted—we wanted—to protect you."

"So you let the ton think he'd ruined *her* instead?" Aunt Genevieve presses.

"I made sure he couldn't ruin her," Mother insists. "And your brother convinced Mr. Pine to propose. It all . . . worked out for the best," Mother says, conviction in her words. "You were safe, she was safe."

"And he got away, again," Aunt Genevieve says.

"What would you have had me do? Tell the ton he'd ruined you and needed to pay for his crimes? Your reputation could never have recovered," Mother says plaintively.

"Surely there could have been—"

"The haberdashery up the street had the perfect sample," Madame Florent announces, flouncing into the shop, the front door tinkling behind her.

Her words land like an icy breeze. Mother scoots back from

Rosalie, and Aunt Genevieve wipes discreetly at her eyes before Madame Florent walks into the seating area.

"Wonderful," Mother says. "Thank you so much. I'll change first, shall I?"

She stands and lets Madame Florent lead her into the fitting room, leaving Rosalie and Aunt Genevieve sitting alone.

"I—" Rosalie starts.

Aunt Genevieve shakes her head. "Later."

Rosalie meets her eyes, wanting to argue, but the anguish on her face stops her cold. "Uncle Walter mentioned you're planting a garden at the estate. What are you having planted?" she asks instead.

Two hours later, Rosalie's stomach is hot with anxiety and she can tell Mother's getting a headache. Aunt Genevieve's personal sitting room is a comfort. Rosalie stares around at the bright paintings of floral gardens and lets herself sink into Aunt Genevieve's worn cream settee. Mother settles in the blue armchair and they sit, waiting, while Aunt Genevieve paces at the end of the low table between the other settee and Rosalie's perch.

"When I came back to Bath, married, why didn't you write to her?" Aunt Genevieve asks.

"She wouldn't have read my letter," Mother says softly. "We spoke only once, after. She told me she never wanted to see me again. And I couldn't—I don't blame her."

"I don't either," Aunt Genevieve says, a bite to her voice that wasn't there before. "She wouldn't have told anyone," she adds.

Mother looks up at Aunt Genevieve. "I know."

"And yet you let my brother command you to ruin her reputation anyway? You took his word, his stupid, irrational, angry— He was so mad, Clara. He wasn't thinking clearly."

"His little sister had been hurt. He loves you so. And he was hurting. I couldn't make that worse. And . . . and Eleanor was fine. Mr. Pine is a *good* man. The man she would have married anyway."

"Then why go so far as to let Captain Daniels ruin another reputation?"

Mother sighs and twists her hands together. "I thought he might get to her before I could convince her. The same way he seduced you. I didn't want to see him hurt someone that I loved again."

"So you hurt her instead," Rosalie surmises, tears pricking at the corners of her eyes. "You chose for her so she couldn't make the wrong choice."

Mother meets her eyes, her own full of anguish. "Eleanor was safe. Genevieve was safe. My two favorite people were settled, even if it meant they were far away. I had to protect them, I just had to."

Rosalie scoots down the settee, reaching out to take her mother's hand, squeezing hard. The gossip, and the social clout, and the endless shopping and fashion—it's all been a way to fill the gaping hole left behind by Aunt Genevieve and Mrs. Pine disappearing. A way to keep herself safe, so she wouldn't be left behind again.

"I'm so sorry." Aunt Genevieve settles on the other settee, reaching out to take Mother's other hand. "I didn't know what it cost to protect my honor. Had I known, I—"

"No," Mother says swiftly. "No. It was worth it. You met Walter. You have a wonderful life. We keep our secrets."

Mother and Aunt Genevieve share a look and Rosalie watches, something catching in her chest. Would Mother protect her like that if she knew how Rosalie truly felt? Are her secrets worth protecting, worth ruining friendships, worth the sacrifice?

"Do you think, if I came with you, we could convince Mrs. Pine to give up on her . . . revenge?" Aunt Genevieve asks gently.

Rosalie's whole body strains to keep still, to keep her hope from bursting from her mouth. She should have told Aunt Genevieve right at the start of the season. Saved herself, and Catherine, and everyone, a whole lot of hurt.

But Mother shakes her head. "It doesn't matter why I did it; she was ruined. You don't forget that."

"Maybe—" Rosalie hears herself say.

"No," Mother says firmly. "She won. Miss Pine can have Mr. Dean, and that will be the end of it."

They sit for a moment in a strangely calm silence. Rosalie should feel relieved, elated. But it all seems so hollow.

"Well, that's one thing sorted, at least," Aunt Genevieve says, her voice loud after the quiet. "And I have my own apology to make, to you," she adds, meeting Rosalie's eyes.

"Pardon?"

"I know your mother thought Mr. Dean a good prospect, but it's been clear for ages that I made a mistake in introducing you. The man is a dud."

"Genevieve!" Mother scolds.

"He is," Aunt Genevieve insists. "He never paid Rosalie the proper attention. He barely pays anyone attention. He would have been an inattentive, vapid husband, and our Rosalie deserves far better. I should have said something a long time ago."

"He . . ." Rosalie starts.

"I suppose I thought finding you someone sensible was safer

than letting you bungle through the world on your own," Aunt Genevieve says.

"You and Mother did all right," Rosalie says. Aunt Genevieve and Mother chuckle wetly.

"Only because we had each other," Aunt Genevieve says.

"And we got lucky," Mother says.

Rosalie turns to look at her, surprised. "I always assumed marrying Father was rather calculated," she admits.

Mother smiles, releasing her hand to smooth Rosalie's hair. It's so gentle. Rosalie's eyes burn and she blinks rapidly. She and her mother haven't sat still like this, close like this, in years.

"If he hadn't been the son of an earl, I would still have been swept off my feet and carried away," Mother says. "I wasn't looking for a love match. I frankly didn't think one was possible." Rosalie's chest clenches; she knows that exact feeling. "But he was so damn charming, and lovely, and kind—I was utterly taken immediately. That he came from such a good family and with such a great sister was pure luck. It was a charmed thing. And you deserve a charmed thing, just like I got," she says softly.

Rosalie's eyes are dangerously close to dripping now. "Really?"

"We'll find you the perfect man," Mother adds. "Someone with whom you can fall head over heels."

The warm, pleasant feeling in Rosalie's chest disappears in an instant. More men? She's finally dispatched of Mr. Dean and they're going to find *more*?

"And we really ought to find someone better for poor Miss Pine," Aunt Genevieve adds. "That could be your penance for what you put Mrs. Pine through."

Mother scoffs. "She'd never allow it. That girl will be the next viscountess. Eleanor always got what she wanted."

"Except when you got what you wanted. Can't we put your stubborn heads together, find these girls something better?"

Mother's laughing, but there's something in Aunt Genevieve's gaze. It's the same little spark she had at the painting tea, when she captured Rosalie and Catherine staring at each other.

"The Hamlen brothers aren't bad to look at," Mother says.

"Oh, goodness, yes, the tall one in particular," Aunt Genevieve agrees, looking back at Mother.

"Well, he'll have to be for Rosalie, then."

"Why must you try to pair the poor thing up with the tallest men? She'll have a permanent neck condition," Aunt Genevieve chides.

Rosalie forces a smile, her stomach clenching with unease. She's gotten Mother to give up on Mr. Dean, which is no small feat. But Mother could have leagues of other men to suggest. Rosalie could be going on courting outings for the rest of her life.

And Catherine will be left either to marry Mr. Dean, or else go on to court yet more men herself.

How long can they knock down suitors? Long enough for their families to give up? Long enough for her and Catherine to figure out a way to convince both their mothers into letting them be spinsters?

They need more time.

Chapter Twenty-Two

Catherine

C atherine bounces on her toes, twisting her hands together as she waits on Amalie's back stoop. Her gray pelisse is getting damp in the light mist, and Miss Teit looks rather miserable waiting behind her in the cramped alley. But she has to try.

Amalie's sly, knowing look from the baths has stuck with her all week as she's followed Mother to event after event, all suspiciously without the Tisends in attendance. She only managed to glimpse Henrietta once in Sydney Gardens. It's like Mother's found a whole other social circle. One that only includes Mr. Dean.

A very tired kitchen maid opens the back door and peers out at her.

"Good morning, is Miss Linet available?" Catherine asks brightly. "Miss Pine calling for a walk," she adds when the short woman just keeps staring at her.

Catherine extends her calling card and the woman takes it, her face entirely blank, before slamming the door in Catherine's face.

In fairness, it is obscenely early. Mother's still asleep; otherwise, Catherine's sure she'd be on her way to a crack-of-dawn knitting circle or something equally ridiculous.

But she just has to know. Has to try. It's been days since she and Rosalie exchanged letters. She's going through withdrawal.

Worse, they're dangerously running out of time.

Amalie opens the door with a frown. She's still in a morning robe over her dress, hair lightly mussed. "It's not even nine yet."

"Want to take a walk in Sydney Gardens?" Catherine asks, eyes big, smile imploring. "On this . . . gorgeous day?"

Amalie squints at her, then looks up at the gloomy, gray sky. "This better be good," she says, shutting the door on her again.

Catherine rocks on her heels, sucking on her cheek. She hopes it is. Hopes she hasn't been reading absolutely everything wrong. Hopes Amalie has come to trust her. Like her. Count her as a true enough ally to bare a soul to.

"Not a lot of morning people in your world," Miss Teit observes after a quiet minute.

Catherine laughs, surprised, and glances over her shoulder to find Miss Teit grinning back at her beneath her short brown bonnet. "I owe you," Catherine says.

"You really do," Miss Teit agrees. But the door opens before Miss Teit can name her price.

Amalie steps out, wearing a pretty blue pelisse and a white bonnet, Mrs. Linet standing behind her, looking exceedingly put together already.

"Miss Pine," she greets.

Catherine and Miss Teit curtsy. "Good morning, Mrs. Linet. Thank you for allowing Miss Linet to walk with me."

"Of course," she says. She and Amalie have the same green eyes and wide smile. "And please extend my congratulations to your mother on your impending engagement. Are you excited?"

Catherine forces herself to smile brightly. Dear God, she hopes she can make this work. "Rather nervous, really."

Mrs. Linet grins. "Of course. The anticipation can be unsettling. But I think soon enough you'll be filled with joy."

"Thank you," Catherine says, hoping she sounds sincere and not simply terrified.

"Shall we?" Amalie prompts.

"Yes. We'll have her back by eleven," Catherine promises Mrs. Linet.

"There is no rush. Have fun."

Amalie takes Catherine's arm and steers her off the stoop and back down the alley, Miss Teit following behind at a leisurely stroll.

Once they've stepped back onto the broad, damp, empty street and turned to head toward the gardens, Amalie squeezes her arm. "So, what's the matter?"

She promised herself she could do this. She could reach out and try, for herself, for Rosalie, and the hazy dream of a someday future. She just has to summon the words.

"Can't a girl just want to take a walk with a friend?" Catherine asks.

"Not before nine in the morning. What's so urgent you had to interrupt my breakfast?"

Catherine swallows against her discomfort. Amalie is her friend. "I need your help."

"That's obvious. With *what?*" Amalie asks.

Catherine glances back at Miss Teit, who's following them at truly discreet distance. Not that she thinks she needs to hide from Miss Teit, but she wants to tell her in her own way, on her own.

"I need you to set up a walk with Christopher."

Amalie stares at her as they walk for a moment. ". . . Okay."

"And invite Rosalie along."

". . . Okay," she repeats.

"We have things to discuss, but my mother doesn't want me writing to Christopher anymore, and I need to—"

"All right," Amalie says easily.

Catherine opens her mouth. That was too easy.

"What, did you expect me to *not* want to go on a walk with Christopher?" Amalie asks. Catherine hesitates. "Did you really need to get me out of the house to ask for this? You could have written a note."

Catherine winces. "Well, I, um, just wanted—"

"Unless there's more to this request than you're telling me."

Catherine stumbles and Amalie catches her. "Like what?" she asks, heart thumping loudly as they stand still on the gray stone sidewalk.

Amalie gives her a shrewd look. "Like maybe whatever you and Rosalie have to discuss is a little more covert than you're letting on?"

"Well—"

"And maybe you and Rosalie would prefer Christopher and I scarper off for a bit while you chat?"

It's like something is squeezing at her stomach, roiling hope and fear and elation together. "I—"

"And you'd like to tell me what's going on, but it feels like Rosalie already should have, and this is rather awkward?"

The words stick in her throat, confusion and relief swirling in her chest.

"It really has been obvious for ages," Amalie says, her voice a bit softer.

"Has it?" Catherine mumbles.

"Rosalie's never been *this* obsessed with anyone. And you may think you're rather sly, but you can't stop staring at her anytime you're together."

Are her cheeks actually bursting into flame? "You don't mind?" Catherine whispers.

Shit. *Shit.* She didn't mean to say—Rosalie's the one who should tell her—she only meant to ask for help, not to—this isn't her secret to—

"Believe me, if Henrietta and I had felt anything the one time we kissed, we'd have run off into the mountains," Amalie says easily, glancing over her shoulder at Miss Teit, who has stopped to pretend to admire a shop window some thirty paces back.

"You and Henrietta?" Catherine manages to ask, her throat tight.

"Once. Just to see what it felt like," Amalie says with a shrug. "You never kissed a friend?"

Catherine worries at her gloves, her face and neck still scaldingly hot. "I did," she admits softly. "She didn't feel the same way."

"And Rosalie does feel the same way?" Amalie asks, her voice lilting, knowing, just shy of teasing.

Catherine shrugs, meeting her eyes briefly. "I won't kiss and tell. At least not if she hasn't."

Amalie shakes her head. She bumps her hip against Catherine's as they head for the entrance to Sydney Gardens. "You both liked it," Amalie says.

"Yes," Catherine whispers, glancing at her to find Amalie looking back, completely at ease, completely without judgment.

"And you don't think it might feel the same with Mr. Dean?" Amalie asks.

"No," Catherine says, quick, easy, sure. "Not at all. I—I don't want to kiss anyone else. Ever," she adds, letting the word slip through unbidden. Giving it joyous voice.

"Good," Amalie says decisively, her calm, measured look melting into a true smile. "Rosalie deserves someone who wants only her."

"I do," Catherine assures her.

Is this what it's like to belong somewhere? To be accepted? Like a warm hug and a hot cup of tea and a beautiful sunrise all at once?

She feels like she could fly. Mother was *wrong*.

"Good," Amalie repeats, squeezing her elbow. "Rosalie's spent our whole lives making sure Henrietta and I end up with the right people. It's only fair she does too."

That warm feeling oozes slowly out of her chest. "I wish I knew how to make it that simple."

Amalie hums. "It is more complicated than letting Mr. Dean pick his prize."

"Oh, ick," Catherine exclaims.

Amalie laughs and leads her across the street and around the Sydney Hotel into the verdant gardens. "I could help you out, if you'll return the favor."

Catherine looks down at her. "Oh?"

"You think I haven't already realized Christopher was inviting you on outings to make me jealous? I'm quicker than you think I am."

"I didn't— He wasn't," Catherine protests. "At least, I don't think he was."

"Oh, Rosalie was, at least," Amalie says with a shrug. "She's effective, but not subtle."

"So it worked?"

Amalie sighs. "Only because I've had my eye on Christopher, and when I decide on something, or someone, I decide. And I act," she adds pointedly.

Catherine bobs her head. She's trying. This is a start. Maybe someday both she and Rosalie can be as decisive as Amalie. Maybe Amalie will help them build a world where they can be.

"Christopher's a good choice."

"He is," Amalie agrees, smiling herself. "And if orchestrating a little liaison for you means Christopher and I might disappear into the woods for a moment . . . I can be persuaded."

The warmth returns to her chest, growing into something brighter, something like fiery hope.

"I have the last volume of *The Children of the Abbey* I can lend you, if that sweetens the deal," Catherine says.

"Done. And I'll bring *my* lady's maid, who will happily go sit by the water and leave us all alone. Though yours seems great too."

Catherine glances over her shoulder to see Miss Teit still standing by the patio of the Sydney Hotel, admiring the flowering trees and paying them no attention whatsoever.

"She is."

"Henrietta's lady's maid is a hoverer, but if you and Rosalie happened to be out with her and Mr. Rile, I doubt she'd notice if you wandered off for a moment."

"Good to know," Catherine says. "And Henrietta wouldn't . . ."

"Henrietta, bless her, has never noticed anything that wasn't right in front of her—the lucky happy thing—but she'll be overjoyed to know Rosalie has found the right person. Whoever he, or she, may be."

She hoped to make friends this season, but she never actually thought she would. Nothing that's happened this season has gone to plan, but it's turned out better than she could ever have imagined. At least if she can manage to dispatch of Mr. Dean.

"Have you and Rosalie talked about the future?" Amalie asks.

"That's what the walk will be for."

Amalie sighs. "Ridiculous. If you need to pass letters, send them to me, and I'll forward them on. You're such smart women, it's a little sad you don't have it all planned out yet."

Catherine bristles for a moment, and then her shoulders slump. "It wasn't . . . We haven't had a lot of time to talk."

"And the time you had you spent a lot of it not talking, I imagine?" Amalie asks with a grin.

"Shut it," Catherine says, laughing.

Amalie looks ridiculously pleased with herself, narrow face set in a smirk. But as she continues to tease, getting more information out of Catherine than she'd have thought possible, Catherine feels like she can breathe again. Maybe they really can make a new life for themselves, and fill it with people who understand. Fill it with the people who already know and care about them.

All they need to do is convince their mothers to throw the old system to the wayside and ignore the gossip. And insult one very boring, very self-centered, very wealthy son of a viscount. How hard could it be?

Chapter Twenty-Three
Rosalie

Henrietta and her mother have strung flowers between the two small oak trees and woven them into the fence. Henrietta's parents are flitting amongst the beautiful tables set up by the back doors, receiving endless congratulations. It's an oversized, joyous celebration packed into a compact space, just like Henrietta. Rosalie can practically feel happiness floating on the air.

Christopher is prattling on at her side, their arms looped together as they make a small circuit of the back garden. She's not paying attention, too busy swiveling her head to try to find Catherine.

She should be here. It's the only thing that's kept Rosalie moving all morning. Mother was too busy to come, Father's back in London, and without word from Catherine for over a week, Rosalie's nearly coming out of her skin. She would have much preferred to stay home and wallow.

But Henrietta deserves to be feted and celebrated and fawned over.

"Mr. Tisend, I need you," Amalie says, appearing on Rosalie's other side.

"All right?" Christopher asks Rosalie.

"Let Amalie steal you for whatever shenanigans she needs," Rosalie dismisses, giving him a practiced smile.

Amalie tuts, but grabs his arm, grinning at Rosalie. Rosalie watches them go, noting the way Amalie's pretty blue dress complements Christopher's starched blue shirt. She wonders if they coordinated.

Rosalie and Catherine could wear beautiful matching gowns, or contrasting colors. Could coordinate their bonnet ribbons to each other's dresses. It would be charming. She wants the opportunity to be that sappy.

But Catherine isn't here. Rosalie has combed her eyes over every inch of the garden, and she and her mother are suspiciously absent. So is Mr. Dean. Rosalie hopes they're at separate functions. Hopes that Mr. Dean isn't presently getting down on one knee.

Rosalie twists her fingers together, trying to focus on the pull of her kid gloves as the fabric bunches between her fingers. She wishes Mother *had* been able to come now. At least she'd have someone to talk to.

She should be used to being left behind. All of her other friends, Jane—they've all left her for happy marriages.

Except this time, she does have someone of her own. She just can't parade her around like Christopher does with Amalie. Can't present her proudly like Mr. Rile will do with Henrietta.

It's then Rosalie realizes she's been standing alone for ten minutes, and not one person has come to greet her. In fact, no one appears to be looking her way at all. But she can see people watching her covertly. Judging. Pitying.

It's dreadfully uncomfortable to be stared at this way. Her stomach clenches unpleasantly. How much worse must it have been for Mrs. Pine?

Blessedly, Henrietta and Mr. Rile finally make their entrance, appearing through the back doors of Henrietta's townhouse to thunderous applause. Henrietta beams out at her guests, holding Mr. Rile's hand. Mr. Rile looks incredibly chuffed, standing there in what must be a new navy tailcoat with a light pink cravat.

It matches Henrietta's stunning pink dress, embroidered up to her thigh with delicate white flowers. Her bright cheeks are stretched wide, eyes shining even at this distance beneath her pink-and-white-trimmed bonnet.

Rosalie listens to Henrietta's parents introducing Mr. Rile as their son-in-law-to-be. She watches Mr. Rile and Henrietta struggle to keep their eyes from each other, barely listening.

Rosalie glances to the side of the patio and notices Christopher and Amalie standing rather close together too, beaming at Henrietta. It might be them next. Which would be wonderful.

She'll be gaining a sister, rather than losing a friend. And Henrietta will still visit.

Amalie catches her eye as the speeches wind down and jerks her chin, summoning Rosalie over. She goes, ignoring the feeling of eyes on the back of her head.

She reaches her brother and Amalie just as Henrietta comes barreling over to them, dragging the still-grinning Mr. Rile behind her. Christopher bumps Rosalie's shoulder.

"Congratulations," Amalie says, taking Henrietta's free right hand. "Let me see."

Henrietta beams, turning her hand so they can look at the beautiful pearl-and-gold engagement ring that adorns her short finger.

"Well done," Christopher tells Mr. Rile.

"She deserves the best," he says, standing flush with Henrietta, his wide cheeks pink.

"You both do," Rosalie says. "I'm so happy for you," she adds, glancing at Mr. Rile before meeting Henrietta's eyes.

"We owe it all to you," Henrietta says.

"We do," Mr. Rile agrees. "You gave me the courage I needed to walk up to the most beautiful woman at that ball."

Rosalie watches them look at each other. It feels different, this time. You can't be forced into love. Both people have to want it. It's work, to make the life you want. She didn't understand before.

"I'll take credit for that first introduction, but the rest was all you," Rosalie says, speaking toward Mr. Rile but staring into Henrietta's widening eyes. "You both braved so many seasons, found each other, and fought to have each other. That is the true accomplishment, and I am sure you will continue to make each other happy in this next chapter of your life together. Because you are wonderful, and beautiful, and worthy of all the happiness to come."

Henrietta bursts into tears, lurching forward to wrap her free arm around Rosalie. Rosalie huffs in surprise, wrapping both arms around her friend while Amalie, Christopher, and Mr. Rile watch in amusement. Henrietta's still holding Mr. Rile's hand.

"Thank you," Henrietta whispers, pulling back, eyes shining, nose a little red.

"Of course," Rosalie says, squeezing her hand before bringing the ring up for closer inspection. "Truly, well done, Mr. Rile."

She glances his way and finds his eyes a little moist too. Her words were meant for Henrietta, but it's good they meant something to him. After all, they're a pair now. He'll always be around as long as Henrietta's in her life. Which Rosalie hopes she is forever.

Henrietta steps back, taking Mr. Rile's proffered handkerchief with a watery smile. "So," she says with a great sniff.

Rosalie catches Amalie wiping at her own eyes. Saps, all of them. She's ignoring her own suspiciously moist cheeks.

"Will Catherine be coming?" Henrietta asks.

All thoughts of tears disappear as Rosalie shifts, uncomfortable. Christopher loops his arm through hers, squeezing, and Rosalie squeezes back.

"Her cousin, Mr. Finch, just returned from London, and they had to spend the afternoon with him," Amalie says.

Rosalie looks over at her too quickly. God, but that actually hurt her neck.

"She sends her deepest apologies," Amalie says, passing a note over to Henrietta. "And an invitation to walk with her on Wednesday."

"Oh, that's lovely of her," Henrietta says.

A sharp twang of jealousy slaps at Rosalie's chest. Catherine's *allowed* to write to Henrietta. And to Amalie, apparently. It's only Rosalie, and Christopher, who are seemingly on Mrs. Pine's unacceptable list.

She wonders how many letters they've exchanged. What Catherine's told Amalie. Is she reading anything new? Has she mentioned Rosalie?

"Perhaps I can reply tonight to confirm the walk," she hears Henrietta say.

"When did you last see Miss Pine?" Rosalie asks, blinking as the words spill too loudly out of her mouth.

They all turn to look at her and Rosalie fights a wince.

"We walked yesterday morning. She asked me to pass this along to you as well," Amalie says, giving her such a look as she hands over another sealed envelope.

Rosalie all but snatches the letter from Amalie's hand, ignoring her friends' inquisitive looks.

"I need to visit your powder room," she says, pulling her arm from Christopher's and turning on her heel to march into Henrietta's house.

She hurries up the stairs and into Henrietta's room, closing the door firmly behind her. She takes a moment to get her breathing in check and lets herself slump against the door.

She combs her eyes over Henrietta's tidy white vanity, the large white four-poster bed pushed into the corner, the armchair beneath the tall window along the opposite wall. Henrietta's beautiful charcoal sketches and watercolors cover almost every surface of the room. Scenes of her garden, Rosalie's garden, Aunt Genevieve's garden, portraits of Amalie, and Rosalie, and Mr. Rile, Henrietta's parents—the room is like a collage of Bath, all from Henrietta's artistic and quirky point of view.

The beautiful art helps her calm down enough to sink into Henrietta's armchair. She opens Catherine's letter with shaking hands, horrified to find herself so excited and anxious over something so simple as a *letter*. But it's been a week. She's starved for news. And she's just left her happy happy friends with their happy happy suitors/fiancés.

Dearest Rosalie,

I hope you won't be upset that I've given Amalie this letter. She is entirely on our side and has promised, with your darling brother's help, to orchestrate whatever we should need to see ourselves through.

I find myself at a loss for exactly what to ask for, but it's a comfort to know our friends will support us.

Rosalie swallows hard. Helping Amalie and Henrietta, giving them perfect lives, has always seemed so much easier than opening her messy chest to ask for what she wants. What she's wanted. To tell them who she is.

She should have asked Amalie and Henrietta to help give her cover with Catherine weeks ago—months, really. She doesn't begrudge Catherine for being brave enough to reach out and ask for help from the people who love them.

I'm hoping they can at least arrange a meeting for us. My father and Lord Dean have been failing to choose a date to confer, but I don't believe we can rely on that forever. One of them will run out of obligations at some point.

I wish Mother would run out of them. I feel like a prized heifer being taken over hill and dale to be seen by the masses. And somehow never where you are set to be. She's kept me so busy I couldn't have written if I wanted to. And any letters Christopher might have sent have not reached me.

Rosalie's heart stutters. If Mr. Pine and Lord Dean meet, and agree upon a dowry, Mr. Dean's proposal truly could come at any point.

Please write me back posthaste.

I miss you most ardently. I think of you each night. And each day, and each hour. I wonder what you'd say when Mother and I are at the modiste, or on promenade, or at a concert. I wonder what you'd think of my Cousin Louis' family home. He brought new books from London. I want to read them with you.

And then at night . . .

Rosalie can't help but blush, looking down at the sizeable gap between that sentence and the next, as if Catherine couldn't quite put her salacious thoughts into appropriate words. Rosalie has a choice few that should never be written down in reply.

> *I have faith in Amalie and Christopher's abilities to or-chestrate a meeting. And frankly, in yours as well. Please make it soon. It feels like it's been years since I saw you.*
> *Whatever have you done to me, lovely Lady Rosalie?*
>
> *Indelibly yours,*
> *Catherine*

Catherine's left an impression of her beautiful full lips at the bottom of the letter, and Rosalie can smell the wafting lilac perfume she must have spritzed on the paper.

Her friends may be able to parade their suitors for the ton to see, but she still gets love letters. Still has her lover. And she's going to keep her lover, come hell or high water.

She stands abruptly and goes to Henrietta's desk. Henrietta may have a talent for drawing, but Rosalie's always been good at faking penmanship. She makes quick work of forging an additional letter from Henrietta, suggesting that she will invite Amalie on her walk with Catherine to celebrate the engagement.

Then Amalie will invite Christopher, and Rosalie's name need not be mentioned to the Pines at all.

Henrietta's signature comes easily. But then Rosalie sits, staring down at her own paper, wanting to be clever, and alluring, and thoughtful, and romantic . . .

But that's a lot to ask of a single letter, and the guests at the party downstairs will start to talk if she dallies much longer.

Darling Catherine,

In missing you—a sensation not unlike having part of my chest kept far from myself—I find I've frozen in place, unsure of how to move forward. Thank you for taking action for us both. I will fight just as hard, and am grateful to know Amalie will be fighting alongside us.

I've no time to enumerate the many ways I think about you, during the day and emphatically at night. Suffice it to say I hope our upcoming rendezvous has many a hidey-hole to steal you away to.

I'll be imagining until I see your beautiful face.

Eternally yours,
Rosalie

She folds the letter up almost before the ink has dried, creasing it into a small square to encase inside her forged missive from Henrietta. She has at least a day to figure out a plan.

Anxiety creeps in immediately and Rosalie taps her foot as she waits for Henrietta's seal wax to melt. She looks up at the sketches above the vanity—a collection of silhouettes and quick likenesses. She and Amalie feature prominently.

Then her eyes fall on a lone sketch of the four of them. The vague background looks like Madame Florent's shop. They're all laughing, Amalie and Henrietta on the outside, Catherine and Rosalie close between them. Catherine's hand is on her arm, and Rosalie's cheeks are a bit pink.

Perhaps Henrietta understands more than Rosalie thinks.

How much longer would Rosalie have sleepwalked through life if Catherine hadn't arrived? Would she be the one getting engaged to Mr. Dean? Living a life devoid of the happiness she can see on Henrietta's face when she reenters the garden? The sly, brimming excitement she can see on Amalie's as Christopher takes her hand to drag her across the lawn?

Melancholy wraps around her chest, but Rosalie pushes it away. She's going to get that happily-ever-after, even if it looks a little different. She just has to reach out and take it.

She just has to be brave.

Amalie and Christopher are at the far side of the garden, setting up for a round of battledore. Just the two of them, happy together. Amalie notices her first and Rosalie squares her shoulders. She can do this. She can walk up to Amalie and pass her the letter, her chin held high.

Amalie takes it, smiling, and then slips it quickly into her bosom, which makes Christopher laugh, his eyes wide. Rosalie rolls her eyes at Amalie's pleased little grin.

"I'm glad you've found someone worthy," Amalie says simply, her voice low but achingly sincere.

Meeting Amalie's eyes cracks something long hardened in Rosalie's chest and she has to swallow thickly against a rush of tears. "Me too."

Amalie reaches out and takes her hand, squeezing hard, and Rosalie squeezes back.

"And likewise," Rosalie adds, smiling at her brother.

Amalie blushes and they stand there together, no further words needed.

"Did I ever tell you two about the time I smuggled a tortoise into the headmaster's office at Eton?" Christopher asks.

It does the trick, and both Rosalie and Amalie burst into laughter, their poignant moment thoroughly ruined. He's such a good brother.

Later, when they're sitting at a table with Henrietta, listening to her and Mr. Rile tell a wildly well-coordinated story about his proposal on the Prior Park bridge, Amalie leans over to her.

"You realize you will now owe *me* for your love match."

Rosalie smiles and bumps her shoulder. She can live with that. As long as she can live with Catherine.

Chapter Twenty-Four

Catherine

Catherine's lip stings. She releases it from between her teeth, smoothing her tongue across the abrasion and staunchly not thinking about how Rosalie bit her lip and did the very same thing. Oh, that she could be back in that room at Blaise House, pretending just for one night that the future was bright and attainable.

Instead, she stares out at the Pump Room, her stomach down by her toes. Mother's peering around hopefully, as if Mr. Dean might pop out of the air and unceremoniously get down on one knee right there in front of everyone.

Not that he *should*, given that Lord Dean and Father have yet to meet. But that doesn't seem to matter. Mother looks so *happy*, basking in the attention from every member of the ton. She's convinced that a proposal will elevate their family status to the top of Bath's social world.

If Mr. Dean dropped to one knee in front of Catherine right now, she doesn't know how she could reject him without ruining the first true happiness she's seen her mother have in God knows how long.

She's getting itchy. Maybe the stress is making her break out in hives.

She hasn't come up with a foolproof plan to suggest to Rosalie on their clandestine walk tomorrow. Worse, even if she *did* have a plan for how to divert Mr. Dean's impending intentions, she doesn't have the faintest idea of what comes after that—of how to build the life she and Rosalie keep promising to figure out together.

Every time she tries to imagine it, she just sees Mother weeping against Father's shoulder, ruined all over again.

"I'm thinking we ought to increase the number of musicians. Go for a sextet, maybe even an octet," Mother says.

Catherine's been thus far ignoring her monologue about their upcoming tea next week, tuning her out so she needn't grapple with the fact that if Mr. Dean were to make a public proposal, it would certainly be at her mother's tea. Which leaves her only a week to figure out her life, make space for Rosalie in it, and convince her parents to let her grow old with her.

"Do you actually enjoy the water?" Catherine asks desperately.

Mother turns her head to meet Catherine's eyes. "What?"

"You savor your cup, but it's so disgusting," Catherine whispers, raising her still-full cup of sulphureous water, which makes Mother laugh.

"You get used to it," Mother promises.

"It's been months and I still hate it. Are you really claiming you still have a tolerance from twenty-five years ago?"

Mother shrugs with a sly smile. "Perhaps."

Catherine rolls her eyes. "I wish that were hereditary."

"Oh, well, you got your father's tongue, then. However much he pretends otherwise, he hates it."

Catherine laughs, thinking of the way Father's face scrunches at even the mention of taking the waters. "At least the baths are helping."

"Yes," Mother agrees. "This has been a most advantageous move all around."

Catherine's shoulders go up. "Have you gotten a chance to read the next chapter of *Trecothick Bower* yet?"

"No. I've not read a book in, goodness, at least a month," Mother says dismissively. "There's always so much to keep up with in the paper, and all the invitations have taken a lot of time, you know."

"Well, I did finish it, and I thought—"

"Oh, those gloves would look lovely on you," Mother says, gesturing with her cup to a young woman and her mother who are sitting on a bench beneath one of the large dreary windows. "Maybe in blue?"

Catherine sighs. They used to spend hours debating the books they read together. Father and Richard would even read a novel now and then and they'd spend whole evenings in fervid family discussion.

But now Mother's content with the gossip columns and invitations and what laces Catherine should have on her slippers, which no one will even see at the tea. Though Rosalie would care. If they could sneak off, maybe she could even see them. Unlace them. Skirt her hand—

Mother comes to an abrupt halt, making Catherine spill her drink down the front of her jacket.

"What—"

She looks up and spots Mr. Dean at the door to the Pump Room, standing beside an elderly gentleman with his same long face, sharp nose, and heavy brow line.

She has water down the front of her dress, Mother's nearly hyperventilating, and there's nowhere to escape. She's stuck here, watching Mr. Dean and his father slowly approach them like the world's worst impending carriage accident.

Mother hastily plops their cups onto a passing porter's tray. She turns to Catherine and grabs her handkerchief, sopping up as much of the water from her dress as she can.

"This could be it!" she whispers excitedly, looking utterly elated.

Surely he wouldn't propose here, not now. Not without formally asking her father. They must be here for the waters. They *must* be.

But there's no time to prepare as Mr. Dean and his father step up to them. Catherine turns, heart in her throat, and forces what must be an uncomfortable-looking smile.

No one seems to notice.

"Mrs. Pine, Miss Pine, may I introduce my father, Lord Dean," Mr. Dean says.

Catherine and Mother curtsy in sync, which is wildly coordinated for how unmoored Catherine feels.

Lord Dean is tall and thin, like Mr. Dean, but with wispy gray hair and sallow cheeks. The two of them side by side look like a painting depicting the ravages of time.

"So pleased to meet you, Lord Dean," Mother says.

"Have we met before?" Lord Dean asks, his voice surprisingly loud for such a frail face.

"I don't believe so," Mother says kindly. Her elbow jerks, almost jostling Catherine.

"I'm sure I've seen your face before," he insists.

"Perhaps when I was a young girl," Mother allows. "Mr. Dean, are you quite recovered?"

"Quite," Mr. Dean says, smiling at Mother. "Father, Miss Pine is the young lady who saved me from choking at our tea. The one I was telling you all about. You've been corresponding with her father to find a time to meet?"

Catherine takes a deep breath through her nose, keeping her smile plastered to her face as Lord Dean's lightly absent eyes track over her.

"Smart young lady," he says.

"Thank you," Catherine replies, glancing at Mother and Mr. Dean, who look ready to recount the entire event, again. "Mr. Dean has spoken of your estate north of York often, and coming from the country myself, I'm so curious. Do you prefer Bath to the country, or vice versa?"

Mother gives her an approving look while Lord Dean ponders her question. She supposes it says something that he hasn't outright dismissed her.

"Father's great-grandfather purchased the Dean estate, and we've summered there every year of my life. In fact, I was hoping your father would be with you today, so they might discuss hunting this summer, amongst other things," Mr. Dean says.

"How lovely," Mother says. "Are you a keen hunter, Lord Dean?"

Lord Dean looks over at Mother, considering.

"Father's won many of our local tournaments," Mr. Dean says. "As a young man, he once brought down a twelve-stone buck."

"How impressive," Catherine says, working very hard not to frown at Mr. Dean. She can't spend the rest of her life with this man, she just can't.

"I'd hoped as well, Miss Pine, that you might accompany your father to our estate if we arrange a hunting trip. Lady Rosalie mentioned often how fond you are of your gothic novels. I think you'd enjoy the Dean manor."

Catherine blinks, startled. "I do love gothic novels. Is it very gothic in design?"

"Exceedingly. Many dark corners and turrets and creepy old attics to explore."

She is absurdly pleased to think maybe Rosalie had been thinking about her just as long as Catherine was obsessed with Rosalie before they owned up to it.

Mother squeezes her elbow and Catherine looks up to find Mr. Dean smiling at her, looking eager. She must look too happy, thinking about Rosalie. She schools her face, giving him a much-smaller smile.

"I know the Dean library is said to be expansive. I'm sure my daughter would enjoy an afternoon lost amongst its shelves," Mother says.

Discomfort twists through her at Mr. Dean's enthusiastic smile.

"Of course. The library looks out on the grounds where we often set up archery. She might enjoy looking out the window every few pages to see us shoot."

She very much would not. Unless it was Rosalie shooting an arrow. Oh, how she'd love to see *that*.

"I'm sure she would. Wouldn't you, darling?" Mother asks.

"I do remember your face," Lord Dean cuts in, suddenly animated. They all turn to look at him, startled. "There were rumors you and that naval fellow—the baron's son—were involved, and then you were caught with him in the bushes and he made a tactical retreat to save his own skin. The Pine boy took pity on you and secreted you away. Never saw your parents again after that, heard they moved away."

His voice booms around the room, stopping all conversation

in its tracks. Every head in the room turns their way, gaping. A horrible, visceral silence hangs around them.

Mother goes stiff beside her, maybe not even breathing. Catherine glances at Mr. Dean, who's staring wide-eyed at his father.

"We—" Catherine starts. "Um, we must—"

"Go," Mr. Dean manages. "My father and I, that is. We must leave for an appointment. A pleasure to see you, and we so look forward to the tea next week. Good day, Mrs. Pine, Miss Pine," he says, his voice high.

Catherine dips into a curtsy, pulling Mother with her. Lord Dean looks quizzically at his son but doesn't fight him. Mr. Dean beats a hasty retreat from the room, frog-marching his father out.

Catherine and Mother stand for a moment, fully exposed, the whole Pump Room staring at them without any effort to pretend otherwise. Mother's pale as a ghost and Catherine isn't feeling much better.

Slowly, and without looking like they're trying to flee the room, Catherine gently guides Mother toward the doors.

Lord Dean being too scandalized by her mother's past to allow his son to propose could be the solution to everything. This could provide exactly the out she and Rosalie have been looking for.

Trying not to smile, Catherine leads Mother out of the Pump Room and around the corner, hiding them in a small alcove until she can be sure Mr. Dean and his father will be gone from the street. She can see the anguish on her mother's face, and her hope curdles in her chest. It's one thing to be the source of her unhappiness. It's another entirely to stand there simply watching the carriage crash happen with no way to help.

"Everything's fine," Catherine hears herself say.

Mother shakes her head, her eyes starting to drip, lips trembling. "It's not."

Catherine takes her shaking hands. "It is," she insists. "You've made so many friends this season. Impressed everyone. Who cares what some bumbling old man thinks he remembers."

"He remembers it exactly," Mother whispers.

"So what?" Catherine says, trying to keep her voice light. "It was twenty-five years ago. You're respectably married now."

"Clearly I can't outrun the idea of being ravished in the bushes."

Catherine squeezes her hands reflexively. "I thought the rumor was only that you kissed."

Mother raises a shoulder. "Rumors always keep growing. By the time your father and I were leaving after our ignominious marriage, I heard that I'd been caught doing . . . well, something no lady should ever do."

Catherine opens her mouth, unsure of exactly what Mother's referring to. Something *worse* than being ravished in public, unmarried, unbetrothed?

Mother lets out a watery giggle. "Oh, darling, I love that you're still so innocent."

Catherine snaps her mouth shut. She's sure there are things about carnality that she still doesn't know. Particularly with a man, she supposes. But she *knows*.

But that's not important now.

"I'm worldly," she says, putting a little extra whine in her voice to make Mother laugh again.

"You are," Mother agrees, looking a smidge put back together.

Catherine smiles. "And because I am worldly, I know that the people who actually matter and care about you won't care a whit that Lord Dean is an uncouth blabbermouth."

"You're right," Mother says, tugging on Catherine's hands to pull her in for a quick hug. "Let's go home to your father, let him tell you all about how he nearly punched a man for saying something similar about a year after we got married."

"Father *what?*" Catherine asks loudly.

Mother laughs, stepping back to lead Catherine down the stairs to the street.

"Who was it?" Catherine asks as they reach the courtyard and start walking back toward home.

"Some second son of a second son passing through on his way north. They met at the tavern. Said your father was lucky to have gotten the spoiled fruit from a titled tree."

"He did not," Catherine says, aghast.

"Your father popped him one, sent him crashing over the bar, and everyone cheered."

"I miss home," Catherine admits, thinking of their rowdy local tavern, full of quarry workers with good hearts.

"I do too," Mother admits. "But we've—well, today not withstanding—we've been doing well here."

"We have," Catherine agrees. "Do you think Father will go over there and punch Lord Dean?"

Mother laughs, the sounding ringing around them. It makes Catherine's shoulders come down just a hair. Even if she couldn't prevent the humiliation, at least she can help cheer her up.

"I'll have to persuade him against it. I am sorry, though," she adds, squeezing Catherine's hand.

"For what?"

"Well, Lord Dean remembering nothing about our family other than my . . . supposed indiscretion might make it harder—"

"It doesn't matter. I don't care," Catherine says, trying not to sound too eager.

"Darling—"

"Anyone who judges you based on something someone said happened twenty-five years ago isn't someone I want to marry, or be related to by marriage."

She said it. *She actually said it.*

"Just wait until the ton sees our tea. Everyone will forget all about him because they'll be so impressed by your hosting skills," she continues, her whole body feeling lighter.

Mother laughs softly. "If you say so."

"I do," Catherine says, watching the way Mother's shoulders roll back, the way she carries herself just a little taller than before. "We'll show them yet."

"We will," Mother agrees, pulling her hand up to tuck their arms together again. "You're right. We can make sure they all forget prior scandals by throwing the best tea they've ever seen."

"Hear, hear," Catherine enthuses, a warmth flooding through her chest. Mother sounds like she used to, back home. Bright, and cheerful, and hopeful.

Maybe everything really will be all right. Maybe this was the best thing that ever could have happened. Maybe she'll get to tell Rosalie tomorrow that—

"A tea so wonderful it'll force Mr. Dean to propose to you, and once you're engaged, his father will simply have to cease discussing the past. We'll be the talk of the town then, for all the right reasons, won't we?"

Catherine withers, forcing herself to nod, her stomach plummeting, hope splintering into jagged pieces. She thought they'd turned a corner here—thought that Mother might finally be willing to stand on her own, be proud of *herself*, without needing Catherine's marriage to be the picture-perfect celebrated story.

Instead, she has a single week to make sure Mr. Dean doesn't propose.

Chapter Twenty-Five
Rosalie

"We couldn't have done this in the afternoon?" Rosalie asks, too exhausted and sweaty to be embarrassed about her petulance.

It's not that she doesn't want to see Catherine. But it's early, and humid, and she feels rather bloated and gross. Worse, she doesn't have a plan. Mother and Aunt Genevieve's story still pierces at her heart. And beside it, guilt for disobeying both of her parents squeezes at her throat.

"Do you *want* Catherine to marry bloody Mr. Dean?" Christopher huffs, breathing hard next to her, while Amalie walks on his other side as if it's no strain at all to climb up the wooded hill on Bathampton Down.

"Your mother would have gotten suspicious if it was any later," Miss Wrigsby says on her other side, looking equally unaffected by their trek.

Rosalie doesn't know which one of them told Miss Wrigsby, but she's oddly grateful to have another adult along for this . . . debacle in the making.

"If we could cease with feeling sorry for ourselves, we could get back to the matter at hand," Amalie says.

"Right," Rosalie says, blowing out a haggard breath as she bats a small branch out of her way.

"You're sure Aunt Genevieve can't convince Mother to just

tell Mrs. Pine? Surely once she understands her reasoning . . ." Christopher says, petering off as both Rosalie and Miss Wrigsby shake their heads.

"She'd rather take it to the grave," Miss Wrigsby says. "You'll have to force her into it, somehow."

"It's the *how* that worries me," Christopher says. "She never does anything she doesn't want to do."

Except for ruining her best friend to protect her sister-in-law-to-be. But Rosalie doesn't think Mother did that truly of her own free will. She didn't see an alternative, trapped into a situation with no good options.

Rosalie knows how she feels.

"Do you think—" Christopher starts, just as they make it to the small clearing at the top of the hill.

But Rosalie's no longer listening. Catherine, Henrietta, and Catherine's lady's maid, Miss Teit, stand in the center of the clearing. Catherine looks a bit worse for wear, her hair frizzy beneath her brown bonnet, cheeks pink. It takes Rosalie a moment to realize she's wearing the cream dress Rosalie bought her, now snagged with brambles beneath her askew gray pelisse. Rosalie's breath catches in her chest.

Henrietta, by contrast, looks entirely unruffled, but Rosalie doesn't care.

She wants to cross the tall grass, crunching twigs and dandelions to run to Catherine. Wants to throw her arms around her. Wants to ask her how she is, and what's been going on. Wants to push her up against the plentiful trees and—

"It's almost worse than watching her kiss her silly, isn't it?"

Rosalie stiffens, looking over to find Christopher and Amalie standing side by side behind her, grinning.

"Well, it's not like they've been subtle about it all this time," Amalie says as they come to the middle of the clearing.

"Hey!" Catherine protests.

"It does rather look like hearts are falling out of your eyes," Henrietta adds.

Rosalie looks back and forth among her friends and her brother. She meets Catherine's eyes and Catherine merely shrugs.

"I do spend an awful lot of time staring at you," she admits.

Catherine looks good enough to eat. Actually, she'd rather like to—

"Before we scarper off and give you two the reunion you're clearly so desperate for . . ." Amalie says.

"Right," Catherine says, cheeks pink. "Well. Henrietta, Miss Teit, and I were talking, and we think the best thing would be to just . . . force our mothers to talk. We just need to figure out how."

"We could forge letters?" Amalie suggests.

"I can do a decent version of Lady Tisend's penmanship," Miss Wrigsby says.

"Oh, I can do Mrs. Pine's. That could be fun!" Miss Teit says.

"Suppose one of them won't open the letter?" Christopher asks.

"We could force them?" Rosalie wonders. Could she, really? Force Mother into opening a letter from Mrs. Pine? Maybe Aunt Genevieve could?

"It seems much more expedient to trap them in the water closet at the Upper Rooms, doesn't it?"

They all turn to look at Henrietta, who stares back innocently.

"I beg your pardon?" Amalie says for the group.

"You trap them in the water closet," Henrietta says. "Catherine got stuck in there at the start of the season. Shouldn't be too difficult to replicate. And then there's little margin for error. As long as you think they'll talk once they're in there."

That's painfully brilliant. So simple. So achievable.

"Trap them in there together, force Mother to explain the whole sordid affair, and get Mrs. Pine to call off the proposal. Ten, twenty minutes," Christopher says.

"More difficult to orchestrate during the tea, but I don't think we'll get another opportunity," Amalie agrees.

But Rosalie's staring at Catherine, who's still looking at Christopher, her mouth slightly open.

"Catherine?" Rosalie prompts.

"Do—did your mother give you a reason?" Catherine asks, ripping her eyes away to meet Rosalie's. "Did she explain?"

Rosalie glances at Christopher, who nods encouragingly. Mother listened to Rosalie's father all those years ago—chose to believe him, and not trust her best friend. But Rosalie can trust Catherine. Can trust Henrietta, and Amalie, and their lady's maids. All these people who have rallied around them.

If she can't trust them, if she chooses to follow her mother's path, she'll only end up alone. She's choosing a better future this time.

"Captain Daniels took advantage of Aunt Genevieve early in the season your mother and mine met him," Rosalie says softly. Even so, it feels like the words land with an explosion. Catherine, Henrietta, and Miss Teit gasp. "Father made my mother promise not to tell yours, to maintain Aunt Genevieve's reputation, but Mother didn't want to risk your mother ending up the same way. So, she spread the rumor, and my father got yours to propose."

She watches as Catherine stands there, taking it in. Henrietta sniffles beside her, and Miss Teit hands her a handkerchief. Catherine meets Rosalie's eyes, tears brimming. Rosalie wants so much to step forward and wrap her arms around Catherine, to apologize for the hurt done to her mother, and the hurt passed down to Catherine that's left them both in this mess together. But she can't find the words, can't move her feet.

What if Catherine never wants to see her again? What if the slight is too great? What if what her mother did is truly unforgivable?

"We owe your family an enormous apology," Christopher says, stepping up beside Rosalie, Amalie in tow. "And I know it cannot undo the damage done, but I will do whatever I can to help you and Rosalie build the life you want."

"Even if it starts with locking you in a water closet with your mothers," Amalie adds.

Her words seem to break the hush that's fallen over the clearing and everyone lets out a startled laugh. Catherine meets Rosalie's eyes again. There's so much she wants to say, so much she doesn't really know how to articulate . . .

"Mr. Tisend, weren't you going to show Miss Raught how to identify edible berries?" Miss Teit asks.

Rosalie feels more than sees Henrietta, Amalie, Christopher, Miss Teit, and Miss Wrigsby exchanging looks. But she and Catherine are still staring at each other, trapped in their mothers' hurt, hoping to escape together.

"You know, I was!" Christopher says, a little overloud. "Follow me, ladies."

"I'd think it might take us about fifteen minutes to find berries, wouldn't you say, Miss Wrigsby?" Amalie adds.

"Perhaps even twenty," Miss Wrigsby agrees, taking Amalie's other arm to follow Miss Teit and Henrietta out of the clearing.

Henrietta glances over her shoulder and meets Rosalie's eyes, smiling tearily at her. Rosalie never actually told Henrietta. Amalie must have. But here she is anyway, helping them. Giving them space. Architecting their madcap plan.

Rosalie smiles back and watches the group leave the clearing, listening until their crunching footsteps fade out of earshot.

"Are you mad?" she whispers.

But it's loud enough for Catherine to hear, her eyes widening. She takes a step forward. "Mad?"

"You'd have every right to hate my mother. To hate me, even, for what she did to yours," Rosalie tells her.

Catherine slowly shakes her head. "I feel sorry for *her*. I can't imagine how awful that would have felt, to save your best friend and lose her all at once."

Rosalie stares at Catherine, punched in the chest by her generosity, her kindness, her lovely wonderful self. "You have a beautiful heart," she says.

Catherine chuckles and they stand there for a long moment, just smiling at each other, the weight of the past sloughing off until brimming promise surrounds them.

Catherine's hands curl and uncurl at her sides, and she huffs lightly. "Have we waited long enough for me to touch you?"

Rosalie can't help but laugh. "Oh, absolutely," she says, finally ungluing her feet enough to rush toward her.

They meet in the middle, Rosalie wrapping her arms about Catherine's waist while Catherine's hands glide against Rosalie's jaw to pull her into a desperate kiss.

Rosalie's whole body slackens. She presses up on her tiptoes, hands curling into Catherine's hips, fisting in her gray pelisse. It's soft, and hot, and lovely, and Rosalie wishes time could just stop altogether, leave them in this beautiful kiss forever.

"Hi," Catherine says when they pull apart at least a minute later.

"Hi," Rosalie whispers back, unable to control her smile.

"Come here," Catherine says, dragging her out of the clearing and up to a big oak tree.

And then they're snogging, Rosalie's back flush against the tree, her arms thrown around Catherine's shoulders, their bonnets knocking, heads tilted to give them the most room.

"I wish they were further away so I could crawl under your skirt," Catherine whispers as she laves kisses up to Rosalie's ear.

Rosalie's knees buckle in surprise. "Jesus," she rasps as Catherine laughs huskily.

She pulls back to meet Rosalie's eyes and they stare at each other, lips swollen, pupils wide.

"I've missed you," Catherine says breathily.

"Oh, I've missed you too," Rosalie agrees, squeezing her waist. "Letters don't do you any justice."

"No, they don't," Catherine agrees, her fingers toying with Rosalie's earlobe in a way that makes her want to melt into a puddle of goo.

She bites at her lip and Rosalie tilts her head, watching her go suddenly shy. "What?"

"It seems silly to say it out loud, because I do think you know. But I want much more than letters with you?"

A sudden wave of relief courses through Rosalie's body. It's a reassurance she didn't realize she needed so badly. So much that she wants to give it back, wants to make Catherine feel just as bright and wonderful and full. "I might want a lifetime of more than letters with you," Rosalie whispers.

Catherine's face breaks into the most beautiful smile, and she leans in to sip a delicate, aching kiss from Rosalie's mouth.

There's so much more she could say. So much more she *should* say.

They really should be using the rest of this visit to plan. It would be prudent, and smart, and expedient.

But when Catherine sucks on Rosalie's bottom lip, her thigh pressing between Rosalie's legs until she's nearly off the ground, both of them panting, Rosalie thinks that just for today, just for right now, perhaps prudent is the least of her worries.

"How much longer do you think they'll be gone?" she gasps against Catherine's mouth.

"Ten minutes, at least," Catherine mumbles back, one of her hands creeping up Rosalie's chest over her dress beneath her pelisse.

"Be a shame to waste ten minutes," Rosalie whispers.

"It really would," Catherine agrees, pulling back to meet her eyes as her hand closes over Rosalie's breast.

Rosalie groans and moves her own hands lower, cupping Catherine's utterly perfect arse.

"We can figure the rest out in letters, can't we?" Catherine asks.

She grinds her thigh upward and Rosalie has to clamp her mouth shut around a loud moan. "Fuck yes," she whispers, leaning up to chase Catherine's mouth.

Ten minutes passes in the heady blink of an eye, and when footsteps loudly intrude upon their quiet, Rosalie finds she no longer cares about her swollen lips, her red cheeks, her wrinkled dress, or her breathless laughter. Catherine drags her back into the clearing, their fingers wound together proudly.

Their friends eye them knowingly, but Rosalie finds she doesn't care. They're going to build the future they both want, together. She's ready to accept the love and help Amalie, Christopher, and Henrietta are offering, so she can have the love she wants for the rest of her life.

And by the way Catherine's gripping hard at her hand, she wants the very same thing.

Chapter Twenty-Six

Catherine

The tearoom looks exquisite. Mother has gone with a silver, lilac, and blue theme, with tall vases of beautiful flowers at the center of every circular table, laid with white tablecloths with blue serviettes. The silverware is embossed with roses, and small violets have been strung around the room with vines along the backs of the chairs.

"Do you think the centerpieces should be shorter?" Mother asks her, toying with the fingers of her delicate lace gloves.

"Everything is perfect," Catherine assures her, taking her hands.

"You are both perfect," Father says, coming up behind Mother and placing his hand on her waist.

She leans into him gratefully. "You have to say that."

"I don't," he insists. "You will absolutely be the most stunning vision anyone has ever seen."

Their dresses, both a pale blue overlaid with white lace threaded with bits of silver, are truly gorgeous. Madame Florent outdid herself. And Miss Teit did wonders with both of their hair, studding little jewels into their elegant braided buns, leaving delicate curls to frame their faces. Father looks great in his new black suit as well.

For a moment, Catherine wishes she could freeze time right here. Stay in the anticipation of everything changing without having to live to see it through. Before she and Rosalie discover whether her mother can really forgive Lady Tisend. And after that, whether she can forgive Catherine for wanting a life so different from the one she's tried to give her.

It makes her stomach tight. But horribly, and thankfully, they can hear the first guests ascending the grand staircase in the hallway.

"Come, come," Mother says, grabbing Catherine's and Father's hands, leading them to the doors to receive their guests.

"Here we go," Father whispers.

Mother gestures to the porters, who open the doors to the tearoom, revealing a line of guests moving up the staircase, led by Mr. Dean and his father.

Rosalie and her mother are, of course, nowhere to be seen. They're either further back, or haven't arrived at all. Catherine's on her own, at least for now.

She pastes on her best smile, trying to look welcoming. One glance at Mother proves she's no more excited to see Lord Dean than Catherine is. But true to form, her gracious "Lord Dean, Mr. Dean, welcome, we are so grateful to have you here with us" sounds positively radiant.

"Thank you for the invitation," Mr. Dean says, taking Mother's hand to kiss it before taking Catherine's. "Miss Pine, you look wonderful," he says.

"Thank you," Catherine says. She knows.

"Have we met?" Lord Dean asks, looking between them.

Catherine stares at Lord Dean, feeling Mother stiffen in surprise. Does he not—

"And Mr. Pine, I am delighted to introduce you to my father," Mr. Dean says quickly. "Father, I believe you knew Mr. Pine's father rather well."

"Pine, Pine. Yes," Lord Dean agrees, shaking Father's hand. "I recall visiting a lake once that was well stocked."

"Our fish are always plentiful," Father says, glancing at Catherine and her mother in surprise before smiling at Lord Dean. "May I escort you in?"

And off they go, leaving Catherine, Mother, and Mr. Dean at the door. They stand for a moment in an awkward silence. Mr. Dean opens his mouth, as if he might offer some excuse, but then shuts it, moving instead to Catherine's side.

She feels his hand at her elbow, a clear request to take her arm—to stand *with* her as they greet the rising tide of guests. Without so much as a word, an apology, an explanation for his father's behavior.

She wants to push him away, but she can't, not yet. She can't publicly snub him. Not until Mother and Lady Tisend have had it out.

So she pushes down her anger and moves her elbow, allowing Mr. Dean to slip his hand through its crook, linking their arms together. She glances up at Mother, but she looks perfectly composed and unaffected. She's even smiling.

How can she be— Catherine turns to the line of mothers waiting for entry. They're all tittering. Mr. Dean is standing beside her, *with* her, to greet the guests. Damn. It's almost as big a statement as a proposal would be.

God willing, this will be the worst of it.

They greet what seems like a never-ending slew of guests, curtsying and smiling. All of them give Catherine significant looks that make her blood slowly fizz.

"Did you buy that lovely dress at Madame Florent's shop?"

Catherine turns, surprised, and looks up at Mr. Dean. "I did."

"It's quite fetching. The lace is very intricate." He almost looks . . . animated.

Like nothing even happened.

"Thank you," she says. She turns back to greet the next guest, unsettled.

"I heard there's to be a shipment of books in to Mr. Weston's shop next week. Thought you ought to know."

Catherine turns to Mr. Dean again, finding him smiling down at her. "Oh, that's lovely," she says. She can't wait to tell Rosalie and Amalie and Henrietta. Assuming they'll still be able to spend time together after tonight.

"What are you reading right now?"

Catherine blinks, working hard to hide her complete bemusement. He's choosing now to take an interest? To care, even a little?

"I've been busy with planning for this tea," she says, hoping it dissuades him.

"Entirely fair. What are you hoping to read next?"

It's somehow even less surprising that he can't take a hint.

"I've three or four titles. I'm not sure I could pick just one," she says, glancing at Mother, but she's entirely engrossed in greeting guests and not any help at all.

As she looks back at Mr. Dean, she finally spots Amalie and Henrietta on the stairs. They wave and Catherine nearly wilts with relief. Reinforcements are coming. She just needs to stand her ground and—

"Shall we head inside to get some refreshment?"

She could scowl. "Oh, I shouldn't leave Mother to—"

"Go, go," Mother says easily. "We shouldn't keep Mr. Dean from mingling."

And so she finds herself back in the tearoom, Mr. Dean squiring her around, and decidedly not heading toward the refreshments along the back wall. She could use a glass of champagne.

"Ah, Mr. Duncan," Mr. Dean says, bringing Catherine over to a circle of young men.

She recognizes Mr. Fortes and Mr. Rile, of course, but the rest are a mystery. She curtsies and then stands there while they talk of hunting and fishing and cards. She could chime in. She's an excellent whist player, especially if she and Father are on a team. But she doesn't want to draw any attention to herself.

As long as she's over here with the men, she's safe from any spontaneous proposals. Though it could just be a matter of time. Father's talking to a younger couple across the room, distracted, and Lord Dean keeps glancing at them, as if he's waiting for something.

She can't imagine he thinks Mr. Dean should propose here, today. He can't seriously think she'd accept without even a brief apology to her mother. But then again, perhaps Mr. Dean will simply pretend it never happened. Pretend he too doesn't remember.

Thankfully, finally, Rosalie, Christopher, Amalie, Henrietta, and Lady Tisend enter the room. Rosalie spots her right away, and she watches with some amusement as a chain of jerking elbows alerts the rest of the group. Amalie and Christopher are arm in arm.

Henrietta waves at her, and then at Mr. Rile behind her. Which should, hopefully, give her some salvation. And sure enough, Henrietta grabs Amalie's hand, tugging her away from Christopher, who pouts. Lady Tisend's too busy looking at the rest of the room with a sour face to notice, but Rosalie's laughing. And that's something, at least.

"Miss Pine, what a delightful room you and your mother have put together," Henrietta announces, stepping right into their circle and forcing all of the gentlemen to make way for her.

"Thank you," Catherine says, watching as Amalie scooches in beside her, ignoring Mr. Fortes' intrigued look. "You both look lovely."

"You certainly do, my dear," Mr. Rile says, beckoning Henrietta to join him across the circle.

Henrietta grins, leaving Amalie beside Catherine. She crosses the circle and slips in flush with Mr. Rile. "You look exceedingly handsome," she says.

The circle chuckles and Mr. Rile blushes. Catherine glances at Mr. Dean to find him frowning, clearly disgruntled at the interruption. Heaven forfend some of the men might *want* to talk to the ladies.

"We've been discussing their upcoming hunting trips," Catherine tells the girls.

"Going north or west, gentlemen?" Amalie asks.

Raised eyebrows all around.

"North," Mr. Fortes says. "To my father's property as usual."

"How lovely," Amalie says without looking at him.

Mr. Fortes looks a little crestfallen. Mr. Rile snickers into his handkerchief and exchanges a look with Henrietta.

"And Mr. Dean, where will you be going?" Amalie asks.

"I'll be heading north as well, starting on the expansive Dean estate, and then working my way eastward again toward Wales. Father has a few cousins with grand lands there as well, and we'll follow the game for the season."

"I imagine that will take you from Bath for most of the summer," Amalie says.

"It will. Though I hope to make frequent trips back to visit."

Catherine can feel him looking down at her and forces herself not to react.

"Excuse me for a moment," Amalie says, ducking out of the circle.

"My father's lands are rich in grouse and deer," Henrietta says. "Mr. Rile will of course be coming to shoot."

"I am most excited to see the Raught lands," Mr. Rile jumps in.

Catherine ignores the way Mr. Dean is holding even more tightly to her elbow, almost as though he's goading her into meeting his eyes. Instead, she glances over her shoulder, trying to spot her mother. The last of the guests have trickled in now, and everyone is merely milling about, waiting to start the tea.

Catherine can't see Rosalie anywhere. They're running out of time.

"Mr. Dean, Mr. Tisend was just telling me how eager he was to show you his uncle's lake," Amalie announces, appearing back in the circle with Christopher in tow, and holding two almost overflowing wineglasses. "Miss Raught," she says, holding one out for Henrietta.

Mr. Rile grabs it for her with a grin, still going on about the Raught lands. Amalie then muscles in next to Catherine, forcing Christopher in beside her.

Mr. Dean frowns over at them. "I'm not sure I'll have the time after all, Mr. Tisend, but I might—"

"Oh, do let me implore you," Christopher says gamely, nudging Amalie to make her stop smiling. "In fact, I've got a schedule planned, if you'd be willing to discuss it. I'm sure we can find a time."

"Now?" Mr. Dean asks, glancing around, his arm still tight on Catherine's elbow. It's starting to hurt.

"My fishing compatriot leaves the day after tomorrow. It won't take but a minute. Miss Pine doesn't mind, does she?"

"Not at all," Catherine says, hoping she sounds demure instead of desperate.

She slides her arm out from Mr. Dean's, forcing herself not to knead at the sore crook of her elbow. Christopher gestures across the room. Mr. Dean nods to Catherine and follows Christopher's lead. Which leaves Catherine, Amalie, and Henrietta standing alone in the cluster of men.

Go, Henrietta mouths at them. "Yes, I think my father's planning to stock the lake," she adds, louder, for Mr. Rile.

"Come on," Amalie whispers, taking Catherine's hand.

And then they're walking the perimeter of the room while Amalie sips her drink, trying not to look like they're searching out Catherine's mother. Catherine notices Rosalie in the far back corner, trapped with her mother and the gossiping Mrs. Plory.

Rosalie catches her eye, giving her a disheartened shrug. Catherine frowns back, but she can't focus on Rosalie's side of the equation, not when the band is striking up in the hallway. If they don't find her mother before Mr. Dean hears the band, she'll find herself seated for tea service and they'll be ruined.

"There," Amalie says urgently, tipping her glass toward where Mother's standing by the doors again.

"Thank Christ," Catherine says, heading across the room, Amalie's hand still clutched in hers.

Now she just needs to work into a good panic and draw Mother back into the cloakroom. Shouldn't be hard; she's been halfway into panic since before they arrived.

"Incoming," Amalie hisses.

Catherine glances to the left and sees Mr. Dean heading for them, slipping something out of his pocket. Oh, God, it's a box. A small box.

"That's a ring box," Amalie whispers.

Catherine keeps moving—what else can she do?—dragging Amalie up to her mother.

"Darling, turn around and smile," Mother says, her eyes alight. "This could be your moment."

Catherine looks to Amalie, horrified. They turn together to see Mr. Dean not ten feet away. Across the room, she can see Rosalie watching, her eyes wide, mouth open in distress.

Did their fathers already talk? Does she turn him down, right here, right now, in front of all of these people? Oh God. She might be sick.

"I'm sorry," Amalie whispers.

Catherine glances at her, opening her mouth to say she is too, before Amalie stumbles. And throws her glass of wine down the front of Catherine's dress.

They stare at each other for a silent moment. Amalie raises an eyebrow. Mr. Dean is still coming toward her. There's wine all over the front of her beautiful dress. There's . . .

Oh.

She lets out a piercing shriek and starts slapping at her dress. "Oh my goodness!" she wails.

Amalie holds her hands up, eyes wide in faux horror. *Go bigger.*

"Why would you *do* that?" Catherine shouts. "Look at what you've done to my dress!"

"I'm so sorry, so very sorry," Amalie says loudly, sounding

properly devastated. "I'll replace it. Mrs. Pine, I am soooo sorry," she adds as Mother steps forward, taking Catherine's shoulders.

"It's *ruined*," Catherine whines loudly. She screws up her face, sniffling. She's not sure she can quite work up real tears, but she can look the part. "Mother, looook."

"I see, darling," Mother says tightly, squeezing her shoulder hard. "It will wash out."

"No it won't!" Catherine cries. "It's ruined. Ruined!"

Out of the corner of her eye, she sees Mr. Dean stop in his tracks, staring at her, before turning on his heel and stalking away, slipping whatever it was back into his pocket.

Score one for female hysterics.

"I'm so embarrassed," Catherine continues, covering her face with her hands.

"Come now, darling. We'll—we'll just step out." Catherine feels pressure on her shoulders and lets Mother start pushing her out of the tearoom.

"I'm so sorry!" Amalie says, almost shouting, following after them. She keeps up a steady slew of apologies until they reach the cloakroom.

"That is quite— Miss Linet," Mother stays, stopping just before the door. "We will get this sorted. Please go enjoy the tea. We will be back shortly."

Catherine gives an exaggerated sniffle and Mother sighs, pushing her into the cloakroom. Catherine looks over her shoulder just in time to see Amalie wink before the door swings closed.

"Utterly ridiculous. You'll bet she's paying for this dress," Mother mutters, pushing Catherine further into the empty cloakroom.

Catherine spins, facing herself in the mirror. There's wine down to her chemise. She'll pay for the dress herself if this works. And get Amalie a present.

"There was nothing on the floor. I don't understand how it even happened," Mother continues, unlacing the back of her dress.

Catherine shrugs. "I don't know." She keeps her eye on the door in the mirror, hoping, praying, that Rosalie will come through.

"Mr. Dean was walking over. Miss Linet is never allowed in our home again."

"That's a bit harsh," Catherine argues.

"He had a ring in his hand, I saw it," Mother says gruffly.

So did Catherine. Thank Christ Amalie had the wits to get her out of there.

"Up," Mother commands.

Catherine lifts her arms and together they carefully maneuver the dress over her head, leaving her in her stays, petticoat, and chemise.

"Maybe I can pat some of it out," Mother says, eyeing the massive stain down the front. "Grab me a towel."

Catherine hurries to the stack of towelettes in the corner and brings two back.

"Here, there's better light," Catherine says, directing her mother to lay the dress on the vanity closest to the water closet, which gets a smidge of sunlight through the transom over the door.

Mother grabs one of the towelettes and they both begin to blot at her dress.

"If we just had some water," Mother mutters, biting at her cheek as she dabs a bit too forcefully.

"There might be some in the closet?" Catherine suggests a little too eagerly.

Mother merely gives her an affronted look. In fairness, it's a terrible idea. But they need to move. If they're in here when—

"I just do not understand why you insist on acting this way," Lady Tisend snaps in a shouting whisper as she backs through the cloakroom door.

Rosalie follows after her, taking in the tableau of Catherine in her shift, bent over her gown and blotting with her mother.

Mother's gaze snaps to the door. Her eyes widen, and Catherine's never seen her move so fast. In a blink, she's got Catherine's dress in her arms, towels and all, and begins shoving Catherine into the water closet.

She goes, trying not to laugh at the absurdity of it. The door swings shut before Lady Tisend turns around, and they're left standing in the cramped water closet, holding her sopping dress. The dim daylight coming in from the high windows only makes it more pathetic.

Catherine glances at Mother and finds her looking far too pleased.

"What on earth has gotten into you?" Lady Tisend's voice is clear as a bell.

"What do you think happened?" Mother whispers, inching closer to the door to eavesdrop.

"You're enjoying this?" Catherine can't help but ask.

They were each in charge of getting their mothers here separately. Who knows what shenanigans might have occurred on Rosalie's end. With Christopher involved, anything's possible. Though Amalie certainly was a wild card.

Catherine needs to stop Mother before she starts to open the door to eavesdrop more effectively. Catherine reaches out for Mother's elbow and the door slams open. Catherine yanks Mother back just in time for Lady Tisend to barrel into the cramped room, Rosalie right behind her.

Catherine and Mother stumble backward. Rosalie pushes her mother into the center of the room, then spins and gives the door a good shove. Catherine hears the squeak of the wood against the tiled doorstep.

It's firmly stuck into place, just like it was when she got trapped at the first ball of the season. Success.

. . . Of course, she didn't imagine success would look quite like this.

Chapter Twenty-Seven
Rosalie

Mother's still practically hyperventilating with rage over Mr. Dean snubbing them in the tearoom. Mrs. Pine looks halfway between hysterical laughter and hysterics, and Catherine's . . . in just her shift and petticoat.

"What happened?" Rosalie asks.

"Amalie threw wine on me," Catherine says simply.

"She *threw* it on you?" Mrs. Pine nearly shouts.

Rosalie just stares at Catherine. Catherine shrugs. "It worked, didn't it?"

Rosalie can't help but laugh a little. "Devious."

"She certainly thought so," Catherine says, running her hand down her stays, a beautiful white set now stained with red.

Momentarily distracted, Rosalie doesn't notice Mother moving behind her to try to open the door until the handle rattles.

"Why won't it move?" Mother mutters, tugging frantically.

"Did you plan this?" Mrs. Pine asks Catherine. "This—with the wine, and the door, and *her*?"

Catherine looks to Rosalie, who can feel her mother boring a hole in her back. Seems like it's now or never.

"Open this door, right now," Mother demands.

Rosalie meets Catherine's eyes, taking strength in the fact that they're in this together. "No."

Mother moves to face her, glaring, and Rosalie takes a step

back. Catherine goes with her until they're standing there staring at their mothers, reluctantly shoulder to shoulder, angry and trapped in the water closet with them.

Rosalie musters every imperious impulse she's ever had. "You are not leaving this water closet until you end this feud. Catherine and I won't play along anymore."

Mother's eyes widen, her nostrils flaring. "Open the door, now."

"It's time Mrs. Pine understands what happened, and why."

She keeps herself tall despite the ice in her mother's eyes, her body screaming at her to cower, to run. But she can't. She has to do this. For Catherine, for Mrs. Pine, for herself.

"You have no right," Mother hisses.

Rosalie stares at her mother, willing her to make the choice herself. Willing her to see reason. "Doesn't she deserve to know?"

Mother's jaw tightens. "Don't you want to tell her? Apologize?"

"Whatever rosy image you have concocted in your head about what happened twenty-five years ago, Lady Rosalie, you are severely mistaken if you think it could be waved away with an insincere apology," Mrs. Pine says, her voice biting. "Your mother's actions were unforgivable, and I won't stand here and listen to you defend whatever you've been told. Catherine, open that door, right now."

"It wasn't unforgivable, Mama," Catherine says, her voice shaking. "You just don't know the whole story."

"You told her?" Mother exclaims, horror and shock and betrayal on her face.

"I had to," Rosalie says. "I couldn't let Catherine end up married to Mr. Dean when she can't stand him just to protect our family."

"What?" Mrs. Pine nearly shrieks, turning wide eyes on her daughter.

"Could you have used a little more tact?" Catherine mutters.

Rosalie sighs, looking among the three of them, all glaring at her now. "If we're making them tell the truth, it's only fair we do as well."

"You could have prepared me," Catherine shoots back.

"You thought we'd get through this *without* that coming out?" Rosalie asks, incredulous.

"I thought we'd get through this first and it would come into the conversation more natur—"

"What the hell are you talking about?" Mrs. Pine shouts.

"I want you to open this door right now," Mother insists.

"Mama, if you would just listen," Catherine says, reaching out to touch her mother's arm.

Mrs. Pine rears back. "Oh no. No, no, I want to know what the hell you're doing colluding with . . . conspiring with—"

"I'd hardly say we're conspiring," Rosalie hears herself say.

"It certainly seems that way," Mother puts in.

"Well, at least they agree on something," Catherine says.

"Stop that!" Mrs. Pine says. "Stop talking to each other like we're not here!"

"And let us out," Mother adds.

Rosalie runs her hands down her face, her pulse starting to race with all the shouting. It's warm in the water closet, and she's getting tired of this. "Would everyone just be—"

The door wrenches open behind her. Rosalie spins around, heart in her throat, stomach at her toes—it's not enough time. They can't get interrupted, not now.

But it's only Aunt Genevieve, looking a bit crazed. She turns and snaps the door shut again. It groans against the wood, and she gives it an experimental tug. It doesn't budge.

She turns back to them, wiping her hands down her green skirt. "So, where are we?"

They all stare at her, the four of them quiet in shock.

"Christopher squealed like a pig when I asked him where you'd gone," Aunt Genevieve says with a shrug.

Rosalie huffs out an incredulous laugh and Catherine snorts quietly beside her. They are so in over their heads, but at least Aunt Genevieve is here too. Which . . . well, she doesn't know how it might change the situation, but it's another variable.

"Are you part of this? Did you agree to . . . to . . ." Mother starts.

"Capture you in a water closet? No, that was all their idea," Aunt Genevieve says, gesturing to Rosalie and Catherine. "Though I agree that it's high time the two of you talked, and if you won't explain, Clara, I will."

Mother glares at Aunt Genevieve. "It's not—"

"Of the three of us, I rather think I have the most right to decide whether it is or isn't Mrs. Pine's business?"

"Would someone like to explain what in the hell you're talking about?" Mrs. Pine demands, glaring at all of them.

Mother stands with her hands on her hips, staring daggers at Aunt Genevieve. "Well?"

"Coward," Aunt Genevieve says coolly, before turning to look directly at Mrs. Pine. "I have come to apologize for the incredible wrong that was done to you twenty-five years ago. I didn't know my brother and soon-to-be sister-in-law would go to such lengths to protect my reputation. Had I known, I would have put up a fight to make sure that your honor was equally protected. I'm sorry I didn't."

Mrs. Pine's tight jaw slowly goes slack, her eyes widening. "I . . . don't understand," she says, her voice much softer. "What—what is she talking about?"

She turns to Mother, who looks between the two of them for a long, painful moment. "When Lord Tisend began courting me, he told me that Captain Daniels had a . . . reputation, and I ought to stay away from him. As should you."

Mother hesitates, looking to Aunt Genevieve, who sighs loudly. "He seduced me," she says, and it comes out too loudly, echoing off the walls.

There's a very uncomfortable silence.

"You were fifteen," Mrs. Pine says, aghast.

Rosalie squirms. She hadn't actually done the math. Catherine winces beside her.

"And very naïve," Aunt Genevieve agrees. "George found out and tried to intimidate him into making me an . . . honest offer. But Captain Daniels was so wretched, he decided it wasn't worth it. Instead, George paid him off to stay quiet, and whisked me up north so rumors couldn't spread."

"But Captain Daniels never left town," Mother says. "And George couldn't go around warning everyone he knew, because he'd—"

"He'd have had to explain how he knew," Mrs. Pine deduces slowly. "Lady Jones, I am terribly sorry that happened to you."

So that's where Catherine gets her kind heart.

Aunt Genevieve waves her off. "I was fine. Silly, and young, and impressionable. A few years with my very strict cousin, and I bounced right back, met Walter, and everything worked out. No one told me that in the interim you suffered on my behalf."

Mrs. Pine's warm regard melts quickly away as she turns to

Mother. "You didn't think to simply *tell* me this? Instead you told the whole ton I'd fallen to him too?"

Mother meets Mrs. Pine's angry gaze, her face cracked, and hurting, and vulnerable in a way that makes Rosalie want to shrink against the wall. She knew it would be painful, but she didn't know how *much* it would hurt to watch her mother live through this.

"George made me promise," she says, her voice brittle.

"I wouldn't have told anymore," Mrs. Pine insists hotly. "I'd have taken that to the grave," she adds, glancing at Aunt Genevieve.

"I know," Mother whispers.

"Then why?" Mrs. Pine demands, her cheeks pink, hands fisted. "Why didn't you trust me?"

"Because I was young, and silly, and in love with a man who said he knew best," Mother exclaims. "I did what I was told."

There's a pregnant pause as those words settle over all of them. Rosalie wonders how many friendships have ended, how much hurt has been wrought, because women are meant to do as they're told.

"I wasn't as headstrong as either of our daughters, it seems, even if I thought I was," Mother continues.

Rosalie glances at Catherine, who shoots her a tentative smile. The sick, twisted feeling in Rosalie's stomach eases just a little.

"You never wrote to explain," Mrs. Pine says. The tone of her voice breaks Rosalie's heart. So much hurt and anger and sadness laced through each word.

"Would you have read a letter if I had?" Mother asks.

Mrs. Pine opens her mouth to snap out a retort, and then pauses. "I don't know," she admits.

"There was no apology I could make that would justify what

I did," Mother says softly. "I knew what I was doing was wrong, and I did it anyway. I did it because I wanted to protect you, and I had no other way, not without breaking George's trust, and jeopardizing Genevieve's future."

"I wouldn't have told anyone," Mrs. Pine repeats, almost plaintively.

"I know," Mother says, reaching up to swipe at her cheek.

She's crying. Rosalie hasn't seen her mother cry in . . .

Catherine's hand slips into hers, squeezing. Rosalie squeezes back, the two of them watching their mothers crack themselves open. It's beautiful, and horrible, and she's glad she's not alone.

Aunt Genevieve glances at them, eyes falling to their hands. She opens her mouth—

"I am sorry I took the choice from you. That I forced your hand," Mother says softly. "It was wrong. I had my reasons. I— God, I loved you both," she continues, looking between Aunt Genevieve and Mrs. Pine. "There hasn't been a day I didn't regret how I went about protecting you."

Mrs. Pine stands there staring at Mother, her lip between her teeth. After a moment, she bobs her head, blowing out a long, forceful breath. "You were between a rock and a terribly hard place. Catherine reminded me the other day that while it was awful when it happened, I have gone on to a beautiful life."

"Can you forgive me for it?" Mother whispers. "I know I can't ever change it, but I am sorry. I am so very, very sorry. I wanted to tell you, I *should* have told you."

"I can try," Mrs. Pine whispers.

They stand still for a moment before Mother moves forward, wrapping her arms around Mrs. Pine with a sob. Slowly, Mrs. Pine hugs her back.

Rosalie lists into Catherine, heart in her throat. Catherine releases her hand to wrap her arm around Rosalie, holding tight and sniffling.

They did this. They made this happen.

It's a strangely wonderful feeling, watching her mother hug her oldest friend. She deserves forgiveness, and happiness, and friendship. Rosalie's not sure she's ever seen the broken-open, carefree smile on her mother's face now as she pulls back, holding Mrs. Pine's forearms.

"You know an excellent way to celebrate this rekindled friendship? We should track down Captain Daniels, see where he ended up, and ruin him," Aunt Genevieve says.

They all burst out laughing, the lingering tension evaporating around them.

"It has been a while since we've been on a trip," Mother says to Aunt Genevieve.

"I hope he didn't hurt you," Mrs. Pine adds, looking to Aunt Genevieve.

"Only my heart. He was—" She glances at Rosalie and Catherine, still standing with their arms around each other, Rosalie's head on Catherine's shoulder.

Their mothers slowly turn to look at them as well, and that elated, carefree air seems to disappear all at once.

They can't—they can't know. Not just from this. They were hugging not moments ago. It's not—they can't—

"I *knew* it," Aunt Genevieve says softly.

Oh, God.

Catherine's grip on her shoulder tightens and Rosalie can feel her own hand fisting into the back of Catherine's shift. Because she's still just in her undergarments, which rather changes the image, doesn't it?

Rosalie knows they should pull away from each other, but

she can't let go of Catherine, can't make herself step away. They weren't planning on doing this now. Today was always supposed to be about their mothers, and hopefully dispatching Mr. Dean. But not this.

Not telling them they're . . .

"Knew what, exactly?" Mother asks, looking to Aunt Genevieve.

Rosalie meets Aunt Genevieve's eyes. Fragile hope rises in her chest that maybe Aunt Genevieve knows what to do, how to say it. That she has the magic fix somewhere within, just like when she tells a well-timed joke to break the tension.

"Tell her," Aunt Genevieve says instead.

Rosalie tries to swallow, but her mouth has gone suddenly dry. She meets Mother's eyes but can't summon the words. She wants to, but—

"Neither of us wants to marry Mr. Dean, and not because he's boring. Well, not just because he's boring," Catherine says, her voice rough but strong.

Aunt Genevieve snorts and Mother's lips twitch. Mrs. Pine's still staring at them, wide-eyed. Rosalie squeezes Catherine's waist.

"We don't want to marry him because we've fallen for each other instead." Catherine says it so simply. So firmly. So beautifully.

"You've—" Mother starts.

"You don't want to marry Mr. Dean," Mrs. Pine repeats slowly.

Catherine takes a deep breath. "I want to be with Rosalie."

Rosalie tugs Catherine a little closer, a strange relief flooding through her chest, even with Mother staring at her like she's gone mad. Some last small part of her heart slips back into place.

Catherine isn't Jane. Catherine is like no one she's ever known before. She's standing here with Rosalie, brave and strong and real.

"I just haven't figured out how to persuade him out of proposing after the whole . . . saving-his-life debacle. Which I still contend is utterly absurd," Catherine adds, glancing at Rosalie.

Catherine's incredulity is enough to make her laugh, just a little, which unsticks her tongue from the roof of her mouth. She can do this. She can be brave too.

"I hope you're not too angry," she says, looking to Mother. "I know this isn't what you wanted. What either of you wanted," she adds, meeting Mrs. Pine's eyes. "But Catherine is the one I want, not Mr. Dean. Not . . . any man."

Neither Mother nor Mrs. Pine seems to know what to say. They're just staring, blankly, both of them. It's unnerving.

"And we don't know—we haven't figured out what it would look like," Catherine says, glancing at Rosalie. "But we . . ."

"We hope you'll both help us figure it out," Rosalie says, her voice small and high. Mother's unflinching stare makes her feel like she's eight again, but instead of asking forgiveness for breaking Mother's favorite figurine, she's asking for help making a life with a woman she adores.

"You're the smartest women we know," Catherine says. "If anyone can figure it out, you can."

Rosalie smiles hopefully at her mother. She needs her help. But more than that, she wants it. Wants her to reach out and hold her the way she held Mrs. Pine. To promise her everything will be all right, and tell her she still loves her. That who Rosalie wants to want doesn't matter.

But the silence stretches on, and on, and *on*. Rosalie's stomach twists and her heart starts beating uncomfortably fast. This isn't the silence of acceptance, of help, of support. It's something else, something she doesn't know if she can face.

Catherine's grip on her shoulder is almost painful now.

Mother suddenly seems to come back to herself, blinking and looking away from Rosalie and Catherine. She pulls herself up tall, putting the armor she wears through the world back on without even a shudder, all the vulnerability she showed with Mrs. Pine gone in an instant.

"Dissuading Mr. Dean won't be difficult, Miss Pine," Mother says, glancing at Catherine before looking at Mrs. Pine. "Lord Dean thinks doing business is quite gauche and will never allow his son to marry into a family that would expect his participation in it. All you'll need to do is suggest that her father will want Lord Dean to invest in his business."

Mrs. Pine nods once and Mother blows out a breath, clapping her hands together. She meets Rosalie's eyes for a moment, opening her mouth, and Rosalie feels her hopes rise—

But then she simply walks to the door, gives it an immense yank, and walks through the doorway without a backward glance.

"Mother," Rosalie calls out, reflexive and terrified.

But her mother doesn't come back.

Her knees go wobbly and Rosalie leans into Catherine, who grips her shoulders. "It's okay," she whispers.

Rosalie turns to meet her eyes. "No, it isn't," she says, and she can hear the tears in her voice already.

Aunt Genevieve moves for the first time in minutes. Rosalie had almost forgotten she was there until she slips her arm around Rosalie's waist, holding her up with Catherine.

Mrs. Pine is still just standing there, staring and silent.

"I've got you," Aunt Genevieve says softly.

Rosalie looks up at her and Aunt Genevieve smiles before turning to Mrs. Pine. They wait, but she doesn't say anything, doesn't even acknowledge Aunt Genevieve's gaze. Catherine's dress is nearly twisted in her hands, forgotten amid everything. She unfurls it haltingly, holding it by the shoulders.

"We should return to the tea, sod the stain," she says to no one in particular.

Catherine slumps against Rosalie with a mewl of despair.

Mrs. Pine looks to them then, finally meeting Catherine's eyes. "We'll dispatch of Mr. Dean tonight, and talk about everything else later."

Her voice is hard, back ramrod straight, but it's something, at least. Watching her walk into the cloakroom doesn't pierce through Rosalie's heart the way her mother's exit did, but it's close.

Rosalie and Catherine stand there holding each other up, everything irreparably different. Rosalie knew this was a possibility. That her mother, and her father, might not approve. That Catherine's parents might not approve.

She just didn't think it would feel like her childhood has splintered in her chest, stabbing every bit of joy and freedom and safety she's ever felt until what's left is bloody and sloshing in her stomach.

"Everything will be all right, I promise you that. Even if I'm not one of the smartest women you know."

Both of them turn to look at Aunt Genevieve. She reaches out to pat Catherine's cheek and then steps back, pushing Rosalie lightly. Rosalie takes the hint and throws her arms around Catherine's shoulders, pressing her face into her neck while Catherine wraps her arms around her waist.

Whatever the future holds, they've chosen each other. Chosen together.

Catherine slowly pulls back. Her beautiful brown eyes are red-rimmed and teary, but she's still here. Rosalie rises on her tiptoes and Catherine meets her halfway in a terrified, devastated kiss.

"We'll make it," Rosalie whispers as they part.

Rosalie can see in her eyes that she has doubts. Rosalie does too. So she kisses her one more time, sliding her hands to hold Catherine's jaw, keeping her close and safe and there with her until Aunt Genevieve coughs quietly.

Catherine presses her lips together and forces a watery smile. And then she pulls away and walks out into the cloakroom.

Rosalie stands there, listening, but either Mrs. Pine is speaking too quietly to hear, or, more likely, Catherine's dressing in horrid silence under her mother's disapproving gaze. Rosalie shivers, bringing a hand up to cover her mouth as the tears finally fall in earnest.

She wants her mother to come back and tell her it's all right. To promise to help. To promise to love her. She wants—

Aunt Genevieve catches her before she sinks to the floor. Rosalie weeps quietly against her chest, hands fisted in the back of her dress. She must be wrinkling it.

She should be grateful to have Aunt Genevieve—grateful she's not alone. But even with Aunt Genevieve holding her up, this hurts so much more than she thought it would.

They fixed their mothers' relationship just like they planned, but somehow they broke everything else in the span of just a few minutes. How has it only been a few minutes?

Chapter Twenty-Eight
Catherine

Every time she moves, she can feel her damp chemise sticking to her skin. The faint stench of wine keeps wafting up to her nose, roiling her already-twitching stomach.

Rosalie and Lady Jones never came back into the room. Christopher, Amalie, and Henrietta have been throwing her confused looks for the last two hours.

She hasn't gotten up the courage to say a thing to her mother. Instead, she's just standing there, her whole body tight and twisted, her heart so sore it feels like she's being stabbed by a dull knife. Because Mother looks like absolutely nothing happened. Her smile while they say goodbye to their guests seems entirely genuine.

Henrietta and her mother approach them with Mr. Rile. Henrietta opens her mouth—

"A marvelous tea, Mrs. Pine. You've really outdone yourself," Mrs. Raught says.

Mother smiles brightly. "Thank you. And thank you, Mr. Rile, for attending."

"Any chance to spend some time with my dear fiancée is time well spent, and the sandwiches, in particular, were scrumptious," he says, his broad cheeks dimpled in a brilliant smile.

Catherine tries to take solace in Henrietta's happiness. Tries to smile genuinely at her even as she gives Catherine a searching look.

"Thank you most kindly," Mother says to Mr. Rile.

Mrs. Raught leads them away before Henrietta can say anything, and Henrietta looks over her shoulder at Catherine until they're down the stairs and out of sight.

Father appears on Mother's other side. "They're leaving."

Catherine opens her mouth, about to ask who he means while Mother glances around at the mostly empty tearoom.

"All right. Do it quietly."

Mr. and Mrs. Flintley approach them and Catherine shuts her mouth, forcing a smile while she watches her father make his slow way across the room to Lord Dean and Mr. Dean, who have been loitering by the dessert table. They sat glaringly separately for the tea. And now Lord Dean is stuffing his face rather conspicuously. Mr. Dean looks a bit embarrassed.

It doesn't deter Father, who steps up to them with a jaunty smile. Catherine notices Christopher and Amalie watching from across the room while Lady Tisend speaks to someone she doesn't know. She's acting like nothing happened too, but hiding it more poorly than Mother. Her shoulders are tense, her smile pinched.

Catherine turns back to Mr. and Mrs. Flintley, trying to focus on whatever they're saying to Mother.

"Sir," she hears from across the room.

Catherine looks back at Father, who's going on to Mr. Dean about something she can't quite make out over by the dessert table. Lord Dean beside them is slowly going red in the face, Mr. Dean glancing at him at intervals.

"Sir, I implore you—"

Father says something else with a little bounce on his toes and Lord Dean slams down the profiterole he was holding, sending crème pat flying onto Mr. Dean's and Father's jackets.

"I will not let this stand!" Lord Dean exclaims, his voice echoing around the room.

Everyone turns to stare at the three of them.

"Whatever do you mean, Lord Dean? I thought we were to have a merry union?" Father asks, glancing over at Catherine and winking.

Her bruised heart soars.

"There will be no union between our families, absolutely not. I cannot have my son involved with business so base."

Mother scoffs beside her, her hand curling around Catherine's elbow.

"Mr. Pine—" Mr. Dean starts.

Father merely shrugs casually, his voice carrying cleanly across the room. "Well, that's rather for the best. I wouldn't want my beautiful, intelligent daughter around any man who would so loudly embarrass my wife. Both of them are more prize than all of the Dean fortune anyway. Good riddance."

With that, Father turns, ignoring Mr. Dean's spluttering behind him and Lord Dean's scandalized face. Father strides evenly across the room, no hint of his limp, grinning.

"That's that, then," he says, taking Catherine's other arm. "We so appreciate your coming to the tea," he adds to the Flintleys, who are staring at them, mouths agog.

He squeezes Catherine's arm as she and Mother curtsy to the Flintleys. They leave quickly without another word.

Catherine can't help but smile at Father. "Thank you," she whispers, refusing to look over her shoulder at Mr. Dean.

"For you, anything," Father whispers back, leaning in to kiss her cheek before turning to a rapidly assembling line of stragglers.

Catherine's chest clenches. Will he still look like that at the end of the night, when Mother has told him everything? Will he still think her such a prize when he knows whom she wants? Does "anything" really mean *anything*?

A few minutes later Lord Dean and Mr. Dean slink past behind the other guests without a word. Mr. Dean doesn't meet her eyes, seeming more bemused than anything else. Which is . . . absolutely fitting.

She wants to tell Rosalie. Wants to see her expression when she recounts the entire exchange. Wishes she could have seen him taken down a peg. Catherine glances over at Christopher and Amalie, who stare back with wide eyes, caught between excitement and confusion. They'll have to tell her.

Mother leaves Catherine's side as soon as the rest of the guests file out. She walks over to bid Lady Tisend adieu where she, Christopher, and Amalie are still hovering at the back of the room. Catherine clutches at Father's arm, watching the stilted way the women speak—watching Lady Tisend lead Christopher and Amalie rapidly out of the room without more than a nod in Father's direction.

Mother stands alone at the back of the hall, staring out the large windows down to the street. She was so excited for this tea. So proud and so brave to face the ton as she has. And Catherine took all of that from her. She thought righting the wrong between Mother and Lady Tisend was what needed to be done—thought it would be worth any of the fallout.

She still thinks it was. At least, she thinks she thinks it was.

She's not sure she'll feel the same way once she's alone. When she can focus on the way Mother avoided her eyes in the water closet. When she can think about the way Lady Tisend ignored Rosalie altogether.

If it were just Catherine's happiness, maybe she could bear it. But even though Father seemed more righteous in the altercation with Lord Dean, Catherine will still be the ridiculous girl who ruined a perfect match. The ton will talk about her family again—a second generation disgraced, just differently.

"Your mother will be fine," Father whispers. They watch Mother wandering the back of the room, just the three of them and the staff now milling about, clearing plates. "Your happiness matters more than any fortune; she knows that."

Catherine forces herself to smile, to look relieved. But it's a long few minutes while Mother liaises with the staff, and longer still as they make their way out of the Upper Rooms, leaving their "triumphant" afternoon behind.

No one says a word in the carriage. Catherine tries to catch Mother's eye, but Mother won't look at her. Father, none the wiser, stares out the window, looking absurdly cheerful. It would almost be funny if it didn't hurt so much.

By the time they arrive home, Catherine feels like she might fly apart with rage and confusion and sadness. The door closes behind them and she stands in the foyer, watching Father help Mother remove her wrap. Like nothing's wrong. Like nothing changed. Like there's nothing to say.

Mother hands her gloves to Miss Teit, muttering something about a very light supper and Catherine feels herself break.

"Would you at least look at me?" she exclaims, her words bouncing around the room.

Miss Teit glances among them and slowly backs out of the foyer and down the servants' hallway, leaving Catherine staring at Mother and Father, chest heaving.

"Are you really going to pretend it didn't happen?"

"Catherine—"

"Just wake up tomorrow and start a list of other suitors? Send me off on more outings, like everything is just as it was this morning?"

Mother finally meets her eyes and Catherine physically steps back. It's a look she's never seen before. Like she's searching Catherine for the woman she knew, when Catherine's still standing there, exactly the same person she was before the tea.

"What did I miss?" Father asks, looking between them.

Catherine opens her mouth, unsure of how to face it—how to tell him—how to risk him looking at her the way Mother is now.

Mother shakes her head. "I need to speak with your father before we discuss this as a family," she says, her tone final. It almost feels like a scolding.

"It's about me, shouldn't—"

"Let me do this, Catherine. Please," Mother says.

Her *please* feels like a physical blow.

Biting at her lip, Catherine watches with dread as Mother guides her confused father up the stairs. She has to support him now, his muscles tired from the tea—from playing host. From saving her so gamely from a life of mediocrity.

When they reach the landing, Father looks down at her and smiles.

Thank you, Catherine mouths. If he feels like it seems Mother does, it may be her last opportunity to say it.

He winks at her, and then they're gone, moving slowly up the next staircase.

What if he never smiles at her like that again? What if everything is different from this moment on? What if they never look at her the same way ever again?

She didn't think about the aftermath, not like this. She never let herself. Forced herself to believe that her parents could only accept her. That it would be hard at first, of course, but it was possible. It was possible they'd help her and keep loving her exactly as they always have.

She just wanted . . . she just *wanted*.

She stands there, trembling, trying not to cry, and Miss Teit comes out of the servants' hallway, wringing her hands.

"Shall I help you undress?" she asks. "We ought to get to that stain."

Catherine looks down at her wine-soaked dress. She'd almost forgotten. Everything started from that stain. From asking Amalie for help. From daring to wonder if there was a different way to live her life—a way that gave her Rosalie, and Christopher, and a bigger, wider, better world than the one she's always been told to expect.

She doesn't know if she can stay in this dress for another minute.

"Here. Spin," Miss Teit says softly.

Catherine realizes then that her chest is heaving and she's sucking in scant air. Miss Teit quickly undoes the laces and helps lift the dress and her petticoat over her head.

The moment the fabric clears her hair, Catherine whispers a choked "Thank you."

Then she's running full tilt up all the staircases, past the sitting room, past her parents' floor, until she hurtles into her room, slamming herself into safe, secluded peace.

It's started raining, water streaking down the window. How fitting. If this were one of her novels . . .

Catherine growls and hurls herself onto the window seat.

She curls up in her wine-soaked chemise and her stays, arms around her knees, staring out at the rain.

Rosalie isn't going to climb into her window in a pair of riding pants and whisk her away to live happily off somewhere. Her parents aren't going to easily turn the other cheek. Society isn't going to magically accept Catherine and Rosalie together. There isn't a fairy-tale ending.

It didn't all have to be tonight. They didn't *have* to upend everything they've ever known all at once. It would have been easier to just keep . . . pretending. Fend off suitors and steal time together.

But as Catherine watches a raindrop slide down the window, she knows she doesn't really want to live a half-life like that. Always stealing time, stealing moments, stealing each other.

Her mother's unsure gaze, her father's confusion, Rosalie's mother's dismissal—they sear at her gut and clench at her heart. But even so, she still wants the opportunity to love Rosalie, really love her. To decide how to start a life and grow together. Live off in the country, run a home—like she would have with Mr. Dean.

The happiness her mother has with her father. The happiness Amalie and Christopher have. She and Rosalie deserve that too.

She wants her mother to visit. Wants her father to send her letters and keep exchanging novels. Wants to watch her brother meet Rosalie. Wants to watch Rosalie beat him at every card game imaginable.

She wants the life with her family she always thought she'd have. Just with a woman by her side instead of a man. Surely it's not so much to ask.

Catherine sighs, resting her cheek on her knee to stare out at the rain.

She's always quietly thought the happily-ever-afters in her novels were disingenuous. That there was too much tumult, too much to the story before the wedding, for everything to end in a sunny *happily ever after.*

She wanted to be the heroine of her own story. Maybe this is the price.

She turns her face into her knees and lets the tears come in full, sobbing until the pain dulls enough to sleep.

Chapter Twenty-Nine
Rosalie

Rosalie stands in her foyer, staring at Mother, Christopher, and Aunt Genevieve. Amalie wanted to come with them; Christopher tried to invite her for . . . more tea. But in the only words she's spoken to them since the Upper Rooms, Mother said they needed to speak as a family on some matters, and Christopher could see her tomorrow.

Rosalie doesn't know if she should be hopeful or terrified.

They're all just standing there, slowly pulling off gloves in the most stifled silence she's ever heard. Rosalie looks at each of them, not sure what to say, not sure what to ask for. She feels numb and frantic all at once.

Mother finally moves, heading for the stairs.

"No," Aunt Genevieve says, her voice like a whipcrack.

Mother pauses and Rosalie takes her first deep breath since the cloakroom.

"We are talking about this. Family meeting, now."

"Genevieve, this can wait until the—"

"FATHER," Christopher bellows. Rosalie, Mother, and Aunt Genevieve jump. "You heard Aunt Genevieve," Christopher says sternly. "Sitting room, now."

Father appears in the hallway from his study, rubbing his hands together eagerly and yawning. He's such a gossipmonger, even exhausted by the trip back from London.

Rosalie might vomit.

"What's the news?" Father asks. "Did anyone choke this time? I hope it was Mr. Martin. He could use a good wallop on the back."

Mother sighs gustily. *Mr. Martin could use a good wallop*, Rosalie thinks idly, swaying in place.

"We've important family matters to discuss, George," Aunt Genevieve says, taking Rosalie's hand. "Sitting room, now."

Rosalie grips her hand, following her upstairs and toward the sitting room. She tries to keep herself calm, to hold on to Aunt Genevieve. If her parents—if this is—

The sitting room is dark and drafty. Christopher hurries to the fireplace and gets a fire going while Aunt Genevieve and Rosalie sit on one of the settees, Mother and Father settling on the other. They don't need the staff for this. This is . . . private.

Christopher comes to sit on her other side. Rosalie wishes they'd gone upstairs to Mother's drawing room so that she doesn't need to stare at where she pushed Catherine up against the bookcases when they kissed for the first time.

"Do you want to start?" Aunt Genevieve asks softly.

Rosalie blinks. Father's leaning in, his hands between his knees, expecting her to provide some salacious season gossip. By contrast, Mother's almost leaning away from her, like she wants as much distance between them as she can get.

Rosalie opens her mouth, parched and horrified. She doesn't know if she can tell him this—can rip his world apart like she's clearly done to her mother. But Father just looks back at her, open and receptive.

They don't talk about important things much, but he always listens to her.

"I . . . don't want to marry Mr. Dean," she hears herself say, struggling to maintain eye contact.

Father blinks back at her. "You don't?"

"No," she says, her voice cracking.

"Well, that is a surprise," Father says, sitting up straight. "Has he done something, other than show a preference for the Pine girl?"

Rosalie swallows hard. It can't be worse than Mother's reaction . . . can it?

"I—I don't want to marry him because of—because I . . ." She can't push it out of her mouth, not with him staring at her like that.

"Rosalie has developed feelings for Miss Pine," Mother says.

Rosalie flinches. Mother doesn't meet her eyes, looking calmly instead at Father, who's staring back at her, mouth gaping. Rosalie's whole body goes stiff with terror. Aunt Genevieve's hand comes to covers hers where she's twisted her fingers into the lace cover of her dress.

"Does Miss Pine share her . . . affection?" Father asks, his voice sounding hollow against the quiet crackling of the fire.

"She does," Mother says. "I suggest we allow them a year, maybe two, together before deciding on the proper future for them. Genevieve has rooms at Jones House. They could return for relevant social functions regularly, so their absence could be easily waved away. And after the various scandals with Mr. Dean that I now realize they architected, it would likely be for the best anyway."

Rosalie's barely breathing. Her body feels frozen, her fingers tingling from where she's holding too tightly to Aunt Genevieve and the settee below her.

Father looks over at her, appraising. Rosalie stares back, desperate to know what he's thinking. She wants to scream, wants to cry, wants to fling her arms around her mother and shake her all at once.

If this was what she was thinking the whole time, could she not have said, instead of storming out of the water closet, leaving Rosalie to think that—to feel—

"Will that suffice?" Father asks, looking now to Aunt Genevieve.

"It's not my choice to make," Aunt Genevieve says firmly. "But I would love to have them."

"Rosalie? Is that what you want?" Father asks.

"Of course it is," Mother says archly.

"Let her have her say," Aunt Genevieve says curtly.

Mother holds up her hands and then waves to Rosalie to weigh in.

Rosalie sits there staring at her parents, hope and relief and a strange rage warring in her chest. Was it always this simple? Was this always allowed? She's been living and preparing for a life she's never wanted for as long as she's been alive. And the whole time, if she'd just said, "I want something else," they would have listened?

She feels betrayed. And angry. And grateful. And, and, and—

"Rosalie," Aunt Genevieve says softly.

"Yes," Rosalie exclaims, almost shouting. Everyone jumps.

She sits for a moment, breathing hard, trying to rein in the overflow of emotion before she starts yelling. But no one else says anything. They're all sitting there, waiting for her to say words she has no idea how to say.

She's known this about herself her whole life, how can she not have the words now?

"Rosalie and Miss Pine told me and her mother that they would like to be together," Mother starts.

"Clara," Aunt Genevieve scolds. "Let her talk."

"Well, she's not saying anything!"

Rosalie cringes and Christopher leans forward. "Perhaps this isn't the easiest thing to discuss. You could give her some grace," he says firmly.

"You already know?" Father asks. He sounds so like his normal self, curious and engaged.

"Of course I know. I've been paying attention. I've been here," Christopher replies, his voice cold.

"My responsibilities in London—"

"And I asked," Christopher says over him. "You decided she was supposed to marry Mr. Boring two years ago and never bothered to ask if she even liked him, let alone if marriage was what she wanted."

Rosalie places her hand on his arm. Christopher looks over at her and she can't help but smile. His defense shifts something in her chest.

"I've never wanted to marry any man," Rosalie hears herself say. "I've known that for a very long time, but I didn't think there was any . . . alternative, until I met Catherine." Christopher takes her hand and squeezes. "She's the most wonderful person I've ever known, and I want the chance to be with her and to decide with her what our life could look like, if all of you and her parents can support that."

Father's lips twitch, almost like he might smile, but Mother's face is still blank. She's still too calm, too collected, and it puts a sliver of doubt into Rosalie's otherwise rising hopes.

"But if the . . . solution you've come up with is that Catherine and I can be together for a few years, but then we'll still be expected to part and marry, I don't want it." Mother purses her lips and Rosalie finds herself leaning forward, pulling Aunt Genevieve and Christopher with her. "It would hurt too much. It would hurt more than losing her now. Can't you see that?"

"If Aunt Genevieve can't have them live at Jones House forever, they can come live with me," Christopher says quickly. "And they'll never have to marry, if that's what they want."

"I never said they couldn't stay with me forever," Aunt Genevieve says, affronted.

"Well, at some point you'll die," Christopher says.

Rosalie gasps and Aunt Genevieve snorts. She thinks she hears Father laugh across from them, but she's too busy staring at Christopher, aghast.

"Well, she will!" Christopher says, meeting her eyes. "I'm the only one who can offer you a permanent residence after the rest of them croak. You'll have to take it."

Mother, Father, and Aunt Genevieve let out varying noises of disagreement. Rosalie laughs, and it's such a freeing, wonderful feeling.

"I already told you I would," she says, gripping his hand.

"You made this offer already?" Father asks, bringing both their gazes back to him. "Where will you live?"

"The northern estate," Christopher says. "Or I'll find another residence if you won't have us there until I inherit."

"You'd be willing to spend your own money to give your sister a safe place to live?" Father presses.

"I'd be willing to spend all of my money to give her a safe place to live," Christopher says simply, as easy as breathing. "If you won't support her, I will."

Rosalie presses her shoulder into his, so incredibly grateful for him, and for Aunt Genevieve, still clinging to her other hand.

Father's stern face slowly cracks into a smile. "I am proud of you," he says.

Christopher's face stills, his hand going slack around her own.

"It seems you've made rather excellent use of this season. I regret that I doubted your intentions, staying here rather than coming with me to London. I will be proud to have you inherit the title, when I finally croak."

It makes everyone except Mother laugh.

"Thank you," Christopher says, his voice trembling. "I would do it for Rosalie even if you hated me for it, though, so don't be too proud."

"I'll be proud of my son if I want," Father argues. "You cannot stop me."

Rosalie stares at him. More words that should have been said so much sooner.

But the way Christopher is smiling now, the way his hand is gripping Rosalie's again, she's grateful. It would have killed her for Christopher to lose their parents on her account.

"Don't you want to run your own home someday? Have children?" Rosalie looks over to find Mother watching them almost curiously.

Rosalie hesitates, glancing at Aunt Genevieve and back to Mother. They're both living lives she's never wanted. Father— she doesn't want to say this in front of him.

"It's all right to want something different," Aunt Genevieve says, giving Mother and Father a pointed look while squeezing Rosalie's hand.

Rosalie sighs and squeezes back, clenching her eyes shut

before meeting her mother's gaze. "It wouldn't feel like it was my life, if I married a man, if I bore his children. I'd be living his life. I know that's what you wanted for me, what you'd planned for me, and I'm so sorry, but I don't want it."

"Rosalie—" Mother starts, but now that she's begun, she can't stop the words from coming fast and sure.

"I have always . . . felt the way you said I would about a man about women. And now with Catherine—I know what it's truly supposed to feel like when you meet someone you want to spend your life with. And I know—I know it isn't the life that would make you proud," she says, meeting Father's eyes. "And I know it isn't the life that will make society happy," she adds, looking to Mother.

"We—" Father says.

"And I am sorry. If I could change myself, I would have, just to make it easier, but I can't. And I don't want to anymore. I'll do as much as I can to help, and find a way to fix what I've broken, but I can't—I can't—"

"You do not need to be fixed," Father says loudly, stopping her tirade, the words hitting her chest like a punch. "You do not need to change, nor to fix anything. To hell with Lord Dean."

"George," Mother exclaims with a laugh.

"He is a mean old man," Father says, turning to Mother. "You heard what he said in the Pump Room about Mrs. Pine. Who's to say he wouldn't say the same about us, or Rosalie, in a moment of inhibition?"

"It was horribly indelicate," Mother agrees.

"Even if Rosalie wanted to marry that boy, I'd have had quiet reservations. But as it is, I'm glad you won't be marrying him," Father says, looking back at Rosalie. "And we shall help you and Miss Pine, whatever you need."

"Really?" she asks, breathless.

"We have not spent our entire lives developing an impeccable reputation, gathering all this power and wealth and social influence just to crush your spirit," Father says, as if it's the simplest thing in the world.

As if it's a given.

That wretched fiery indignation rises again. "Just like that. After all these years—all the etiquette lessons, and all the time spent making me into the perfect little wife—all the lectures about *what we do*—it's perfectly all right that I don't want to marry?"

She winces as it comes out loud and rough, but her parents don't yell back. Instead, Father turns to look at Mother, almost imploring. There can't be more family secrets. Rosalie glances at Christopher, who stares back, equally at sea. Can there?

"You might not be as alone as you think," Aunt Genevieve says.

Rosalie turns, looking up at her aunt, one of her very favorite people in the world. Desperate, shocking yearning rises painfully in her chest.

"Do you—have you felt like this?" Rosalie whispers.

Aunt Genevieve gives her the softest smile she's ever seen. "No, darling, I haven't," she says, her voice achingly gentle.

It does nothing to stop the painful, stabbing feeling in her stomach. She didn't know she *wanted* someone else to feel like this. Didn't know what the hope of having someone to talk to would feel like. Even fleetingly, it was wide and wonderful and absurdly comforting, and its loss hurts almost as much as Mother walking out of the water closet earlier in the night.

"But I have."

Rosalie turns slowly to find Mother staring back at her, eyes wide and brimming. It can't—she can't—

"I was so angry at myself earlier," Mother says.

"Angry at—" Rosalie starts, breath bated, hope and that raw, wounded pain pushing at her chest.

"That you felt you had to hide this from me. That you didn't think you could talk about it. That I never sat you down and told you—" She breaks off, using her free hand to wipe at her cheek.

Mother has felt like this for a woman? And she never said? All this time, all of the courting, all of Rosalie's *life* they could have shared this, and she never said?

Mother blows out a shaking breath as she meets Rosalie's eyes. "It didn't seem fair to burden you with a secret so large," she says, her voice cracking.

"I wouldn't have told anyone," Rosalie says, unable to keep the hurt from bleeding through.

"Nor would I," Christopher adds beside her, his arm coming around her shoulders. "It's not what we do," he adds, voice sharp.

"We know you wouldn't have," Father says as Mother stares at both of them, her lips pressed tightly together.

"You knew, this whole time?" Rosalie stares at her father in shock, in wonder, in anger. It's like she's seeing her parents as entirely new people. "And it didn't matter?"

Father shakes his head with a sad smile. "I loved your mother from the very first night we danced. Everything about her. That she'd loved before me didn't matter. Who she loved before me didn't matter. Just that I was her greatest and her last."

Rosalie feels a tear slip down her cheek and tries to reach up to wipe it away. Both Christopher and Aunt Genevieve whip out handkerchiefs for her. She takes Christopher's with trembling fingers.

"And you—Father—" Rosalie starts, looking back at her

mother, who's gripping Father's hand so tightly. "It doesn't matter that—you feel the same way for him that—" She can't seem to find the proper words.

There aren't proper words for any of this, because it's never discussed.

Mother swallows hard, meeting her eyes. "For me, I think, it matters more who the person is than whether they are a man or a woman."

"Oh," Rosalie says.

She didn't know. What else doesn't she know?

"Had the girl I loved once stayed—had I had your bravery, darling, to go after her when she left, I don't know where I'd be today," Mother says, and Rosalie's heart stutters.

Who was she? What tore them apart?

Could she have sobbed in her mother's arms when Jane left?

"That I fell madly in love with your father was purely luck. I could just as easily have fallen for another woman—for someone I could not love loudly and with my entire chest. The way you have with Miss Pine."

Rosalie stares at her mother, feeling so wonderfully seen, and somehow yet so entirely other. "I don't think I could fall in love with a man," she whispers. The words still carry around the room.

"And you do not have to," Father says immediately.

But Rosalie's still watching her mother, who smiles so softly at her.

"All we care about is that you love whomever you choose to spend your life with," Father continues.

"Do you love Miss Pine?" Mother asks.

They've avoided such words, but Rosalie does. She does. Ardently, and passionately, and fully.

"I should probably tell her first," Rosalie whispers.

Aunt Genevieve chuckles. "You should." Rosalie turns and meets Aunt Genevieve's eyes. "I have a feeling she feels the same way."

"I hope so," Rosalie says.

"You don't risk your whole life on someone you don't love," Mother says, a promise there in her slightly teary voice.

Rosalie turns to look at her, a catch in her chest.

"I'm sorry it wasn't clear that you could tell me," Mother adds. "That I made you go through this all alone."

Rosalie doesn't know what to say. She didn't know there was any other option until tonight. She's grieving something she never knew existed. Where does all that pain go?

"We'll make it up to you now," Father says.

"All of us," Aunt Genevieve adds. "Because it is far less lonely, isn't it, for our loved ones to know who we truly are?" Rosalie looks up at her and finds her watching Mother.

Rosalie turns and Mother meets her eyes. "It is."

A short sob erupts unexpectedly from Rosalie's chest. Aunt Genevieve wraps her arm around Rosalie's shoulders and she leans into her, trying to calm down, handkerchief pressed to her lips.

Her parents just watch, eyes shining, their hands clasped together. She doesn't want to make anyone sad, or hurt, or worried. But the feelings feel too big. She could sob into Aunt Genevieve's shoulder for hours and never get them all out.

"I feel left out," Christopher exclaims. He throws his arms out and huffs. "Everyone has secrets but me."

They all burst into laughter. Aunt Genevieve grips at Rosalie's shoulder to keep them both upright. Mother and Father fall into each other in giggles. Christopher grins at Rosalie, who wipes at her dripping nose, beaming back.

"Is there something you would like to share with the family that, while not scandalous, is still important, to feel better included?" Father asks.

Christopher's silly smile disappears and he looks at Father and Mother almost hesitantly. Rosalie reaches out to take his hand again. They really can't take more secrets or surprises.

"I'd like to ask Amalie—Miss Linet—to marry me, actually," he says. "With your blessing."

"Oh," Mother says, her face breaking into a smile.

"Though I should admit that she was my partner in crime in tonight's reconciliation."

"What reconciliation?" Father asks. They all turn to him, flabbergasted. "How, exactly, did it come out that Rosalie and Miss Pine are in love?"

"We didn't actually—"

"Amalie threw wine on Miss Pine, so Miss Pine and her mother had to go into the water closet, and Rosalie tricked Mother into going in there, and then I sent in Aunt Genevieve to end the feud," Christopher says. Like it was all his plan.

"There was a little more nuance than that," Rosalie says as Father looks between them. Not much, but still.

"So you and Eleanor made up?" Father asks Mother.

"We did. Which should help," Mother says, gesturing to Rosalie.

"Good," Father says, then looks to Rosalie. "Excellently done."

"A little more dramatic than we anticipated, but thank you. Amalie ruining Catherine's dress was not actually part of the plan."

"But wonderfully executed," Christopher says.

"I believe we've swerved off the point," Aunt Genevieve says.

"Ah, yes," Father says, smiling at his sister before looking back to Christopher. Mother squeezes his hand. "You, of course, have our blessing, on the condition that Miss Linet is equally prepared to have Rosalie and Miss Pine in residence should they choose, and that you both will swear to take care of them until the day you die."

Christopher looks to Rosalie, who grins back at him, feeling light and excited and so terribly exhausted all at once.

"She is," Christopher says as the same time Rosalie says, "She will."

Father and Mother laugh. "Then we'll arrange a wonderful ceremony as soon as you propose," Father says.

"Yay," Christopher says, reaching out to hug Rosalie, who leans into him, smiling as Aunt Genevieve jostles his shoulder in congratulations.

"We'll need to find Mother's ring for her," Aunt Genevieve says.

"You have her jewelry box," Father says.

"I'll check tonight. And perhaps on my way home, I ought to deliver a letter to the Pine residence?"

Rosalie's good cheer dims a little. It's all well and good that this family meeting has gone spectacularly well, but the Pines are another matter entirely.

"I'll write one before you leave," Mother says. "Our plan is perfectly reasonable; they should have no cause to object to the girls living with you for a few years, and it will be easy enough to orchestrate smoothly."

"Leave the details to your mother," Father tells Rosalie. "It's easier." Mother elbows him. "She can see the whole chessboard.

Always has done, even when it's cost her," he says, meeting Mother's eyes. "It's one of the things I love most about her."

"No one will be sacrificing happiness for reputation anymore," Aunt Genevieve says firmly. "If we do this right, Rosalie and Miss Pine can be happy and save face, with saving face being the far less important of the two."

Rosalie smiles up at her. Christopher pulls her backward until they're slumped against the back of the settee, and they listen exhaustedly as Mother and Aunt Genevieve begin a rapid discussion of furniture, annual events, and décor. Father smiles at them and gets up to fill his pipe.

Rosalie sniffles against Christopher's shoulder. She didn't know the pain of what could have been would be as fierce as the excitement for what will be. That learning she and Mother could have celebrated knowing they were alike in this way would *hurt*. Everything is a messy ball of joy and sadness in her head.

"You think she'll want the blue room or the yellow?" Christopher wonders. Rosalie nudges his chin in question. "You'll have a wing at Aunt Genevieve's. Does Catherine like blue or yellow more?"

Rosalie smiles despite the tumult of emotions coursing through her. "The yellow," she whispers.

Once she stops crying, she knows she'll be desperate to see Catherine again. To get to spend a life with Catherine. To see her face as they explore Aunt Genevieve's estate. As they build a beautiful future together.

But for now, she's going to let herself doze against Christopher's shoulder while her mother and aunt argue over drapes. It turns out getting everything you've always wanted feels suspiciously like falling and flying all at once.

Chapter Thirty
Catherine

Sunlight filters in through the crack in the curtains, and Catherine turns her face into her pillow. Even a bright, sunny day cannot fix what's been broken. The pain of yesterday still flares hard against her chest and all she wants to do is lie in her bed until darkness takes over again.

"You will not!"

Catherine squints toward the door, muted yelling finally permeating her bubble of sadness. What on earth?

She shuffles out of bed, pulling her dressing gown over her chemise. She hurries down the stairs, tying her robe and running an anxious hand through her hair. Are her parents fighting about her? Has Father decided he's on her side? Does Mother want her out of the house? Will they ever let her see Rosalie again?

"Will you stop insisting you're right for two blasted seconds?"

"Not if you're just going to insist they stay here!"

That's not Father's voice. Nor Miss Teit's. The screaming keeps going, melding into a muddied furor until she hits the final landing, staring down the staircase into their bustling and crowded foyer.

The entire Tisend family stands there in jackets and bonnets and pelisses. Her mother and Lady Tisend are circling each other in the middle of the room, still shouting at each other, while Christopher, Father, Lord Tisend, and Lady Jones linger to the side, watching.

"Genevieve has an entire wing for them, and they can live there for as long as they want until Christopher inherits," Lady Tisend shouts.

"Longer, if they want," Lady Jones puts in.

Both Mother and Lady Tisend glare at her and she holds up her hands.

"Staying in Bath will be far less conspicuous than up and leaving together after the mess they've made with Mr. Dean!" Mother insists.

Lord Tisend and Father exchange a look, both slightly amused and a little frightened. Of course, Christopher's just grinning like it's all *funny* somehow.

No one has noticed her yet. No one has told her anything. No one came to wake her so she could be part of this yelling match. No one has bothered to ask her anything.

Does no one care how she feels about having her life decided?

"You are doing it again," Mother yells.

"Doing what?" Lady Tisend yells back.

"Declaring what you feel is proper for my family without even asking. You haven't the right—"

"The only right answer is for the girls to go north with Genevieve, so neither of them has to live the same scandal—"

"That *you* put me through! It's entirely proper for them to live at home. I don't know why you're so eager to send your daughter away—"

"I am not eager for her to leave!" Lady Tisend shouts. "I'm not," she adds, looking toward the door, where Catherine finally notices Rosalie hovering uneasily in the shadow of the large vase they keep to the side of the entry, watching the exchange with wide eyes. She's holding her bonnet, worrying it with anxious fingers.

As if she can feel Catherine's gaze, Rosalie looks up. The moment she sees Catherine, her face lights up, eyes hopeful, cheeks lifting. Catherine's just in her robe and chemise, her hair probably still messy from sleep, but she feels beautiful under Rosalie's gaze.

It makes her brave.

She's been waiting all season for the impossible. For someone to swoop in and save her, to tell her what to do and make it all right. But that's not going to happen. This imperfect life with their mothers screaming, their fathers amused and useless, Christopher snickering—this is her goddamned romantic novel, and she's not letting their mothers decide what becomes of them without asking them first. She's going to save herself, and Rosalie, and rewrite this damn ending.

"You don't get to decide what happens to our lives, to *my* daughter," Mother starts.

"Enough!" Catherine hears herself yell, marching down the stairs.

Her voice rings around the foyer and everyone turns to look at her. She stops on the bottom step and stares around at all of them with her hands on her hips. "You cannot unilaterally make decisions about my life, about Rosalie's life—however well-meaning."

"Exactly. It is not your—" Mother starts.

"You can't make decisions like this for us either. Much less without even talking to me about it," Catherine adds, looking to her mother, forcing the words out, even though they come out choked and tight.

Mother looks over at her. "Catherine—"

Catherine shakes her head and steps off the stairs. She takes a deep breath and gestures to the second floor.

"If everyone would please make their way up to our sitting room, so we may discuss this like civilized people for the love of all that's holy."

Christopher and Lady Jones both laugh while Mother and Lady Tisend just stand there staring at her.

"Now, if you would," Catherine prompts.

She waits, tapping her toe, while Lord Tisend and Father come and take their wives' arms. Both of them grin at her while leading Mother and Lady Tisend toward the stairs. Christopher and Lady Jones follow them up, giving her proud nods and smiles, and Catherine feels the tension begin to leach out of her shoulders.

She doesn't think she's ever been that loud before.

She watches almost hazily as Rosalie drops her bonnet and walks quickly across the foyer, the two of them alone now. Catherine opens her mouth, to laugh, to sob, to greet her, but Rosalie doesn't give her a chance. She reaches up and cradles Catherine's face in her hands, pulling her into a deep, needy kiss.

Catherine wraps her arms instinctively around Rosalie's delicate shoulders, holding on tight as her tongue slicks into Catherine's mouth. They both groan, the sound loud in the now-empty foyer, but it doesn't matter. They're together, and they're kissing in the middle of her house, unafraid. Catherine could stay just like this forever.

Eventually, Rosalie pulls back, looking up at her, her eyes wide and dark, lips red. "That was by far the hottest thing I have *ever* seen."

Catherine laughs, leaning in to rest her forehead on Rosalie's. "Yeah?"

"You should be bossy more often," Rosalie says eagerly.

Catherine leans down for one more kiss. "I'll try," she says, stepping back so she can take Rosalie's hands. "Would you care to tell me what the hell is going on?" she asks, instead of pushing Rosalie against the railing and rucking up her skirts.

"Well, my mother has decided we're to move in with Aunt Genevieve for the foreseeable future and be scandalously in love away in the country, if you're interested."

Catherine blinks at her. "Oh, um—"

"While your mother would much prefer we stay here, figure things out, and live at home, separately. I suppose we'd slowly have to win her over to get to stay the night at either house together."

"That sounds—"

"I'm a bit more partial to being lovers in the country, if you are."

Catherine pauses, squeezing Rosalie's hands. "Wait. You said we'd be scandalously in love in the country?"

Rosalie's eyes go wide. "Oh. Yes. Um, if you'd like. I—I'd love to . . . love you in the country, if you're willing."

Catherine feels the grin spread across her face, her chest loosening, a giggle falling from her lips. "I'll be in love with you wherever we are, but the country would be nice."

Rosalie's face splits in an answering, beautiful, glorious smile, and they grab at each other, pressing their smiles together, too happy to kiss properly, laughing.

She's never felt this happy before. She's never felt so herself. Never felt so supported, so cherished, so loved. And loving Rosalie—it's like breathing the most wonderful mountain air, expanding, and brimming, and just on the pleasurable side of fabulously painful.

"I can't wait to keep loving you," Rosalie whispers as they pull apart to meet each other's eyes.

"It'll be a wondrous adventure," Catherine agrees. "That we'll start by . . . facing our mothers, together?"

"Exceedingly romantic," Rosalie says, laughing as Catherine wrinkles her nose. "But like you said, we'll decide together. I'll learn to speak up to my mother like you did, for you."

Catherine sighs, smoothing Rosalie's hair from her face. "Speak up to your mother for yourself." Rosalie frowns. "You can pretend it's for me, for a while, for good practice."

"Deal," Rosalie says, her hands sliding down Catherine's chest to tighten the belt of her dressing gown. "We decide?"

"We decide, together," Catherine agrees.

Rosalie takes her hand and they turn and head up the stairs, fingers interlaced. Their slightly damp palms pressing tight help bolster Catherine as they come around the staircase on the second floor, staring down the hall toward the sitting room where Mother and Father are hovering just outside, the Tisend family's voices murmuring within.

"I'll be right inside," Rosalie says as they reach the doors.

She squeezes Catherine's hand and then lets go, walking into the sitting room, head held high. Catherine watches her go, elated, and bereft without the press of her fingers. Then Mother shuts the door, leaving them in the relative silence of the dim hallway.

Father glances at Mother, nudging her gently. Mother opens her mouth, but nothing comes out, and the happy bubble in Catherine's chest starts to deflate.

"I know this isn't what you wanted," Catherine starts.

"We never said that," Father says.

Catherine glances at him, calm and smiling, then looks back to Mother, who's still just standing there, blank.

"I know it will be more difficult," Catherine continues. "And it won't look the way you envisioned for my future but I—I truly hope you'll still—that you can . . ." She falters as Mother just continues to *stare* at her. She can feel tears pricking at the corners of her eyes again.

Father sighs and releases Mother's hand to step forward, wrapping Catherine in his arms. The moment her cheek hits his shoulder, she loses the fight with her tears, fisting her hands into the back of his simple brown housecoat.

"If she makes you happy, that's all that matters," Father whispers. "Didn't I tell you that yesterday?"

Catherine sniffles, pulling back to meet his eyes. "I wasn't sure if—I wasn't sure you'd feel that way about Rosalie," she says, glancing at Mother over his shoulder.

She's still painfully unsure.

Father scoffs and Catherine looks back at him. He takes her hands and squeezes. "All I've ever wanted was for you to find someone to love and build a life that made you happy. You haven't chosen the easiest path."

"I know," Catherine says, gripping at his hands, afraid they might slip away.

"But it's brave of you," Father says firmly. "All I ask is that you be cautious with whom you trust, and you visit us very often."

"That I can do," Catherine promises, watching the way he smiles at her. Like nothing has changed. Like she's still the girl he's known all her life.

"She'll come around, I'll make sure of it," he adds, softer.

Catherine blinks, watching more than feeling his hands slip

away. He steps back to wrap his arm around her mother's waist. Mother's still not smiling. Still barely moving.

"Mother?" Catherine hears herself say.

"This is not the choice I would make," Mother says, her words soft. Still, they echo around the hall, bowling into Catherine's stomach.

"I know," Catherine says haltingly.

"You're giving up so much."

Her mother's eyes are wide and shining, grieving the life she wanted for Catherine. The marriage, the babies, the social status. But those were *her* dreams, *her* happy ending.

"I know," Catherine repeats, stronger. "But they're not things I want. Can you—" She hesitates. Father nods at her and Catherine takes a deep breath. "Can you—will you still help me, even if it's not what you want for me?"

Mother meets Catherine's eyes, so much brimming between them. So much now so broken between them.

"She will," Father says.

Catherine glances at him, Mother and Lady Tisend's fight echoing in her head. "Not just because he tells you you have to?"

Father opens his mouth, affronted.

"Will it change your mind if I won't?" Mother asks.

Catherine pushes through the knot in her throat, disappointment flooding through her veins. "No," she says. It's cracking, and bruised, but it's true.

Catherine will love Rosalie, will choose Rosalie, whatever the cost, but she had . . . she hoped—

Mother nods slowly, her body still so stiff, face still so blank. "I have never regretted marrying your father, but I do regret the manner in which it happened. I was backed into the decision. It was the right one, but not how I wanted to make it and

I—" She glances at Father, whose face has softened, and takes a deep breath. "I want you to have the choice." Her eyes meet Catherine's. "I don't agree, but neither will I stand in your way."

It's not a weeping hug and unquestioned support. It's not the two of them, girls together against the world, anymore. It's not the fairy tale.

It's not what she wanted.

But it's a start.

"Thank you," Catherine says, grateful, and grieving, and wounded, and hopeful all at once.

They stand there staring tearfully at each other, learning each other all over again.

"Well," Father says, smiling at them both. "I suppose we should go deal with our guests. Can't leave Lord Tisend to referee your mother and Lady Tisend on his own."

Mother huffs and Catherine lets out a small laugh. Some things never change, at least.

Mother steps away from Father, opening the door to the sitting room. She glances at Catherine and nods once before heading inside.

"She'll come around," Father repeats, stepping forward to squeeze Catherine's hand.

"I know," Catherine says, squeezing back. "Thank you."

Father smiles, his eyes crinkling, and then lets go, heading inside.

Catherine remains just outside the doorway, alone. She takes a deep breath, trying to let the onslaught of elation, and hurt, and exhaustion, and hope cascade off her until she feels steady again.

Taking her happiness, choosing her happiness, comes at a

cost. It isn't perfect. It isn't painless. It isn't without sacrifice. But it's her choice.

"All right?" Catherine blinks as Rosalie slips out into the hallway. "I was eavesdropping," she admits, stepping forward to wrap her arms around Catherine. "I'm sorry."

Catherine holds tight to her shoulders, pressing her face into her hair. She's sorry too. But she's also so incredibly happy.

"I love you," she whispers, pulling back to meet Rosalie's eyes. "And the rest will come."

Rosalie smiles, reaching up to brush the remaining tears from her cheeks. "The rest will come."

Catherine lets the sparkle in Rosalie's eyes fill her up. There's a lot of life to be lived together. A lot after their happy-ever-after to get to.

She takes Rosalie's hand and strides into the sitting room, looking around at the Tisends and her parents, gathered on their two worn settees, Christopher and Lady Jones in the armchairs between them. Wholehearted acceptance might not be in the immediate offing, but they're all here.

Christopher beams at her beside Lady Jones. Christopher, Amalie, and Henrietta—they'll build a better world with them, whether all of their parents ever come around or not.

Even so, the words stick momentarily in her throat. Rosalie squeezes her hand, and there's a tingly feeling that flows from the touch of her palm, the press of her fingers, the heat of her body close against Catherine's arm.

They'll do this together. They'll choose the future, together.

Rosalie nods up at her once, smiling.

Catherine takes a deep breath and turns back to their families, determination spreading through her. "So."

Acknowledgments

It's wild to say this is the third book I've gotten to write while working with this spectacular team. Every part of delivering this book and getting to collaborate with this wonderful group of people has been a joy and an ongoing dream come true.

To Allie, my fantastic editor, thank you for believing in this story, for your enthusiasm, your thoughtful input, your laughter, and your joy. It's been a true delight to work on Catherine and Rosalie's story with you, and I look forward to many more!

To Stacy, my dream agent, thank you for your ongoing support, your vision, your laughter, and your drive. Being on this ride alongside you is such a treat.

To Sydnee, thank you for all of your help, your thoughtful notes, and your enthusiasm. I'm so very grateful to get to work with you.

To Larry, my fabulous manager. It's been the best decade. Thank you. Here's to more to come. And to Devra, thank you for absolutely everything.

To Wayne, attorney extraordinaire, thank you for all of your guidance and our wonderful chats. I always look forward to them.

To Leni Kauffman, my amazing illustrator, thank you for yet another AMAZING cover! It continues to be the most unreal thing to get to work with you and have you bring my characters to such spectacular life.

To the Vitamin String Quartet, who have provided the soundtrack while I've written all three of my books, from the bottom of my heart, thank you.

To the fantastic publishing professionals who have touched *Like in Love with You,* and with whom I'm so grateful to keep getting to publish books, thank you: May Chen, Tessa Woodward, Linda Sawicki, Christine Vahaly, Diahann Sturge-Campbell, Shelby Peak, Amy Halperin, Sophia Lee, DJ De-Smyter, Jes Lyons, Ronnie Kutys, Andy LeCount, and Caroline Bodkin.

To my ever-amazing beta readers, Abby, Becca, Ben, Lindsay, Stacy, and Sydnee, I just wouldn't be the writer I am without you. Thank you for reading my stories, giving me such thoughtful feedback, and just being the best dang group of people. You rock. So hard.

To my friends. I write about found family in all of my books. It's my favorite thing. And it's truly surreal and wonderful that I have a found family in my life that's just as vibrant, loving, and real as anything in fiction. I feel so lucky to know you, and I love you.

To Dani, to whom this book is dedicated, I am so incredibly grateful you are in my life, and that I get to call you my sister. I love you so very much.

To Dylan, the best big brother, thank you for always cheering me on, and for being my friend. I love you.

To my parents, no words seem adequate enough to thank

you for the life I lead, the love we share, and how much I adore you, but I'll continue to try to find them.

And to you, my lovely reader, thank you for coming on Catherine and Rosalie's journey with me. Thank you for supporting queer and diverse stories. Thank you for reading. Let's keep going together.

About the Author

Emma R. Alban is a *USA Today* bestselling author and screen-writer. Raised in the Hudson Valley, she now lives in Los Angeles, enjoying the eternal sunshine, ocean, and mountains. When she isn't writing books or screenplays, she can usually be found stress-baking with the AC on full blast, skiing late into the spring, singing show tunes at the top of her lungs on the freeway, and reading anywhere there's somewhere to lean. She is the author of *Don't Want You Like a Best Friend* and *You're the Problem, It's You.*

Read more from
EMMA R. ALBAN

YOU'RE THE PROBLEM, IT'S YOU
The enemies-to-lovers queer Victorian romance follow-up to *Don't Want You Like a Best Friend*, in which a young lord and a second son clash but find themselves thrust together again and again by their meddling cousins.

DON'T WANT YOU LIKE A BEST FRIEND
A swoon-worthy debut queer Victorian romance in which two debutantes distract themselves from having to seek husbands by setting up their widowed parents, and instead find their perfect match in each other—the lesbian *Bridgerton/Parent Trap* mash-up you never knew you needed!